Dear Reader:

Fire Song first came out in 1985. It's the second novel in the Medieval Song Quartet. I've updated the language a bit, and hummed with pleasure at the beautiful new cover.

Lord Graelam de Moreton first appeared in *Warrior's Song*. He was a warrior, a man both hard and ruthless, a man who took what he wanted and never looked back. He was, and still is, a very bad boy. But things change and Graelam finds himself in a situation he never anticipated: he has gotten himself a wife through no fault of his own.

Kassia de Loris of Brittany is gentle and yielding, untested in the ways of men. She cheats death only to find herself wedded to a stranger.

When the two meet as husband and wife at Graelam's castle of Wolffeton in Cornwall, Kassia is prepared to give obeisance to this man her father chose for her. Graelam is willing to accept her as she appears—a lady as innocent and guileless as rainwater flowing through his fingers.

But things change again. Graelam comes to believe she has betrayed him. It's time for Kassia to prove her mettle.

You'll be seeing Graelam and Kassia again in *Earth Song* and *Secret Song*. Do enjoy and let me know what you think. Write me at P.O. Box 17, Mill Valley, CA 94942 or e-mail me at ReadMoi@aol.com.

Catherine Coulter

Titles by Catherine Coulter

Fire
Song

Catherine Coulter

A SIGNET BOOK

SIGNET
Published by New American Library, a division of
Penguin Group (USA) Inc., 375 Hudson Street,
New York, New York 10014, USA
Penguin Group (Canada), 90 Eglinton Avenue East, Suite 700, Toronto,
Ontario M4P 2Y3, Canada (a division of Pearson Penguin Canada Inc.)
Penguin Books Ltd., 80 Strand, London WC2R 0RL, England
Penguin Ireland, 25 St. Stephen's Green, Dublin 2,
Ireland (a division of Penguin Books Ltd.)
Penguin Group (Australia), 250 Camberwell Road, Camberwell, Victoria 3124,
Australia (a division of Pearson Australia Group Pty. Ltd.)
Penguin Books India Pvt. Ltd., 11 Community Centre, Panchsheel Park,
New Delhi - 110 017, India
Penguin Group (NZ), 67 Apollo Drive, Rosedale, North Shore 0632,
New Zealand (a division of Pearson New Zealand Ltd.)
Penguin Books (South Africa) (Pty.) Ltd., 24 Sturdee Avenue,
Rosebank, Johannesburg 2196, South Africa

Penguin Books Ltd., Registered Offices:
80 Strand, London WC2R 0RL, England

Published by Signet, an imprint of New American Library,
a division of Penguin Group (USA) Inc.

First Signet Printing, February 1999
First Signet Printing (Revised Edition), November 2002
10 9 8 7 6

*To Randi and Bob Kerlan,
friends for life.*

1

"By all the fires in hell, Guy." Graelam pointed between Demon's flattened ears. "A dozen bandits against a merchant and six men." He wheeled around in his saddle and yelled back to his men, "Let's show these damned French bastards what the English are made of." Even as he spoke, he dug his heels into his destrier's sides, smoothly unsheathed his gleaming sword. Demon thundered down the grassy rolling hill into the small valley below, his silver-studded bridle glittering in the bright sun.

"*A Moreton, A Moreton!*" Graelam shouted. He clapped his visor down and swung his huge sword in a wide vicious arc. His two knights and dozen men-at-arms closed behind him, their cries echoing his own. Graelam coolly studied the band of men thinking they had chosen an ideal spot for their attack. And one of the men under attack was no merchant, he realized, as Demon crashed into a horse, tossing the rider high into the air. The man was richly garbed in wine velvet over his chain mail, and sat astride a magnificent bay stallion. He obviously had a knight's training, for his sword was flashing like silver as at least six of the bandits circled him, four of them on horseback. But despite his prowess as a warrior, unaided he would soon be cut to pieces.

Graelam yelled again, "*A Moreton! A Moreton!*", and half of the bandits, no fools, dashed toward the forest, while six others continued their furious attack on the lone man.

He fights well, Graelam thought, and in the next moment he rode into the fray, a grim smile on his face as his sword sank into a man's throat. Blood spurted upward, splattering Graelam's mail, but he ignored it, riding Demon straight into another horse. Demon rose to his hind legs, slashing with his forelegs at the horse's neck. At the same moment, Graelam sliced his sword through the man's chest, sending him spinning to the ground, a thin, surprised croak tearing from his throat. He closed beside the warrior, protecting his flank, and laughed aloud as the remaining men, screaming from wounds and fear, fled after their fellows into the forest.

The fighting had lasted five minutes, no more. Save for the groans of the wounded, all was silent again. Graelam handed his bloody sword to one of his men-at-arms, then dismounted and turned to Sir Guy de Blasis, one of his knights.

"Only Hugh is wounded, my lord," Guy said, panting a little, "and not badly. The bandits were cowards."

Graelam nodded and approached the richly clothed man. "Are you hurt?"

"Nay, but I would be fodder for the crops were it not for you. My thanks." He pulled off his helmet and shoved back the chain mail covering his head. "My name is Maurice de Lorris, of Belleterre." He smiled at Graelam, eyes twinkling.

He fights like a much younger man, Graelam thought, taking in the close-cropped graying hair and the deep lines radiating from his very green eyes. He was still a well-looking man who had not grown soft in the manner of many older warriors. He had not an ounce of fat on his wiry body and Graelam could see the play of firm muscles in his shoulders and arms. "You are breathing hard, my lord," Graelam said. "Come, rest awhile and tell me why a party of bandits would attack you."

Maurice nodded and dismounted, aware that his heart was pounding in his chest and his breathing was coming in short gasps. But Christ's bones, he thought, it had been a good fight.

"You are wounded."

Maurice looked stupidly at the bloody rent in his velvet surcoat, and cursed softly. Kassia would have difficulty repairing the jagged tear. "It is nothing," he said, shrugging it off.

"Guy," Graelam called. "Have one of the men bring me some water and cloths."

He smiled down at Maurice. "I am Lord Graelam de Moreton, an Englishman, returning from the Holy Land. I was beginning to believe that I was traveling through an Eden," he continued, looking around at the rolling hills of Aquitaine. "Bloody boring it was becoming. I thank you, my lord, for the sport."

"Your timing bespeaks divine intervention to me," Maurice said, wincing as one of Graelam's men ripped the velvet surcoat beyond repair to clean and bind the wound in his arm. "You say you were in the Holy Land?" he asked, looking more closely at the large English warrior who had saved his life. At Graelam's nod, he said, "Word reached me about

King Louis dying like filth in that godforsaken land. A saint among men, but now what does it matter? Your valiant Prince Edward, did he survive?"

"He did indeed. But enough talk for you until you are stronger, my lord."

Maurice found himself leaning gratefully against Graelam's chest. Graelam eased him down beneath an oak tree, then rose to survey the damage wreaked by the bandits. He pulled back his mail and ran his hands through his matted black hair. "Guy," he called, pointing toward a mortally wounded man who was groaning on the ground, "dispatch him to hell."

It was odd, Graelam thought, but none of the wagons had been touched. He pictured the battle in his mind, recalling the six men who had attacked Maurice de Lorris. If contraband had not been their goal, then—He shook his head and continued his inspection. Three of Lord Maurice's men were dead, two wounded. He gave his men further instructions and walked back to Maurice, whose arm now rested in a sling.

Maurice studied the man who had saved his life. English or no, he was a splendid specimen, and a fierce fighter. And, Maurice thought, squinting against the afternoon sun, he was young and healthy, his chest solid as an oak tree. He was a man well used to command, a man one could trust. He saw Graelam's frowning brow and said, "I know your thoughts, my lord, for they echo my own. There are thieves aplenty in this world, but this attack is unusual. Aquitaine is well-governed. It stretches the imagination to believe I was attacked by such a collection of men for a mere three wagons of wine."

"You have enemies," Graelam said matter of factly.

"It would appear so." Maurice shrugged and looked directly into Graelam's dark eyes. "What man does not?"

"An enemy who also is too cowardly to do the work himself.

"So it would appear." He looked thoughtful for a moment. "I have no proof," he said finally. "There is but one man who would go to such lengths to have me removed from this earth."

With the excitement of battle receding, Graelam felt weary, more from the weeks trekking from Sicily than from wielding his sword. He rubbed his hand over the muscles knotted in his neck.

"I had forgot," Maurice said. "Your Prince Edward is now king. Does he return soon to claim his crown?"

"Nay. He has the wanderlust. And there is no need. England is at peace and his uncle, the Duke of Cornwall, will protect what is Edward's."

"But you, Graelam de Moreton, I hear in your voice that you wish to be home."

"Aye. Fighting the heathen in the Holy Land was an exercise in bloodletting and disease and frustration. The treaty Edward negotiated with the Saracens will keep the Christians safe for some time, at least."

Maurice looked thoughtfully at the English knight. "We are but three days from my home, Lord Graelam," he said. "Will you accompany me to Belleterre?"

"It will be my pleasure," Graelam said.

"Good," Maurice said, his thoughts turning to Kassia. He would have three days to determine if this Englishman would prove a worthy husband for his only daughter. He asked, not meeting Graelam's eyes, "I suppose you have a family eagerly awaiting your return?"

"Nay, but my castle, Wolffeton, is likely falling to ruin. A year is a long time to be gone."

"Ah," Maurice said, sat back against the oak tree, and closed his eyes.

2

Kassia shrugged out of her ermine-lined cloak, folded it carefully, and laid it across the saddle in front of her. It was much too beautiful to wear, she thought with a smile, remembering her father's sly looks when he presented it to her on her last birthday. She had teased him that it was a gift for a princess and not a simple maid living in the wilds of Brittany. As for her nurse and maid, Etta, she had tisked behind her hand, claiming the master was spoiling her baby, but Maurice had only laughed.

Kassia raised her face to the brilliant sun. It was a beautiful spring day, white clouds dotting the blue sky, and air so pure and clean she couldn't seem to breathe deeply enough. She turned slightly in her saddle and looked back toward Belleterre. Four round towers rose high to guard the surrounding countryside. Thick gray stone walls, aged to mute grace over the last hundred years, connected the huge towers, forming a large square atop the rocky hillock. Belleterre was not only her home but also a strategic fortress, commanding the River Morlaix. No enemy could sail from the sea up the river without the soldiers of Belleterre knowing of it. And no enemy could escape detection landward, no matter how stealthfully they tried, for the castle commanded the highest hill in the area. As Kassia gazed beyond the thriving town of Morlaix, toward the sea, she remembered the stories her father had told her of the violent past when powerful men had fought to gain control of Brittany. Belleterre had survived, for even the stoutest war machines had faltered and failed before they could draw close enough to harm Belleterre with their flaming balls of fire. Siege was their only fear and her father would remind them of it every year when the crops were safely stored. Kassia, every bit as fine a housekeeper as her grandmother had been, would ensure that the outbuildings were well-stocked with wheat and fodder, the meat cured, and enough flour and salt purchased to withstand the forces of the King of France himself.

Thomas, one of her father's squires, reined in beside Bluebell, drawing Kassia from her thoughts. "My lady," he said, pointing to the east, "a group of men is approaching. We should return to Belleterre."

She nodded, remembering her promise to her father, and urged Bluebell into a canter back to Belleterre. She smiled, thankful that he would be home within the week. Home with enough wine from Aquitaine to last him a decade.

Pierre, the porter, raised the portcullis, and their small troop rode into the inner bailey. As always, Kassia felt a sense of accomplishment when she viewed the cleanliness of the outbuildings and the well-swept cobbled ground that slanted gently downward to the outer bailey so that rain could not collect and stagnate. There was no filth, no untidiness in her home, and all who lived within the keep were well-fed, and clothed in stout wool. A group of children were playing near the large well, and Kassia waved to them. They also were a part of her huge family, and she knew each of them by name. "We live in a rabbit warren," her father would complain with a smile. "Sometimes I cannot even relieve my bowels without someone about."

"Thomas," she said after he had helped her to dismount, "have Pierre close the gates until we know who our visitors are."

"Yes, my lady," Thomas said, unable to entirely keep the worship from his voice. He was Kassia's age, and his father held sizable lands to the east, but he knew, sadly, that Kassia regarded him as a brother. It was just as well, he thought, turning to speak to Pierre, that he would win his spurs within the year. He did not think he could bear to be around when her father gave her in marriage to another man.

"Damned whoreson," Pierre said, watching the dozen riders approaching Belleterre. "It's that miserable Geoffrey de Lacy. I recognize his standard. It should be a weasel and not a proud eagle. How I'd like to tell the lout to keep his hide away from Belleterre and my lady."

"I will see what Kassia wishes," Thomas said.

But Kassia had heard, and she called to him to open the gates. Geoffrey was her cousin, son of her father's sister, Felice. Evidently his disagreeable mother had not accompanied him this time. Thank the saints for one small favor. If only her father were here. She climbed the wooden stairs to the outer wall and watched Geoffrey draw his small troop to a halt at the base of the hill. He was richly attired, as usual, in dark blue velvet, and she imagined that he had long before calculated the worth of Belleterre. She chewed on her lower lip, wishing she could refuse him entry. But, of course, she could not.

"Kassia, it is I, Geoffrey," he called up to her. "May I take my rest for a while?" She did not even bother to call back to him, Geoffrey noted, his lips thinning with annoyance. Proud little bitch. Once he was wed to her, he would teach her manners. He could not prevent his eyes wandering lovingly over every inch of Belleterre as he and his troop of men rode slowly upward toward the massive gates. It would be his soon. He would be lord of Belleterre and away from his mother's infernal harping.

He straightened his shoulders, pasted a smile upon his face, and rode his destrier into the inner bailey to where Kassia now stood awaiting him. He had not seen her for nearly six months, and he felt a tingling of pleased surprise as he noted her breasts were fuller now, more womanly. He admired her chestnut hair that caught the sunlight in its thick strands, falling in lazy waves down her back. But he did not like her eyes. Though they were a brilliant hazel, wide, framed with dark lashes, they looked at him too straightly, directly into his face, into his mind. She was forward for a woman; his damned uncle had coddled her, not teaching her her place. But on this visit Geoffrey had no trouble smiling as he viewed his future home and his future wife.

"Kassia," he said, dismounting to stand beside her. "You become more beautiful with the passing months."

"Geoffrey," Kassia said disregarding the possessive tone of his voice. "My father has not yet returned from Aquitaine."

"Ah, it is not just your father's company that draws me."

"What does draw you, Geoffrey?"

His lashes lowered over his eyes, hiding his irritation. "The lovely day, and you, my cousin. May I spend an hour with you? Unfortunately, I must return to Beaumanoir by evening."

Kassia nodded, picked up her skirts, and led him up the winding stairs into the great hall. "I trust your mother is well," she said.

Geoffrey laughed. "My mother is always in good health. She is particularly in fine fettle when I am about, a likely candidate upon which to vent her spleen."

"Well," Kassia said, bending a bit, "she treats you better than she treats me. Imagine her telling my father that I am far too young to manage Belleterre. As if I were some silly twit raised in a convent."

Geoffrey relaxed at the honest laughter in her voice, and her eyes were twinkling in a very acceptable way. It was wise of him, he thought, to come here today. He would be the one she would wish to see when she heard about her father. He would have her, willing or unwilling, but he preferred her to want him, to accept him. The thought of forcing a lady was distasteful to him. She motioned him to a chair and he again noticed, with pleasure, the fulness of her breasts as she gestured with her hand.

"You have not grown taller," he said.

"No, I fear it is my fate to forever be at the level of my father's Adam's apple. Would you care for some ale, Geoffrey?"

He nodded and sat back comfortably in the high-backed chair. It felt like home already. It was not her father's chair, but nonetheless it was solid and intricately carved, and lasting, like Belleterre itself. He watched Kassia give orders to a serving girl, her voice gentle, pleasing. "Kassia is like her mother, Lady Anne," his mother would snort upon occasion. "Soft and spineless and without spirit." But Geoffrey knew she was wrong. Kassia was gentle because she had been raised gently. She appeared soft because her father treated her with unstinting affection. He doubted if anyone had ever spoken roughly to her in her life, except of course, his mother. But she had spirit, perhaps too much for a girl. His eyes drifted down to her hips. So slender she was. He wondered if she would bear him sons without dying in childbirth as her mother had. His own mother had informed him that Kassia was late in developing into a woman, and he winced, remembering her crude discussion of Kassia's monthly flow of woman's blood, not begun until she had passed her fourteenth year.

Kassia handed him a goblet of ale, a slab of cheese and freshly baked bread. "I am certain that Thomas will provide your men with refreshment." She sat down across from him in an armless chair and looked at him with her direct gaze. "Why are you here, Geoffrey?"

"To see you, cousin," he said, breaking off a piece of bread.

"My father would not approve."

"Your father is wrong not to approve. I have never done him ill and he is my uncle, and I am his heir."

"Nay, Geoffrey," she said steadily. "I am his heir."

Geoffrey shrugged. "Let us say that your husband will be his heir."

She knew well what he was thinking and it angered her. She said, gazing straight at him, "It is so sad that my brother did not live. Then no man would look at me and at Belleterre as one and the same."

"You do not hold yourself in sufficient esteem, cousin. Believe me, I value you for yourself alone."

She wanted to laugh in his face for the blatant lie, but she felt a tingling of fear and rising gooseflesh at his words. Geoffrey was smooth as oil, but today his meaning was all too clear. He was eight years her senior and she remembered him clearly as a boy, tall and gangly and mean, particularly to her brother, Jean. She knew that her father had blamed Geoffrey for her brother's drowning, and because her father believed him responsible, so did Kassia. Maurice had forbidden Geoffrey to come to Belleterre for five long, very peaceful years, until his sister's merciless harping made him relent. But every time Geoffrey came to Belleterre, her father would mutter about vipers and bad blood.

Kassia wondered now at Geoffrey's motives, and decided to push him. "Yes," she said. "I suspect that one day I will have to wed. But of course, my father will select my husband."

"Or perhaps the Duke of Brittany will."

"That could only happen if my father were dead."

"We live in uncertain times," Geoffrey said. "Just last week one of my men, a strong fellow and young, fell ill of a fever that wasted him within a week. Yes, life is quite uncertain."

"Surely such a philosophy isn't at all comforting," Kassia said. "Do not you believe that God protects those who are good?"

"You speak like a child, Kassia. God has little to

do with the affairs of men. But enough of grim subjects. Tell me how you are amusing yourself during your father's absence."

Although Kassia knew that Geoffrey wasn't at all interested in her activities, it was, nonetheless, a way of passing the time until he left. She told him of her herb garden, of the medicinal properties of certain substances her nurse, Etta, had taught her about, and the construction of a new outbuilding for their temperamental cook, Raymond. She gazed at Geoffrey beneath her lashes. He was beginning to drowse in his chair. Kassia took pity on him and halted her monologue.

"When Father returns," she finished, her eyes lowered to hide the laughter, "I am certain that we will all become drunk as jongleurs with the wine he is bringing."

She did not see the look Geoffrey shot her, a look that softened briefly with regret. "A pity that I will not be here to join in your festivities," he said only.

"Yes, isn't it? Oh my, the hour has flown by with amazing speed. You must, I suppose, be on your way."

She rose, and Geoffrey, seeing no way of delaying, also got to his feet. He looked down at her face, remembering clearly how he had thought her as plain and unappetizing as monk pudding but two years before.

"You will send a messenger to Beaumanoir if ever you wish to see me?"

Kassia cocked her head to one side, thinking it an odd question, and a most unlikely circumstance, but said, "Indeed, Geoffrey. I bid you Godspeed."

She watched him mount, returned his wave, and

walked to the top of the east tower, not leaving until he and his men were specks in the distance.

She ate her evening meal with Thomas, raised her voice just a bit to a serving maid for an unmended rent in her gown, and went to bed, a headache beginning to throb at her temple.

The next morning Kassia felt oddly weak, but she ignored it and prepared to ride Bluebell, as was her habit. The morning sun was bright overhead, yet she felt cold, and her throat was feeling scratchy. "You are being silly," she said aloud, for she could count on her fingers the number of days she had been ill during her life. When Thomas prepared to help her into the saddle, she could not seem to grasp Bluebell's reins. With a small cry she fainted, falling backward into his arms.

3

Maurice cursed loudly and fluently as one of the wagons mired itself deeper into the muck. And still the rain poured down upon them in thick, cold sheets. They were circling the Noires mountains, more like barren saw-toothed crests than mountains, Graelam thought, and the rain had turned the narrow winding trail into a quagmire.

Graelam, weary and drenched to the skin, dismounted and added his strength to the back wheel. He wished he were home. But as he pushed with all his might, he thought philosophically that he would have been sodden with or without Maurice's company. The thick mud made a sucking sound and he heaved again with the men. The wheel, once freed, jumped into the air, and three casks of wine tumbled to the ground.

"Tonight, by God," Maurice said as the casks of wine were loaded again into the wagon, "we will be dry. 'Tis near to Beaumanoir we are, and I plan to ignore my witch of a sister and drink away my damp bones. And you, my lord, are my guest."

"Where is your sister's keep?" Graelam asked.

"Near to Huelgoat. I pray the damned lake hasn't flooded the countryside."

Graelam, who had never heard of Huelgoat or its lake, merely grunted. During the past three days, he had learned a great deal about Maurice de Lorris, and even more about the long-lived antipathy between him and his nephew and his sister, Lady Felice de Lacy. "She had the nerve to insult my Kassia's housekeeping," Maurice had told him. "My Kassia, who could manage your king's Windsor Palace."

Graelam thought cynically that *his* precious Kassia was assuming saintlike stature with every word from her sire's mouth. He was regretting his agreement to stay at Belleterre, even for a few days. This Kassia was likely a rabbit-toothed female, indeed, so unattractive that Maurice was courting him, Graelam de Moreton, an Englishman and a virtual stranger, as a possible husband for his daughter.

But he liked Maurice. He enjoyed his wit and the outrageous tales he spun. He hadn't even lost his sense of humor when the skies opened up and made the entire troop feel like drowned rats. And, Graelam knew, under Maurice's skillful probing he had likely told him all Maurice wished to know. He wondered, smiling to himself, if Maurice would like to know that his first wife had had a wart on her left buttock.

"As for that nephew of mine," Maurice had said in disdain the afternoon before, "he's naught but a worthless fool."

"Mayhap a dangerous one," Graelam had said calmly.

"Aye, it's possible," Maurice had agreed. "Slimy bastard." He had told Graelam about his son, Jean, a fine lad, who, he had long suspected, had been left to drown by the jealous Geoffrey. "He lusts after Belleterre, and his mother has encouraged him. She had the effrontery to tell me to my face that her son was my heir. My heir, all the while looking at Kassia as if she were naught but a fly on the ceiling. Aye, I know what is in both of their minds. Kassia wed to that malignant wretch and my sister lording it over everyone at Belleterre."

"Why," Graelam had asked Maurice, "did you not remarry after the death of your son?"

The veil of pain that had fallen into Maurice's eyes had shaken Graelam, and he needed no words to answer his question.

And now he would meet Maurice's sister, Lady Felice, and perhaps the nephew, Geoffrey.

Beaumanoir was a small castle, of little strategic importance, Graelam saw, set near the edge of a narrow lake. The water was dirty brown and churning, but had not yet flowed over its bounds. Nor did Beaumanoir appear to be a rich keep. The surrounding countryside was dotted with hilly forests of beech, oak, and pine, and the rain-drenched soil looked poor. He was aware of ragged serfs, shivering and miserably clothed in the inner bailey. He followed Maurice up the stairs into the hall, Guy at his heels.

"Brother dear," a tall woman said. "What a pleasant surprise. My, how very wet you are, Maurice. I hope that you will not die of a chill," she added, her smile ruthlessly insincere.

Maurice grunted. "Felice, this is Lord Graelam de Moreton. We are both in need of a hot bath and dry clothes."

She was a tall, slender woman, Graelam saw, and

not unhandsome, even though she must be over forty. Her hair was hidden beneath a large white wimple.

"Certainly, Maurice." Felice glanced more closely at Graelam de Moreton and felt a quickening of blood in her veins. Lord, but he was a man, and handsome. Felice gave sharp instructions for her brother's bath to a serving wench and walked toward Graelam, her hips swaying gracefully. "You, my lord," she said, "I will see to personally."

This is all I need, Graelam thought, to be seduced by Maurice's sister in my bath. He was tired, and all he wanted was to drop in his tracks. Aloud he said, "You are all kindness, my lady."

He left Guy in front of the open fire in the hall, a shy serving wench hovering over him, and followed Lady Felice to the upper chambers.

"Your son is not here, my lady?"

"Nay," Felice said. "He will be sorry to have missed his uncle."

If Geoffrey were behind the ambush in Aquitaine, Graelam thought, it did not appear that his mother knew about it.

"I am certain," Graelam said, "that Maurice is of the same mind."

Felice did not notice the sarcasm in his voice, her attention on lighting the candles in her chamber. "Ah, my lord, it's not elegant, for I am but a poor widow." Her voice rose sharply toward a serving girl: "Betta, see that Lord Graelam's bath is prepared, immediately. Now, my lord, let us ease your discomfort."

She is very efficient, Graelam thought, as she deftly assisted him out of his sodden surcoat. She unlaced his mail, clucking at its heaviness, and gently laid it in a corner. To his chagrin, she knelt before him and unfastened his chaussures. It was common practice for a lady to assist a visitor in his bath, but her hands were anything but matter-of-fact, and made him aware that he hadn't had a woman in several long weeks.

When he was naked, he felt her eyes upon him, studying him, he thought, as if he were a stud for her stable. Belatedly she handed him a thick wool cloth to wrap about himself.

"I see that you have known much battle, my lord," she said, her voice low and throaty. She reached out and touched the long scar that ran along his left side and disappeared beneath the cloth.

"Aye," Graelam said, wishing only for the serving wenches to return with the hot water.

Felice did not move away from him. She breathed in the male scent of him, the fresh rain smell mixing with his sweat, so potent that she felt her senses reel.

She stepped away from him when three serving wenches hauled buckets of steaming water into her chamber and heaved them into the wooden tub. She herself added cold water and tested the temperature of the bath. Satisfied, she rose and beckoned Graelam with a smile.

"Come, my lord, this will revive you."

Graelam pulled off the cloth and stepped into the tub. The feel of the hot water made him draw in his breath with sheer pleasure. He leaned his head back against the edge of the tub and closed his eyes.

"I did not know that my brother called an Englishman friend," Felice said, her voice too close.

"We have traveled together from Aquitaine,"

Graelam said, wishing that the woman would leave him in peace.

He felt a soapy sponge drift slowly over his shoulder and forced himself to keep his eyes closed.

"I see," Felice said, moving the sponge over his chest. Her finger tingled at the touch of him. "Lean forward, my lord, and I will wash your back."

Graelam did as she bid. "Aye," he said, "I will journey with Graelam to Belleterre. He wishes me to spend some time there."

Did he imagine her sucking in her breath? "Aye, I wish to see his daughter, Kassia. I have been told that she is a beautiful girl."

The sponge halted a moment on his back. "Kassia," Felice said, "is a sweet child, though my brother spoils her shamefully. Once she is wed to Geoffrey, I fear I will have to teach her many things. As for her looks"—he could feel her shrugging— "she resembles her mother, so of course my poor Maurice is somewhat prejudiced. Only passable, one would say. Now, my lord, lean back and I will wash your hair."

Graelam knew he should mind his own business, but her matter-of-fact assumption that Maurice's daughter was to wed her son aroused his curiosity. He had gotten the distinct impression that Maurice would send his daughter to a convent before he would allow such a thing. But then, had Maurice died, Kassia would be at the mercy of her aunt.

He leaned his head back and reveled in her fingers rubbing soap into his scalp. Though it was none of his business, he said, "I did not realize that Geoffrey was a suitor for Kassia's hand."

"Oh," Felice said, "Maurice will come about. He

has this odd dislike for his own nephew, but it will pass. After all, Geoffrey is his heir."

She rinsed his hair and bade him to rise.

"Heir?" Graelam asked, aware of the sponge descending slowly over his belly. "I would have thought that his daughter is his heir."

Her hand paused, and he felt her fingers softly tangling in the thick black hair of his groin. His sex swelled.

"How magnificent you are, my lord," Felice said, and to Graelam's surprise, she giggled like a girl.

"The air is cool, my lady," he said, gritting his teeth. "I would wish to be done."

"Certainly, my lord," Felice agreed, but she continued her assault on his body, touching and exploring every inch of him.

"Should you not see to your brother's comfort?" Graelam asked, an edge of desperation to his voice. He was not made of stone, but the thought of bedding this woman left all but his brainless sex cold.

"My brother," Felice said dryly, "is likely enjoying the services of Glenna. I will fetch you one of my son's bedrobes, my lord."

Graelam took the cloth from her and dried himself, relieved that finally she had left him in peace. It was in his mind to relieve himself to prevent further unwanted reactions from his body, but she returned too quickly, a rich burgundy velvet robe in her hands.

"I fear, my lord," she said in a clipped, almost angry voice, "that my brother is demanding that you come to him." She ran her tongue over her lips, but his attention was on the robe.

Graelam smiled at her, a slow, seductive smile that made her knees tremble. "Perhaps," he said, "if Maurice is not with this Glenna, I could enjoy her services."

It was cruel and he knew it, but he refused to spend the night half-awake, waiting for her to crawl into bed beside him.

Two spots of color flagged her cheeks and she wheeled about and left the chamber.

Graelam walked quickly down the stairs into the hall, still wearing Geoffrey's bedrobe. He heard Maurice's voice: "You did not tell me, dear sister, where my nephew is. Does he take no interest in his home?"

"I do not know where Geoffrey is," Felice said, watching him tear the chicken meat off a bone with his strong teeth. Damn him, she thought enviously. Just last week she had lost another tooth, this one dangerously close to the front of her mouth.

She saw Graelam approach and felt fury course through her. She had offered herself to him, and he had refused her. She touched her fingers unconsciously to her jaw, feeling the slack flesh, and winced. Soon he would be comparing her to Kassia.

Maurice smiled, his mouth full, and motioned Graelam to join him.

"Did my lord Graelam tell you, Felice, that he would be spending some days with Kassia and me at Belleterre?"

She heard the malicious tone, but forced herself to smile.

"Aye," she said. "Geoffrey rode to Belleterre but a few days past. It seems that Kassia was very pleased to see him."

Maurice howled with laughter, a piece of bread flying from his mouth. "Kassia," he said, "is her father's daughter. Her pleasure in her cousin's company can only reflect her sire's pleasure in his nephew's company, and that, my dear sister, is nil."

"You Maurice, are merely jealous that you have a worthless girl. Geoffrey is a warrior and is rising in favor with the duke."

"I am not surprised, if he has his father's oily tongue and your cunning, sister."

Graelam chewed thoughtfully on his meat, watching the two of them spar. At least, he thought, it appeared that Lady Felice had all but forgotten him. He cast an eye about for the wench Glenna as he drank his ale.

"If only," he heard Felice say angrily, "I had not been born a female, Belleterre would be mine. And you, Maurice, you would sell your homely daughter's hand to the devil to keep Belleterre from its rightful heir."

"You are never satisfied, sister. It was you who insisted upon wedding Gilbert de Lacy. His was the bed you wanted, so now you may lie in it."

"Where is Guy?" Graelam asked Maurice in a brief moment of silence.

Maurice said absently, "Glenna found the fair Englishman much to her taste. She is likely teaching your knight a thing or two."

So much for that, Graelam thought, and downed the remainder of his ale. He rose and laid his hand on Maurice's shoulder. "We've a long ride tomorrow, and I, for one, am ready to take my rest."

Maurice shot a snide look toward his sister. "If you don't mind, dear sister, my lord Graelam and I will sleep in Geoffrey's chamber. As an Englishman, he is too polite to protect himself."

Felice gave Graelam a venomous look and Graelam a disappointed smile.

"I thank you, my lady," Graelam said, "for your hospitality. The bath was refreshing and the meal sits well in my belly."

"And he wants nothing else sitting on his belly, sister."

Felice said something, but Graelam could not make out her words. He found himself wondering if the two of them had argued and baited each other all their lives. He was mildly disappointed that Geoffrey had not been present. He would have liked to take the man's measure himself.

The rain, thankfully, had stopped during the night, and the sun was fast drying the muddy road by the time they left Beaumanoir.

"It's a relief to be away from that viper's nest," Maurice said.

Graelam cocked a thick black brow. "You gave as good as you got, Maurice. Indeed, I fancied that you were enjoying yourself."

"Aye," Maurice said. "Felice has never bored me. I gave her two casks of wine for her hospitality."

As for Guy, Graelam found the young knight heavy-eyed. He'd evidently not slept much.

They passed through hilly forests of oak and beech, cut through by gorges, ravines, and tumbled rocks. Untilled moors dotted with yellow gorse and purple heather stretched to barren summits, giving views of tilled green valleys beyond. Maurice grew more excited as they drew closer to Belleterre. "We are near the Morlaix River," Maurice said. "You can nearly smell the sea. The soil is rich here, fortunately, and our wheat crops are plentiful in most years. We also have cattle and sheep aplenty, and their noxious smell and loud baas fill the air in the spring."

Graelam nodded. "It's like Cornwall," he said. "The beggers also abound there. It is a difficult task to keep them out of the crops. God be praised that we grow most of our wheat and barley in a valley, protected from the salty air and the sea winds."

Twilight was falling when they crossed the final rocky rise. "There"—Maurice pointed proudly—"is Belleterre."

Belleterre was not a sprawling pile of stone, as was Wolffeton. Nor did its aura of strength lessen its beauty. Graelam's military eyes took in its battlements and its prominence in the countryside and the river. Belleterre was a fortress of no mean value.

As Graelam turned to tell Maurice some of his thoughts, Maurice shouted, dug his heels in his destrier's sides, and rode like a wild-eyed Saracen up the steep path to Belleterre. The rest of his men, save those driving the wagons, fell into line behind him, all of them shouting and waving.

Graelam said to Guy, "When you are within the walls, I want you to examine the fortifications. Wolffeton is in need of repairs. Perhaps you will learn something useful. As for me, I fear that I will be drinking a lot of wine and smiling at Maurice's precious daughter until my mouth aches."

"Glenna told me that Kassia de Lorris is a gentle girl and possessed of considerable beauty."

Graelam grunted. "I care not if she be as winsome as Queen Eleanor or a crone with no teeth," he said.

As he rode under the iron portcullis into the inner bailey, he noted the winching mechanisms and the thickness of the inner walls with approval. The inner bailey itself surprised him. It was flawlessly clean and orderly. Even the cobblestones were set into the earth on a slight incline so that rainwater would not collect. He was examining the outbuildings and the stables when he heard Maurice shouting at the top of his lungs, "Kassia! Kassia!"

There was something wrong. The many people who were in the inner bailey were strangely quiet, staring toward Maurice or talking in whispers to each other behind their hands. They had the look, Graelam thought suddenly, of sheep who had lost their shepherd. He dismounted from Demon and handed the reins to one of his men.

He looked upward at the huge keep, and the winding thick oak stairs that led to the great hall. Suddenly he heard an anguished cry. "Kassia—"

Graelam ran up the stairs to a huge, high-vaulted chamber. He was vaguely aware of the smell of lemon, and sweet rosemary from the thick rushes that covered the stone floor. There were exquisite tapestries covering the walls next to a cavernous fireplace. He saw Maurice stride toward an old woman and begin to shake her shoulders.

"My lord," Graelam said, closing his hand over Maurice's arm. "What is the matter?"

Maurice made an odd keening sound and released the old woman. "It's Kassia. I am told she has a fever and is dying."

He rushed like a madman toward the stairs that led to the upper chambers, Graelam at his heels.

Graelam drew back when Maurice flung open the door to a chamber at the top of the stairs. The room was filled with a sickening sweet scent of incense, and the myriad candles cast long shadows on the walls. There were four women surrounding a raised bed. The silence was shattering. Two coal braziers burned next to the bed, and the heat was stifling. Graelam found himself walking forward toward the bed.

Maurice was bowing over a figure, his sobs painful to hear.

"My dear child, no—no," he heard Maurice say over and over. "You cannot leave me. No."

Graelam moved closer and stared down at Kassia de Lorris. He felt a knot of pity in his belly. The pitiful creature was a parody of life. Her hair had been cut close, and the flesh of her face was gray. He saw Maurice clutching at her hand. It looked like a claw. He could hear her pained breathing. Suddenly Maurice jerked back the cover, and Graelam stared in horror at several leeches that were sucking at the wasted flesh of her breasts.

"Get them off her," Maurice yelled. He clutched at the blood-engorged leeches, ripped them from his daughter's flesh, and hurled them across the room.

The old woman, Etta, touched his shoulder, but he threw off her hand. "You are killing her, you old crone. God's bones, you are killing her."

The girl could be fifteen years old or a hundred, Graelam thought. He could even see the blue veins standing out on her eyelids. He wondered briefly what Kassia de Lorris had looked like before she had been struck down. Poor child, he thought, his eyes narrowing in pity on her face. He wanted to do something, but knew there was nothing he could say, nothing he could do. He turned slowly and left the chamber, the sound of Maurice's curses and sobs filling his ears.

Guy was speaking to a serving wench. When he saw Graelam, he quickly walked over to him and said quietly, "The girl is dying, my lord. She came down with the fever some four days ago. She is not expected to last through the night."

Graelam nodded. Indeed, he was surprised that she still clung to life.

"The serving wench thinks that the priest should be fetched."

"That is Maurice's decision." Graelam ran his hand through his hair, realizing that Maurice's thoughts were all on his daughter. "Have the priest brought here."

He and Guy ate a silent meal, attended by quietly crying servants. Graelam wondered where all Maurice's men were, but didn't ask the servants.

"It's a rich keep," Guy said, looking around the great hall. The trestle table shone with polish and there were cushions on the benches. "I am very sorry for Lord Maurice."

"Aye," Graelam said, his eyes resting a moment upon the two beautifully carved high-backed chairs that stood opposite each other not far from the warm fire. Between the chairs was an ivory chessboard, the pieces in place. He tried to picture Maurice and Kassia seated opposite each other, laughing and playing chess. His belly tightened. Damn, he thought, he didn't want to be touched by the girl's death. He felt suddenly as though he were trespassing. He was, after all, a stranger.

He found himself drawn to the chairs, and he eased himself down, a goblet of ale resting on his knee. He found his eyes going every few minutes toward the stairs. The priest arrived, a bald, watery-eyed old man whose robe was tied loosely about his fat stomach.

The time passed with agonizing slowness. Graelam dismissed Guy and found himself alone in the great hall. It was near to midnight when he saw Maurice walk like a bent old man down the stairs. His face was haggard and his eyes swollen.

"She is dying," Maurice said in a strangely calm voice. He sat down in the chair opposite Graelam and stared into the fire. "I found myself wishing that you, my lord, had not saved me. Perhaps if I had died, God would spare Kassia."

Graelam clutched Maurice's hand. "You will not say that, Maurice. A man cannot question God's will." His words sounded empty, even to his own ears.

"Why not? She is good and pure, and gentle. It is not right or just that she be cheated of life. God's blood, do you understand? I wanted you, the man who saved my life, a strong warrior who knows no fear, to take her to wife. To protect her, and Belleterre, to give me grandchildren. God be cursed. It's an evil that takes her from me."

Graelam watched helplessly as Maurice dropped his face into his hands and sobbed. He pictured the small girl in the chamber above and felt pity choking in his throat. He had seen horrors unimagined in the Holy Land, but it had been the utter waste that had disgusted him, not the actual misery of the people. He did not want to be affected by the death of one girl. By the saints in heaven, he did not even know her.

"Maurice," he said urgently, "what will happen you cannot change. Belleterre is yours. If you wish it to remain yours, you must remarry and breed more children of your own. You must not give up."

Maurice laughed, a humorless, bitter sound that made Graelam wince. "I cannot," he said finally, very quietly. "I contracted a disease some ten years ago. It left my seed lifeless."

There was nothing to say. Graelam closed his eyes, leaning back in the chair, only the sounds of Maurice's ragged breathing breaking the silence of the hall. He felt the older man's hand upon his arm and opened his eyes to see Maurice looking at his face with feverish intensity.

"Listen to me, my lord," Maurice said, his fingers tightening on Graelam's arm. "I will repay my debt to you. Belleterre is near to the coast and thus not far from your lands in Cornwall. Even if my Kassia's blood cannot flow in the veins of Belleterre's descendants, yours will. It's noble blood you carry, my lord Graelam, and I would call you my son and heir."

"That is not possible, Maurice," Graelam said. "I am an Englishman, and your liege lord would never grant me your lands. Nor do I deserve to have them. Maurice, I would have saved your life had you been a merchant. You must make peace with yourself, and perhaps with your nephew. There is no choice."

Maurice's eyes glistened with purpose. "Nay, my lord, attend me. If you wed my Kassia this night, you will be her husband and entitled to Belleterre upon my death."

Graelam drew back appalled. "No. By God's teeth, Maurice, you aren't thinking. Your daughter is dying. Leave her in peace."

"You would not be burdened with a wife unknown to you. You will have only the responsibility of Belleterre. What matters it to Kassia if she is wed before she dies? What matters it to you?''

Graelam hissed out his breath, his body hard with tension. ''I will not marry the child. I buried one wife, I will not wed another only to bury her within hours. See you, Maurice, it is madness, it's your grief.''

Maurice drew back in his chair, but his eyes never wavered from Graelam's face. ''Hear me, my lord. If Kassia dies unwed, my own death warrant is signed. Geoffrey will not wait for my body to rot with age. He will take what he believes is his. But with you as Kassia's husband—''

''Widower.''

''—widower, Geoffrey will find himself helpless against a powerful English nobleman. I cannot save my daughter, but I can save Belleterre. Marry her, Graelam, then you will go to the Duke of Brittany and swear your fealty to him. I ask nothing more of you. You can return to England with naught but honor, and the promise of rich lands for your sons.''

Graelam rose swiftly from his chair and paced to and fro in front of the older man. ''You do not even know me,'' he said, striving for cool reason as he came to an abrupt halt in front of Maurice, his arms folded over his powerful chest. ''I was a stranger to you until less than a week ago. How can you trust your lands to a man who could, for all you know, be the biggest scoundrel in all of Christendom?''

''I would rather trust my fortunes to an unknown scoundrel than to a known one. Be you a scoundrel, my lord?''

Graelam gritted his teeth. ''Leave be, Maurice. If you fear your nephew, I will kill him for you before I leave Brittany. Does that ease your mind?''

"Nay. Belleterre must have its lord, and he must be strong, ruthless, and a fearless warrior. You must be the future Lord of Belleterre."

Graelam stared at him, stunned.

"Even now," Maurice continued, "Kassia could be drawing her last breath. If you do not wed her, my lord, I will lose everything I hold dear in his wretched world. By all that's holy, man, do I ask so much of you? I take nothing from you, only give. You do not lose your vaunted honor. You suffer no shame."

It was not Maurice de Lorris' passionate words that decided Graelam at that moment. It was the unashamed tears that streaked down his cheeks.

"Let us get it over with," Graelam said.

Graelam held Kassia's hand in his as the priest said his marriage lines in the early hours of the night. He felt the delicate bones and knew a moment of utter pain. Maurice's scribe had hastily penned the marriage contract, and in the bleak silence of the stifling hot chamber, Graelam de Moreton signed his name and titles. He watched silently as Maurice guided Kassia's hand over the parchment.

"My daughter writes," Maurice said, his voice quavering. "I taught her."

It was done. Graelam heard the soft rattling deep in her chest and knew the end was near. Slowly he drew off his ring, thick pounded gold inset with onyx, the deep imprint of a wolf raised on its surface, and slid it onto Kassia's middle finger. He closed her fingers into a fist to keep the ring from sliding off, and gently laid her hand over her chest.

"Come, my lord," Maurice said. "There is much to do before I grieve."

Graelam took one last look at his wife, then followed Maurice from the chamber.

"It will be morning soon, my lord. You must journey immediately to St. Pol-de-Leon on the northern coast. The Duke of Brittany is at his castle there. You will only tell him that you have wed Kassia de Lorris and present to him the marriage contract."

"I am known to the duke," Graelam said. He remembered the powerful Charles de Marcey, a proud man, but a man Edward approved. Graelam had bested the duke in a joust. He wondered if de Marcey would remember.

Maurice's eyes glittered and he rubbed his hands together. "Excellent. You must swear fealty to him. Kassia's death will be kept a secret for as long as possible."

"Very well, Maurice. I will return—"

"Nay. There is no need, my lord. I will bury my daughter and you will continue on your way." He paused a moment, his eyes lowered to his gnarled hands. "I wish to grieve alone. I will be safe from Geoffrey, for your marriage will be proclaimed far and wide. I thank you, Graelam de Moreton."

Graelam saw a tear fall on the back of Maurice's hands. He felt a portion of his grief, but he knew no words to ease it.

"I wish you well, Maurice," he said. He took the older man in his arms and pressed him tightly. "I will share some of your pain, my friend."

"I thank you," Maurice said again, and drew back, his shoulders straightening. "You must leave now. Godspeed, my son."

Graelam halted his small troop to gaze back at Belleterre bathed in the crimson streaks of dawn. It was a magnificent castle, and he could not prevent the surge of pleasure that one day Belleterre would belong to one of his sons.

"Guy," he said to the silent young knight beside him. "You know what has passed. I wish you to keep all to yourself. Ensure that the men keep silent also."

"Aye, my lord," Guy said. "I am sorry, my lord."

"Yes," Graelam said in a harsh voice. "So am I."

He wheeled Demon about and dug in his heels. The powerful destrier bounded forward, and soon Belleterre was lost to view in a cloud of dust.

4

Charles de Marcey, Duke of Brittany, slouched in his chair, his thoughts not on the two knights squabbling before him, but on his wife, Alice, and her unending demands. Always another jewel, or a new gown, always something. Damn her for a bitch, he thought, and shifted in his chair. She dared to berate him for taking a willing girl to his bed, when she, frigid witch that she was, refused him. His sudden movement momentarily silenced the two knights, and they looked at him expectantly.

He waved his hand, frowning. "Continue," he said. And to his scribe he said, "You, Simon, are recording the essence of this problem?"

"Aye, my lord," Simon said, crouching again over the small table in front of him.

Poor Simon, he grew hunchbacked in Charles's service. He sighed, wishing he were hunting, for it was a beautiful spring day, the air fresh and crisp. Anything but listening to squabbles about a keep small enough to fit in his hauberk. The two young men needed bloodletting and he wondered idly if he shouldn't let them go at each other. He was aware that Simon was giving him one of his looks, damn the old man, and pulled his attention back to the two men.

The morning hearings droned on. Charles informed the two knights that he would consider their respective claims and waved his hand in dismissal.

"My lord," Robert de Gros, his closest friend and chamberlain said, approaching him. "An Englishman is here, claiming to know you. He says it is a matter of some urgency."

Charles raised a thick auburn eyebrow and looked from Robert toward the doorway to the chamber.

"Graelam de Moreton. By all that's holy." Charles roared, leaping up from his chair. "I had thought we would be lucky and your hide would be skinned in the Holy Land."

Graelam strode forward, relieved that Charles remembered him and appeared glad to see him. "The Saracens cannot fell an Englishman, my lord," he said.

Charles grasped him by the shoulders. "Do you never learn to show respect to your betters, Graelam?"

"Edward," Graelam said, "never had any reason to complain. How the devil did you know I was in the Holy Land?"

Charles laughed, buffeting Graelam's shoulder. "Your King Edward has scribes to write letters, my lord, unlike the rest of his illiterate followers. I hear that you, Graelam, are one of the few to return with riches from the Holy Land."

"Aye," Graelam said, "perhaps even a jewel for your wife's lovely throat."

"That," Charles said, "is the best news I have

heard today. Come, my lord, let us speak in private and I will hear this urgent business of yours."

Graelam followed Charles from the suffocatingly ornate hall filled with chattering lords and ladies into a small chamber that held but two chairs and a single table. The court life Charles led was making him soft, Graelam thought, studying the Frenchman. Although he was but five years Graelam's senior, lines of dissipation marred his handsome face, and a paunch was beginning to thicken his belly. But his thick auburn hair was unmarked by gray and his dark eyes were sharp with intelligence, his boredom of a few moments before replaced with interest. He certainly looked prosperous enough, with his rich crimson robe and full ermine-lined sleeves.

Without pause, Graelam handed Charles the marriage contract. "I am wed to Kassia de Lorris of Belleterre. I am here to swear fealty to you as my liege lord and gain your official sanction."

To Graelam's surprise, Charles threw back his head and roared with laughter. "That sly old fox," he said, tapping his finger against the parchment. "Ah, I cannot wait to see the fury on poor Geoffrey's face."

"Geoffrey de Lacy is here?" Graelam asked, feeling a tingling of anticipation.

"Sit down, Lord Graelam, and I will tell you about the nest of hornets you have stirred."

Charles bellowed for wine, then eased back in his chair, his hands folded over his belly. "How timely your announcement, my lord. My coffers don't yield enough."

"They never did," Graelam said. "Unfortunately, the riches I gained in the Holy Land must be spent in reparation of Wolffeton. What I offer you in return for recognizing my marriage is a strong sword arm and fighting men to protect your lands. I am at your disposal, say, one month of the year. And, of course, a ruby perhaps for your wife."

"Well, that is something, I suppose," Charles said, sipping at his wine. From the corner of his eye he saw the serving wench hovering near the doorway, doubtless one of his wife's spies. He turned a narrowed eye on the wench and she quickly disappeared.

"My wife," he said, "likes to be informed of everything. I should not wonder if she knows when my bowels move."

Graelam cocked a disbelieving brow. "You, my lord, under a woman's thumb? You tell me that age will shrivel my manhood?"

"It's my manhood I protect." He sighed. "I once believed her so lovely, so innocently sweet. And her body still tempts me mightily."

"Your lady's body is yours," Graelam said, waving a dismissing hand. "Saint Peter's bones, Charles, beat her. A man cannot allow a woman to rule him, else he is no man."

"Ah," Charles said, not offended, "thus speaks a man who has never known a tender emotion. Though," Charles added, frowning into his wine, "the saints know that emotion doesn't last long. The troubadours have done men a great disservice. Their verses make the ladies dream of softness and love, and a man, witless creature, plays the part to get what he wants."

"In England men are not such fools."

"Still so harsh," Charles said. "Let us say, Graelam, that one must suffer a wife's inquisitiveness if she is to suffer his dalliances."

"A woman should have no say in a man's affairs," Graelam said, impatience clear in his voice. "If I remember aright, you were surrounded in England by ladies who wanted naught but to share your bed."

"Aye," Charles said, his eyes growing soft with memory. He sighed again. "Alas, a man grows older, and must take a wife."

"I would beat any woman who dared infringe on my wishes, wife or no. A woman is to be soft and yielding, her duty to see to her master's pleasures and bear him sons."

"And your dear young wife, my friend? Is she gentle and submissive enough to suit you?"

Graelam was silent for a moment, seeing the gray death pallor of Kassia's face. "She is what she is," he said.

"I can almost pity the girl," Charles said. "There is no chivalry in Englishmen. I hope you did not rip her apart on your wedding night with that huge rod of yours."

"Maurice de Lorris sends his greetings," Graelam said. "And his continued pledge of fealty."

"As does his beloved nephew, Geoffrey de Lacy," Charles said. "Geoffrey, until your arrival, Graelam, had convinced me that he should have Kassia de Lorris's hand. He also pledged fealty and other things."

"Then he lies," Graelam said. "I have visited his keep, Beaumanoir. His serfs are ragged wretches, what men I saw appeared swaggering louts, and his mother—"

"The less spoken about Lady Felice, the better."

"—and I would willingly dispatch Geoffrey de Lacy to hell as meet him."

"I imagine Geoffrey will feel the same way—until he sees you, that is. He is brave enough, but not stupid. It's odd what you say about Beaumanoir, for Geoffrey possesses wealth. Lord knows he is lining my pockets. Very well, Graelam de Moreton, what's done is done. You have my official sanction and I accept your pledge of fealty. Breed many sons, Graelam, for the line of Belleterre is a noble one, old and proud."

Graelam bowed his head, and if Charles chose to think it silent agreement, it was his right. The only way he could hold Belleterre after Maurice's death, Graelam knew, would be to kill Geoffrey. The thought gave him no pause of regret.

"Now, my lord Englishman, tell me about your adventures and how you gained your riches. Mayhap I can still relieve you of some of them."

Graelam obliged him, recalling the long, desperate months in the Holy Land, and the outcome, the Treaty of Caesarea. "The Holy Land is replete with fools, Charles, greedy fools who care naught for anything save filling their coffers. They ignore the misery and death that surround them. The treaty"—he gave an ironic laugh—"will protect the fools for another ten years. As for my riches, my lord duke, I gained those in a raid on a Saracen camp."

He looked into the swirling red wine in his goblet and shook his head, not wanting to share that particular adventure with Charles.

He said abruptly, "And you, how many sons now carry your proud name?"

"I am cursed with three daughters and but one

son. Ah, Graelam, the adventures we shared. Do you remember that merchant's daughter in London, the one with the witch's black hair?"

"Aye, the little tart nearly exhausted me."

"You. Ha, it was I who shared her pallet and her favors."

"You rearrange the past to suit yourself, my lord duke." Graelam rose from his chair and proffered Charles a bow. "But since you are my liege lord, I will not trifle with your fanciful memories."

"You are a dog, Graelam," Charles said. He lowered his thick auburn brows and said in a sly voice, "Do I take it as the new bridegroom you will remain chaste during your visit here?"

Graelam refused to be baited, and gave Charles a crooked grin. "I have no taste for the pox, my lord duke. My carnal needs can wait."

The duke roared with laughter. "Ah, Graelam, I cannot wait until the evening dinner to see how you avoid the amorous advances of all the ladies. Alas, I am weak of flesh. I will have my chamberlain show you a chamber."

"I must leave on the morrow, Charles, but I gladly accept your hospitality this night."

"Back to your blushing bride?"

Graelam paused but an instant. "Aye," he said. "I must get back."

Graelam was markedly silent the following morning when he and his men left St. Pol-de-Leon. The coast was barren, battered ceaselessly by the merciless sea winds. Jagged cliffs rose to savage splendor about the rock-strewn beaches. There were no bushes or flowers to soften the bitter landscape. Graelam was impervious to his surroundings, his thoughts on his encounter the previous evening with Geoffrey de Lacy. The great chamber with its huge trestle tables held enough food to supply Edward's army in the Holy Land for at least a week. The duke had taken great delight in introducing Graelam to Geoffrey de Lacy, enjoying the other man's rage, for enraged he was.

"You must welcome Lord Graelam de Moreton to the family," Charles said, eyes alight with deviltry on Geoffrey's pale face.

Geoffrey felt such fury that for a moment he could do nothing but think of the dagger in his belt. His long fingers unconsciously stroked the fine-boned handle.

"I have heard much about you," Graelam said, studying Geoffrey as he would any enemy. Geoffrey de Lacy was about five years his junior, Graelam guessed, a tall, slender young man blessed with broad shoulders and a pleasing face. His hair was dark brown, but it was his eyes that held Graelam's attention. They were a pale blue and shone from his face like slivers of blue ice. He wondered cynically, remembering Lady Felice's randy disposition and dark coloring, if Geoffrey had inherited his features from his father or another.

He watched Geoffrey run his tongue over his lower lip. "I did not know," Geoffrey said, his voice as icy as his eyes, "that my esteemed uncle knew any Englishmen."

"Ah," Graelam said easily, knowing that the duke was enjoying himself immensely, "I did not meet him until very recently. Indeed, I saved him from being murdered by a band of ruffians in Aquitaine."

Maurice's conjectures were right, he thought, catching the flicker of guilt in Geoffrey's eyes. And dismay and frustration.

Geoffrey realized that he must get a hold on himself, for the duke was standing near, all attention. He stared at the harshly handsome man who was looking him with something close to contempt. How he would like to slit the English bastard's throat.

"His gift to me," Graelam said, "was Kassia's fair hand and Belleterre. I shall cherish my possessions."

"Kassia is too young," Geoffrey said, pain and fury breaking his voice. "She is innocent and trusting—"

"No longer," the duke said, laughing, a leering gleam in his dark eyes. "Innocent at least. Lord Graelam is a man of strong passions, as I'm certain his young bride realizes now."

Geoffrey pictured Graelam naked, his powerful body covering Kassia's, pictured him thrusting between her legs. "Kassia was to have been mine," he growled, unable to contain his rage.

"I suggest that you forget both Kassia and Belleterre," Graelam said. "Your own keep, Beaumanoir, is much in need of your attention. Of course, I did not see many of your men. Perhaps they were off elsewhere, following your orders."

"You make insinuations, my lord," Geoffrey said, his hand going to his dagger.

Before he knew it his arm was caught in a grip of iron. "You, my puppy, had best forget your plans and disappointments, else I will break your neck. If ever Belleterre tempts you again, you will find yourself with your face in the dirt."

Geoffrey tasted fear like flaky ashes in his mouth. Hatred boiled inside him, making him tremble. "You will regret what you have done, my lord," he said. He pulled his arm from Graelam's hold and strode from the chamber.

A fine drizzle began to fall and Graelam pulled his cloak more closely about him. He cursed, unable to keep the image of Kassia de Lorris's ravaged face from his mind. He could still hear the soft rattle rising over her labored breathing. She was dead and buried now, poor child, beyond Geoffrey's twisted desires. He found himself worrying about Maurice, and wondered if he shouldn't return to Belleterre. But no, Maurice had been adamant. He had wished to grieve alone, and Graelam knew he must respect his wishes. He wondered how long Kassia's death could be kept a secret. He imagined that within the year he would be returning to Belleterre to defend it from Geoffrey. He smiled at the thought of running Geoffrey cleanly through with his sword.

5

Kassia was trapped in darkness. She realized that her eyes were closed, but she hadn't the strength within her to open them. She heard a hoarse, whimpering sound.

"Hush, my baby." She heard a soft, crooning voice, Etta's voice, and she quieted.

She felt a wooden object pressing against her lips.

"Open your mouth, Kassia. It's beef broth." She did as she was bid. The delicious liquid coursed down her throat.

"Papa," she whispered.

"Yes, *ma chère*. I am here. A bit more broth and you can sleep again."

Maurice gently wiped the trickle of broth from her slack mouth and raised worried eyes to Etta.

"Time, my lord, it will take time. The child will live. She's a de Lorris."

"Aye," Maurice said, his voice sounding as tired as he felt, "a de Lorris." But Jean, his son, had been a de Lorris, and he had died. So young he was, so innocent and helpless.

He sat back in his chair, his eyes upon his daugh-

ter's ravaged face. He wondered idly if the final abso-
lution the priest had granted would serve her when
the time came for her to really leave this earth.

"Fool," he said to himself. "Your brain is becoming
fodder for the cows." He thought of Graelam de
Moreton, and felt a shudder go through him. He
would not think of Graelam now, nor what that
proud warrior would think or do when he discovered his wife lived.

"Papa?"

"Aye, poppin."

"It is raining. It's a marvelous sound."

Maurice kissed her. There was a sparkle in her eyes
again, and her face had lost the gray hollowness.

"You look tired," Kassia said, her eyes narrowing
on her father's face.

"You worry about yourself, Kassia, and let this old
man be. By the saints, child, I have prayed until my
knees are knobby and stiff." He clasped her fingers,
gently stroking them. He felt such happiness that he
could burst with it. Her fingers, of course, were bare.
He had tucked Graelam's ring into a leather pouch
in his chamber.

"I have had such dreams, Papa," Kassia said. "I
remember your voice, of course, but there was another as well. A voice I did not recognize, speaking
in a soft way."

"It was likely one of the women you heard," Maurice said.

"Nay, it was a man's voice, deep and slow."

"A dream," Maurice said. She was still too weak
to know the truth of the matter. He could not believe
that she remembered Graelam.

"Aye," Kassia said, her lashes sweeping over her eyes, "it was a dream."

The days flowed into nights. Kassia slept, spoke briefly to Etta and her father, and ate. At the end of a week she had strength enough to raise her hand and scratch her head. Her fingers slid beneath the simple cotton wimple and touched short tufts of spiky hair.

Maurice entered her chamber to see tears streaking down her face.

He rushed to her bed, guessing their cause when he saw the wimple lying beside her. "Fie, Kassia," he said. " 'Tis but a head of hair, naught of anything. I had not believed you so vain."

Her tears stopped, and she sniffed.

"Within a month you will have soft curls and look like a sweet choir boy."

Suddenly she smiled. "Perhaps you should invite Geoffrey to Belleterre. Were he to see me like this, he would soon lose his desire to wed me."

"There, you see," Maurice said, "there is always a bright side to things. As for Geoffrey, that whoreson dare not show his face here. Now, Kassia, I've brought you another goblet of sweet wine from Aquitaine."

"I think I've already drunk a cask, Papa. If I continue swilling I will have a veined red nose."

She sipped the wine, enjoying its smoothness and warmth. "Papa," she said. "I want a bath. I cannot continue to lie here and wallow in my own filth. Then I want to lie in the garden and feel the sun upon my face."

Maurice beamed at her, feeling his heart swell. "You shall have whatever you desire, poppin." He wrinkled his nose. "You are right about the bath. That must be first."

It was a golden day in Cornwall. The sun shone hot and bright overhead and the stiff sea breeze smelled as sweet as the clumps of wildflowers that grew on the surrounding hills.

Graelam felt utter contentment as he drew Demon to a halt at the edge of the sloping cliff and stared down at the white-crested waves that crashed against the rocks below. From St. Agnes Point, a sharp jutting finger of land, he had a view of at least thirty miles of northward coastline. The rugged cliffs gave onto land so savage and desolate that even the trees were stunted and twisted from the westerly gales that pounded them. Beyond St. Agnes Point lay the small fishing village of St. Agnes, as desolate and rugged and timeless as the craggy cliffs it hugged.

Graelam remembered his hikes along the winding footpath below St. Agnes Point when he was a boy, exploring the caves and calmer coves that indented the coastline, and felt the savage beauty of Cornwall burn into his very soul. He turned in his saddle. Inland, beyond the ragged cliffs, were rolling hills where sheep and cattle grazed, and between the hills, in narrow valleys, farmers tilled the land. His land. His home. His people.

Rising behind him like a rough-hewn monolith stood Wolffeton, fortress of the de Moretons since Duke William had deeded the lands to Albert de Moreton after the Battle of Hastings over two hundred years ago. Albert had torn down the wooden fortress of the Saxons and had erected a stone castle that would defend the northern coast of Cornwall

from any assaulting forces, be they marauding Danes
or the greedy French. On stormy nights lamps were
lit in the two seaward towers, warning off ships from
the deadly rock-strewn waters.

In the distance he could make out the stonemasons
repairing the seaward wall, eroded over the two cen-
turies by the ferocious sea storms. The jewels he had
brought with him from the Holy Land had brought
a respectable price, enough to repair the walls of
Wolffeton, the outbuildings, his men's barracks, and
to purchase sheep, cattle, and a half-dozen horses.
As for the Great Hall and the upper chambers, they
had not changed much since Albert's days. That had
never mattered to Graelam before, but upon his return a month before he had found Wolffeton lacking.
The long walls beneath the soot-covered beams in
the Great Hall looked primitive and bare. The rough-
carved trestles and benches, even his ornately carved
chair, were equally bare, with no thick velvet cushions to soften their lines. The rushes strewn across
the stone floor had not the sweet smell of those at
Belleterre, and there was not one carpet to deaden
the heavy sound of booted feet. There were no comforts, even in his huge bedchamber. His long-dead
first wife, Marie, had not seemed to care, nor had
her half-sister, Blanche de Cormont. He was growing
soft, he grunted to himself, wanting the exotic luxu-
ries he had grown used to in the east.

Rolfe, his trusted master-at-arms, had certainly
maintained the discipline of Wolffeton during Graelam's year away in the Holy Land. But there had
been problems awaiting his return, problems that an
overlord's absence engendered. There were judg-
ments to be rendered, feuds to be settled, laxness

among the castle servants to be halted. Blount, his steward, had kept his records well, but even he could not force a greater production of cloth or discipline the wenches whose job it was to keep the castle in good order. But it gave Graelam a good feeling to be thrown back into the management of his keep and lands. The vast number of people who spent their lives at Wolffeton were his responsibility and his alone.

He thought again of Blanche de Cormont. He had returned to Cornwall a month before to find her wringing her hands when she saw him, tears shining in her eyes. He had not recognized her until she had reminded him that she was half-sister to his first wife. Soft-spoken, shy Blanche, a widow now and with no kin to take her in, none save him. She had come to Wolffeton some three months before his return home. Blount hadn't known what to do with her, so she had remained, awaiting Graelam's return. She was not old, perhaps twenty-eight, but there were faint lines of sadness etched about her mouth, and her brown eyes, when they rested upon him, were liquid with gratitude. Her two children, a boy and a girl, she had told him, her mouth trembling, were being raised by her cousin Robert, in Normandy. She, their mother, had not been welcome, particularly, she had added sadly, touching her hand to her rich raven hair, by Robert's young wife, Elise, a woman jealous of her husband's affections.

Well, Graelam had thought then as well as now, there was no harm in her residing at Wolffeton. She waited on him, served his dinner herself, and mended his clothing. It was odd, though, he thought, that the castle servants did not seem to like her. Why,

he could not guess. She seemed unobtrusive enough
to him.

Graelam's thoughts turned to the Duke of Cornwall's impending visit. King Edward's uncle had always seemed like a second father to Graelam, indeed,
more of a father than his own had been. Though
the bond between them was deep and affectionate,
Graelam devoutly prayed that the duke was not coming as his overlord to request his services. A year of
his life spent in the Holy Land fighting the heathen
Saracens was enough for any man.

He turned Demon away from the cliff and rode
northward back toward Wolffeton.

At the sound of approaching hoofbeats, Blanche de
Cormont pulled the leather hide from the window
opening in her small chamber and watched Graelam
gallop into the inner bailey of Wolffeton, his powerful body at ease in the saddle. She felt a surge of
excitement at the sight of him, and her fingers
twisted at the thought of running them through his
hair. How alike and yet different he was from her
husband, Raoul, curse that bastard's black heart. She
hoped he was rotting in hell. Like Raoul, Graelam
expected her to serve him as unquestioningly as any
servant, but unlike Raoul, he was a virile, handsome
devil whose bed every young serving wench at Wolffeton had shared willingly. And, of course, Graelam
hadn't once raised his hand against her. But then,
she thought cynically, she was not yet his wife. A
wife, she knew from painful experience, was like any
other of a man's possessions. As long as she kept to
her place and was exacting in pleasing her husband,
she was treated as well as his hunting dogs or his
destrier.

Blanche gnawed on her lower lip, wondering how much longer she should pretend the shy, self-effacing widow's role she had instinctively assumed when Graelam returned to Wolffeton. Her first husband, Raoul, had painfully taught her that her high spirits, her occasionally stinging tongue, and her pride were not acceptable in a wife. And her stubbornness. She supposed she was being stubborn where Graelam was concerned, but she wanted him and fully intended to have him. A widow and a poor relation had no real place, her children no real home or future. Perhaps it was time to give Graelam some encouragement, perhaps even slip into his bed, if she could find it empty one night.

She would wed Graelam and then bring her children to Cornwall. She missed them, particularly her son, Evian, a bright lad of eight years, but her decision to come to Cornwall was all for his sake. He would become Graelam's heir, for Blanche intended to bear no more children. The pain of her daughter's birth still made her grit her teeth. At least childbirthing hadn't killed her as it had Marie, her long-dead half-sister. Blanche shook off old memories and turned away from the window. She would meet Graelam in the Great Hall, send the sullen serving wenches out of the way, and serve him some ale herself. She gazed one last time in her polished silver mirror, and curled an errant strand of black hair around her finger. I must please him, she thought, I must.

To her disappointment, Guy de Blasis accompanied Graelam. She was wary of Guy, despite his good looks and polite manners, for she sensed that he guessed her plans and disapproved. Still, she pasted a welcoming smile on her face and walked gracefully forward, her soft wool gown swishing over the reed-covered floor.

"Good day to you, my lord," she said, smiling shyly up at Graelam.

Graelam pulled his attention from Guy and nodded. "I have news for you, Blanche. The Duke of Cornwall is paying us a visit next week. I do not know the extent of his retinue, but doubtless he will bring half an army with him, it is his way. At least," he continued, now to Guy, "the barracks will be finished, so his men will not have to sleep in the keep. We will go hunting again before he arrives. Let us pray we bag more than a rabbit."

"A deer at least, my lord," Guy said, "if we divide the men into three separate hunting parties."

"Some ale, my lord?" Blanche asked.

Graelam nodded, his thoughts elsewhere. "Ah, and some for Guy too, Blanche."

Blanche saw Guy grinning at her, and she frowned at him, but she nonetheless left the hall, her discomfiture kept to herself.

Guy waited until Blanche was out of hearing. "Have you heard anything from France, my lord? From Maurice de Lorris?"

"Nay, but then, what would I hear? If there is a message ever from him, it will doubtless be to inform me that Geoffrey is trying to steal Belleterre from him. I pray that de Lacy will keep his treacherous sword sheathed until Wolffeton is fully restored."

"I doubt he would try an outright attack," Guy said. "His way is to sneak about and hire men to do his dirty work." He fell silent a moment. "That poor girl," he said at last. "I, of course, did not ever see her, as did you, my lord, but the servants talked to me of her, as did her father's men. They all believed her a sweet child and kind and full of laughter. Aye, it is sad to die so young."

Graelam pictured Kassia's lifeless fingers held in his hands as the priest droned out the marriage words. He had only time to nod when Blanche reappeared carrying a tray with two goblets filled with ale.

"Thank you, Blanche," Graelam said, his tone holding dismissal. Blanche saw Guy quirk a fair eyebrow at her and for a moment she frowned at him. Damn him, was he guessing her thoughts?

"Certainly, my lord," she said. "Perhaps, Graelam, when you have finished speaking with Guy, you can spare me a few moments? To speak of the entertainment for the duke."

Graelam. She had used his name but the week before and he had not seemed even to notice her familiarity. Perhaps she was making headway with him.

"Perhaps this evening, Blanche," Graelam said as he wiped the white foam of the ale from his upper lip. "I have a new mare to inspect."

Guy laughed aloud, his eyes on Blanche's face. "Do you mean, my lord, that lovely little Arabian, or that equally enticing little two-legged filly named Nan?"

"Both, I fancy," Graelam said, and rose from his chair. "Nan you say her name is, Guy?"

"Aye. No virgin, but again, lovely as a rose whose petals sparkle with the morning mist. And quite young, my lord," Guy continued, knowing that Blanche was listening. It was not that he disliked Blanche, he thought, as he followed Graelam from the Great Hall down the thick, well-worn oak stairs. She was indeed lovely, his body recognized that, but she felt she must needs playact with Graelam. Guy knew she wasn't the meek, gentle creature she showed to Graelam when he had come upon one of the serving wenches in tears, a livid bruise on her cheek from the slap Lady Blanche had given her. He had told Graelam of the incident, but his master, after speaking to Blanche, had told him that the wench had deserved the slap for insulting his sister-in-law.

It was odd, Guy thought as he walked beside Graelam into the inner bailey, how his master enjoyed women in his bed, pleasuring them until they yelled, but had little understanding of them outside his bedchamber. To Lord Graelam, women were soft bodies and little else, save for the one, Chandra de Avenell, Graelam had tried to steal and wed nearly two years before. But even that beautiful creature, though she had doubtless intrigued Graelam with her warrior ways, had been only a challenge to him, like an untamed mare to be covered and broken by a stallion. He suspected that Graelam's black fury following his failure had resulted more from wounded pride than injured feelings. But now Chandra de Avenell was Chandra de Vernon, and Graelam had made peace with both her and her husband in the Holy Land. She was nothing more to him now, Guy knew, than a vague shadow of memory.

The wench Nan appeared none too clean, Graelam thought as he watched her, her arms pressed against her breasts to better entice him as she drew the bucket of water from the well. Her thick long dark brown hair would be lovely were it not lank and stringy from lack of washing. Her face was a perfect oval and she smiled at him pertly.

"If she were bathed," Graelam said to Guy, "I wouldn't kick her out of my bed."

"Nor would I," Guy said, laughing.

"How many men have enjoyed her favors?"

"Not many, my lord. She was married quite young, when she was fourteen, to a young man who worked with the armorer. He died some two months ago from the wasting disease. According to my knowledge, she has kept her legs together, awaiting your return."

Graelam gave the girl a long, slow smile, then turned away toward the newly repaired stables. "Now, Guy," he said, "it's time to see the four-legged mare."

A gale blew in that evening, and the shutters banged loudly in Graelam's bedchamber. He had spent the past two hours trouncing Guy in a game of chess and drinking more ale than was his habit. He was not overly surprised to find Nan lying in his bed.

Indeed, she did have lovely hair. It was now clean and shining and he wondered idly how long she had spent in a bathing tub to prepare herself for him. He strode to the edge of the bed and smiled at her as he stripped of his clothes. He watched her eyes widen when they fell to his swollen sex.

"Ye are huge, my lord," she said, and never looked away.

"Aye," Graelam said, "and you'll soon know every inch of me."

He drew back the cover and studied her plump white body. "Aye," he said, his dark eyes caressing her, "every inch."

He fondled her and kissed her, pleased that her breath tasted fresh. Her flesh was soft beneath his fingers and his mouth. When she was ready he went into her, hard and deep. She held him close, wrapping her legs about him, drawing him even deeper, and he realized vaguely, not particularly displeased, that she was as experienced as any whore. He reared back, thrusting deep, and felt his body explode. He rolled off her onto his back. He wondered if her soft cries of pleasure had been real or feigned.

"My lord?"

"Aye?" he said, not turning to her.

"May I rest with ye the night? It's cold and the storm frightens me."

"Aye, you may stay."

He felt her fingers running through the thick tufts of hair on his chest. "But expect, my pet, to be awakened during the night. My appetite for you is but momentarily sated."

Nan giggled and stretched her length against his side, hugging herself to him. She had pleased him. Now life would be better for her. Aye, much better. She smiled into the darkness at the thought of the sour looks Lady Blanche would give her. The old bitch wouldn't dare to touch her now.

"Well, Graelam," the Duke of Cornwall said as he tilted his goblet to his mouth, "I have seen several wenches' bellies swollen with child."

"And you're wondering if it is my seed that grows in their bellies?"

The duke shrugged. "It matters not. What does matter is that you have legitimate heirs for your lands, not bastards."

"Ah," Graelam said with a grin, "I was wondering when you would tell me the reason for your visit to Wolffeton. Not, of course, that I am not delighted to greet you."

The duke was silent for a moment. He and Graelam were alone in the Great Hall, sitting opposite each other next to the dying fire. The trestle tables were cleared of the mountains of food from dinner. The jongleurs Graelam had hired were long in bed, as were all of Graelam's men and the duke's.

"I have heard from Edward," the duke said. "He and Eleanor are still in Sicily. I carry the responsibility for his children whilst he must travel. And England's coffers pay for his adventuring."

"I have certainly paid my share."

"That you have, my boy."

"It is because of your strength and honor, my lord duke, that Edward need not come running back to England to fight for his throne. The barons are content. England is at peace. He knew great disappointment in the Holy Land, and if he chooses to travel to mend his weary spirit, so be it."

The duke sighed, raising an age-spotted hand. "Aye, it's true. Edward has grown into a fine man. Men follow him and trust him. Once I feared that he would be weak and vacillating, much like his poor father."

Graelam said, "As much as you hated Simon de Montfort, my lord duke, it was from him that Edward learned his administrative ability. It held us in good stead in the Holy Land. There is no doubt in any man's mind that Edward the king can be trusted and obeyed. He is also a valiant warrior."

"Aye, I know." The duke shook his white head. "I

become an old man, Graelam, and I am weary of my responsibilities."

"And I weary you with this late night. Perhaps, my lord," Graelam said, a glint in his dark eyes, "before you retire, you would care to tell me the reason for your visit."

"I have found you a wife," the duke said baldly.

Graelam was not surprised by his words. Indeed, during the past five years, the Duke of Cornwall had upon several occasions presented him with likely heiresses. Graelam cocked his head at the duke, saying nothing.

"Her name is Joanna de Moreley, daughter of the Earl of Leichester. She is young, comely, rich, and above all, appears to be a good breeder. It's time you wed, Graelam, and produced heirs for Wolffeton."

Graelam remained silent, staring into the graying embers in the fire.

"You still do not hold Lord Richard de Avenell's daughter dear, do you?"

"Nay," Graelam said. "Do you forget, my lord, the Lady Chandra wed Sir Jerval de Vernon? He, not I, managed to tame her. To my ultimate relief, we all parted friends."

"So I hear," the duke said, "which brings me back to the Lady Joanna. Do you deny that you have need of heirs, Graelam?"

"Nay."

"Is there another lady who has caught your fancy?"

Graelam smiled at the impatience in the duke's voice. He shook his head again, and shrugged. "A wife is a burden, my lord duke, a burden that chills my guts."

"You are nearing thirty years old, Graelam. Do you wish to be an old man like me before you see your sons become men?"

And there must be an heir for Belleterre, Graelam thought suddenly.

"You begin to convince me, my lord," he said.

"Forget not," the duke said, more tolerant now, for he scented victory, "that even the wealth you brought from the Holy Land does not go far enough to provide you comforts within your keep." He looked pointedly at the bare stone walls and the reed-covered floors, and doubted not that there were lice mixed with the refuse and bones. The furniture was scant and roughly hewn, with no soft cushions for a man's weary buttocks. The beamed ceiling was black from years of neglect, and the wall sconces were as black as the mutton-fat rushes they held. "A wife who brought a fat dowry and housewifely skills would make Wolffeton a truly noble keep."

"But a wife," Graelam said, leaning his head back against the high-backed chair. "It's something that haunts a man all his days."

"As I said, the Lady Joanna is comely. Perhaps you would learn to care for her."

"Care for a woman?" Graelam arched a black brow up a good inch. "If she were a good breeder, it would have to be enough. Why does Leichester choose me?"

"As one of the king's closest friends," the duke said, "as well as being my vassal, Leichester need look no higher. Any of his neighbors would think twice before encroaching on Leichester's lands with such a powerful son-in-law."

"You have yourself seen this Lady Joanna?"

"Aye, once about six months ago. As I said, she is comely, and built just like her mother. And, I might add, that woman has borne with ease five sons, four of whom have survived."

"I suppose she would expect to be wooed and have songs written about her eyebrows."

"You are a hard man, Graelam. I offer you a rich plum and you complain about playing the suitor."

"And if I beat the wench for disobedience, I suppose I can expect tears and reproaches and her father upon my neck."

"Just keep her belly filled with children, and she'll have no time for disobedience. As to wenches you take to bed, it would be wise to be somewhat more discreet once you have a wife."

Graelam thought of Nan, who was now likely to be sleeping peacefully in his bed. "I must think on it, my lord," Graelam said, rising and stretching.

The Duke of Cornwall rose also and faced the young man he loved more than his own worthless son. He gave him a wide smile. "Think quickly, my lord, for the Lady Joanna will arrive next week, ah, for a visit. She will be accompanied by some of her father's men as well as her ladies. If you suit, the wedding will be attended by her parents and me, of course."

"You wicked old man," Graelam said, a dull flush of anger rising over his face. "You woo me with reason, then clamp down your chains."

"Plow the wench in your bed well, Graelam, for it would be wise to forgo your appetites once the Lady Joanna has arrived." He clapped his hand to Graelam's shoulder. "Don't be angry with me, my boy. It's for the best."

"Christ's bones," Graelam growled. "Best for whom?"

But the Duke of Cornwall only laughed. "You'll make a lusty husband for the girl, Graelam. Be content."

6

"The Duke of Cornwall has arranged a marriage for me," Graelam said to Blanche. "Lady Joanna and her retinue will arrive next week. Can you make preparations for her comfort?"

Blanche stared at him, unable to take in his words. Married? She wanted to scream and cry at the same time, and strike Graelam until he bled like she was bleeding inside. She lowered her head, running her tongue over her suddenly dry lips, and listened to him continue, his voice as indifferent as if he were discussing the weather.

"If the girl is pleasing enough, I will wed her."

Blanche clutched at his words like a lifeline. "You do not know her, Graelam? You have never seen her?"

"Nay. I know nothing about her, save she is an heiress." Graelam shrugged. "If she can breed me sons, I suppose it is enough to ask. Her father is interested in gaining me as a son-in-law because of my friendship with the king and the Duke of Cornwall."

Blanche's thoughts raced. Surely all was not lost.

Graelam cared naught for this Joanna, had never even seen the wench. She still had time. "My lord," she said finally, her head lowered modestly, her voice soft and shy, "it is likely that the Lady Joanna, being such a young girl, knows little of managing a keep the size of Wolffeton. If it pleases you, it would be my honor"—she nearly choked on the word—"to assist her in gaining the necessary knowledge."

Graelam gave her a perfunctory smile, thinking absently that she was a gentle, accommodating woman. "Thank you, Blanche." He wondered briefly if she knew herself how to manage a keep, for Wolffeton had certainly not changed since she had come here, and he had given her free rein within the keep. Perhaps, he thought, not wishing to be unfair, the food had improved somewhat.

Blanche retired to her small chamber, gently closed the door, and smashed her fists against the wall. How could he be drawn into a marriage, and it not be to her? She had been too shy, too modest, she realized when she was calmer. She had not given him enough encouragement, and thus he saw her as a mere adjunct to his household and not as a desirable woman. Damn him. Her lineage was every bit as respectable as this Joanna de Moreley's. The fact that she was not an heiress as was Joanna did not hold long in her mind. Graelam must be made to realize that she, Blanche, would be the right wife, the only wife for him. But Graelam had mentioned breeding sons off his wife, and that stilled her a moment.

She walked to the small window, pulled back the wooden shutter, and stared down toward the practice field. She saw Graelam, stripped to the waist,

wrestling with one of his men. She could see the
sweat glistening off his back, the twisting of his powerful muscles. Ah yes, she would teach this Joanna a
thing or two. Her fingers clutched the edge of the
window, as if they were touching Graelam. "Damn
you, my lord," she said.

Much later, when Blanche lay in her narrow bed,
alone, she considered her son. She would write a
message to her cousin and have him send Evian to
Wolffeton. Once Graelam had met her son, perhaps
he would forget his desire for his own son. After all,
the boy was also his half-nephew. She realized that
she was assuming she could still gain him as her
husband. She would be his wife, and if he demanded
it, she would bear him a child. She hated the thought
of the inevitable birthing pain and the bulk of a child
in her body. For a moment she rebelled against her
woman's lot, against the sheer helplessness of it. But
she would win, she had to. Her son's future and her
own lay in the balance. She fell asleep somewhat
calmer.

The next morning Blanche had to contend with the
servants, Nan in particular. They had supposed that
she would become the future mistress of Wolffeton
and had thus given her grudging obedience. She
trembled with rage when Nan, the wretched little
slut, said in a snide voice, "If ye want a new gown,
mistress, ye'd best ask his lordship. Likely he'll buy
his new young bride anything, but his *old* sister-in-
law, who will be but his poor relation—?" Her voice
fell away like sharp droplets of rain dripping off
stone.

"You little bitch," Blanche said, her voice
trembling, hating both Nan and herself for the truth

of the wench's words. She reached for Nan's long braid, now clean from weekly baths, but Nan was faster. She scurried out of the chamber, laughing aloud.

"I'll have you flogged," Blanche yelled after her, knowing full well that it was an empty threat.

"The master won't allow that," Nan said from a safe distance. "He likes me smooth and soft. He'll not let ye beat me."

"Slut. Just wait until your belly swells with child. You'll see then how much the master cares about you and your soft hide."

"He'll give me a fine cottage and mayhap a servant of my own," Nan retorted.

The other servants snickered behind her back, but at least they obeyed her orders, albeit with the slowness of mules trekking up a cliff. She ground her teeth and bided her time until Lady Joanna de Moreley came, and Evian. Graelam had seemed reluctant to have her son come to Wolffeton, but Blanche had managed to cry, an altogether honest reaction, and he had finally agreed.

Graelam grunted and heaved as he helped the masons fit a huge slab of stone into place on the outer eastern wall of Wolffeton. He stepped back and dashed the sweat from his forehead with the back of his hand. He felt exhilarated from the physical labor, for it had kept his mind off Joanna de Moreley's impending visit, which he dreaded. He thought of the message he had sent to Maurice de Lorris several days before, and felt a spurt of unwanted pain for what had happened. He heard nothing from Maurice, and assumed that Geoffrey had made no move on

Belleterre. Surely it could not be long now before Geoffrey found out about Kassia's death. Belleterre was not that isolated, and over two months had passed.

Graelam stretched, enjoying the pull of his tired muscles, and headed toward the cliff path that led to the narrow beach below. The surf pounded against the naked rocks, splashing spray into wide arcs in the air. He stripped off his clothes and waded into the tumbling water. Feeling the powerful tug of the tide against his legs, he let himself be dragged forward with the outgoing waves. The water was cold, raising gooseflesh on his body, but he ignored it and plunged facedown into a high-crested wave.

Some minutes later he heard a yell from the cliff above him and saw Guy waving toward him. He started to answer, but a huge wave smashed against his back and sent him sprawling onto his face. When he fought his way out of the sea, his face smarting from the coarse rocks and sand, he heard Guy's laughter. He strode onto the narrow beach and shook himself, like a mongrel dog.

"My lord. Dress yourself before your bride sees you in your natural wonder."

Graelam cursed. The girl was two days early. He did not doubt that his days of peace were over. He dressed himself quickly and strode up the cliff path.

"My lord," Guy said, a wide grin splitting his well-formed mouth. "I fear the Lady Joanna will see us side by side and send you about your business." Guy preened in his green velvet and patted his hand to his golden hair, his laughter ringing above the raucous sound of the seabirds.

Graelam didn't rise to the bait. Instead he asked, "Is all in readiness for the lady?"

"Do you mean has Blanche swallowed the prune in her mouth and managed a welcoming smile?"

"If you had something to offer her, you conceited buffoon, you could take that lady off my hands."

"It's not my bed Blanche seeks, my lord." Guy straightened suddenly, a slight worried frown puckering his brow. "It was a mistake allowing her to send for her son."

Graelam felt thoroughly irritated. "For God's sake, Guy, leave be. Blanche is comely and endowed with the proper shyness and modesty a lady should have. If I wed Lady Joanna, I shall find Blanche a husband. With her son in tow, it proves she is a good breeder."

Many of the servants would applaud that decision, Guy thought. Blanche had not been overly patient with any of them, so awash was she in her disappointment. He felt a tug of pity for her, as well as something else he was loath to examine. He shrugged. It was none of his affair. He said aloud, "Nay, my lord, do not waste your ill-humor on me." He paused a moment, then added, "There is but one thing that bothers me."

"I suppose I must ask you what it is, else you'll bury me in hints."

Guy gave him his sunny smile. Their relationship was more in the manner of an indulgent brother toward a younger sibling, not liege lord to one of his knights. "Why did you agree to this match when it so obviously displeases you?"

Graelam had asked himself the same question many times during the past weeks. "A man must have sons," he said finally. "Now, let me meet my sons' mother."

*　　*　　*

Kassia walked slowly through the apple orchard, her face lifted to the bright sun overhead. She smelled the sweet scent of the camellias, hydrangeas, and rhododendrons she herself had planted, and heard the comforting drone of the bees in the hives just beyond the orchard. Hugging her arms around her, feeling the sun warming her bones, she knew the joy of simply being alive.

Her favorite gown of yellow silk still hung loose, but it didn't bother her. She smiled at the thought of her father, ever watching her with worried eyes, encouraging her to do naught but rest and eat. She looked up to see her nurse, Etta, who was now walking purposefully toward her, a bowl of something doubtless very nourishing and equally distasteful held in her hands.

"You should be resting, mistress," Etta said without preamble. "Here, drink this."

"Another of your concoctions," Kassia said, but obligingly downed the thick beef broth. "I need to prune my fig trees," she said, handing the bowl back to Etta.

"Fig trees." Etta said on a mighty sigh.

Kassia cocked her head in question. "I am well enough to do just as I please now. Come, Etta, you know you enjoy my delicious figs."

"Aye, my baby. It's not your figs that are on my mind at the moment."

"What is on your mind?"

"Your father. Another messenger arrived a while ago."

"Another messenger? I did not know there was even a first, much less a second."

"Aye," Etta said. "He does not look happy."

"Then I shall go to him and see what is wrong."

"But you should rest."

"Etta, you and Father are treating me like a downy chick with no sense. I am feeling much stronger, and if I keep eating all the food you stuff in my mouth, I shall be fat as my favorite goose."

Maurice had dismissed the messenger and sat staring blindly in front of him. He didn't realize he was wringing his hands until he felt his daughter's fingers lightly touch his shoulder.

"Father, what troubles you?"

He managed to wipe the worry from his face and smiled at her, drawing her into his lap. She was still so slight, weighing no more than a child. But her vivid hazel eyes were bright again with glowing health, and her beautiful hair now capped her small face in soft, loose curls. He thought of the message and pulled her tightly against him. Time had run out.

He felt her small, firm breasts pressing against him, reminding him yet again that she was no longer a little girl. She was a woman and a wife. He drew in a deep breath and pulled back from her so he could see her face.

"You are feeling well, *ma chère*?" he asked, avoiding the issue.

"Quite well, Father. Much better, I gather, than you are. Now, what about this messenger? Etta also let slip that this was the second one. Is it Geoffrey?"

Kassia could see the beginnings of deception in her father's eyes and said, "Nay, Father. I am no longer at death's door. You must tell me what troubles you. Please, I feel useless when you treat me like a witless child who must be protected and cosseted."

He knew there was no help for it. None at all. Slowly he said, not meeting her eyes, "Do you remember telling me that you dreamed of a man's voice? A man you did not know?"

"Aye, I remember."

"You did not dream him. There was such a man. He is an Englishman, Lord Graelam de Moreton. He accompanied me to Belleterre. You see, I was attacked in Aquitaine by brigands, and Lord Graelam saved my life, he and his men. He is an honorable man, Kassia, and a fine man, a warrior who was just returning from the Holy Land. I found myself telling him about that whoreson Geoffrey, and indeed, we stopped at Beaumanoir one evening. He met your aunt, and managed politely enough to avoid her bed. I will not deny that by the time we reached Belleterre, I was thinking of him as the perfect husband for you. I told him about you. When we arrived, I was told that you were dying. Indeed, there was no doubt in my mind that you would not survive that night."

Kassia was looking at him with such incomprehension that for a moment Maurice couldn't continue. He coughed, raked his fingers through his hair, and said something under his breath.

"Father," Kassia said, "I do not understand. What of this man, this Graelam de Moreton?"

"He is your husband."

Kassia went still, her eyes wide and disbelieving on her father's face. "My husband," she said.

"Aye." He pulled her tightly against him again and breathed in the sweet scent of her flesh. "Aye," he said again. "Let me explain what happened, my love. I was convinced that you were going to die.

And I also knew that Belleterre would be lost to Geoffrey. I convinced Graelam to wed you before you died. It would be he, then, who would have Belleterre, and not that bastard Geoffrey. He argued with me, Kassia, but I wore him down, with guilt. He finally agreed. The next morning he left with the marriage contracts to go to the Duke of Brittany. The duke approved the marriage, and Graelam, according to my wishes, returned to Cornwall. I did not write to tell him that you had lived. I saw no reason for it until you regained your strength."

Married? She was married to a man she had never even seen? She heard herself say, "But why didn't you tell me, Father?"

Maurice shifted uncomfortably in his chair. "I did not want you to become upset, not when you continued so weak."

"But you are telling me now. What has happened?"

"The messenger who arrived today was from Lord Graelam, informing me that his master is to wed an English heiress."

"I see," Kassia said. One shock after another. Married, she thought again, and to an English lord. She stared at her father, trying to understand.

"There is more, Kassia. The first messenger was sent by the Duke of Brittany. Evidently Geoffrey found out that you were still living at Belleterre, that you had not accompanied your husband to England. He has tried to convince the duke that your marriage was all a sham, a plot by me to keep you and Belleterre out of his hands. The duke demands an explanation. If the explanation pleases him not, he threatens to have the marriage annulled and wed you to Geoffrey."

"Is this English lord, this Graelam de Moreton, strong enough to protect Belleterre from Geoffrey?"

"Aye," Maurice said, "he is strong enough."

It was odd, but Kassia felt the stronger of the two now. He looked ill with worry, and, she realized, he was dreading her anger at what he had done. Perhaps, she thought, she would have done the same thing were she her father. She loved her father more than anyone else in the world, more than herself. And she loved Belleterre. She thought of Geoffrey, sly, greedy Geoffrey, and felt a rippling of a shudder at the thought of him as her husband. She said, very firmly, "I understand, Father. I do not blame you for what you did. Do not distress yourself further."

She slid from his lap and forced a calm smile to her lips. "I must prepare myself, Father. I will return with this messenger to England, to my husband. It would not do at all for him to take another wife."

Maurice gaped at her, wondering why she was not in tears, remembering her mother's tears, shed so quickly and with such devastating effect.

"I think also that you should pay a visit to the Duke of Brittany. You could tell him, I suppose, that I fell ill and was unable to accompany my husband back to England. There is some truth to that. And, Father, you must not worry about me. I had to marry someone, and if you believe this Lord Graelam to be a fine man, then I am satisfied. I only wish he were French and lived near. I shall miss Belleterre."

"Cornwall is not so far away," Maurice said. He suddenly realized that he did not know Graelam all that well. He was a man's man, a brave warrior, strong and proud. How would he deal with a wife he had believed dead within hours of his marriage?

Kassia was so innocent, so very young. He had protected her, guarded her, shown her only gentleness and kindness. My God, he thought, what had he done? He rose with sudden decision. "I will accompany you, Kassia, to Cornwall."

"Nay, Father. You must protect Belleterre from Geoffrey. You must see the Duke of Brittany."

Maurice continued to argue, but Kassia knew that he had no choice in the matter. She knew she had no choice either. She felt tears sting her eyes, and resolutely blinked them back. She pictured this Lord Graelam and imagined him to be no different from her father. "Is he old?"

"Graelam? Nay, daughter, he is young and well-formed."

"A kind man, Father? Gentle?"

"I trust so, Kassia."

She smiled. Young and well-formed and gentle, like her father. All would be well.

"Graelam gave you a ring upon your marriage. I have kept it safe for you."

"I suppose it would be wise to have it. I imagine that I look a bit different than I did on my wedding night."

Kassia left her father and hurried to her chamber, calling Etta. "Imagine," she said as she shook out a yellow wool gown, "I am married, and I didn't even know it. Etta, did you see this Lord Graelam?"

"Aye, my baby. He was gentle when the priest said the vows. He held your hand through it all."

"And he is young and handsome?"

"Aye," Etta said. He was also formidable-looking, a huge man who could crush her gentle mistress like a fly. "Aye," she said again, "he is as your father described him." Likely, Etta thought, Lord Maurice was quite flattering in his description of his son-in-law. After all, Lord Maurice was a man, just as was the powerful English nobleman. And did he have any choice? "Now, my baby, I will send some servants to assist you. I must pack my own belongings."

Kassia smiled and threw her arms about her old nurse. "We shall conquer England again, Etta, just as did Duke William two hundred years ago."

7

Joanna de Moreley held the hooded peregrine falcon gracefully on her wrist and eyed the wretched Blanche from beneath her lowered lashes. Miserable bitch. Her mare suddenly sidestepped and the falcon shrieked, digging his claws into her thick leather glove. Joanna would have liked to fling the falcon into the nearest pile of dung, but Lord Graelam was watching her. She smiled prettily, but jerked the mare's reins, hurting her tender mouth.

Graelam turned away, a frown gathering on his brow. Although the mare belonged to Joanna, it angered him that she would so mistreat the animal. He wished he were miles away from Wolffeton, in the heat of battle, breaking heads with his ax, feeling sweat trickle down his face and back with exertion. Anything but playing the gallant to this ridiculous vain girl. She was not ill-looking, he admitted to himself, and he supposed that her arrogance, bred by an overly doting father and mother, he could control soon enough, once she was his wife. Her hair was fair, so blond in fact that when the sun shone down upon her head, it appeared nearly white. He had always been partial to fair-haired women, until now. Her best feature, now covered with a wimple that appeared like stiff flapping wings, left him little to admire. He had eyed her body carefully and noted the wide hips, well-suited for childbearing, and her abundant breasts. Perhaps her excellent opinion of herself would turn to passion once he had her in his bed, but he doubted it.

He heard Blanche question Joanna in her soft-spoken way, and winced at Joanna's patronizing tone when she answered. It hadn't taken long for Graelam to realize he would have no peace in his own castle until Blanche was gone. Unfortunately, he had had two weeks to compare the two women, and to his mind, Blanche, already gentle and sub-missive, would make his life less troublesome. At least Blanche was no budding shrew. He hardened his jaw. If Joanna proved difficult, he would beat her. The thought of her dowry had not swayed him; indeed, the jewels he had brought back from the Holy Land had provided him enough to finish the work on Wolffeton, enough to buy sheep and more cattle for his freehold farmers and two villages, and finally enough to bring at least another dozen men-at-arms into his service. No, it was the Duke of Cornwall who had pressed him into this alliance. With Edward still out of England, it would not be wise to anger the king's uncle.

"My lord," he heard Joanna lisp in that affected way of hers, "I grow overheated. My mother does not like me to spend too much time in the sun."

Graelam grunted and turned his destrier back toward Wolffeton. Damn the Duke of Cornwall any-way. He had chosen to accompany Joanna's parents and their impressive retinue to Wolffeton for the wedding. The duke was no fool.

Joanna looked ahead at Graelam's back. He was rather boorish—no lovely compliments coming from his mouth, unlike some of the young knights at the king's court—but he was handsome and strong. She would mold him to her liking once he was her husband. As for that witch Blanche, she would see her soon gone. She stared toward his castle, Wolffeton, and shuddered. It was a monstrosity, a graceless heap of gray stone in the middle of nowhere that boasted no comforts for a gently reared lady. Joanna smiled. Where her husband would be stupid and boorish, she would be witty and cunning. She would rule him as easily as she ruled her father. She would not suffer by spending her years immured in Wolffeton. Perhaps a few months of the year, but that was more than enough.

Her smile began to hurt, but she did not know when or if Lord Graelam would swing about in his saddle to say something to her. Her eyes bored into his back. She had grown up with too many brothers and she knew well what power a woman could wield with her body. She had seen Graelam once without his shirt and had felt a gentle tingling in her belly at the sight of his chest and arms, tanned by the harsh wind and sun. Her eyes had roved downward and she had shuddered slightly in anticipation. She was not a virgin, having lost that commodity some four years before in the eager arms of one of her father's knights. She doubted that Graelam would know the difference in any case, and if he suspected that her cries of pain were feigned, she would have a small vial of chicken blood ready to blotch her thighs.

Blanche rode beside Sir Guy, wishing she could take his knife and hurl it into Joanna's back. And he knew what was in her mind, damn him! She realized quite clearly that her ploys during the past two weeks had failed miserably, even though her gentle manners had shown in clear opposition to Joanna's snideness, winning her approving looks from Graelam. It was clear to the meanest intelligence that Lord Graelam spent less and less time with his betrothed as the days went by. But it did not matter. There was but one recourse open to her now. She raised her chin, and her eyes gleamed with decision.

"Dare I ask what you are planning now?" Sir Guy said, drawing his destrier closer to her mare.

Blanche gave him a dazzling smile and quirked a beautifully arched brow at him. "For a boy, you show great interest in things that do not concern you."

"And for an older woman," Guy said, "you show too much interest in my lord. I tell you, Blanche, you have lost. Accept your defeat. Graelam will find you a husband." He felt himself frown slightly, disliking that thought.

"You are a fool," Blanche said, her smile never slipping.

"It is you who are the fool, my lady," Guy said, his voice gentling, for he knew well her distress. Why, he wondered, would she not accept the truth? "Lord Graelam is honorable. He has agreed to the marriage. He will not break his word."

Aye, Blanche thought. It was Graelam's honor that would play to her advantage.

Blanche wished that stupid old man would keep his bony hands to himself. She looked at Joanna's father, Lord Thomas, from beneath her lowered lashes. She would have liked to slap his hand away and tell him what an old fool he was, but she kept still, slewing her eyes toward the acrobats performing in the Great Hall. She found no amusement in them. She felt a knot form in her throat as she looked at Graelam, and a renewal of her determination. At least he did naught but drink wine and speak to the Duke of Cornwall, paying no attention to his betrothed. Joanna's lips were in a tight line at being ignored, and that made Blanche's mood somewhat better. Damn her, Blanche thought. Joanna knew that Graelam didn't want her. She signaled to a serving wench to refill Graelam's goblet. She felt Lord Thomas's bony hand once again trail up her thigh and she shifted away from him. His wife, Lady Eleanor, seemed oblivious of her husband's vagaries, content to speak softly with Sir Guy and look about the Great Hall of Wolfeton with a satisfied and proprietary eye.

Finally, Blanche thought, finally, she could excuse herself. She curtsied gracefully and left the hall. She heard Sir Guy laugh.

It seemed that she waited in the darkness of her small chamber for hours. She had begun to sweat and quickly rose from her bed to pat a damp cloth beneath her arms. She paused a moment and stared at herself in the polished silver mirror. She was tall, large-breasted, with full, rounded hips. There were faint lines from childbearing on her belly, but in the candlelight he would not see them. She began to hum softly to herself as she slipped a sheer silk shift over her head. She patted her soft hair into place and walked quietly to the door and opened it. All was quiet at last.

She carried the candle, protecting its thready flame with a cupped hand, and sped toward Graelam's chamber. She unlatched the door quietly and slipped inside. She paused a moment, then smiled at the sound of his snoring. He had drunk a lot of wine. He would likely not come to his senses until it was too late. And as Sir Guy had told her, Graelam was an honorable man. If he took an unmarried lady in his bed, he would also take her hand in marriage. Why, she wondered, had she not thought of it before? She stifled her guilt and her sudden apprehension, and raised her chin.

She walked quietly to his huge bed and stared down at him a moment, the candle held high. He lay naked on top of the covers, for the night was warm. She was not immune to his male beauty and let her gaze rove the length of him. Even in sleep, she could see the ridges of muscle that banded his belly. Lower, she saw a long jagged scar, running from the top of his thigh to near his groin, showing white through the black hair. His sex lay soft and flaccid in the thick matting of hair and she felt the urge to touch him, to caress him, to bring him to life. She set the candle down on the small table beside his bed. Slowly, ever so quietly, she slipped the shift over her head. She prepared to crawl into bed beside him, when a sudden gust of wind came through the small window. The candle flickered and died. She cursed to herself, but quickly realized that the moonlight would be ample for her purposes.

She lay down beside him, pressing her body along his side. Slowly she leaned over him and ran her fingers lightly down his chest. He sighed in his sleep but did not awaken. Blanche sent her fingers lower until they curled around him. She began to stroke and caress him.

"Nan," she heard him mutter, still half-asleep, "I told you that we would bed together no more. Leave off."

Her fingers tightened abut his swelling sex and she smiled as he groaned. Suddenly his arms were around her, drawing her on top of him. She felt his mouth, hard and demanding, close over hers. She quickly parted her lips. She felt his hands stroking down her back to her buttocks, kneading them fiercely, pressing her against him.

Soon, she thought triumphantly, soon she would cry out, but not until Graelam's seed had burst in her belly. She could not wait to see the look on the Duke of Cornwall's face.

"God's bones." Graelam shook his head, clearing away the dregs of wine that clouded his mind. "Blanche."

She had no time to say anything. His hand clamped over her mouth and he threw her onto her back, one massive leg thrown over hers. She knew a moment of fear; then she relaxed and smiled up at him.

"What the devil are you doing here?"

Blanche moved against him, changing her plans abruptly. "I love you, my lord. Do not marry that—"

He interrupted her, appalled. "Shut up, woman. Have you no sense, no pride? Jesus, Blanche, I very nearly took you."

"You may take me, my lord, if you will but marry me." She rubbed her breasts against his arm.

Graelam cursed long and softly, surprising even Blanche with his coarse fluency. "I cannot marry you.

I will not marry you. For God's sake, woman, get out of here before someone discovers you." As if he knew she would not obey him, Graelam rose off the bed, jerking her with him. He leaned down and picked up her shift. "Put it on. And go quietly. I will tell no one, and neither will you."

"Do you not want me, my lord?" Blanche said rather desperately, thrusting her breasts out so that she brushed his naked chest.

Graelam felt his outrage and his anger dissolve. Blanche was such a gentle creature and he saw tears glistening in her eyes. He said quietly, more calmly, "It is not meant to be, Blanche. I am sorry, but I am promised. You cannot be my mistress. You are a lady. It's a husband only who can know you."

I would never be your mistress, she wanted to yell at him, but her body was still shuddering from her brief moment of pleasure. She felt tears of disappointment and despair streak down her cheeks.

Graelam pulled the flimsy shift over her head, for in truth, his body was reacting to hers and he had no intention of shaming either himself or her. "Come," he said, "you must return to your chamber. We will both forget this, Blanche."

She wanted to scream, to bring Joanna or her ferret-faced mother running, but she knew she could not. He would strangle her if she did, particularly since he was full-witted again. It wasn't fair, none of it. What would become of her now? What would become of her poor son? At least she could show a bit of pride. She squared her shoulders.

Graelam watched her silently slip from his chamber. He walked back to his bed and threw himself down on his back, his arms pillowing his head. Jesus, he thought, women. But that wasn't fair. Blanche was so sweet and shy. He mustn't blame her overly for her actions. She only thought she loved him. He would find her a husband, and quickly. He remembered the feel of her body against him, the touch of her fingers caressing him. Her body was full and round, the way he liked his women. He realized with a start that if he had indeed taken her, the consequences could have been enough to make the bravest man shrivel. He thought idly that perhaps it would have been just as well, if he could have survived the pandemonium that would doubtless result. He would, he decided, prefer Blanche to wive, rather than Joanna. He flipped over onto his stomach and willed himself back to sleep. It was over and done with and his fate was decided.

Kassia felt dazed from weariness, but she forced herself to sit straight on Bluebell and gaze ahead at Wolffeton. It was a huge fortress, as solid and lasting as the rugged countryside surrounding it. When their vessel had arrived four days before on the southern coast of Cornwall, she had eyed the odd foliage and trees—palm trees, she had been told—and the calm, warm countryside, so different from Brittany. The closer they had drawn to Wolffeton, the more at home she had felt. It was unforgiving, demanding country, and if she were not so dreadfully weary, she would have delighted in every coarse-haired sheep and fat-bellied cow they had seen. They were riding close to the rocky cliffs and she could hear the battering rush of the waves against the rocks. Wolffeton, the home of Graelam de Moreton, her husband—now her home. She felt a surge of fear so

strong she wavered in the saddle. She was in a foreign country, going to a man she had never seen
before. It was lunacy, sheer lunacy. Her courage had
left her slowly, seeping away just as her strength
over the past week and a half. Now all she wanted
to do was turn tail and hide.

"My lady."

"Nay, nay," she managed, getting hold on herself.
"I am fine, Stephen." She smiled at one of her father's oldest and most trusted retainers. "Just tired,
that is all. It has been a long journey."

Too long for his slight mistress, Stephen thought,
worried. And what would her reception be like? His
jaw hardened. No one would insult his young mistress, no one. His gloved hand dropped unconsciously to his sword.

He saw the uncertainty in her eyes, and the fear.
She was only a young girl. How could Lord Maurice
have allowed her to journey here without him? But
of course, Stephen knew the answer to that. That
whoreson Geoffrey.

"Rest a moment, my lady," he said to Kassia. "I
will see that the men look fit to greet Lord Graelam."

Kassia nodded, nearly beyond words now. She
looked back toward the small litter and wondered
what Etta was thinking now. She watched Stephen
ride among their twenty-odd men, doubtless cursing
some, praising others. Their journey had been thankfully uneventful. No brigands would dare to attack
such a large force. But she was so tired; she wanted
to slip from her saddle and sleep. But she could not.
She could not shame her father or her men. Kassia
forced her back to stiffen. She was dirty and travel-
worn. She was afraid to ask Stephen how she looked.

She waited patiently for Stephen to join her at the head of their troop. She lightly tapped her heels into Bluebell's fat sides and her mare broke into a rocking canter.

They rode through the small fishing village of St. Agnes, so like the villages along the coast of Brittany that Kassia felt no ill-ease at the dour glances of the villagers. The only difference, Kassia thought, smiling to herself, was that at home the villagers would pull their forelocks at her presence. The rutted road continued eastward from the village, up a winding incline toward Wolffeton. Kassia became more impressed and awed the closer they drew to the thick, massive outer walls. No one could take this castle. She felt a moment of pride, then laughed. This great keep was not hers. She felt her blood curdle at the thought that had not been far from the surface during her journey. What if Lord Graelam de Moreton had already married?

Stephen raised his arm for the men to halt. Kassia watched him ride toward the man who was leaning from one of the great towers. She did not hear their conversation. The man disappeared and Stephen rode back to her.

"The fellow thinks me mad," Stephen said, a half-grin splitting his wide mouth. "I told him that his master's bride was below."

"Mad indeed," Kassia said. She turned back at the sound of the thick oak drawbridge being lowered. It came down over the dry ditch with a heavy thud. She urged Bluebell forward, but Stephen's hand came out to clutch at the reins.

"No, my lady, not yet."

They watched in silence as the iron portcullis was slowly winched upward.

Stephen eyed her for a minute. "Remove your cloak from your head, my lady. No man would attack when a woman was present."

Kassia obligingly lowered the rabbit-lined hood.

Stephen nodded slowly, but motioned her to ride behind him. They rode over the drawbridge, the horses' hooves pounding with a deafening roar on the thick wood planks. It was a warrior's keep, Kassia thought as they slowed their horses to a walk. The outer courtyard was not precisely filthy with its dry mud ground, it was simply that there was no sign of care. They continued through another, narrower arch into the inner bailey. There were at least fifty men, women, and children staring at them silently. Loudly squawking chickens strutted about and several cows mooed impatiently, doubtless wanting to be led to the grassy field outside the castle walls. A dog barked loudly at a black cat. There were several old outbuildings, for cooking, laundry, and storage, and a new barracks sat next to a low thatched-roof stable. She became aware of the soldiers, standing stiffly all around them, eyeing them as possible enemies.

Kassia had no more opportunity to examine her surroundings. Her eyes went to a tall blond man, quite handsome, who stood on the lower steps of the keep, waiting for them to come to him. Her father had told her that Lord Graelam was comely. He was indeed. And he looked gentle and kind.

He came down the steps when they halted and she had a moment to admire him. He was younger than she had expected. He walked directly to her and raised his arms to help her down from Bluebell.

He stared at her for a long moment, as if trying to remember her.

"Lady Kassia," he said, more a question than a statement.

"Aye, my lord." She saw he had deep blue eyes, kind eyes that laughed, and she relaxed even further.

"You are something of a surprise, my lady. We had believed you—"

"Dead? Nay, my lord, I survived." Kassia looked down at the chipped cobblestones beneath her feet. "I am pleased that you are not angry, my lord. But I could not allow you to wed, not when you had a wife who still lived."

"You mistake the matter, my lady."

Kassia raised her eyes to his face.

"I am not your husband. I am Sir Guy de Blasis, one of Lord Graelam's knights. At your service, my lady."

Guy bowed to the young girl before him. It had not occurred to him that she would mistake him for Lord Graelam. But then again, she had never even seen his master.

Kassia swayed where she stood and Guy quickly caught her arm to steady her. "There is no reason for you to be afraid, my lady," Guy said. "Lord Graelam is within and he is not yet wed. Your timing, in fact, is exquisite. The wedding is tomorrow." As he spoke, the enormity of the situation broke over him. Poor Joanna. Poor Blanche. He wanted to laugh, but he saw the pain of utter weariness in Kassia's eyes, and gently cupped her elbow, pulling her forward. He spoke to one of Lord Graelam's men and motioned him toward Stephen.

"Your men will be taken care of, my lady. Now it is time for you to meet your husband."

Kassia felt the warmth of his hand through her

cloak. But still she felt cold, icy to her very bones. Where was her pride? Her feet obeyed, yet each step upward was a terrible obstacle to overcome. She stepped into the massive hall. It was darker and cooler within, and for a moment she could see nothing for the dim light. She shook her head, allowing Guy to lead her toward the end of the hall. She saw a man seated in an ornately carved high-backed chair. Next to him, seated in a smaller chair, sat a young woman with blond hair so light that it looked nearly white. There were at least fifty men and women standing about, some richly garbed. She became aware suddenly that all the voices were dying away. Closer and closer they came to the man. She could see him clearly now. He was as dark as Guy was fair. He appeared too big, even seated, and he looked stern, forbidding.

"My lord," Guy said in a loud voice, "may I present your wife, Lady Kassia de Moreton, to your guests."

The young woman seated beside Graelam let out a shriek and jumped to her feet. Lord Graelam merely looked at her, his face telling her nothing.

There was a suddenly furious babble of voices, all of them raised, all of them outraged. Kassia was vaguely aware of an older man, richly garbed, stepping toward her.

It took a moment for Guy's words to sink in. Graelam looked at the slight girl, covered from throat to toe in a dusty cloak. He saw the short curls capping her small head. He ignored the strident, angry voices about him, ignored the cries from Joanna and the guttural moans from Joanna's mother, Lady Eleanor. Slowly he rose from his chair, his eyes never leaving her face. It was the short, curling chestnut hair that made him believe it was Kassia de Lorris, for he could not place this girl into the wraith's body he had seen at Belleterre.

Suddenly he could not help himself. He threw back his head and roared with laughter. Laughter at himself, laughter at the uproar this girl had caused, laughter at the sudden inevitable turn his life had taken.

Kassia gaped at the too big man whose whole body was convulsed with laughter. She felt the hostility and the blatant disbelief of the people around her.

"I carry your ring, my lord," she said in a loud, clear voice.

She slid it off her finger and thrust it out toward him.

Graelam stopped laughing. He stared down at his ring, banded with thick horsehair to keep it on her finger.

He heard Lord Thomas shrieking like an idiot woman, demanding to know the meaning of this outrage. He heard Joanna or perhaps Blanche, he couldn't tell which, yelling insults at the girl. Another woman, likely Joanna's mother, was wailing with piercing loudness.

"Graelam," the Duke of Cornwall said in a voice of awful calm, striding forward, "perhaps you will tell me the meaning of this? Who is this girl?"

Graelam ignored him. He stepped closer to Kassia and gently cupped her chin in his hand, drawing her face upward.

His dark eyes searched her face. She could not bring herself to look up at him. Why did he not say something?

"My lord," Joanna yelled, "I will not allow you to have your whore here. How dare you."

Blanche was laughing, her eyes alight with malicious joy on Joanna's contorted face. "Well, my *lady*," she said to Joanna, "it appears your wedding must be to another."

"You bitch," Joanna said furiously, turning on Blanche, "she is but a whore. She will be gone soon, and forever. My father will not allow her to remain."

Kassia was not deaf. *A whore*. She turned angry eyes toward the women, but no words came to mind. Her husband still had said nothing. She felt herself again begin to tremble. What was going to happen to her? The light seemed to grow dimmer. The terrible women seemed to weave before her eyes.

"I—I am sorry," she said, her eyes going to her husband's face. For the first time in her life, she welcomed the blessed darkness that was welling up within her, letting her escape from this nightmare. For the second time in her life, Kassia collapsed where she stood.

Kassia felt great weariness, but the blackness was receding, bringing her back to consciousness. Slowly she opened her eyes. For many moments everything was a blur. Then she saw a man—her husband—beside her, his dark eyes expressionless on her face. She made a small gasping sound and tried to pull herself up. She felt ashamed that she had fainted like a silly sheep in front of all those people.

"Nay," Graelam said, "lie still."

"Where am I?" she asked, hating herself for her pathetic little voice.

"In my chamber, or rather I should say, our chamber. Are you still ill?"

His voice was still gentle and she managed to meet his eyes. She could read nothing. His face was impassive, giving her no clue.

"I'm sorry. I am not given to fainting, but the journey was long."

She felt his fingers lightly touch her arm and she tensed. He released her, a slight frown on his forehead. "There is much we have to say to each other, my lady. Your arrival was unexpected. But first, I will leave you to rest and regain your strength."

"I'm sorry," Kassia said again. "There was no time to give you warning. Please do not blame my father. He sought only to protect me."

"Doubtless he did," Graelam said. He picked up her hand and gently slid his ring back on her third finger. "Your nurse, Etta, is outside. Shall I bring her to you?"

Kassia's head throbbed, and she blinked rapidly to keep his face in focus. "What will you do?"

"That, my lady," Graelam said, standing to stare down at her, "will be interesting to see. I but hope that you will not become a widow just as I believed myself a widower."

He turned with those words and strode across the chamber to the thick oak door. He did not look back at her.

Kassia was aware of Etta bending over her, gently soothing her brow with a damp cloth. "Rest, my baby," she heard her nurse say, and she willingly obliged.

Graelam left his chamber thoughtfully. Lord, what an ungodly mess. Never, he thought, for as long as he breathed, would he forget his first sight of Kassia, standing beside Guy, holding herself so straight, fear dilating her eyes. Yet she had come, bravely. Nor would he ever forget the sight of her quietly crumbling, all life gone from her. Nor the feel of her in his arms as he carried her to his chamber. His wife, he thought, shaking his head. A scrawny girl, and now she was his responsibility. He gave another spurt of laughter. He had, after all, succumbed to Maurice's arguments, and done himself in. He pictured her face again, so quiet in repose, for he had studied her carefully before she had regained consciousness. He had wanted to feel anger, to rage at her, but when she had finally awakened and he saw the deep uncertainty in her eyes, he had felt compelled to treat her gently. He was a fool. What in God's name was he to do? He had ignored his gloating sister-in-law and the moaning Joanna, and carried Kassia out of the hall. He supposed, as he took the final step into the hall, that he would rather face an army of infidels than this group.

8

The thread of flame from a single candle broke the darkness. Kassia blinked, stared a moment into the flame, remembering quite clearly everything that had passed since her arrival at Wolffeton.

"How do you feel, my baby?"

Kassia smiled wanly at the sound of her old nurse's soft voice. "Alive, Etta," she said, "alive. Is it very late?"

"Nearly ten o'clock in the evening. You slept for six hours. I have food and mulled wine for you."

Kassia slowly pulled herself up and Etta quickly came to place pillows behind her head. "What I really want," she said, staring at her dirty fingernails, "is a bath."

"First you eat," Etta said, "then I will have those lazy sluts bring you hot water."

"Lord Graelam," Kassia said, hearing the thin thread of nervousness in her voice, "where is he?"

To her surprise, Etta laughed. "Ah, your lord. What a man that one is."

"What do you mean?"

"I will tell you while you eat. I kept the victuals

warm over a small brazier. This great keep will vastly improve with you as mistress, my baby. The food is barely edible, and the servants do naught unless Lord Graelam is about."

"You are too stern, Etta," Kassia said, but the pork was clearly stringy and overcooked.

Etta regarded her young mistress with a worried eye. She had been raised in the midst of people who loved her and obeyed her because they loved her. But Wolffeton was vastly different from Belleterre. "Tell me now, Etta," she heard Kassia say. "What happened whilst I slept?"

Etta eased herself into the one chair in the large chamber. "Well, after I was certain that you were all right, I slipped into the hall below. I have never heard so many people arguing at once in all my life. And the screeching from Lord Graelam's betrothed."

Kassia felt a surge of guilt, but it was tempered with the anger she had felt at the insults that lady had hurled at her. She sipped at the warm wine. "I hope her heart is not broken."

"Ha, that one. Lord Graelam should kiss your feet, for you saved him from a wretched existence. As to the other one, well, we shall have to see."

"What other one?"

"Lady Blanche, Lord Graelam's sister-in-law."

Kassia frowned. "I don't understand."

"Lord Graelam, I discovered from one of the servants, was married before, a long time ago. His wife's half-sister came to Wolffeton some three or four months ago to live. Why, I don't know." Etta shrugged. "She did seem quiet enough and quite the lady during all the shrieking and arguing. Eat the sweet bread, my lady," Etta added, her eyes upon Kassia's trencher.

The bread was grainy, Kassia found, but she would not give Etta the pleasure of admitting it.

"Now, where was I? Aye, your husband is quite the man. He had to roar for quiet but once, and all obeyed him, even the Duke of Cornwall. Aye, you stare, my baby. The king's own uncle. It was he, according to what I heard, who arranged the marriage with the heiress. His face, I tell you, was a bright crimson. As for Lord Thomas, Lady Joanna's father, he looked for all the world like a boiled turnip. But Lord Graelam soon took care of all of them. Told them, he did, all that happened at Belleterre. He even produced the marriage contract so there could be no doubts as to your status as his lady wife. At that, Lady Joanna was forced to close her mouth, but her mother kept wailing in the most ridiculous way. Lord Thomas finally slapped her. That shut the old harridan up, you may be certain. He announced to the Duke of Cornwall that he would not remain at Wolffeton another day. Then he took his wife on one arm and his daughter on the other and marched them out of the hall. I know Lord Graelam was smiling, though he tried to hide it. Praise be to Saint Anne that you'll nay have to see any of them again."

Kassia did not admit her overwhelming relief at Etta's words. She still shuddered at the thought of standing before them in her travel-stained clothes. It appeared that her husband had protected her.

"Etta, where is Lord Graelam? Is this not his chamber?"

"He is in the hall, speaking, I believe, to the Duke of Cornwall. All the others have retired, thank the Lord."

Kassia shoved the trencher off her lap. "My bath,

Etta. I will not face him again looking like a dirty urchin. Nay, do not argue with me! I am not ill."

Graelam sat in his ornately carved chair across from the Duke of Cornwall, a goblet of wine in his hand. The hall was quiet at last, with but the two of them.

"St. Peter's bones, Graelam, this has been a fine day." The duke said acidly, his thick gray brows drawn together.

"Aye, it has certainly been a day I shall not quickly forget."

"This girl, Kassia de Lorris—"

"Lady Kassia de Moreton," Graelam said.

"It's true you only saw her once?"

Graelam nodded. He felt oddly exhilarated, as if he had just fought in a battle. "She was near death. I would not have recognized her save for my ring and her short hair. Her hair had been shorn, you see, from her fever."

"She is quite young, Graelam," the duke said. "Aye, quite young. You never bedded her."

Graelam arched a thick black brow. "Indeed, my lord."

"Then you can still be rescued from this mess," the duke said. "Annulment. The marriage was never consummated. It will be an easy matter, and the girl will soon be on her way back to Brittany."

Graelam looked thoughtful, then said slowly, "Belleterre is an impressive holding, my lord duke. The keep is magnificent, the lands rich. Upon Lord Maurice de Lorris's death, it will come to me. If you will, the girl is as much an heiress as Joanna de Moreley."

"But she is French."

Graelam merely cocked a brow at the duke.

"You will not have this travesty of a marriage annulled?"

Graelam stroked his fingers across his jaw. "I will speak to the Lady Kassia again tonight. Tomorrow, my lord duke, I will tell you my decision."

But the Duke of Cornwall was not finished. His fury had calmed, but he still felt the fool, a feeling he did not appreciate. "I do not know why you couldn't have told me of the damned girl," he said, "and your ridiculous midnight marriage."

"As I said, my lord duke, I believed her dead. What reason was there to tell you?"

"I cannot believe you prefer her to Lady Joanna," the duke said, ignoring Graelam's question. "She has not half Joanna's beauty. Indeed, she looked like a skinny boy, and a dirty one at that."

"She has been quite ill," Graelam said mildly. "Some food will fill her out and a bath will take care of the dirt."

The duke knew he was losing, and it galled him. Abruptly he said, "What if her illness rendered her barren? Ah, I see you had not thought of that."

Graelam did not immediately reply. He was seeing Joanna's distorted features, hearing her venomous words. Even a barren wife would be preferable to that shrew. "Nay," he said finally, "I have not given that any thought as yet."

"You must," the duke said, rising from his chair. "Give it a lot of thought, Graelam, before you make your decision. You told me yourself that your only reason for marrying was to breed sons."

"Aye," Graelam said. "That is what I told you."

Graelam saw the duke to his chamber, then drew up suddenly outside his own. By God, he thought, his wife was within. His *wife*. He quietly opened the door and stepped inside. He blinked rapidly at the sight of Kassia in his wooden bathing tub. He could see naught but her thin white shoulders. Slowly he backed out and firmly closed the door. At least the girl didn't appear ill.

He returned after some fifteen minutes. "My lady," he said quietly, not wishing to frighten her.

Kassia jumped, dropping her tortoise shell comb to the floor. She tried to rise, but Graelam waved her back into the chair. He glanced at her old nurse and curtly nodded toward the door. "I wish to speak to your mistress."

The duke, Graelam thought, would perforce change his opinions if he were to see her now. She looked like an impish girl, with her large eyes staring at him, unblinking, and her short damp curls framing her face.

"How old are you?"

"Seventeen my lord." He continued to look at her, and Kassia touched her fingertips to a thick curl that fell over her forehead. "It's my hair." She raised her chin. "Father told me I must not be vain. My hair will grow, my lord."

He wanted to laugh at her show of defiance. Instead, he only nodded and walked to the bed. He saw her wary look, but ignored it, and sat down. "I saw your nurse below during the discussions. I imagine she told you what happened?"

"Aye."

Graelam saw her clutch her bedrobe across her breasts, her eyes never leaving his face.

"Are you cold?"

"Nay, my lord," but she pulled the protecting cover over her legs.

"I am twenty-eight years old, Kassia," Graelam said. "A great, venerable age to one so young."

"My father is forty-two," Kassia said. He saw the barest trace of a dimple near her mouth when she added, "It is Etta who is the venerable age, my lord. She is near to fifty."

Graelam was silent for a moment. "The Duke of Cornwall wishes to have this marriage annulled."

Kassia cocked her head to one side. "I do not understand, my lord. My father told me that our priest wed us."

"Aye, but our marriage was not consummated." Still she looked at him with innocent eyes.

"That means, Kassia, that I did not take you to my bed."

He watched a flush creep over her cheeks.

"It means that we are not truly man and wife until I do. Are you a virgin?"

"No man has touched me, my lord."

He was tempted to smile at the display of defiant pride. He had never doubted she was a virgin, yet he had purposefully embarrassed her. He was not certain why he had done it.

"Enough of that for the moment," he said. "Now, you will tell me why your father did not send me a message that you lived."

"My father loves me, my lord. He feared that such news, until I was completely well again, would harm me. I did not even know you existed—save for my dream—"

"What dream?"

A flush warmed her cheeks. "I told my father that I had dreamed that another man had been near me. A—a man with a gentle voice."

Graelam had been called many things in his life, but never gentle. "Continue," he said.

"It was nearly two weeks ago that he told me of your message. But that was not all, my lord. My cousin, Geoffrey de Lacy, had somehow discovered that I was still at Belleterre and had not accompanied my husband to England. He evidently convinced the Duke of Brittany that our marriage was a sham. My father feared that the duke would set the marriage aside and wed me to Geoffrey."

Graelam heard the fear and distaste in her voice. "Aye," he said. "I know about Geoffrey."

Kassia sat forward, her voice earnest. "You must understand, my lord, it was never my father's intent to harm you in any way. He much admires you. There was simply no time when your messenger arrived. He wanted to accompany me, but of course it was not possible. Whilst I traveled here to Cornwall, my father went to see the duke."

"Geoffrey is dangerous, albeit a coward. He will not give in so easily."

"I know that, my lord. But my father told me you were a strong warrior, that you would protect Belleterre if Geoffrey tried treachery."

"Do you wish to remain here at Wolffeton as my wife?"

"Why, of course," she said, her voice strong and sure. She cocked her head at him. "If my father chose you for my husband, my lord, I would never gainsay his wishes. And," she added, "Geoffrey must never have Belleterre."

Aye, the girl would follow the devil if her father asked it of her. It disturbed him that she saw him through the eyes of her father. "You have ridden through my country, Kassia. It is not gentle, but savage and rugged."

"It reminds me greatly of Brittany, my lord. It was the southern coast I found unlikely."

Graelam nodded and rose from his bed. "You will rest and not leave this chamber. I am informed by my former betrothed's father that they will leave on the morrow." He paused a moment, his eyes sweeping over her. "And you will eat. You are still very thin; a strong wind could blow you away."

She nodded. As he turned and strode away from her, she felt a wave of guilt that she had taken his bedchamber. He opened the chest at the foot of the bed and drew out a blanket. Without looking at her again, he left the chamber. For the first time, he was real to her, this man who was her husband, this man who now controlled her life and her destiny. She felt no fear, for after all, her father had picked him for her. She slid down under the covers and fell into an exhausted sleep.

Graelam wrapped the blanket closer about him and pressed his back against the stone wall. He had dismissed all the men and servants from the Great Hall to ensure privacy for his conversation with the duke. But now they were back, and he had had to step carefully over the snoring men. The lord of Wolffeton, sleeping on the floor. And all for the scrawny girl who slept in his bed and was his wife.

9

Graelam leaned against the northern stone tower and watched Thomas de Moreley's retinue disappear in whirls of dust over the rocky hill toward St. Agnes. He found, somewhat to his surprise, that Joanna's departure had lifted almost a physical weight from his spirit. She had eyed him glacially as she sat her palfrey in the inner bailey, her gloved hands clutching at her riding whip.

"I bid you Godspeed, Joanna," he said.

Joanna quivered with humiliation and rage; he could see it clearly in her face as she had said, "And I wish you to hell, Lord Graelam, you and that skinny little slut you claim as your wife."

Graelam shook away the image of Joanna, clapped Arnolf, the porter, on his stooped shoulder, and quickly made his way back to the Great Hall. It was early and he found he was ravenous. He bellowed for food.

"A blessed escape," Guy said as he seated himself across from Graelam at the trestle table.

Graelam swallowed the crunchy heel of bread and downed the remainder of his ale. "Perhaps," he said, wiping the back of his hand across his mouth. "One woman is much the same as another," he added on a shrug, disregarding the relief he had felt upon her departure. "Joanna would have suited me, eventually. Her body was pleasant enough. Should you like me to talk to the Duke of Cornwall for you, Guy? Mayhap you would make Lady Joanna a suitable husband."

"I would take to my heels," Guy said, laughing. "You speak of a wife like one of your destriers, my lord. Surely a woman is not an animal to be broken."

"Mastered, Guy."

"What if the lady is already as gentle as a soft summer rain?"

"Without guile you mean? I have known but one woman who was as true as a man, and she, Guy, was about as gentle as a viper."

"Ah, Lady Chandra de Vernon."

"Aye, a prince among women."

"Your wife, my lord," Guy said suddenly, his eyes gazing beyond Graelam's left shoulder. He rose quickly. "I bid you good morning, my lady."

Graelam swiveled about to see Kassia standing at the foot of the stairs. In truth, he had forgotten about her. She was looking toward him hesitantly.

"Come," he called to her. "We will start fattening you up this instant."

He could not be certain, but at his words, he thought she blushed. She is graceful, he thought, watching her walk toward him. She was wearing a gown of soft blue wool, belted at her waist. Her short chestnut curls glistened in the morning light and for a moment he wondered how soft they would feel in his hands. He frowned at the thought, for as she drew closer, he saw that she appeared very fragile, her delicate bones too prominent. He felt an unwanted surge of guilt, for he saw her suddenly as she was at Belleterre.

Kassia saw her husband's frown and her steps slowed. She saw a sympathetic smile curl up the corners of Sir Guy's mouth, then, unwillingly, she turned her eyes back to her husband's harsh face.

"My lord," she said shyly, and proffered him a deep curtsy.

"You are well, my lady?" Graelam asked, his eyes on the curls that caressed her small ears.

"Aye, my lord, quite well." She nodded to Sir Guy and to the dozen men-at-arms who sat at another trestle table, staring at her with open curiosity. She did not see Stephen or any of her father's men.

"Stephen, my lord?"

"He has already broken his fast, my lady," Sir Guy said, "and is seeing to the supplies for his return to Brittany."

"He—he plans to leave soon?"

"I will tell him when he is to leave," Graelam said. He rose and it took all of Kassia's resolution not to cower. Which was foolish, he had been naught but kind to her, but he was so large, so hard. "You will eat now, Kassia," he said to her. "I must see to the Duke of Cornwall. He also wishes to depart today. Guy, take the men to the training field. With all the festivities, they have grown fat and lazy."

He strode out of the hall without a backward glance, leaving her to the mercy of utter strangers. Guy did not want to leave the shy girl, but he had no choice. He motioned to the men, smiled once again at Kassia, and left the hall.

Kassia slipped into the smaller chair next to her husband's. She glanced at the crusts of bread and the pale unripened cheese and shuddered.

"It is not good enough for ye, my lady?"

Kassia tensed at the barely veiled insolence in the serving girl's voice. The girl was as young as she, and quite pretty, as rounded and plump as Kassia was thin. And, Kassia thought on a silent sigh, her hair was thick and long, flowing down her back.

"What is your name?" she asked quietly.

"Nan, my lady."

Kassia suddenly remembered a serving wench who had remained but three days at Belleterre. She had insulted Kassia, thinking the twelve-year-old girl too young to retaliate. Kassia now smiled at the memory. "Nan," she said, "I would like a glass of fresh milk and three slices of freshly baked bread. As for this cheese, you may eat it yourself, or feed it to the pigs."

Nan stared at the little upstart. She was smiling sweetly, but there had been a tone of command in her voice that made Nan start.

"There are cows to be milked, are there not?"

"Aye," Nan said, her eyes narrowing. "But there's no more bread, not until this afternoon."

"Fetch me the milk and I will see to the baking of bread myself." Kassia nodded dismissal to the girl, praying silently that she would obey her. To her relief, the girl, after shooting her a venomous look, flounced away. Kassia forced herself to eat the cold bread left by her husband. She was aware of at least a dozen servants skulking about the hall, all wanting a glimpse of her, she supposed. Her housekeeper's eyes took in the reeds scattered haphazardly over the stone floor. They were not filthy, at least they didn't offend her nose, and that was probably because of the wedding guests at Wolffeton. But they were dull, and there were no sweet-smelling herbs. She ran her hand over the table. It was badly gouged, old and battered, and this was the master's table. She shook her head, shocked at the lack of care. The wood beams overhead were black with years of smoke and soot, making the hall even darker than necessary, and there was a feeling of damp and cold. Two old-fashioned lavers stood near her table. They had seen no polish in years. She wanted to set the servants to work immediately, but it was her husband's face that stilled her. He was the master here. Until he gave her permission to attend to his keep, she would be wise to keep her mouth shut. She closed her eyes a moment, wondering if her husband would indeed keep her. Annulment. He could set her aside, he had told her that himself, unless the marriage was consummated. She could not prevent the shudder at the thought. She was ignorant, but not stupid or blind. She had seen animals mate and knew that somehow men did much the same thing to women. But she had never seen a naked man, and thus was uncertain just how they accomplished the sex act. Well if mares could tolerate it, so could she. And, she must tolerate it to save Belleterre from Geoffrey. She became aware of the serving wench, Nan, standing at her elbow, and she flushed, wondering if the girl could see the terrifying thoughts in her eyes.

"Yer milk, my lady," Nan said. She set the goblet in front of Kassia, none too gently, and some of the warm milk spilled onto the table.

Kassia wanted to slap the insolent girl. There was

probably a lot of that around. She was saved from a decision by the appearance of her husband, accompanied by an older, fierce-looking man, the Duke of Cornwall. She turned to dismiss Nan, when she saw the girl's eyes resting possessively and intimately upon Lord Graelam. Ah, she thought with no particular emotion, so that was why the girl was surly and insolent. She smiled and rose, curtsying deeply to the older man.

Graelam said calmly, "My lord duke, this is Lady Kassia, my wife."

The Duke of Cornwall felt a tug of surprise. The slight little creature standing so resolutely before him, her large eyes fastened upon his face, bore little resemblance to the dirty urchin who had so insolently forced her way into the hall the day before. She was a lovely girl, and had an air of great sweetness about her. And uncertainty.

He felt a tug of protectiveness that surprised him. He was too old to be such a fool. But nonetheless he said in a very gentle voice, "Lord Graelam is blessed in his bride, my lady. Allow me to welcome you to England."

"Thank you, my lord duke," Kassia said. "Even in Brittany, your name is much revered. My father used to tell me that you should have been the King of England, for you are brave and decisive, and fair to all your people."

The duke laughed. "It is God who decides these matters, my lady." But nonetheless, Graelam saw him preening at her praise. He wasn't certain whether to be annoyed at her flattery or pleased.

"My father also says that our own king, the sainted Louis, was too much in God's service. That God should have released him to rule his people."

"And what do you believe, my lady?"

"I, my lord duke? It is my belief that there is quite enough misery and injustice at home to keep the most sainted of men well-occupied."

"Well, my lord," the duke said to Graelam. "Perhaps it is your wife who can convince Edward to return to take his throne. I will remember your words, my lady, when next I write my nephew."

Kassia flushed at his kind words, and said quickly, "There is but bread and cheese to offer you, and fresh milk."

Graelam frowned. It was a miserable offering to the king's uncle. "Nan, bring food for the duke."

"Fresh milk," the duke mused aloud. "It has been a long time, my lady. Yea, a very long time."

"It is very beneficial to your health, I am told, my lord duke. Please, will you not be seated?"

Graelam eyed his wife. She was acting every bit the lady of the castle, and for some reason, that angered him. Perhaps her pleasing hesitancy before him was all an act. Perhaps she was just as much the shrew as Joanna.

"I will see to your milk, my lord," he said to the duke. "This glass is for my wife." He thought perversely that she was more in need of it than the duke.

Kassia looked quickly up at her husband. He was kind, she thought, and she had no reason to fear him. He could not, after all, help his harsh looks and too big body.

The Duke of Cornwall chuckled at Graelam's retreating back and obligingly settled his old bones into Graelam's chair. "Tell me of Brittany, my lady," he said, drinking the milk she handed him.

"It reminds me of Cornwall, my lord," she said,

sitting on the edge of a bench, all the world like a precocious child eager to please. "Perhaps a bit colder." She shivered, her eyes upon the damp stone walls of the hall.

"Wolffeton has long been without a mistress, my lady," the duke said kindly. "Lord Graelam is a warrior and thus pays heed only to his fortifications. And his sojourn in the Holy Land left Wolffeton in my nominal care. The serfs have grown lazy, I fear."

"I know nothing of fortifications, my lord," Kassia said firmly, "but I will endeavor to make Wolffeton more pleasing for you on your next visit."

The duke shifted slightly in his chair. He had thought Kassia a pleasing child, but without spine. Now he saw differently and he felt concern for her. Graelam was no gentle man to be ruled by a woman.

The duke's silence made Kassia say, "Has my husband accepted me, my lord duke?" She was unaware that her fingers were clutching the wool of her gown.

The duke frowned. "So he spoke to you of an annulment," he said.

Kassia nodded. "Aye, last evening." She raised her head and gazed at the duke directly, her eyes proud and intense. "He must accept me, my lord duke. My father chose him to be my husband and the protector of Belleterre. Perhaps he prefers Lady Joanna, but I will bring him wealth and much valuable land."

"Aye, he told me as much." The duke set down the empty goblet and hunched forward in Graelam's chair, his bony fingers tapping together. "My lady," he began, "your husband is a powerful man. The alliance with the de Moreleys would have added to his power and his wealth. He is a close friend of my nephew, the King of England. You offer him land, it's true, but to hold it, he will undoubtedly have to fight. And that, my lady, requires fighting men."

"You are telling me, my lord duke, that my father asked too much of Lord Graelam?"

The duke chuckled. "Nay, dear child, Graelam is not a man to be led by the nose. He is more comfortable bashing heads than sitting in his castle. He is a man bred to war. It's just that I would prefer he fight in England, if need be, or in the service of the king. I tell you this so you may understand. A marriage is an alliance between two houses, each bringing value to the other. You have brought Lord Graelam value, but to keep it, he will tempt his unscrupulous neighbors to take advantage of his absence."

"You believe," Kassia said slowly, "that I should allow my marriage to be annulled?"

"Nay, child. You are being too fair. You cannot protect both your father's interests and Lord Graelam's. I suspect that your loyalties still lie with your father. After all, you do not know your husband. Allow Lord Graelam to decide, and do not interfere." The duke sat back a moment, watching Kassia think about what he had said. She was intelligent, he thought, not particularly discomfited by the fact even though she was a woman.

"I believe," Kassia said finally, "that Lord Graelam has already decided. He presented me to you as his wife."

"Aye, he has decided, my lady. But your problems are not yet solved. There is still Charles de Marcey, the Duke of Brittany, to placate. This cousin of yours appears to have some part of the duke's ear. You must bear a son within the year, my lady, else Charles may still believe your cousin's charges that this marriage is a sham."

A child. Kassia's hands moved unconsciously to her belly.

"Ah, Graelam, I was just giving your bride an old man's advice."

Graelam set another goblet of milk before Kassia. He cocked a black brow at the duke, saying nothing.

"It would perhaps be worth the trouble to take Kassia for a visit to Belleterre and to the Duke of Brittany when she is carrying your child. Her swollen belly would do much to still her cousin, I believe."

Graelam slanted a look toward Kassia at the duke's blunt words. She was sipping her milk, her eyes downcast. "You're right," he said. "But first my lady must regain her health and her strength."

"I am strong and healthy now, my lord," Kassia said, her chin up.

The Duke of Cornwall threw back his head and laughed. Graelam saw Kassia's face drain of color. He grinned, knowing she had not realized the import of her words. "It is wise, is it not, Kassia," he said, "to think carefully before you speak?"

He was teasing her, Graelam thought, somewhat surprised at himself. Rarely had he jested with a woman. He turned to the duke and assisted him out of his chair.

"I will take my leave of you, Graelam," the duke said. "I have but one word of advice to you, my lord," he added, his eyes resting for a moment on Kassia. "Wolffeton now has a mistress—"

Aye, Kassia thought, likely several mistresses, given the look on the serving wench's face.

"—a lady to add comfort to your keep." The duke paused, seeing Graelam frown. It was true, he thought, he was meddling. It was none of his affair.

"Aye," he said, "a lovely mistress. Perhaps I will see you both in London," he added, "if I can but convince my nephew to return to England. I plan myself to oversee his coronation."

"Edward loves splendor and ceremony," Graelam said. "Make your letters to him reek of this and perhaps you'll seduce him home."

"Aye, mayhap I will." The duke rubbed his hands together. "Mayhap I will hint to him of rebellion. Edward is like you, Graelam. He prefers nothing more than fighting. I must take my leave. My lady, I came to Wolffeton expecting to be bored with ceremony. You provided a charming diversion."

10

Kassia carefully held up her skirts, not wanting to dirty them in the muck from the rain that had fallen earlier in the afternoon. It was disgraceful, she thought, filth so close to the cooking outbuilding. Her husband obviously had no interest in the place where his meals were prepared, but Kassia kept her thoughts to herself, for the moment.

"You are not overtiring yourself?"

"Oh no, my lord," Kassia said. "Your keep is surely vast, but I wish to see all of it."

"Even the armorer's?"

There was a touch of amusement in his deep voice, and Kassia, emboldened by it, smiled impishly up at him. "Aye," she said, "even the armorer's. Perhaps I can give him some suggestions to improve your gear."

They toured the falconery after the armory, and Graelam, seeing Kassia's excitement, gave her a peregrine falcon for a gift.

"He is mine?" she asked, gazing at the beautiful bird, who was in turn regarding her with an unblinking stare.

"Aye, he is yours."

"Oh, thank you, my lord." Without thought, Kassia clasped his arms in her delight at his generosity.

"Do you hunt?" he asked, smiling down at her.

She nodded happily and turned quickly away from him to croon soft words to her falcon. "What is he called, my lord?"

"Strangely enough, his name is Hawk."

Her tinkling laughter rang out. "Ah, you are much too noble to carry such an insulting name," she said to her falcon.

"When you are stronger, we will hunt," Graelam said. "Hawk can bring down a heron without breaking his speed."

Kassia wanted to tell him that she was strong as a mule, but indeed she was tiring. The long journey had weakened her. That, and coming face to face with a man who was her husband, and a stranger.

"I thank you, my lord," she said. "You are very kind."

Her voice rang with sincerity and Graelam felt inordinately uncomfortable for a moment. "Your father, my lady, was perhaps overly generous in his view of me."

"My father," Kassia said firmly, "is never wrong about a person's character."

"Thus I am kind because Maurice tells you so?"

"Aye, and of course, you did give me Hawk."

"I did, did I not?" Graelam said. "Come, Kassia, it is beginning to rain again. I do not wish you to become ill."

Graelam strode toward the keep, Kassia hiking up her skirts to keep up with him. He turned at a sharp cry and saw her stumble on a slick cobblestone. He caught her easily and lifted her in his arms.

"I'm clumsy," she said in a breathless voice.

"And you weigh no more than a child."

Kassia turned her body against him and he felt her soft breasts against his chest. His body reacted immediately. She was his wife and he could take her now, if he wished. His breathing quickened.

Unaware of his thoughts, Kassia said, "When I was recovering from the fever, my father was forever pouring his Aquitaine wine down me. I feared I would become a drunkard with a red nose. I promise that I will be plump as a spring goose before long, my lord."

He didn't reply but Kassia was content. He was kind and strong and he appeared to at least like her. She felt his arm tighten beneath her thighs and flushed. She ducked her head down against his shoulder. They had entered the hall, yet her husband still held her close.

"Good afternoon, my lord."

Graelam's hold on her eased and he let her down. "Blanche," he said. "Have you yet met Kassia?"

"I bid you welcome," Blanche said sweetly. She stared at the girl standing so close to Graelam. She looked for the world like a boy with her tumbled curls, and skinny. Blanche smiled. She knew Graelam preferred women with more ample proportions. He could not be pleased with this sorry excuse for a wife. During the long preceding night and the equally long day she had finally accepted the fact that she would never be mistress of Wolffeton, and Graelam's wife. It was, she supposed, her fervent dislike of Joanna that had kept her from seeing the futility of her wishes, that and the growing dislike she saw Graelam evince toward his betrothed. But Joanna was gone and Kassia was here, already wed to Graelam. But what of her son?

Her smile didn't reach her eyes, but Kassia, still flushed at her reaction to her husband's arms, did not notice. "Thank you," she said quietly.

"I am Lord Graelam's sister-in-law," Blanche said. "Blanche de Cormont. Would you like a cup of ale, my lord?"

"Aye, Blanche," Graelam said. He looked down for a moment at Kassia. "And a cup of wine for Kassia."

Kassia watched Blanche give instructions to one of the serving wenches. The girl appeared sullen, her eyes darting toward Kassia before she took herself off.

Blanche walked gracefully to Graelam's chair and carefully pulled it away from the trestle table.

"I understand," she said to Kassia, "that you have been quite ill."

Kassia nodded, pleased that Graelam motioned for her to sit beside him. "Aye," she said. "But I am well now."

"Perhaps not entirely, yet," Graelam said.

Blanche took the goblet of ale from the serving girl and handed it herself to Graelam. She nodded to the girl to give the wine to Kassia.

"You still look pale and thin," she said, sitting herself near to Graelam. "Perhaps, my lord," she continued, "you wish me to continue in my present duties until she is stronger?" *Why am I doing this to myself when there is no hope?*

Kassia stiffened. She shot a look toward her husband, waiting for him to tell his sister-in-law that she needn't bother. To her chagrin, Graelam said, "Aye, thank you, Blanche." He downed his ale, wiped his hand across his mouth, and asked, "Where is Guy?"

"I don't know," Blanche said, her lips thinning. How he must be laughing at her now.

Graelam rose from his chair. "Kassia," he said, "I must meet with my steward, Blount. Why do you not rest for a couple of hours?"

Kassia didn't know what to say. She was too uncertain of her husband to tell him plainly that she wished to direct the servants, but without his permission, she could accomplish nothing. She knew Blanche was watching her. She nodded, saying nothing, and watched her husband stride from the hall.

"We have the evening meal in two hours," Blanche said. "Would you like me to have one of the serving wenches show you to your chamber?"

Perhaps she is his mistress, Kassia thought, and thus her power with him. But no, that made no sense. Lord Graelam would not take his own sister-in-law, and a lady, to his bed. She looked about the hall, seeing at least a dozen servants watching them. Did they expect her and Blanche to fight?

"Not as yet," Kassia said.

"You are scarce more than a girl," Blanche continued after a moment. "Your marriage to Lord Graelam came as a shock to everyone. I shall try to shield you from the unkindness of the servants and Lord Graelam's men."

For a long moment Kassia gave Blanche a puzzled stare. "Why should anyone be unkind to me, Blanche? I do not understand your concern."

"Wolffeton is a very large keep. There are many servants to direct. I doubt that you have the experience to make them do your bidding."

Kassia laughed warmly. "My home in Brittany— Belleterre—is as vast as Wolffeton. My mother died when I was quite young and I have kept my father's castle for a number of years. Indeed, I read and write and keep accounts. My husband did not ally himself to an orphan waif, Blanche." She was tempted to ask what experience Blanche had had, for the keep did not show a woman's caring attention.

"I am pleased," Blanche said. She dropped her eyes to her lap to cover her sharp disappointment and frustration.

"My lord Graelam," Kassia said after a moment, "did he care mightily for Lady Joanna?"

"Lady Joanna is very beautiful," Blanche said honestly. "Her hair is long, to her hips, and nearly silver, it is so light. Aye, he has—had—very strong feelings for her."

Kassia unconsciously touched her fingers to her own short curls. "I see," she said, and felt miserable.

"Lady Joanna also has strong passions. In that, she was well-suited to Lord Graelam. He is a very demanding man, so I have heard. I hear the serving wenches gossip—only the comely ones, of course. He is evidently so large a man that he has hurt some of them. And, of course, he never tires."

Blanche saw that Kassia was staring at her, uncomprehending. So it was true, just as she had heard. Graelam had not taken his young wife as yet. The thought of Graelam coupling with Kassia made her continue. "You are very small," she said, leaning close to Kassia. "I hope that you will be brave enough to bear the pain."

"My lord is kind," Kassia said.

Blanche heard the uncertainty and fear in her voice. Graelam deserved a shrinking wife in his bed, damn him. "Of course," she said, and rose. "Now

that he is wed, perhaps his other women will be relieved of their duties, for a while at least." She knew
she was being cruel, utterly mean, in fact, but she
stifled her guilt at her lie, for her own disappointment was too fresh to bear in silence. She left Kassia,
now parchment pale at her words, sitting rigidly in
her chair, her hands twisting in her lap. At the very
least, Graelam would regret not taking Blanche to his
bed when she had offered herself to him. Perhaps
his innocent little wife would quickly come to despise him. It would be her revenge. She had nothing
else, at least for the moment.

Graelam frowned toward Kassia's bent head. She
was pushing her food about on her trencher, paying
no attention to her food, to him, or to anything else
in the noisy hall.

"Why are you not eating?" he asked. "Are you
feeling ill?"

Kassia looked at his large hand lying lightly on
her arm. He had introduced her formally as Lady
Kassia de Moreton to all his men-at-arms, and all the
servants. His wife. His possession. He would hurt
her. She forced herself to look at him. She saw concern in his dark eyes, and blinked. Blanche had to
be wrong. He was kind. He would not harm her.

"I—I am a bit tired, my lord, that is all."

"You may retire in a few minutes. I will join you
later."

No. Her tongue slid over her lower lip in her
nervousness.

It was an unconsciously sensuous gesture and
Graelam turned quickly away from her. He called
out to Rolfe, his master-at-arms, "What have you

heard of de Fortenberry? Has he kept to his own lands?"

"Aye, my lord," Rolfe shouted back, above the din of voices. "The man is many things, but he is no fool. He knows you would burn his keep down about his ears if he dared to attack any of our demesne farms."

"I have head," Guy said, "that Dienwald de Fortenberry buried his wife some months ago. Perhaps he would be interested in the Duke of Cornwall's assistance in finding him another."

Graelam merely grinned and said, "I wish another twelve or so men, Rolfe. Many men lost their masters in the Holy Land and have become no more than vagabonds."

Kassia listened to their talk. She wished she could ask Graelam to direct some of his wealth toward the keep. She became aware that Blount, the steward, a cadaverous man of middle years who was once, she had heard, a priest, was speaking to her and turned politely to attend him.

Blanche slipped from the hall and made her way to her chamber. So de Fortenberry had no wife, she thought, hope beginning to stir through her. Nor did Graelam, not really, not yet. Despite what she had told Kassia, she doubted Graelam would take his young wife until he believed her strong again. She sat on her narrow bed picturing Kassia's pale face at her words. If he were tempted, perhaps the girl's fear would stop him, at least for a while. Unwanted tears spilled onto her cheeks. She was a wretched witch, yet she couldn't seem to help herself.

Kassia's fear had quieted. Her husband was still below in the hall discussing various matters with his men. He had gently patted her hand when she had excused herself, but he had appeared distracted. Surely he would not harm her. She tightened the sash of her bedrobe more tightly about her waist and snuggled down under the covers. She was nearly asleep when she heard the bedchamber door open. She sat up, drawing the blanket to her chin. Graelam entered, holding a candle in his hand. His dark eyes locked on hers from across the room.

"I had hoped you would be asleep," he said.

She wanted to ask him where he was going to sleep, but the words lay leaden in her mouth. She said only, "Nay."

"Do you miss Belleterre and your father?"

She nodded, praying he would not see her nervousness.

He set the candle down atop a chess table and began to take off his clothes. He had stripped to the waist when he heard her gasp. He turned to see her staring at him.

"Did you never attend your father or his guests in their bath?"

She shook her head.

"You have never seen a naked man?"

A chestnut curl fell over her forehead as she again shook her head.

Graelam was silent for a moment, watching her. He knew fear when he saw it. He slowly walked to the bed and sat down beside her. He could feel her tense, though she didn't move away from him.

"Listen to me, Kassia," he said quietly. "You are young and innocent. Your husband is a stranger, and you are living amongst strangers. You have also been very ill." He paused. "Must you stare at my chest?"

Her eyes flew upward to his face. "I am sorry, my lord," she whispered.

He felt a surge of impatience at her for acting like a whipped puppy. "You have nothing to be sorry about. I fully intend to sleep in my own bed, with you. I will not take you. But you will become used to me. When you are well again and have added flesh, you will become my wife."

He rose and pulled off the rest of his clothes. "Look at me, Kassia," he said.

Kassia raised her eyes. He was standing by the bed, sublimely indifferent in his nakedness. He felt her eyes roving over his body, and despite himself, his member swelled. He quickly eased into bed beside her.

"The scar, my lord?"

"Which one?"

"The one on your leg that goes to your—"

"My groin?"

"Aye. How did you get it?"

"In a tournament in France, some eight years ago. I was careless and my opponent was quick to take advantage of it."

"And the scar on your shoulder?"

He was silent for many moments. "That," he said slowly, "was a gift from a lady."

"I do not understand."

"It's a very long story. Perhaps someday I will tell you about it. Now go to sleep, Kassia. Tomorrow, if you are feeling strong, we will go riding."

"Yes, my lord."

But she did not close her eyes until she heard his deep even breathing. She pictured his body, so different from hers, and felt herself grow hot. She had been taught modesty. Evidently men were not. Blanche was right, she thought, huddling near the edge of the bed, her knees drawn to her chest. He would hurt her. She tried to imagine him covering her as a stallion would a mare, and penetrating her body. She quivered. How would she bear the pain?

11

Graelam turned in his saddle at the sound of Kassia's bright laughter. A sea gull was swooping down, nearly touching her shoulder, and she tossed another bit of bread high into the air. The gull squawked loudly, and dived to catch it.

She guided Bluebell forward to escape the half-dozen gulls now gathering behind her, and reined in beside him, her eyes filled with pleasure.

Graelam gazed at her, remembering again how she had looked early that morning, her legs drawn to her chest, her pillow hugged in her arms. He had reached out his hand and gently touched the soft curl over her temple. A sudden fierce protectiveness had flooded him and he had quickly drawn back his hand, angry at himself for his weakness. His abruptness with her when she had come into the Great Hall to break her fast had made her draw back. He had left the hall quickly, aware that Drake, his master armorer, and Blount, his steward, weren't pleased.

Damn them for not minding their own business, he thought now, but he smiled back at her, unable to help himself.

"Oh. Look, my lord."

He followed Kassia's pointing finger to the sea lion who was diving in the waves. They had ridden to the southern boundaries of Graelam's land, then turned downward along the coastline.

"Would you care to rest awhile?" he asked her.

She nodded happily, still watching the sea lion.

He swung off Demon and tied him to a wind-bowed cedar, then clasped his hands around Kassia's waist and lifted her down.

She walked quickly to the edge of the cliff while he secured Bluebell's reins. It was a bright, windy day and Kassia lifted her face to the sun, feeling it warm her. She turned to see Graelam unfasten his cloak and spread it on the ground.

She sat down and crossed her legs in front of her. Graelam joined her, stretching out on his back, resting on his elbows.

"The man who was hurt this morning," she said. "Is he all right now?"

"Aye," Graelam said shortly, disliking to be reminded of his own stupidity. He had pushed his men too hard after he had left the hall, until one of them, careless from fatigue, had been hurt.

Kassia lowered her eyes to the rocky cliff edge but a few feet away. "I'm sorry if I offended you, my lord."

"You did not offend me," he said roughly. "I had much on my mind this morning." It was a half-truth and as much of an apology as Graelam had ever offered to a woman. After a moment he asked abruptly, "Do you believe Geoffrey was responsible for your brother's death?"

Her eyes clouded for a moment. "If he was," she

said slowly, "it would mean that he is evil. I remember the day very clearly. My brother, Geoffrey, and I had a small boat and we would take turns rowing it to the mouth of the cove and fishing. On that day, Geoffrey and Jean ran ahead. My father and I were nearly to the cove when we heard Jean scream. Geoffrey was standing at the edge of the water, and he started yelling and pointing when he saw us. My father watched his son drown and there was naught he could do.

"He ordered the boat brought to shore after my brother had been buried. There was a jagged hole in the bottom."

"Surely that is not proof enough," Graelam said.

Kassia shook her head sadly. "But you see, I had taken the boat out the day before. It did not even leak. And there is more. Evidently Geoffrey could swim. Yet he had stood on the shore watching my brother drown. He could have saved him. When my father found out, he went into a rage and ordered Geoffrey from Belleterre. That was eight years ago. My father's sister, Felice, kept after him to allow her to visit Belleterre occasionally. She and Geoffrey have been allowed to visit three times in the past three years."

"How old was your brother?"

"He was but eight years old when he died. I was nearly ten years old. I am not certain that Geoffrey did kill my brother. Perhaps he did not rip the hole in the boat. Perhaps his only fault was that he was a coward, and was afraid to try to save him. I don't know."

"Geoffrey is still a coward," Graelam said. "I'm glad you're safe from him now."

His voice was warm and Kassia turned to face him, her eyes glowing with pleasure. "You sound like my father," she said.

"I am not your father," Graelam said harshly. His eyes fell to her breasts, the wool of her gown outlining their small roundness by the wind. "Tell me about your mother."

Kassia cocked her head at him, wondering at his constantly shifting moods. "She was very loving and gentle. I do not remember her very well, but my father has told me often of her goodness. And what of your mother, my lord?"

"Her name was Dagne, and unlike your mother, she was not particularly loving and gentle. My father had oft to chastise her for her disobedience and ill humor."

Kassia stared at him. "You mean he *struck* her?"

"Only when she had earned his wrath."

"And when your father earned her wrath, did she strike him?"

"She was a woman. Of course she did not strike him. But I recall her tongue was very sharp on occasion." That was half-truth if ever there was one. His mother had been about as soft-spoken and gentle as a snake. Not, of course, that his father had ever done anything to call forth kind emotions from her. He shrugged that thought aside as Kassia said sharply, "That, my lord, is hardly the same thing. My father would never harm someone smaller and weaker than he. Surely a man could not love a woman and still wish to hurt her."

"Kassia, you do not understand," Graelam said patiently. "It is a man's responsibility to discipline his wife. It is her duty to obey, to serve him, and to bear his children."

"Being a wife does not sound very pleasant," Kassia said. "I think that I should prefer being a dog. At least he is petted and allowed to run free."

"There are benefits to being a wife rather than a dog," Graelam said.

"Oh?" Kassia asked in a tone of disbelief.

He raised his hand and lightly stroked his fingertips over her jaw. "When you are ready, I will show you the benefits of being a wife."

Her eyes widened as she remembered Blanche's words. She blurted out, without thinking, "Oh no. That is not a benefit. That is worse than a beating."

Graelam dropped his hand and stared at her. "Kassia, it is natural for you to be nervous, perhaps even afraid, of what you do not understand. But lovemaking is not a punishment, I promise you."

"Why do you call it lovemaking?" she asked rather wildly. "It is like animals, and it hurts, and there is no love."

Graelam could not believe his ears. Nor could he believe his patience. "What did your father tell you?"

She shook her head, refusing to look at him. "Nothing. He said nothing."

"Then why do you believe it will hurt?"

Kassia bowed her head. "Please," she whispered. "I will do my duty when I must. I know that you want sons."

"Who told you it would hurt?"

"A—lady," she said. "She told me that you—that men were demanding and cared not about a woman's pain. She told me I must bear it."

Graelam cursed long and fluently, the more foul of his curses thankfully whipped away by the wind. "This lady," he said finally in a very calm voice, "was wrong to say such a thing to you, and she lied." He sighed, knowing he had not been truthful. "There are some men who are not interested in a woman's feelings, but not all men are like that."

Kassia turned wide, innocent eyes to his face. "Are you like these men, my lord?"

"I will not hurt you," he said.

She well remembered him naked, his swollen sex thrusting out. She remembered his strange abruptness with her that morning. She said nothing.

"Perhaps you misunderstood this lady," he said. "There is a bit of pain the first time when your maidenhead is torn. But if the man is gentle, pleasure quickly follows and the pain is forgotten."

She was gazing at him, disbelief written clearly in her eyes.

"There is no reason for you to disbelieve me. I am your husband."

"You are so different from me," she whispered.

"Aye, God willed it so." His voice was clipped, for his patience was near an end. Still, it bothered him that she should fear coupling. "Kassia, you have seen animals mate." She continued staring at him, mute. "You have seen me naked. My sex will enter you. Do you understand?"

"I have seen a stallion cover a mare. Will it be like that?"

He wanted to laugh. "Sometimes," he said. "But usually you will be on your back, beneath me."

"Oh."

"The proof will be in the doing," he said, and rose. She stared up at him. He blocked out the sun.

"Kassia," he said, "you cannot remain a child. Come, it is time to return." He stretched out his hand to her. She hesitated a moment, then thrust her hand into his. "Your hand is cold," he said as he drew her to her feet. He pulled her against him. She was stiff as a board. Slowly he began to stroke his hands down her back. "A wife is her husband's responsibility," he said. "I will take good care of you." He felt her ease against him and lay her cheek trustingly against his chest. "Tonight you will become a wife. No, don't stiffen." He smiled over the top of her head. "Did you not tell me that your father trusted me to be kind to you?"

He felt her hesitation, then felt her nose nodding up and down against him. "It is not your monthly flux, is it?"

He heard a small gasp; then she shook her head, burrowing her face into his tunic.

"Look at me, Kassia." When she hesitated, he gently cupped her chin and raised her face upward. "Now, hold still and relax." He touched his fingertips to her lips, then slowly lowered his head.

Kassia jumped when his mouth touched hers. It was not unpleasant. His lips were warm and firm. She felt his tongue glide over her lower lip, and frowned, wondering at the sudden warmth burgeoning low in her belly. She felt his fingers tangle in her hair; then he released her. "That was not so bad, was it?"

"Nay," she said, her head cocked to one side, her eyes studying his face intently. "My stomach feels warm. It is very odd. I've never felt that before."

He grinned, a boyish grin that made him look very young. "Come," he said. He lifted her onto her mare's back and swung into his own saddle. During their ride back to Wolffeton, he wondered at himself.

Never had he had such a discussion with a woman. But there was something so vulnerable about Kassia, and it made him furious at himself, yet still protective of her. He supposed it was simply her innocence that made him babble like a fool. Oddly, he did not want her to fear coupling with him. He would arouse passion in her, he had the skill and he would force himself to patience. She was young, malleable, and he did not doubt that she would be easily molded into an obedient, gentle wife. The future stretched out pleasantly before him in his mind.

Graelam wooed his young wife that evening. He gave her all of his attention at dinner, ensuring that she drank two goblets of sweet wine and ate most of the spicy stew that he shared with her. And he touched her, light caresses that brought color to her cheeks.

"You have eaten almost enough," he said, and sopped a bit of bread in the remainder of the stew and fed it to her himself. She smiled at him. He drew a deep breath and it was her sweet scent that filled his nostrils. Her chestnut curls glowed with reddish glints in the rushlight.

"My hair will grow," Kassia said, aware that he was staring at her.

He wrapped a loose curl around his fingers. "Your hair is so soft," he said. "As fine as a babe's."

A dimple he had not noticed before deepened beside her mouth. "But, my lord," she said, "you do not want a babe for your wife."

He chuckled and ruffled her curls. "You are right, my lady, particularly tonight."

Her eyes widened, but she did not draw away

from him. He was pleased. He turned and nodded to a minstrel, Louis, a Frenchman he had invited to stay at his castle in Cornwall for several days. The small dark-eyed man, sun-baked from his travels, had been playing softly throughout the meal, and now moved forward to sit on a stool in front of Graelam's daised table. He smiled toward Kassia and played several haunting cords on his lute. "To your lovely bride from Brittany, my lord," he said, and bowed his head, strumming the strings lightly. "I have christened it *Fire Song*."

> *'Tis a fire in the blood that draws me*
> *to thee, my maid of Brittany.*
> *A softness in your eyes that makes me*
> *Dream of nights in your gentle arms.*

His voice, soft as spring rain, filled the silent hall. At his words, Kassia smiled at her husband.

> *Your woman's beauty meets my hungry eyes*
> *calling me, my maid of Brittany.*
> *'Tis a fire in the blood that makes me*
> *yearn to hold thee close.*

Graelam pressed his shoulder against hers and gently squeezed her hand. "A fire, my lady?" he said. "Soon we will know if he speaks true."

> *The sweetness in your smile draws me*
> *to thee, my maid of Brittany.*
> *'Tis a fire I long to give thee*
> *the fire of my song and my heart.*

Louis kept his head down as he softly played a crescendo of minor chords. At the finish, he raised his eyes and bowed his head to Kassia.

"That was well done, Louis," Graelam called out over the clamor of the men. "I am pleased as is my lovely bride."

"It is my pleasure, my lord," Louis said. He began again, this time a song of the great Roland and his death fighting the Saracens at Roncesvalles.

Graelam said quietly to Kassia, "Go to our chamber, Kassia. I will come to you soon."

Kassia rose and nodded to Blanche, who was sitting quietly beside Blount, the steward.

"God give you sweet sleep, my lady," Guy said, smiling at her. He watched her wave a slender hand at him, then turn and walk from the hall. His eyes went back to Graelam. He had never before seen his master treat a woman so gently. It boded well.

Graelam lifted his goblet and sipped the sweet wine, his eyes thoughtful. A woman should want a man. He would make Kassia respond to him, make her moan, and make her forget her maiden's fear. The fire in his body would warm her. He downed the rest of his wine and rose from his chair when Louis finished his song. He saw a speculative look on Blount's craggy face, an open smile on Guy's, and knew that all his men were in no doubt about how he would spend his night.

"Please continue, Louis," he said to the minstrel. "As to the rest of you louts," he called out to his men, "listen well and learn." He strode from the hall, feeling something of a fool, for everyone knew he was going to his wife. He took the stone steps two at a time. He opened his chamber door and saw Kassia seated on the bed, wrapped in her blue wool bedrobe.

"Come here, Kassia," he said.

She slipped off the bed, clutched her robe closely to her, and walked to him on bare feet. He held out his arms and she moved against him, wrapping her arms about his waist. He closed his arms about her back, and began to stroke away the tension he felt in her shoulders.

"You smell so sweet," he said, inhaling her lavender scent. He stroked his long fingers through her hair, massaging her scalp, tangling the soft curls about her ears. He drew her more tightly against him, lifting her against his hardening sex.

Kassia raised her head from his shoulder and looked into his dark eyes. Slowly, without instruction from him, she closed her eyes and pressed her mouth against his. She felt again that strange warmth flow through her.

Graelam swung her up in his arms and carried her to the bed. He laid her on her back and sat beside her. Slowly, he untied the sash about her waist. She gave a soft distressed gasp, and he stopped.

"Did I tell you about my destrier, Demon?" he asked.

She stared up at him, blinking in surprise. "Nay, my lord."

"He was bred near York," Graelam said. "His sire was called Satan and his dam, Witch." He lowered his head and gently kissed her closed mouth. He licked her lower lip, all the while talking about his stallion. "He saved my life in the Holy Land when a Saracen would have carved me. He reared up and stomped the fellow." He realized belatedly that though he spoke softly, his words were anything but seductive and soothing. Why the devil was he talking to her about his damned horse? He shook his head at himself. "I want to see you, Kassia," he said, and drew her robe apart.

Her hands fluttered up, but he stilled them, clasping them lightly above her head. "You have beautiful breasts," he said.

"I'm small," Kassia said, "but I will be larger when I gain flesh."

"You are perfectly shaped," he said, surprising himself. He did not like slight women, but somehow, Kassia's delicately rounded breasts appealed to him. And the soft pink nipples, so smooth now, not yet taut with passion.

"You're staring at me,"

"Aye." He grimaced at the memory of Maurice tearing the leech from her breast and flinging it across the chamber.

"I do not please you, my lord?"

"You please me well," he said. He lowered his head and kissed the column of her throat. Slowly he touched his lips to her soft flesh until he lightly flicked her nipple with his tongue. She gasped and he raised his head to see her staring at him, a stunned look on her face. He smiled and lowered his head to suckle her gently. He could feel the pounding of her heart against his cheek.

"Someday," he said, lifting his face to look at her, "our babe will suck at your breast thusly."

He felt her hands stroking in his hair, pulling him closer to her breast.

"Oh."

A look of pain flashed across her face.

"What is the matter?"

"I—I don't know." A cramp twisted in her belly and she cried out.

Graelam sat up and laid his hand to her cheek.

She suddenly lurched up, her face ashen. "I'm going to be sick."

He handed her the chamber pot just in time. She retched until there was naught left in her belly.

"I'm sorry, my lord," she whispered, and moaned, drawing her knees up against the vicious cramps.

"Hush," he said. What had she eaten that he had not, he wondered, worry gnawing at him. Had he forced her to eat too much? Had her fear of him made her ill? He dampened a cloth and gently wiped her sweating face. "Lie still. I will get your nurse."

He watched helplessly as Etta crooned over Kassia, feeling her belly with gentle hands.

"What is wrong with her?"

Etta shook her heard. "She ate something that was bad, I think." She rose. "I will make her a potion, my lord."

At that moment, Graelam felt a cramp in his belly, and doubled over. "Christ," he muttered, and strode quickly out of his bedchamber.

At least, he thought a few minutes later, his belly empty, it wasn't her fear of him that had made her vomit. He checked with his men in the hall. None were ill. The cramps continued and he gladly drank the potion Etta handed him.

"It was the stew," he said. "Only Kassia and I shared it, and she ate the most of it."

She was moaning, her arms wrapped around her stomach. His cramps were lessening, yet he knew what she felt and it frightened him. She was so slight, and had not half his strength. He sat beside her and pulled her into his arms, rocking her.

"She will sleep soon, my lord," Etta said, hovering protectively close to her young mistress. "And she has nothing foul left in her belly."

Kassia's head lolled back against his arm. She said vaguely, "I shall hang the cook up by his heels with his head in the stew."

Graelam was thinking of a more ferocious punishment for the cook.

"You will be all right tomorrow, my baby," Etta said, gently wiping the damp cloth over Kassia's forehead.

"I'm so ashamed." Kassia burrowed her face against Graelam's arm.

"Don't be a fool. Can you sleep now, Kassia?"

"Aye."

He laid her on her back and drew the covers over her. "I will call you if she worsens," Graelam said to Etta.

The night was a long one. Kassia awoke every several hours, her belly convulsed with cramps. Graelam forced her to drink, but she could keep nothing down. Finally, toward dawn, she fell into a deep sleep, and he allowed himself to relax.

It was near to noon the next day when Graelam entered to find Kassia awake. The chamber reeked of sickness and he felt nausea rise in his belly at the stench.

"She has drunk some broth, my lord," Etta said.

"She will not keep it down if she must remain in here," Graelam said. He strode over to his wife and wrapped her up in blankets. "I am taking her outside. Clean the chamber and open the windows. Burn incense, whatever, just get rid of the stench."

Graelam carried his wife out of the keep. He ordered Demon saddled.

"What are you going to do with me?" Kassia asked, clutching at Graelam's sleeve. Now that the cramps were gone, she felt mortified. He had held her whilst she had retched. All night he had cared for her. She wanted to bury her face in his shoulder and never look him in the face again.

"Perhaps I shall toss you over the cliff," Graelam said, hugging her tightly against his chest.

"I would not blame you," she sighed. "I have not been a very good wife to you."

Graelam laughed deeply. "You have not been a wife at all. Now keep quiet."

He held her in his arms as he guided Demon over the lowered drawbridge. "Breathe deeply, Kassia," he said.

He rode to the cliff and dismounted, tying Demon to a low juniper bush. He eased himself down against a bowed pine tree and settled Kassia in his lap. "Now," he said, "you will think about being well again."

"I am so ashamed," she said.

"I was also ill. We have both survived. Now, I want you to be quiet and breathe the clean air."

He felt her burrow trustingly against him, her fist closing about his tunic. He dropped a light kiss on her forehead and leaned back against the tree trunk and closed his eyes.

"My lord."

Graelam opened his eyes and looked up at Guy. He shook away the remnants of sleep.

"It grows late," Guy said quietly, for Kassia was still quiet.

"I will come soon, Guy."

"Is she all right?"

"Aye, thank God. Did you speak to the cook? What is that varlet's name?"

"I gave him—Dayken is his name—the flat of my sword against his fat buttocks. He swears the meat was fresh. I do not understand it. It's almost as if—" He broke off, shaking his head.

"As if what?"

"Nothing, my lord."

"If you have something to say, Guy, say it."

Guy scratched his ear. "I like not that only the two of you fell ill."

"I like it not either," Graelam said. "The only question is who, Guy?"

"A woman's jealousy can lead her to do vicious things, my lord."

Graelam grunted. "So who is this woman, Guy?" he asked.

"Not Blanche, I am certain of that." Indeed, he had spoken to her, watching her beautiful eyes for signs of deception. He did not want to admit to his profound relief when he realized she was innocent. Guy shook his head, perplexed. "All knew you were to bed your lady last night." He flushed as his master's eyes narrowed on his face.

"It need not have been a woman, Guy," was all he said.

Kassia stirred in his lap and raised her head from Graelam's shoulder. "My lord?"

"It's nothing, Kassia," Graelam said. "How do you feel?"

She smiled, and the dimple deepened beside her mouth. "Hungry," she said.

"Excellent. I am certain that your nurse has a pot of broth awaiting you. Your belly isn't cramping anymore?"

She flushed, seeing Guy, and shook her head.

Graelam rose easily, and shifted Kassia in his arms. The blankets fell away and Guy saw the white curve of her breast.

"I'll get Demon, my lord," he said quickly, and strode to his master's destrier.

12

The afternoon was overcast and a chill wind blew from the sea. Kassia stood watching Graelam, his powerful chest bared, wrestling with one of his men, a huge fellow who had the look of a mighty oak tree. The men formed a half-circle, calling out explicit and coarse advice.

Kassia moved closer. She saw the concentration on her husband's face as he circled the other man. He lunged so suddenly that she blinked in surprise. He gave a fierce yell as he hooked his leg behind his opponent's and toppled him to the ground. He slammed down on top of him, pinning his shoulders.

The men cheered and Graelam stood up, offering his hand to his man. He met Kassia's eyes at that moment, and smiled.

She waved to him shyly and called, "We have a visitor, my lord."

Graelam spoke to his men, then strode to his wife, flexing his shoulder muscles. He looked at her closely, studying her face for any signs of lingering illness, and satisfied, asked, "Who comes, Kassia?"

"Blanche's son, my lord."

Graelam frowned a moment, having forgotten the boy.

"Blanche is smiling. I am pleased her son is here." *Her son will give her something to think about other than you.*

One of Graelam's men tossed him his shirt and tunic. "Wash me down first, Kassia," he said, and walked beside her to the well in the inner bailey.

Kassia filled the bucket and poured it over her husband's head and back as he leaned over. He shook himself and donned his shirt.

"My tunic, Kassia," he said.

"Oh." She had been staring at his chest, wondering why it made her heart pound to think of tangling her fingers in the dark curling hair, or suckling at his nipples as he had hers.

Graelam wondered at the sudden flush on her cheeks as he pulled his tunic over his shirt.

They walked into the hall. Blanche was talking to three men, all travel-stained and weary-looking. A slender boy, some eight years old, clung to the side of one of the men.

"My lord," Blanche called out. "My son is here. Evian, this is Lord Graelam de Moreton, your uncle by marriage."

The boy peeped from behind the man. The man gave him an indulgent smile and shoved him forward. "He's a bit shy, my lord. I am Louis, from my lord Robert's household in Normandy."

"I bid you welcome, and thank you for delivering the boy safely," Graelam said, then squatted down to the boy's eye level. He had his mother's dark eyes and dark hair, but was saved from being pretty by a square jaw and a broad forehead. "You will be my page," Graelam said. "If you are competent at your duties, you will one day be my squire. Does that please you, boy?"

"Aye, my lord," Evian said. He studied Lord Graelam with intelligent eyes and became his slave at that moment. Graelam dropped his hand on the boy's shoulder, patted him, then rose. "You have already met my wife, Lady Kassia?" he asked.

Evian nodded, his eyes turning toward Kassia. She was giving him a welcoming, open smile, and he gave her a tentative one in return.

"You are very welcome, Evian," Kassia said.

"I am nearly as tall as you, my lady," Evian said.

"Aye, in another year or so, it is I who will be looking up at you."

Blanche grabbed her son's hand. "He can sleep in my chamber, Graelam."

"Nay, Blanche. Guy, come and meet my new page. The boy will sleep outside my chamber, on a pallet, and take his meals with the men."

"I have been living with my mother's cousin," Evian said confidentially to Guy, "in Normandy."

"Evian, I would like to speak to you."

The boy turned large reluctant eyes back to his mother, wishing she would not treat him like a little boy.

"Nay, let him go, Blanche," Graelam said, to Evian's immense relief. "You can cosset him later." He turned to Louis. "Come have some ale, your men also. Nan, bring drink."

"He is a fine lad," Graelam said to Blanche that evening. "Your cousin has raised him well, but it's men's company he needs."

Blanche forced a bright smile. Graelam was pleased with her son, just as she had hoped he would be. But it was too late. "You are very kind, Graelam," she said. Such a pity that Nan had not mixed more of the vile herbs in the stew. Blanche knew the wench had done it, for Nan was unable to keep the smug, triumphant grin off her face when she believed no one was looking at her. Blanche frowned, lowering her eyes. Jealousy was a terrible thing, and it made her writhe in self-reproach, hating herself for her feelings, even as she searched for ways to undermine Kassia. Life had not been fair to her, she would tell herself over and over, the litany her excuse.

Kassia watched Graelam and Blanche speaking together, and felt a strange burst of anger. Unlike her, Blanche was endowed with a full and rounded woman's body and her long dark hair glistened in the rushlight.

"Your thoughts are not pleasant?"

Kassia turned to Guy "Blanche is very beautiful," she said honestly, bewilderment at her jealousy sounding in her voice.

"That's true," Guy said. "But she need never concern you, truly. Lord Graelam could have wed her had he wished to."

Kassia gave him a sad little smile. "It appears that my lord could have wed any lady he wished. It's his misfortune that he came upon my father in Aquitaine, and that I didn't die."

"Lord Graelam saw much misery in the Holy Land," Guy said pensively, "disease, starvation, butchery that seemed to know no end, but never did it really touch him. Yet I tell you truthfully that after he came from your chamber, believing that you were dying, I was in anguish. You touched him as no other ever has—man or woman. Even now he treats you gently, carefully, and my lord is not a particularly gentle man. When you fell ill from the food, he was distraught. He told me that it was not fair that you should regain your health, only to come to Wolffeton and lose it again." Guy paused a moment, watching Kassia's brow furrow deeply in thought at his words. "Lord Graelam is also a man of strong appetites, yet he is more concerned with your well-being than his own needs."

"But I am well now," Kassia said, and turned red.

Guy grinned at her and raised his goblet in a silent toast. "Your noble husband approaches, my lady."

Kassia raised her face to her husband. She looked like such a naughty child that Graelam laughed.

"I have been telling her of your prowess, my lord," Guy said.

Kassia choked, and Graelam arched a thick black brow. His eyes fell to Kassia's trencher and he frowned. "What have you eaten?"

Kassia, who had consumed chicken and fruit, merely shook her head at him. "I have been a glutton, my lord. May I serve you now?"

He nodded and sat himself beside her. "The boy, Evian," he said to Guy, "we must begin to toughen him up."

Kassia looked down the trestle table at Evian, who was leaning sleepily against Drake's massive shoulder.

"The lad seems willing," Guy said, "though his mother would like to turn him into a lapdog."

Graelam merely grunted, and talk turned to de Fortenberry and his ever-nearing raids. It seemed to

Kassia that Graelam was looking forward to crossing swords with the man; indeed, he hoped that de Fortenberry would attack some of Wolffeton's outlying demesne farms. She watched her husband, and saw that he was not eating as much as he needed. It was the wretched cooking. She must see to her responsibilities as chatelaine soon. If only Graelam would cease treating her like an invalid. He still looked to Blanche, and Kassia found that she did not like that at all. She had noted during the day that the servants heeded Blanche's orders, but slowly and sullenly. Her housewifely hackles rose. They would obey her, and promptly, or she would know the reason why.

She leaned over to pick up an apple from the plate in front of Graelam. Her breast accidentally brushed against his arm. She felt him stiffen and he paused perceptibly in his speech. She turned her head, unaware that he looked at her speculatively for a long moment.

Graelam was surprised at the surge of lust he felt, thinking again that Kassia had scarcely enough womanly curves for his taste. Yet, thinking of her lying soft and yielding in his arms, her trusting eyes upon him, made him anxious, as he had never been before. Tonight, he thought, tonight, he would take her. He must take her.

"Your hand, Kassia," he said, laying his own palm-up on the table beside her.

She tentatively laid her hand in his and watched as his fingers closed around hers. A frown crossed his brow and she held herself very still, not knowing what he was thinking.

She is so slight, he mused, curling his fingers around her slender wrist. He had promised her there

was no pain in coupling, and hoped he was right—
that his size wouldn't hurt her. He must go easily
with her. He felt a renewed tightening in his groin
at the thought of her naked beneath him. He said
abruptly, releasing her hand, "Go to our bedchamber
now, and ready yourself for me."

Kassia knew that her face was red. She remembered quite clearly the odd sensations she had felt
before she had fallen ill, and she knew that Graelam
wanted to make her his wife this night. She walked
from the hall, imagining that all the men knew exactly what was in her mind and in her husband's.

Etta awaited her in her bedchamber.

"Ah, my baby," the older woman said. "You're
tired. You should have stayed abed as your husband
wished you to."

"Nay," Kassia said. "I'm not tired, but I would
like a bath."

Etta shooed Nan and another girl, Erna, pointed-
chinned and scraggle-toothed, from the chamber after
they had filled the wooden tub, then scented the hot
water liberally with lavender, Kassia's favorite scent.

As Kassia disrobed, her eyes kept flying toward
the chamber door. She did not luxuriate in her bath
as was her wont, but scrubbed herself quickly. She
turned to ask Etta for her towel and became mute at
the sight of her husband standing in the doorway,
his arms crossed over his chest, looking at her.

"Is the water still warm?" Graelam asked.

She nodded, sinking down in the wooden tub until
only her head was showing.

"Will you scrub my back?"

He had moved out of her range, and Kassia eased
up a bit to find him. "Aye," she said, "I will." He

was tugging at the ties on his tunic. As he pulled it over his head, she scurried out of the tub and grabbed at the linen towel.

"Kassia, help me."

The tie on his chaussures was knotted. She wrapped the towel securely around her and dropped to her feet before him, her fingers nimble on the knot. She could feel the heat from his body; had she the courage, she could touch the growing bulge in his groin. She stilled suddenly at the touch of his fingers in her hair.

"Soft as a babe's," he said. The knot untied, Kassia lowered her arms, resting her cheek against his thigh.

"Come," he said, and lifted her to her feet. He drew off his chaussures and strode naked to the tub. Kassia giggled at the sight of him, his knees thrust upward, as he settled himself into the tub.

"I amuse you, wench?"

"You are so large, my lord." She smiled as she soaped a sponge and began to stroke it down his back. She soaped his thick hair, careful to keep the lather from his eyes. "I used to shave my father," she said as she rinsed his hair.

"Did you now?" he said, swiping the water from his eyes. His eyes crinkled as he looked up at her. She had time only to gasp in surprise. He jerked the towel from her, grabbed her about her waist, and swung her into the tub onto his lap.

Kassia fell forward, her arms looping about his neck to steady herself. "Oh," she said helplessly, her mouth but a breath away from his.

"Aye." He pressed his hand against the back of her head, bringing her to him. He pressed his mouth against hers, undemanding. He drew her closer until her breasts were pressed against his chest.

"A small wife is not such a bad thing," he said, nibbling on her earlobe. He lifted her carefully so her hips were resting on his belly. "Give me your mouth, Kassia."

"I don't know what to do," she said, feeling like a fool.

"I will teach you," he said. "Part your lips."

She did as he bid her and drew back startled at the touch of his tongue against hers. "That feels strange," she said as her hand stroked through his wet hair without instruction from him.

"Strange good or strange bad?"

"I don't know. Can you do it again, my lord?"

"A willing pupil," he said against her parted lips. He wrapped his arms around her back and pressed her tightly against him, deepening the pressure with his lips. He eased instantly when he felt her stiffen, and was rewarded soon with a quiver that ran the length of her. Slowly, he thought to himself, go very slowly. He felt gooseflesh rise on her arms and laughed. "How the devil do I get you out of this thing?"

He lifted her above him, only to have her slip in a welter of arms and legs. She landed flat against him, her belly against his swollen manhood. Her eyes flew to his face and she knew a moment of fear when his hands pressed against her buttocks, molding her against his hard flesh, and he moaned roughly deep in his throat.

"The water grows cold," she said in a thin, high voice.

Graelam closed his eyes tightly for a moment, getting a hold on himself. The last place he wanted to take his virgin bride was in a tub of cool water. And

she was frightened, he heard it in her voice. He
kissed her lightly on the tip of her nose and thrust
her away from him. Kassia grabbed the towel and
quickly twisted it around her. But she didn't avert
her eyes when he stood in the tub.

"I wish that I looked as beautiful as you," she said.

He stared at her a moment. No woman had ever
before told him he was beautiful. He said as he
stepped from the tub, "A scarred, hairy warrior?"

"Aye," she said, "and endowed with great power
and strength." She handed him a towel. "My father
told me once that the more valiant the knight, the
more gentle he was in his physical strength. I think
he must have been thinking of you, my lord."

"Your father did not know me, Kassia." It made
him uncomfortable to be cast in a chivalrous hero's
mold. "I am as I am. Don't grant me virtues I own
not."

"No, my lord," she said, but he saw the dimple
deepening beside her mouth.

He drew on his bedrobe and strode to the chamber
door, yelling for the servants to empty the tub.

"Get into bed," he called over his shoulder to Kassia. "I do not want you to take cold."

Because she was nervous, it seemed but a moment
of time before they were alone, the door firmly
closed, her husband walking toward the bed.

"I play chess quite well."

He merely grunted, knowing there was nothing he
could say to ease her wariness of him. "How does
your belly feel?" he asked, drawing off his bedrobe
and sitting down beside her.

He laid his hand on her belly and probed lightly.
"I am truly all right," she said.

"You are so small," he said on a frown, his eyes on his splayed hand. He could touch her pelvic bones with the tips of his stretched fingers.

To Kassia's surprise, she felt a bolt of heat sear through her stomach and her eyes flew to his face.

He lifted his hand and she knew a moment of disappointment. He saw it in her eyes, and was pleased. She was innocent of a woman's pleasure, but not cold.

He stretched out above her and stroked his fingers along the column of her throat.

"Should I not douse the candle?"

He shook his head, leaning down to kiss the pulse in her throat. "Nay, I wish to see all of you, wife, even to the soft white flesh between your thighs." She quivered at his words, and he continued in a deep, tantalizing voice, "I want you to watch me looking at you. I will know your body better than you will know yourself. You are so soft." He cupped his hand slightly over her woman's mound and rested it there.

"Open your mouth for me, Kassia."

He touched her even teeth with his tongue, then took her warm mouth. He clasped her in his arms and pulled her onto her side against the length of him.

"Be at your ease, dearling, I will not hurt you."

She believed him and came to him, slipping her arm around his ribs to stroke over his back.

"I want to feel you against me," she said when he released her mouth for a moment.

He quickly loosed the sash of her bedrobe and flung it open. He pushed the robe from her shoulders, pausing a moment to look down at her breasts.

"You are so delicate," he said, more to himself than to her. "So soft, like the Genoese velvet I bought in Acre." Slowly, his eyes on her breast, he stroked his fingertips over her flesh, drawing closer and closer to her nipple. He felt her tremble and leaned his head down to take her into his mouth. He pushed her breast upward to better possess her. He felt her arch her back and slipped one arm beneath her. To his delight, he felt her hand glide down over his hip, gently kneading his muscles, exploring his body as he was hers. As her searching fingers neared his groin, he thought he would spill his seed.

"Touch me, Kassia."

She touched his hard sex, and heard her breath jerk as she tried to take him in her hand. "Don't be afraid, sweetheart," he said between nipping kisses on her throat. "You'll be ready for me. Let me show you."

She grew utterly still as his hand roved over her ribs to her belly. He kneaded the soft flesh a moment, then laid his hand over the curling hair of her woman's mound. "You are holding now a man's desire," he said. "I am an obvious being with no hidden treasures. Unlike you." Gently he probed until he found her. "Here is your woman's place of pleasure. A small treasure, of infinite beauty and enchantment." He swallowed her gasp of surprise when he kissed her, even as his fingers continued to caress her rhythmically. "Does that please you?" he asked into her mouth.

Kassia could think of no words. Her hips were pressing up against his fingers and the only sound from her throat was a pathetic groan.

"I feel so odd," she said. She tightened her hold

on his sex, making him jerk. He prized her fingers loose, aware of her disappointment that his fingers had left her. "I would look at you now, sweeting."

He reared up, parting her thighs. "Open your eyes and look at me, Kassia. There is no shame between husband and wife."

He touched his fingertip to her and watched her hips twist. He slowly parted her, and was startled at the provocative beauty of her. She was all delicate soft pink. Slowly he lowered his head and gave her his mouth. Kassia nearly leapt off the bed, and yelled to the rafters. "Oh no. My lord, you must not— please." She hit her hands against his shoulders.

"Hush, Kassia, do not interfere with a man's pleasure."

"But you should not—surely."

He laughed, his warm breath making her tingle. He continued to nuzzle her, explore her, but she would not ease, her embarrassment too great. He sighed, knowing he should not expect her to fall like a ripe plum into his mouth. He left her and lay beside her, drawing her into his arms. He began to kiss her deeply, even as his fingers caressed her, and he felt her slowly ease, tentatively returning his kisses.

"Kassia. Look at me."

She clutched at his hand that rested on her belly.

"Feel how soft and ready you are for me." She felt his finger slip inside her. She gasped, tried to pull away.

"Nay, little one." She was very small, stretching to hold his finger. He pushed deeper inside her until he felt her maidenhead. He probed gently against it, but it held fast. He cursed silently. She was stiff and afraid, and there was nothing he could do about it, save get it over with. Slowly he drew up, parted her thighs, and guided himself into her.

Kassia's eyes flew to his face. She tried to hold herself still, but she felt a pressure building inside her, felt herself stretching painfully. She gasped and tried to twist away from the pain. "Kassia," he said, kissing her. "Hold still."

She blinked at the tears filming her eyes. "It hurts."

He couldn't help himself, and moved deeper, butting her maidenhead. She was stiff and tense beneath him; he gritted his teeth against the overwhelming urge to drive forward. He held perfectly still, hoping she would become accustomed to the feel of him. He pressed harder against her maidenhead, but the barrier was as strong as an Amazon's shield. "Sweeting, I must cause you but a moment of pain. Hold onto me, Kassia." He looked down at her as he spoke and saw that her eyes were firmly closed, her face pale. What stopped him cold was the tears slowly snaking down her cheeks.

He could not explain his action to himself, for never before had he forgone his own pleasure. He pulled out of her, feeling her flinch, and pulled her tight against him.

She clasped her hands around his back and pressed her face against his shoulder. He stroked her, calming her, until she eased.

"It was not so bad," she said, pulling away from him slightly to see his face. "I'm sorry I'm such a coward. You did not hurt me greatly, truly, my lord."

He wanted to laugh and to curse at the same time. Instead, he kissed her until she was breathless. At least, he thought, he had stretched her somewhat.

When she lay snuggled against his side, her breathing even in sleep, he stared into the darkness, cursing himself for seven kinds of a fool. He should have gotten it over with. A woman's tears had never before touched him with such devastating result.

A wife's maidenhead was a man's pride, yet he would have gladly forgone that small barrier to save her pain. That realization made him frown. She was, after all, but a woman, his possession, a creature whose only purpose was to give him pleasure and provide him with sons, and see to the management of his keep. But rant as he would at himself for his display of weakness, he could not dismiss the pain he had caused her. Ignorant little wench, he thought. She did not even realize she was yet a virgin.

13

She seemed so proud of herself, Graelam thought, both amused and puzzled, as he watched Kassia chew on a piece of warm bread the next morning. With sudden insight he realized that she believed herself a woman now, a wife, and was pleased with her accomplishment. She was more confident, teasing his steward Blount as if she had known him all her life. And the old man was grinning back at her as if she were giving him a great treat.

Damn. How was he supposed to inform her that her maidenhead was still firmly in place? He sighed. He didn't want to tell her, but neither did he have any intention of letting this state of affairs continue. It had been his fault, of course, all because he had not wanted to cause her more pain. Abruptly he said to her, "Kassia, I wish to ride. You will accompany me, in an hour."

She met his eyes shyly, but with wicked knowledge in hers that made him want to laugh. "It would be my pleasure, my lord," she said, and he saw the dimple peeping out.

Exactly an hour later, Kassia, a triumphant smile

on her lips, walked to the stables to meet Graelam. So much for Blanche and her attempts to frighten me, she thought, unconsciously squaring her shoulders. She had not meant to say anything to Blanche, but the sight of her giving the servants orders had made her feel mean. She was now the mistress of Wolffeton, and its management was her responsibility.

She had said calmly to Alice, a woman of middle years who seemed to have common sense and the respect of the other servants, "I wish to inspect the looms after I return from my ride with my lord. I think all of us need new garments."

"I doubt," Blanche said, before Alice could speak, wondering at this show of spine from the skinny twit, "that your husband will approve. He little appreciates unnecessary expense."

"It is the Wolffeton sheep and their wool that are of concern," she said. "I doubt my lord cares a whit, and I would trust that he would not concern himself with household matters."

"The old woman who did all the weaving died some months ago. There is no one else to assume her job."

Kassia gaped at her in astonishment. "That is ridiculous."

"I fear it's true, my lady," Alice said.

"Aye," Blanche said, a pleased smile on her lips. "I, of course, asked Graelam for funds to hire a weaver to come to Wolffeton, but he refused."

"Well, I should think so," Kassia said. "I will, of course, teach the servants to weave and sew properly. If you please, Alice, see that all is in readiness for me when I return." She knew she should keep her mouth shut, but she felt really mean. When Alice was out of earshot she said, "I wonder that you do not possess such skill, Blanche."

"I am not a servant."

"A wife's responsibilities number many things, amongst them the knowledge to train servants. Just as a wife also enjoys many benefits, such as pleasure in her husband's company."

Blanche paled. So Graelam had taken the girl, and evidently he hadn't hurt her. "Perhaps," she said in a voice meaner than Kassia's, "when your belly swells with child, you will not so much enjoy your husband's lusty company. Whilst you retch and grow fat, you can rest assured that he will not be so concerned. Perhaps he will even provide you with another chamber, so he can continue to enjoy himself with his other women."

"You speak as if you know," Kassia said, her heart pounding as hard as her anger.

"I?" Blanche laughed. "I am simply not a silly little girl who believes her husband is a gallant lord. I doubt Lord Graelam was faithful to my half-sister for above a month."

"Graelam," Kassia said, "is an honorable man. I cannot, of course, say anything about your half-sister, but I know he would never break faith with me." Guilt was beginning to win out over the anger. She knew that Blanche had wanted to wed Graelam. "Blanche, let us not disagree. You should not have lied to me about coupling."

Blanche shrugged. "So you are larger than you look. I did not lie to you, I merely did not want you to go blindly like a sheep to slaughter."

"Thank you for your consideration. Now I must go."

Kassia felt pleased with herself. As to Blanche's terrible accusations, they were the result of jealousy. Coupling wasn't the terrible ordeal Kassia had believed it would be; his part of it had hurt a bit, but nonetheless, she had felt some pleasure when he'd touched and kissed her.

"You're looking thoughtful."

Kassia's face turned red at her husband's voice. "Oh. I was just—that is, you were—It is a lovely morning, is it not?"

A thick black brow went up. Graelam reached out his hand and cupped her chin. "If I threaten to beat you, will you tell me what your thoughts were?"

She smiled, rubbing her cheek against his palm. "It was wool, my lord, pure and simple wool."

He leaned down and kissed her. "My thoughts, also, were pure and simple."

She laughed. "I don't believe you. Mayhap you have simple thoughts, but never pure ones."

"Perhaps I should beat you," Graelam said. "A man does not want an impertinent wife."

"Behold, a docile creature," Kassia said. She dropped him a deep curtsy.

She no longer fears me, he realized. He supposed it pleased him—at least, that she did not fear him sexually. And she made him smile.

He said nothing as they rode from the keep southward along the coast road. The day was deliciously warm, for which he was greatly relieved. He shook his head at himself. Never before had he approached coupling with less passion and more planning. He gave Kassia a sideways look, but she seemed to be memorizing the scenery. The road roughened downhill, then flattened out, swinging toward the cliff edge. To Kassia's surprise, Graelam left the road, slowing Demon to a walk, and disappeared for a moment over the edge. She followed him without question and saw that there was a well-worn path down the cliff to the beach below.

"It's not steep," Graelam called over his shoulder, "but go easy."

When they reached the pebbly beach, Kassia drew in her breath in pleased surprise. "Oh, how lovely," she said, slipping off Bluebell's back.

The beach formed a deep half-circle, its arc protected by the overhanging cliff. Scraggly bushes and a few bowed trees provided more protection. As Graelam tethered Bluebell and Demon on long leads, Kassia walked around the beach.

"This was my own private place when I was a boy," Graelam said, coming up behind her.

Kassia raised her face to the bright sun overhead and closed her eyes. The only sounds were the crashing waves and the squawking of the seabirds. "It is so peaceful," she said, turning to face him.

"I am pleased you like it."

"We should have brought some wine and bread."

"Kassia," he said suddenly, "how do you feel?"

"My lord, I am as healthy as my fat Bluebell. You needn't concern yourself further."

"Are you sore?"

"Sore?" She cocked her head to the side, a habit he found charming.

"From last night," he said.

"Oh." She pressed her hands against her cheeks and shook her head.

"As I said," Graelam said, "this is a very private place. No one will disturb us here."

She looked utterly taken aback. "You wish to couple with me now?"

"Aye," he said baldly.

"But it is daylight. You can see—Surely you cannot—"

"Hush, Kassia," he said. "Come here."

She had not considered that her husband would wish to take her again so soon. She supposed that one coupled occasionally, when the man wished it, but—"I feel so stupid," she said, and stepped against him, her head lowered against his chest.

She felt his arms go around her, pulling her more closely against him. "Why do you say that?" he said, kissing the soft curls at her temple.

"You will laugh at me, I know it." She raised her face and felt an odd longing as she stared up into her husband's dark eyes. "I did not believe that one coupled frequently. Perhaps just once, to create a babe."

He looked startled; then he squeezed her until she squeaked. "Creating a babe, Kassia, usually takes a lot of effort. It is a task that most men willingly seek. And, dearling, it will be up to me to make you want to couple too, quite often."

She looked doubtful, but did not further question him, particularly when he lowered his mouth to hers. She stood passively, aware of his hands stroking down her back to cup beneath her. Now that she knew about a man's lust, she knew from his hardness against her belly that he wanted her. She remembered Blanche's taunts about Graelam sleeping with other women. If a man was always so eager to couple, was a woman, any woman, merely a convenience?

Graelam released her and spread two thick blankets on the ground.

Never, Graelam thought again as he smoothed them out, had he approached coupling with less enthusiasm. He was well aware that Kassia had not responded to him. Damn her, she could have at least pretended. No, he wanted no acting from her. Indeed, he was pleased that she was too ignorant to feign pleasure. It meant that when he brought her to pleasure, he would know it. Patience, he had to have patience.

He sat down on the blanket and patted the place beside him, then leaned back on his elbows and watched her approach warily, slowly.

When she eased down beside him, he did not touch her. He was surprised when she said, "Have you known many women, my lord?"

"There is one more that I would know," he said. He turned on his side to face her and gently drew her down onto her back. "This morning, you were not afraid of me. You were, if I'm not mistaken, quite pleased with yourself over sharing my bed, over becoming a wife to me."

"Aye, it's true," she said, frowning at his ease in reading her thoughts. "And I don't believe I've ever really feared you, my lord."

"When all I wish to do is give you pleasure, it is foolish for you to do so." He was stroking her hand as he spoke. Very slowly he eased his fingers over her belly and began to gently knead her.

Kassia had closed her eyes and she knew the moment he leaned his head over hers, for he blotted out the sun. Unconsciously she ran her tongue over her dry lips. She heard him suck in his breath, then felt his on hers. He did not have to tell her to part her lips. She felt an urge to do so. He did not ravish her mouth, merely teased her with his tongue.

Kassia wanted more. She raised her arm and pressed her hand along the back of his neck and brought him down. He deepened the pressure and the odd ache she'd felt briefly the night before raced through her.

"Oh," she said into his mouth. He lifted his head and smiled down at her. "Please, my lord, do not stop."

His fingers were pressed together, lightly resting in a wedge between her thighs. "What do you want me to do, Kassia?"

Her hips jerked upward against his hand, and she nearly swallowed her tongue. "Everything," she said.

Graelam laughed, a pure, deep sound, and hugged her against him. "You are too warm," he said, and began to unfasten her tunic. She squirmed against him, unable to help herself. Soon she was lying beneath him in naught but her thin linen shift.

For a long moment he merely stared down at her, his eyes roving from her face downward until they came to rest at her belly. Slowly he lifted her shift until she was naked to her waist. He did not mean to think her beautiful, but oddly enough, he found her so. Her legs were long and straight; he touched his hand to her white flesh and gently stroked downward. It was rare that he spent so much time seducing a woman, but he realized vaguely that somehow his own pleasure was tied to hers. Slowly, gently, he continued exploring her, then parted her thighs with his fingers. The heat of her made him smile with satisfaction. She began to shake as his fingers neared the soft, hidden seat of her pleasure, but instead of giving her what she wanted, he rose suddenly and jerked off his clothes. Nearby he laid down a small jar of cream, not letting her see it.

"Sit up," he said.

She did as he bid. He slipped her shift over her head, then pressed her again onto her back. He lay beside her, and let his fingers rove again over her belly. He kissed her, letting her deepen the pressure. He felt her hands clutching at his back.

"Kassia," he said, "I would love you now. You will not feel embarrassment or guilt."

She stared up at him, not understanding, only knowing that her body was somehow an instrument she didn't control. He watched her as his fingers caressed her. When he dipped his fingers into the cream and slowly entered her she sucked in her breath, eyes flying to his face. She grabbed his arm, but he merely eased more deeply into her, easing his way.

His fingers pressed against her maidenhead, but not hard enough to hurt her. Her muscles tensed around his fingers, and he groaned at the thought of her doing that to his sex. Damn, he hadn't felt such lust since he was a boy. He lowered himself over her, careful not to hurt her with his weight, and slowly eased down her body until he was on his knees between her parted thighs. She tried to jerk away from him when he nuzzled his face against her, but he merely tightened his hold, drawing her upward.

Despite what he had said, she froze with embarrassment, her passion crushed. Surely he should not be doing that to her, not with his mouth. She tried to pull away from him, but he held her firm.

"Give in, Kassia," he said, his warm breath touching her intimately. "Relax."

Graelam willed her to respond to him, but she didn't. Time, it would take time to make her at ease with him. He left her reluctantly, desire roaring in his head. The softness of her, the taste of her, her woman's scent made him wild. Slowly he parted her thighs and eased into her. The cream soothed his way.

He kept his eyes on her face. "Kassia," he said, holding himself perfectly still.

Kassia felt the pressure of him inside her, but there was no pain, only a fullness that was not at all unpleasant. She opened her eyes and smiled up at him.

"Sweeting, I must cause you bit of discomfort. Hold onto me. It will be over quickly."

She clasped her hands around his back, not understanding. He tore through her taut maidenhead, seating himself to his hilt within her. He took her cry of pain into his mouth. He knew he couldn't leave her, not again. He kissed away her tears, trying to keep himself in check. But it was no use. He moved slightly, feeling her squeezing him, and that sent him over the edge. He drove deep, groans tearing from his mouth.

It was many minutes before Graelam could raise himself on his elbows and look down at her. "You are mine now," he said, and generations of possessiveness sounded in his deep voice.

"Why did you hurt me?"

He kissed her lightly on her mouth, a slight smile curving his lips. "You were still a virgin, sweetheart."

She blinked at him. "But last night—you came inside me, you—"

He carefully eased out of her and lay on his side beside her. "Last night," he said slowly, "I did not finish what I started. I could not, for I was hurting you too much. That is why I brought you here today. I wanted to get the damned business over with. Kassia, did you feel any pleasure?"

She nodded.

"When next we couple, there will be only pleasure, I promise you. Will you trust me?"

"How can there be pleasure?" she managed, her eyes fastened on his chest. "You are large and will remain so."

"It was the rending of your maidenhead that caused most of the pain, and now I promise you it is no longer there. That small barrier did not wish to allow a man within."

"Even my husband?"

He smiled, relieved. "We will use cream until you are well used to me."

He was stroking her hair and she turned her face to nuzzle her cheek against his palm. "Did I please you? I am so ignorant. I didn't know what to do."

"You pleased me. You will respond to me, Kassia, once you forget your embarrassment."

"Do I not need skill, my lord?"

He thought of her killing hold on his sex the night before, and grinned. "Aye," he said, "I will teach you."

"When?"

"Greedy wench." He squeezed her until she yelped for breath. "When you are no longer sore from this plowing, sweetheart."

14

Graelam led his fatigued men into the inner bailey, a smile leaping to his eyes at the sight of Kassia, clutching her gown above her ankles so she would not trip, hurtling down the steps of the Great Hall toward him. He quickly dismounted, tossed Demon's reins to the stable hand, and caught her up in his arms. He held her above his head for a moment, feeling her warm laughter flow over him like soothing balm.

"Welcome home, my lord. Did all go well at Crandall? Who is the new castellan? There was no fighting, was there? You were not hurt?"

He gave her a quick kiss and set her down, aware that every eye in the castle was enjoying their reunion. "So many questions," he said. "Everything is fine, Kassia," he added, seeing her pale at the dried blood on his sleeve.

"But your arm—"

"I took a fall when Demon slipped, it's naught. Such a welcome, and I was away but four days."

She laughed and hugged him. "When I was told you were approaching, I ordered water taken to our bedchamber for your bath. Or would you prefer some ale first? Come, my lord, and I will attend you."

He smiled at her excitement. "I will follow in a moment. First I must see to Demon. I fear his hock is bruised."

"May I help you, my lord?"

Graelam turned to Evian. "Well, boy, you are looking fit. Aye, come with me. My lady, soon." He added, his voice low, "It's more than a bath that I desire."

He patted her shoulder, and strode toward the stables, Evian trying to keep pace with him.

"You are looking well, my lady," Guy said, drawing her attention from her husband's retreating figure.

"What? Oh, Guy."

"You are not concerned about my health, my lady?"

"You, sir," she said, "are but a worthless knave. It is your responsibility to see that my lord comes to no harm."

"True," Guy said. "I fear Graelam's thoughts were on other things, thus his clumsiness. He is the only one of us who has shucked off his fatigue like an old cloak, and all at the sight of you."

Kassia laughed, and turned pink with pleasure at his words.

"I see Blanche hovering about like a disapproving abbess," Guy said.

Kassia's smile faded.

"Has she been a trial to you, my lady?"

"Nay, truly, it's just that she—well, she is unhappy, Guy."

"I imagine she tries to treat you like an unwanted guest," he said. "Graelam should find her a husband, and soon." But something deep within him hated that thought. Damn her, he thought, irritated at both himself and her. Why couldn't she let go? But he knew the answer to that. Blanche was strong-willed and determined. She could see no other course open to her.

"She spends much of her time in the chapel," Kassia said. "I fear she is praying not for a husband, but for ways of doing me in. But enough of my woes, Guy. What happened at Crandall?"

"All went just as Graelam thought, and I will leave your husband to tell you about it."

"No fighting? No attempt at treachery?"

"Nay, it was revoltingly tame."

"You may be disappointed because there were no heads to knock together, but I am relieved. Just you wait for supper. It's my major accomplishment in the four days you have been absent."

"Strung that varlet Dayken up by his worthless heels?"

"Nay, but I did discover that one of his assistants, a poor fellow who spent most of his time being kicked about and cursed, is really quite accomplished. It is he who now does the cursing."

The roast pork was tender, well-seasoned, and altogether delicious. Graelam saw that Kassia was looking at him for all the world like a child waiting for her parent's approval, her own food untouched. He sampled the other fare whilst he talked with Blount.

"The merchant Drieux would settle at Wolffeton,

my lord," Blount said. "He of course brings some dozen or so men with him."

"And their families?"

"Aye, my lord. As you know, we need no more labor in the fields or in the mill. Our wheat production already exceeds our needs."

"I know it well, Blount. What we do need is money and the ability to trade our excess wool. Prepare a charter. I will meet with Drieux when it is done to settle on terms."

"If it is successful, my lord, it is likely other craftsmen will make their way here."

Graelam nodded, then turned to Kassia. "Did you procure some new wine, my lady? I believe I find something of an improvement."

Her lips tightened until she saw he was laughing at her.

"The merchant Drieux, you know, my lord," she said. "He wished to be in your good graces. The wine is from Bordeaux."

"You lie as fluently as do I," Graelam said, smiling at her.

"But imagine how fluent I shall be when I have gained your years, my lord."

Blount said quickly, "Nay, my lord, it's not the wine that is different. My lady but jests."

Graelam turned a surprised look toward his steward. "It's the pork, my lord!" Blount yelled.

Graelam felt a shock when he realized that Blount was trying to protect Kassia from his wrath, that he had, indeed, expected Graelam to be furious at his wife's teasing. But Graelam wasn't angry. He had, in fact, been on the point of continuing the jest with his wife when Blount interrupted.

"And the bread and vegetables and pheasant pie," Kassia added on a laugh, wondering why the well-spoken, polished steward was fumbling about for his words.

"I imagine," Graelam said, "that there is even an improvement in the apples. Do they taste redder, Kassia?"

"Actually," Kassia said, leaning toward her husband, "I did polish yours on my sleeve."

Graelam claimed her hand and slowly raised it to his lips. "I doubt," he said, "that this excellent meal—aye, I did notice, you may be certain—could taste as tempting as do you."

"Oh," Kassia said as his tongue brushed over her palm. Her brain died in her head, but Graelam merely sat back in his chair and grinned shamelessly at her. He was relieved that his robe was full cut, for his body was reacting just as shamelessly to her.

"He is bewitched," Blanche said just loud enough for Guy to hear her.

Guy turned thoughtful eyes to her. "You must cease this, Blanche," he said. Christ, if only he had something to offer her. "Listen to me," he said in an urgent voice. "Kassia is his wife. That is an end to it. And he appears quite pleased with her. How oft must I remind you?"

"Things change," Blanche said. "Aye, he will soon grow bored with her."

"It would make no difference in any case."

"Mayhap he would send her back to her father, or she would leave."

"I doubt, Blanche, that you will still be at Wolffeton should such a thing occur."

"You take her part too. Can it be, Sir Guy, that you are also bewitched with the skinny little—"

"Blanche," he said, now thoroughly irritated, "I would that your temper matched your outward beauty. Stop being such a bloody shrew." Guy turned away from her, his eyes upon his master and mistress.

Graelam bid an abrupt good night to his men, and rose, holding Kassia's hand. "At last," he said, drawing her arm through his.

"Does your arm pain you, my lord?" Kassia asked as she skipped up the stairs to keep up with him.

"Nay, it's other parts of me that are in dire pain."

"Pray tell me. If I cannot ease you, surely Etta will know of a suitable remedy."

"Presently," he said.

Once inside their bedchamber, he firmly closed the door and leaned against it, watching her. "I have missed you," he said.

"And I you, my lord." She smiled up at him, but he saw that her hands were twisting in the folds of her gown.

"Four days and you fear me again?"

She shook her head. "Nay, I do not fear you, my lord."

"I am relieved. You do know, do you not, how you will ease me?"

Her eyes flew to his face. "Your arm. You will hurt your wound."

"There are few stitches to rend, and the bandage is secure. I would ask that you help me out of my clothes."

She did as she was bid, saying nothing until he stood in front of her naked. His desire for her was obvious and she backed away. "Chess," she said. "I am really quite good, my lord. Would you like to—"

"Kassia, I do not want to play chess. I want you naked and in my bed."

She was a fool to have wished him home so quickly. "My lord," she said as calmly as she could manage, "I do not wish—that is, I cannot be naked!"

His frown deepened. "You cannot still be sore from our last coupling. It was nearly five days ago."

"Nay, I am not sore."

"Kassia, look at me."

She wanted nothing more than to sink into the fresh reeds beneath her feet and disappear through the floor. Slowly she raised her face, so embarrassed she thought she'd choke on it.

"I told you that our coupling would not hurt you again." It bothered him that she did not want him.

"I know," she said. "I would willingly come to you, my lord, but I cannot. Please, I—"

He burst out laughing, and grabbed her, pulling her tightly against him. "You're silly, Kassia," he said. He cupped her face between his hands and lowered his face to kiss her. He felt her start, as if in surprise, and for a moment she responded to him. Then she stiffened, a small cry of distress muffled in his mouth.

"Sweetheart," he said, smiling down at her, "it is your monthly flux, is it not?"

She nodded, mute with embarrassment.

"That is no problem, you will see. Come now, I will help you undress."

She stood still as a stone.

Graelam slowly loosed his hold on her. He guessed that her embarrassment could not be easily overcome. He felt his desire fading. Oddly enough, he did not want to force her, did not want to ease himself in her without her feeling equal need for him. "Do you feel discomfort in your belly?"

"Nay, it's not that, my lord."

"I know." He sighed and stepped away from her. "How much longer, Kassia?"

"Another day or so."

"Come to bed when it pleases you." He sank down into the soft feather-and-straw mattress and forced himself to turn on his side away from her. When she finally slipped into bed beside him, she was wearing her bedrobe.

He turned and pulled her against him. She was stiff as his shield. He kissed her on her forehead.

"I'm sorry," she said against his chest. "It's just that I have never spoken of such things, save with Etta."

"I am your husband," he said. "You must learn to speak to me of everything."

"That is what my father said."

"Your father?"

She did not reply and Graelam continued to stroke her back. "You see," she said finally, propping herself up on her elbow, "I did not become a woman for a very long time. There was a count from Flanders who saw me at Charles de Marcey's court when I was fifteen, and asked my father about marriage. It was Etta who told my father that I must have more time. He was upset with me for not telling him myself. But I was so ashamed." She burrowed her face into the hollow of his neck.

"What happened to the count?"

"Once Father and I returned to Belleterre, I worked very hard to convince him that I was indispensable to his comfort. He forgot the count."

"And will you prove yourself just as indispensable to me?"

"Of course," she said, and he could picture the smile on her face. "Did not your wine already taste better?"

Graelam grinned into the darkness until his mind finally convinced his body that he must wait another day—or so. "Perhaps we will play chess tomorrow night," he said.

Graelam stepped into his bedchamber, a frown on his face, for he was worried about Demon's still swollen hock. Also Nan had purposefully brushed her body against him, an invitation clear in her eyes. It was a nuisance that his body had leapt in response. And there was Blanche, sobbing her heart out against his tunic. He sighed, drawing up at the sight of Kassia, so immersed in her sewing that she didn't hear him. He drew closer, smiling at her look of intense concentration. His eyes fell to the garment in her lap, and his smile faltered, then disappeared entirely. It was a singularly beautiful piece of burgundy velvet that he had brought back from Genoa.

"What are you doing?"

Kassia jumped, jabbed the needle point into her thumb. "Oh," she said, and quickly licked away the drop of blood before it fell to the velvet.

"I repeat," Graelam said, pointing to the velvet on her lap, "what are you doing with that?"

"I wish you had not come in so stealthily, my lord.

Now I am found out." She smiled up at him. Her smile began to crack.

"I do not recall having given you permission to rifle my trunk and make yourself free with my belongings."

She cocked her head as was her unconscious habit, but he felt no tug of amusement, not this time. "Well?"

"It did not occur to me, my lord, that you would be—upset at my taking the velvet. It is a lovely piece and I thought—"

"What is mine is mine," he said. "If you wished to make yourself a new gown, you should have asked me."

"I thought," she began again, raising her chin just a bit, "that I shared in your possessions, just as you share in mine."

"Your father," Graelam said, his voice colder, "did me a great disservice. What is yours is mine, my lady, and what is mine remains mine."

"But that is hardly fair."

"God's bones," Graelam said. "Just because I have allowed you to play at being mistress of Wolf-feton—"

"Play?" Kassia jumped to her feet, the precious velvet falling to the floor.

"You will not interrupt me again, madam. Pick up the cloth. I do not wish it to become soiled. And remove your stitches."

She stared at him, so indignant that she could find no words. His kindness to her since his return was forgotten. "And what, my lord," she said at last, "did you intend the velvet for?"

It was Graelam's turn to stare at his wife. He had

likely been a fool, to treat her so indulgently. And poor Blanche. Had Kassia treated her as unkindly as Blanche had sobbed to him? He gritted his teeth. "Pick up the velvet," he said, "and let me hear no more."

Etta was standing still as a tombstone outside the bedchamber door, listening. Seldom had her gentle mistress ever spoken in anger to anyone. She ran through the open door just as Kassia, too angry to be afraid, shouted, "No."

"My baby," Etta said, rushing toward her mistress. "Have you nearly finished with your lord's tunic? He will be so pleased. Oh, forgive me, my lord. I did not know—my eyes—I did not see you."

Graelam was stopped cold. His eyes narrowed on the old nurse's face, then back to his wife. Slowly he leaned over and picked up the velvet, spreading it out over his arm. He looked at the exquisite stitching, traced his fingers over the width of material, and felt a fool. Without raising his head, he said in Etta's direction, "Get out."

Etta, clutching her rosary, fled the bedchamber, praying that she'd saved her mistress.

"It is a tunic for me," Graelam said.

"Aye. You are so large, and your shirts and tunics so worn and ill-fitting. I wanted you to be garbed as you should be."

He looked at her for several moments, trying to still his guilt. "You will ask me in the future," he said, and tossed the velvet to her. "And, my lady, you will answer me honestly when I ask you a question."

With those words, Graelam turned on his heel and strode from the bedchamber, leaving Kassia to grind her teeth and jab her needle into the velvet. Upon reflection, she knew she should have told him immediately that it was not a gown for herself she was making. But how dare he treat her so. Looking down, she realized she had set several very crooked stitches and jerked them out of the velvet.

15

Graelam stood on the ramparts, looking east toward rolling green hills. He had tried to concentrate on the problems Blount had brought him: two peasants who wanted the same girl for wife; a dispute over the ownership of a pig; and a crusty old man who had wanted to sell Graelam his daughter. But it was no use.

He turned westward and watched the sun make its downward descent. A slight breeze ruffled his hair, and he pushed it out of his eyes.

"My lord."

It was as if he had willed her to appear. Slowly Graelam turned to Kassia, standing some distance away from him.

"My lady," he said, his voice clipped.

"The baker has made some pastries I thought you would like—almond and honey, your favorite."

Graelam cursed under his breath. "Can you not come closer?"

She obeyed him, but her step was hesitant. He watched the sunlight create glints of copper and gold in her hair. He felt a pang of guilt and it angered him.

"I don't want the pastries," he said when she came to a halt in front of him.

"I did not really come for that reason," Kassia said, raising her head.

She was pale and he saw the strain in her eyes. Damn, he had but chastised her for taking the cloth. "Why did you come?" he asked.

"To tell you I am sorry. I should not have taken the velvet without your permission."

"Then why did you do it?"

"I wanted to surprise you." She looked at him searchingly, hopeful of some bending, but his face was impassive. "I meant no harm."

Kassia turned away from him, not wanting him to see her cry. Her anger at him was gone, and she had hoped that he would smile at her again and dismiss the entire incident. But he looked all the more grim.

Graelam cursed, and grabbed her arm. "I did not give you permission to go," he said. He closed his hand more tightly about her arm, feeling her delicate and fragile bones that would snap like a twig under his strength. "Why do you not eat the pastries? By all the saints, you are so slight that a breeze could sweep you away."

Kassia did not understand him. He sounded furious, yet his hand had eased on her arm, and his fingers were gently massaging where he had clasped her.

"Truly, my lord," she said at last, "I did not mean to anger you. I did not think—"

"No, it's obvious," He dropped her arm and turned slightly away from her. "You gave orders to have the outbuildings whitewashed."

"Aye," she said in a small voice, cursing herself at

the same time for her cowardice. Were she at Belleterre, she wanted to shout at him, not only would she have given orders to whitewash the sheds, but she would have also overseen, with her father, the drawing of the charter with the merchant Drieux. Would he give her authority to act as mistress of Wolffeton one minute, and withdraw it the next?

Silence stretched between them. "Have I your permission to go now, my lord?"

"Why, my lady?" he asked, turning to face her again. "Do you not find my company to your liking?"

"I must tell the servants not to whitewash the outbuildings."

"I want it done. Leave be."

Her eyes flew to his face. He smiled at the spark of anger he saw there. But it immediately recalled another matter to mind. "What did you do to Blanche in my absence? She was very upset."

She cocked her head to one side, clearly puzzled. "I don't understand."

"She was crying earlier." Indeed, she had wet his tunic through. "You are not to give her orders, Kassia, or make her life unpleasant. She is a gentle lady, and deserving of kind treatment."

Surely, Kassia thought, he could not be talking about his sister-in-law, Blanche? Before she could stop herself, she said, "Which Blanche do you mean, my lord? One of the serving maids?"

"Perhaps," he said, "Blanche could teach you submissiveness and the proper respect for your husband."

She felt such a surge of anger that she feared what she would say if she remained with him. She swallowed her rage, turned on her heel, and ran as fast as she could back along the narrow walkway.

"Kassia. Come back here."

She tripped on her long gown at his voice, and swayed for an instant, the cobblestones of the inner bailey rising upward toward her.

"Hellfire, you stupid wench." Graelam's gut cramped at the sight of her weaving toward the edge of the rampart. He grabbed her arm, and jerked her back. "Have you no sense?" He was shaking her so hard her neck snapped back.

She cried out, a broken sound that froze him. He stared down at her white face, cursed savagely, and pulled her against him, unconsciously rocking her. She leaned pliantly against him, her cheek pressed against his shoulder. He could feel her small breasts heaving against him as she tried to stop her panting. He felt a bolt of lust so powerful that he was stunned. He realized vaguely that it was born of fear for her, and anger, but it didn't matter. She was his wife, dammit, and he had not possessed her for six days.

In one swift motion he lifted her over his shoulder and strode toward the steep wooden stairs that led down to the inner bailey. He paid no attention to the scores of gaping servants or to his men who watched his progress. He was breathing hard when he finally reached their bedchamber, but not from exertion. He kicked the door closed behind him and strode to the bed. He eased her off his shoulder and laid her on her back. He pulled his trousers open, his hands shaking, then turned back to her. He jerked off her leather slippers, pulled up her clothes, baring her to her waist, and flung himself down over her.

"Damn you," he said, and kissed her brutally.

Kassia felt suspended, as if time had stopped, and she was another, looking down on the furious man savaging a girl who was no longer she. She felt his hands upon her, roughly jerking her legs apart. When he reared over her, she realized starkly that he was going to force her. Still, her mind held her utterly still, like a stick puppet with no will of her own. She felt his fingers parting her, felt his rigid sex drive inward. A tearing pain threw her mind back into her body. She screamed, a high, thin wailing sound. She began to fight him, striking his shoulders and back with all her strength, but it made no difference.

Thrusting his full length, Graelam seated himself to his hilt. Her fists made no impression on him as he sought to force her to utter submission. He flung himself onto her, grabbed her face between his hands, and kissed her hard. At the taste of her tears, his mind balked, but his body, intent upon release, rammed into her until his seed burst from his body. He was insensate for several moments. It was her helpless moan that jerked him to awareness. He raised himself over her and stared down at her face. Her eyes were closed, her thick lashes wet spikes against her cheeks. There was a spot of blood on her lower lip, bitten in pain.

He closed his own eyes for a moment, wishing he could close out the enormity of what he had done.

"Kassia." Her name was a growl of pain on his lips. He withdrew from her, feeling her shudder, and drew her into his arms. She lay utterly still, unresponsive even as he smoothed the curls back from her forehead.

"Look at me, damn you. Kassia, open your eyes." He clasped her jaw and shook her head until her lashes fluttered and she looked up at him.

What he saw chilled him. She was staring up at him, and he knew that the wide, unseeing look in her eyes reflected her thoughts.

"Stop it." He shook her shoulders, but she didn't respond. For the first time in his life, he felt himself to be despicable, a brute who had hurt someone who had not half his strength. He knew a fear that made him tremble. "Kassia," he said, and buried his face in her hair.

"You hurt me."

Her voice made him jerk his head up. The blind look was gone from her eyes and she was looking at him like a child who does not understand why the parent has struck him.

"You promised you would never hurt me again. You lied to me."

He wanted to beg her forgiveness, but the words stuck in his throat. Never in his life had he uttered such words to a woman. Images of his father telling him that a wife was her husband's possession, to do with as he pleased, careened through his mind. A woman had no will; she existed only through her husband and through her children. He was struggling with himself when she spoke again, her voice holding no anger, no reproach.

"You told me that being a wife was better than being a dog. You told me that there were benefits to being a wife."

"Aye," he said, "I told you that."

"I think," she said very clearly, "that I should prefer being a dog."

"You have no choice in the matter. You are as God fashioned you."

"Must I also blame God?" She moved away from him and he let her go. She pulled her clothing down and stood a moment by the bed. She looked remote, yet utterly calm. "Have I your permission to leave now, my lord? There is the meal to see to. I would not want you displeased."

He stared at her, frustrated, sunk in his own guilt. "Go," he said. She turned away without another word. He saw her weave a moment, then stiffen and walk slowly toward the door.

Graelam closed his eyes a moment. He pictured the Earl of Drexel in his mind, the man whose page and squire he had been, the man who had knighted the very young Graelam for saving his life at the Battle of Evesham. He had attended him after the battle, as was his wont, and watched his blood lust become sexual lust. It did not surprise him, for he had seen his lord take both willing and unwilling women. But the peasant wench had screamed and fought. The earl had merely laughed, cuffing her senseless. "What else are women good for, lad, if not for a man's pleasure? The stupid wench wasn't even a virgin." He had shaken his head, perplexed. The fat priest with them had said nothing. It was a point of debate among Church prelates whether or not women possessed a soul. Then why, Graelam thought, did he feel so despicable, like a rutting animal? Kassia was his possession. There would be no one to say him nay or even look at him askance if he beat her within an inch of her life, with or without just cause.

Why then did he feel as if he had destroyed something precious, as if he had wantonly crushed a rare flower underfoot?

He rose slowly, like an old man, and straightened his clothes. He paused, seeing blood on his sex. He cursed softly to the silent chamber.

Blanche smiled and said gaily to the stone-faced Sir Guy, "Such a shame, is it not, Sir Guy?"

"I do not know what you are talking about," he said, not looking at her.

She laughed. "Ah, such a pity. But I don't suppose you heard her screams? And look at her now. No longer the proud, preening little fool she was."

Guy had been looking at Kassia. She looked dazed, her face so pale as to be waxen. He saw Graelam lean toward her, and felt himself stiffen as she jerked away. Everyone in the castle knew that Graelam had abused his wife. To Guy's surprise, only a very few of the men had appeared untouched by his actions. Most of them had been tense and silent. Blount, Graelam's crusty steward, had tightened his thin lips in anger. Of course Blanche was delighted. He turned to her, and felt his own anger near the boiling point at her smug smile. He wanted to shake her until her teeth rattled and kiss her until she was breathless.

"To anger Graelam so quickly," she said, shaking her head. As to her own stirring performance, she firmly repressed her guilt, saying over and over in her mind that she must see to herself and her children, for there was no one else to. She understood why she acted such a witch in front of Guy—it was because he championed Kassia. It angered her that he did, but she refused to examine why this was so. After all, he was merely a landless knight. She saw him looking toward Kassia, and angry words came from her mouth. "I heard that she had stolen some precious cloth from his trunk. Perhaps he will send her back to her home, where she belongs. Surely, Guy, you do not defend her?"

She supposed she achieved what she wanted. Guy was white with anger. His calmly spoken words took her off guard. "Do you know, Blanche, I am tempted to marry you myself. Were you my wife, I would beat you senseless."

"If the girl were not such a fool," Blanche said, wishing his words did not dig so deeply, and hating the response they aroused in her, "Graelam would not have struck her. She thinks herself above all of us. My lord would not long tolerate such airs."

Guy closed his eyes a moment against the temptation to haul Blanche over his shoulder that very instant and carry her from the hall. What he would do with her once he had done this, he didn't know. He forced his attention back to Graelam. He could not understand the lord of Wolffeton. Until today, Graelam had been so gentle toward his lady. There was no doubt in Guy's mind that he had missed Kassia during their absence from Wolffeton. His greeting of her upon their return was proof enough. What, he wondered, was in his lord's mind?

Graelam speared a bit of tender fish on his knife, and thrust it into his mouth. He could feel the tension radiating from Kassia. The fish tasted of fear, her fear, of him.

Damn her. He didn't want her to be afraid of him. He wanted to hear her laugh again, to see the dimples deepen in her cheeks.

I have no choice, Kassia was thinking. No choice

at all. I do not understand him, yet I must bear whatever he metes out to me. The events of the day had effectively destroyed all the budding happiness she had known since she had come to Wolffeton as his wife. Why had he been so gentle with her at first, if it was his intention to become a ravening beast? She closed her eyes, knowing that soon she would have to share his bed. Would he force her again? She picked up her goblet of wine, but her hand was shaking so badly, she quickly lowered it back to the table. Where was her pride? Would she spend the rest of her days cowering, wondering if he turn on her again if she serve him a meal not to his liking or speak to Blanche in a voice he didn't like?

Her chin went up, and she sat straight in her chair. Slowly she turned to face her husband.

"My lord," she said quietly, drawing his attention from his baked heron.

She had to call upon a strength she had not known she possessed not to cower. "Aye?" he asked, his expression impassive.

"I would like to—understand my role at Wolffeton."

He felt a moment of pleasure at her defiance. But she was a woman, and that meant she must never dictate to her husband. "Your role," he said, "is to see to my pleasure."

Her eyes remained steady on his face. "You told me that you had allowed me to play at being mistress at Wolffeton. I know that I am young, my lord, but I managed Belleterre since my mother's death, a holding just as vast as this keep. Is it your pleasure that I indeed be the mistress of Wolffeton?"

She saw his eyes go briefly toward Blanche, and

felt a surge of fury. She spoke without thought. "Why did you not wed her, my lord? Why did you not allow our marriage to be annulled?"

It was odd, Graelam thought, but he did not have an answer to her question. Indeed, how dare she even question him?

"You are the mistress of Wolffeton," he said. "But you will not harm those less fortunate than you. Do you understand me?"

She said, sarcasm thick in her voice, "I, fortunate, my lord?"

"Enough, Kassia." His voice, a low hiss, slammed into her. He clutched her arm, and her courage, illusory at best, faltered. She knew she could not try to jerk away from him, not in front of fifty people. Not in front of Blanche or the serving wench, Nan.

"As you wish, my lord," she said. "As mistress of Wolffeton, I will need funds to see to improvements within the keep."

"There are none."

"Soon you will sign the charter with the merchant Drieux. In my experience, the charter will bring you immediate access to goods."

"In your experience? A woman should not understand those things," he said slowly. He saw the mounting frustration in her eyes, and shrugged. "Very well, you have my permission to speak with Blount. But, my lady, you will not instruct him."

"Aye, I understand," she said. "He is a man, and thus far superior to me. I am not to annoy him with my silly questions and demands."

"You understand well," he said. "See that that sarcastic tongue of yours stays quiet in your mouth."

Her hand balled into a fist in her lap.

"Aye, and watch Blanche. I find her attitude and demeanor much to my liking."

"As you wish, my lord. It will be just as you say, my lord. May I now be excused now, my lord? I wish to retire."

She was mocking him. Her submissiveness was feigned. It both pleased him and angered him. She was unlike any woman in his experience. She was gently bred, and yet he had treated her cruelly. He sighed. "You may go."

Kassia endured Etta's worry and clucking advice all during her bath.

"Please, leave off, Etta," she said, wrapping her bedrobe securely about her.

"But, my baby, you cannot continue to challenge your lord."

"I did not say that I had."

Etta shook her head sadly. "There is no need. I know you."

"Would you prefer that I lie down upon the floor and let him tread over me like a rug?"

"He is not your father, my baby. He is a man who is used to command, a man who—"

"Odd," Kassia said in a low voice, cutting Etta off, "until this day I had begun to believe him as kind and gentle as my father. I was a fool."

"He owns you."

"Aye, what a joy to be owned by a man who hates me."

Graelam paused a moment, her words stark in his mind, then pushed the bedchamber door open. "Go," he said to Etta, his eyes upon Kassia.

Etta cast her mistress a pleading look, and took herself off.

Kassia could not look at him. She felt utterly vulnerable, clothed only in the flimsy bedrobe, and alone with him. He took a step toward her, and she stepped back.

"Get into bed," he said, standing motionless before her. "And take off that robe. You will wear nothing unless it is your monthly flux."

She didn't move. She saw herself as she had been today, lying helplessly beneath him. She winced at the memory of the pain.

"Is that order so difficult for you to understand?"

Even as the words flew from her mouth, she knew that she was a fool to try to bargain with him. "Only if you swear to me that you will not force me again."

He cursed. "I will take you whenever it pleases me to do so!"

"No."

He froze for an instant, then took another step toward her, only to halt again when he saw tears in her eyes.

"Go to bed, Kassia," he said, and turned away from her.

He heard no sound or movement. "Do as I tell you," he said over his shoulder.

"I'm afraid of you."

The whispered words made him close his eyes over a pain that he didn't understand.

"I swear I will not force you," he said. Perversely, the moment the words were out of his mouth, he felt that he had given in to her, and saw himself as one of those weak men he despised. He added, knowing well the cruelty of his words, "You are a child, and as unresponsive as a nun. It would give me no pleasure to take you again. You do not have a woman's grace, a woman's yielding, or a woman's softness.''

She wanted to scream at him: *Like your slut Nan?* But she said nothing. She walked slowly to the bed, slipped between the covers, and pulled them to her chin.

She listened to him splash in the tub. Slowly, without wishing to, she stroked her hand over her body. I have the body of a child, she thought. Would he have been more pleased with her if she were full-fleshed like Blanche? Her hand paused a moment in the valley of her belly. Her pelvic bones were still prominent when she lay upon her back. She tensed and quickly whipped her hand away when her fingers touched herself. She didn't want to touch where he had. When she saw him step from the tub, she closed her eyes.

She heard his footsteps come toward the bed. She was terrified that he would not keep his word.

But he did nothing. He lay on top of the covers on his back, motionless. Suddenly he turned toward her. Startled, she rolled to the side of the bed.

He cursed, but made no move to touch her. Kassia did not relax until she heard his breathing become slow and regular in sleep.

16

"What lovely stitches," Blanche said. "I can scarce see them. You sew them much more proficiently than I."

Kassia's fingers froze over the material. She looked up warily at Blanche. "Thank you," she said finally, her voice clipped. The last thing she wanted to endure was more baiting and insults from that lady. But Blanche was smiling at her.

"Do you mind if I sit with you for a while? I have a rent to mend in my tunic. Perhaps I can improve my stitches if I watch you closely."

"What do you want, Blanche?" Kassia asked without preamble.

Blanche lowered her head a moment. She said softly, "I want us to be friends, Kassia. I know that I have not been kind to you."

Kind? You have treated me like a tethered goat.

Blanche persevered, her voice liquid with shame. "It was jealousy that made me act as I did. I wanted Graelam, but he chose first Joanna, then you. It was not well done of me. I wish there to be peace between us."

Kassia did not think herself a gullible fool, but she
was lonely, and terribly unhappy. The past week and
a half had dragged past even though Blount had enthusiastically approved everything she wished to do
within Wolffeton, and work had begun. It was not
that she was bored or felt useless. No, never that.
She was the mistress of Wolffeton. She remembered
how Graelam had watched the great hall scrubbed
clean of years of filth, sniffed at the fresh reeds that
were scattered with a special mixture of sweet rosemary, lavender, and other herbs and flowers handed
down from Kassia's grandmother. She had waited for
him to say something, anything, but he had merely
grunted, ignoring her.

Blanche saw Kassia look toward the far whitewashed wall and guessed the direction of her
thoughts. She said, "You have performed wonders. I
had not believed Wolffeton could be so beautiful."
She forced herself to sigh softly. "And the servants
respect you and obey you. I wanted to make changes,
you know, but they would not heed me. And the
cushions you are making. How often I have wished
to be more at ease in my chair."

That brought a smile to Kassia's lips. "Aye," she
said with a bit more enthusiasm, "I have felt the
same way."

"Will you let me help you?" Blanche asked. "I do
have some skill with a needle."

"Aye," Kassia said again slowly, still wary of the
incredible change in Blanche. "If you would like, it
would make us all more comfortable that much
sooner."

The two women sewed together companionably
until the light faded. "Just a few more minutes,"

Kassia said, "and I shall be through with this cushion."

"It is for your lord?" Blanche asked, her voice sympathetic.

"It is," Kassia said, wondering what Graelam would say, wondering if Graelam would even notice.

She jumped when Blanche reached over and patted her hand. "All will be well between you, Kassia. You will see. Graelam is a man unused to gently bred ladies, but your care of him will soon change his thinking."

Kassia felt tears blind her. "Perhaps you are right, Blanche."

"Of course I am right," Blanche said. "Whilst you finish your lord's cushion, is there something you would like me to do?"

Kassia sniffed back her tears. "Nay," she said, managing a wan smile. "The servants have things well in hand. I do thank you, Blanche. I really do."

Graelam noticed the rich red velvet cushion immediately. It was thick and soft, stuffed with goose down, and beautifully made. He ran his hand over its smooth surface.

"I have begun another cushion for the back of your chair," Kassia said.

He heard the wariness in her voice but ignored it. "Will you make more cushions? For your chair as well?"

"Aye, but it will take me several weeks."

"The material appears very valuable. Did Blount approve its purchase?"

Kassia wanted to throw the cushion in him. She fought down anger at his barely-veiled accusation, but was saved from answering him by Blount himself.

"Aye, my lord," he said. "I agreed with your lady that Wolffeton should boast only the best. With her skill, it is achieved."

Graelam grunted and sat down. "It is an improvement," he said, and reached for his wine goblet.

Blount gave his master an incredulous look. He caught Lady Kassia's eye, and bit back his words. He did not understand Lord Graelam. He had been in a black, savage mood for so long now that the household was afraid to come near him. His bellows of anger made their blood run cold. But to treat his gentle lady as he would his servants. Blount shook his grizzled head and walked slowly down the trestle table and seated himself down on the bench beside Sir Guy.

Kassia waited until Graelam had drunk two goblets of wine. "My lord," she said carefully.

"Aye?"

He can't even bring himself to look at me? She gritted her teeth. "The merchant Drieux assures me that we can barter wool for carpets from Flanders. The carpets at Belleterre come from Spain, but he tells me that Flanders weaves beautiful ones as well. I thought crimson, to complement the chair cushions."

"Carpets, my lady?" Graelam asked, turning slightly in his chair to face her, his dark brows raised. "Is it your desire to turn this keep into a palace? Do you find Wolffeton so much to your distaste?"

Damn him. She knew that Graelam had been to the Holy Land and admired the comfort and luxury of the furnishings there. Her father had told her so.

"Aye," she said, chin up. "If you do not wish to

barter wool, I will send a message to my father. Surely he will be most willing to fill Wolffeton with beauty."

"You will send no message to your father." He hit his fist against the trestle table, making his trencher tremble.

"Very well," Kassia said calmly, forcing herself to hold firm. "What is your wish then, my lord?"

I am spiting myself, Graelam realized suddenly, and the little witch knows it well. God's bones, he wanted to break her. How dare she criticize his home? She had held her little chin high and ignored him during the past days, knowing that she was safe from him at night, for, fool that he was, he had sworn he wouldn't force her. The power he had given her unthinkingly. He was an idiot.

He was saved from a reply by Guy's laughter. "My lord. You have the look of a man whose buttocks are content. Will you grant your lesser men such comforts?"

"All you deserve, Sir Guy," Graelam shouted back, "is the flat of my sword against your buttocks."

There were hoots of laughter from the men, and Drake, the armorer, slapped Guy on the back. "I'd say," he said, "that yer young butt needs nothing more than a good strapping."

Graelam turned back to his wife. She was laughing, and there was a smile in her eyes. He followed the direction of her gaze and stiffened. Guy? She was smiling at him openly. Anger burned in his gut.

"Kassia."

She flinched, her smile dying on her lips. She forced her eyes to his, and waited for him to continue.

"Fetch your cloak. I wish to speak to you."

She hesitated, cursed herself for a coward because she was afraid of his intentions.

He lowered his voice. "Would you prefer the privacy of our chamber?"

She jumped up from her chair. Nan stood closest to her, and she called to the serving girl, her voice hard in her fear. "My cloak, Nan. It's in my chamber."

Nan gave her a venomous look before leaving the hall.

Kassia downed the remainder of her wine, willed herself to calm.

"Are you always so sharp with the servants, my lady?"

She gave him a wide, uncomprehending look.

"*My* servants?"

"You mean your slut," she said, but she shook her head, her eyes lowered.

Kassia felt Guy looking at her as Graelam led her from the hall, his hand cupping her elbow. She looked at him, afraid to smile.

Graelam jerked her arm. She was nearly running beside him down the deep-set stairs and into the inner bailey. The moon was nearly full, silver light over the keep.

She drew a deep breath. "Where do you wish to go, my lord?"

"To the ramparts."

Would he throw her over? She pictured herself flailing through the empty air, hurtling toward the ground. She shivered.

When they reached the east tower, Graelam

stopped, clasped both her arms, and turned her face to him.

Slowly he eased his hands down her arms, his dark, brooding eyes never leaving her face. She felt his fingers circle her throat and tighten slightly.

"You will not escape me to another man," he said, his fingertips lightly stroking her neck.

"I do not know what you mean, my lord," she whispered.

"Do you not?" He stared down at her pale face, and he smiled an awful smile. "A woman is born with lies already forming in her mouth. Most women, I fancy, have the wit to hide their coy looks in their husbands' presence. But you, Kassia, you were blessed with a father who could not believe ill of you. Listen well, my girl. I will not tolerate being made the cuckold."

Kassia could only stare at him. He believed she wished one of his men as her lover? The only one of his men she spent any time with at all was his steward. It was so ridiculous as to be laughable. She said sharply, forgetting her fear of him, "Am I no longer to smile, my lord? Am I no longer to speak to Blount? By all the saints, he is old enough to be my father."

"It wasn't Blount who won your smile, my lady. You will cease your deception. You will never lie with another man, and if it is your wish to have your belly plowed, it is I who will do it."

"No. You promised me."

"Think you I will allow Guy to enjoy you when my back is turned?"

"Guy," she repeated blankly.

"Aye, even his name sounds like lust on your lips."

"You are ridiculous," she said, drawing out each word.

Graelam jerked her against him. She struck his chest, but he only tightened his hold and her arms fell to her sides. He lowered his head, and she twisted back, feeling his kiss land on her throat. His hand wound in her hair, holding her still, and she sobbed when his mouth crushed down. His tongue pushed against her lips. She pictured herself when last he had taken her: docile as a stick, passive, enduring the pain without fight. *Let him beat me.* She parted her lips slightly, and when he thrust his tongue into her mouth, she bit down on it, hard.

He drew back from her in fury. "You little bitch." He touched his mouth. Grabbing her shoulders, he shook her until her head lolled back on her neck. Suddenly he dropped his hands and took a step back from her.

"And will you force me again? Rape me? I want no man to touch me, do you hear? No man. You are all brutes, selfish animals. You spoke once to me of pleasure. Ha. There is none for the woman. She must lie still and endure your cruel rutting. You have done naught but lie to me, Graelam. I hate you."

He raised his hand, wanting to cover her mouth, to shut out her words, to bring her against him again. She jerked away. "Kill me then. I care not."

His eyes narrowed on her face, dark as the night. Without a word, he turned away from her and strode down the wooden walkway to the inner bailey. He paused but a moment, her sobs reaching him, and cursed under his breath.

She is but a woman, my possession, damn her. Her

worth is only what I choose to grant her. Still, he could not shut out her crying, after he was too far away to hear them.

Kassia rose slowly, aware suddenly that she was shivering from cold. She pulled her cloak more closely about her shoulders and walked back toward the keep. Graelam's men-at-arms were in the inner bailey, and she squared her shoulders and walked up the deep stairs into the great hall, ignoring them. Servants were clearing off the trestle tables. She saw Blanche from the corner of her eye, but did not stop. She reached the bedchamber, but her hand froze on the huge brass handle. No, he was inside. She couldn't bear to face him now. She turned away and walked toward the spinning room. Moonlight streamed through the unshuttered windows as she stepped quietly into the dark room. She heard strange grunting sounds coming from the corner where bolts of material were stacked.

She saw them clearly. Graelam was astride Nan, his powerful naked body thrusting between her white legs. Nan was groaning, her hands stroking frantically over his back, her legs wrapped around his flanks.

Kassia felt bile in her throat. She wasn't aware that a keening sound came from her mouth. She jerked around and ran from the room.

Graelam's lust drove him blindly. He was intent upon exorcising Kassia's pale, distraught face from his mind. He heard the odd wailing sound, and turned quickly to see Kassia flee from the room. His lust disappeared as if it had never existed. He jerked out of Nan's body, and rolled over, staring toward the door.

"My lord," Nan whispered. "Please—"

He wanted to vomit, to curse, to rail at himself for being such a bloody fool. He said nothing, merely rose and began to pull on his clothes.

He heard Nan call out to him, but he ignored her. He strode to his bedchamber and flung open the door. Kassia was not there. He called out her name, hating the fear in his voice. She was not in the keep. He ran toward the stables, knowing well that she could not simply ride away from Wolffeton, for the porter would never raise the portcullis or lower the drawbridge for her. The postern in the eastern wall. His blood froze as he remembered how he himself had shown Kassia the hidden entrance into Wolffeton. Her mare, Bluebell, was gone. He drew a deep steadying breath, knowing that she had only minutes on him, and quickly drew on Demon's bridle. He swung himself onto his destrier's broad back.

He saw her quickly enough, riding along the cliffs, too fast. He yelled her name, but she didn't slow.

He leaned down close to Demon's neck and urged him forward. The mare was no match for the powerful destrier.

Kassia heard the pounding hooves behind her. She didn't look back, for she knew it was Graelam. She dug her heels into Bluebell's sides, her sobs echoing with her mare's labored breathing in the still night.

Graelam tried to grab the mare's reins, but Kassia pulled her sharply, jerking her so close to the edge of the cliff that Graelam felt his blood turn cold. He dared not crowd her. He kept pace until the ground evened out, then turned Demon sharply toward the mare and grabbed Kassia about her waist and lifted her off Bluebell's back. She fought him, struggling wildly, hitting at his chest. He pulled Demon to a halt, pressed Kassia tightly against him, and jumped to the ground.

"You little fool." He tightened his hold about her ribs. "God's bones, you could have killed yourself."

"I don't care."

He eased her back to look into her face. He expected tears, waited for her to plead with him. To his utter surprise, she drew back her foot and kicked him in the shin. He grunted with the sharp pain.

"You test the fates," he said, his voice low and calm.

She said nothing, merely stared up at him.

"Did you really think to escape me? By yourself? Have you no wits at all?"

"What could have happened to me, my lord? Mayhap brigands would have caught me. What could they have done to me? Beat me? Rape me? Cut my throat?" She shrugged, looking away from him, out over the white-capped sea.

"You saw me in the weaving room."

She cocked her head, her eyes cold. "Yes, I saw you." She heard him draw in his breath, but continued in a calm voice, "Forgive me for interrupting your pleasures." She shrugged again. "At least it keeps you away from me."

"You angered me," he said.

She looked at him then. "Will you send me home, my lord? Back to Belleterre? It will still be yours. My father would not renege on your agreement."

"No."

"Why not? You care nothing for me."

"You are mine," he said, "and what is mine I keep. Never again try to escape me, Kassia, else I will lock you away."

Unbidden, the image of Graelam thrusting into Nan rose into her mind, and she felt such fury that she felt she would choke on it. She drew back her hand and slapped him as hard as she could.

"Now you will either kill me or let me go."

No woman had ever struck him. One man had, once, long ago, and he had died very quickly. She was so small, fragile. He could kill her with one blow. He did not move. "You will bend to me," he said finally, very quietly. "Aye, you will bend to me, for I am your master and your husband."

She stood stiff as a stone before him, silent as the night.

"Come, Kassia," he said, taking her arm quite gently. "We are returning to Wolffeton before my men mount a search."

She knew she had no choice. If she struggled with him, he would subdue her.

As she rode beside him back to Wolffeton, she felt the maze of anger and shock recede. Dear God, what had she done? She did not want to be a prisoner; she did not want him to beat her. She ran her tongue over her dry lips.

"What will you do?"

He heard the thread of fear in her voice. She will bend to me, he thought. But he hated her fear.

He said nothing. When they rode into the inner bailey, Guy rushed toward them, his face drawn with worry. Graelam saw him look toward his wife, and felt a renewed surge of anger.

"My wife wished for a midnight ride," he said.

"See to our horses," he said to the stable boy. He pulled Kassia of Bluebell's back and led her into the keep.

Blanche watched Graelam draw Kassia toward the stairs. She stayed in the shadows of the hall, a small smile lifting the corners of her mouth. Soon, she thought. Very soon.

17

Graelam stood against the door of his bedchamber, his arms crossed over his chest, watching Kassia walk slowly toward his chair and ease down on its edge.

"Why did you run from me?"

She did not look up. He saw her hands twisting in her lap.

"Why?"

"I don't know."

His dark eyes gleamed. "Could it be, my lady wife, that you were jealous? Nan is a comely wench, and enjoys a man well."

Her head shot up, and he saw the incredulous look on her face. Was she so impervious to him then?

"Aye, jealous," he said, more softly this time.

The words tumbled out before she could stop them. "Jealous because my husband takes another woman? Nay, my lord. If you do not choose to honor our marriage vows, who am I to gainsay you?"

"Then why did you run from me?"

"I did not wish to stay," she said, knowing he could see the lie in her eyes. She could not answer his question, even to herself. She had felt fury and such unhappiness that she had not thought clearly. She had thought only to escape.

"Ah, Kassia," he said, striding toward her. "You begin to try my patience." He saw her eyes darken as he approached her, and she stiffened. He stopped. "You are such a curious little thing," he said, stroking his chin thoughtfully. "You strike me, revile me, and tremble with fear before me. And you lie to me. Come here, Kassia."

She heard the steel in his voice, even though he had spoken softly, almost meditatively. Slowly, hating herself for her cowardice, she rose and walked to him. He closed his hands over her arms.

"Look at me," he said.

She looked.

"Listen well, Kassia, for I will not tell you again. You will keep your smiles to yourself, and away from Sir Guy, or any other of my men for that matter. And, Kassia, if ever you do something so stupid as attempt to flee from me, I will treat you like an ill-broken mare." His hands tightened on her arms. "Do you understand me?"

"I understand you," she whispered.

"Do you? Do you really? I wonder. Your father was like soft rain flowing through your small fingers, wasn't he? He suffered your woman's demands, your woman's wiles, without complaint. Indeed, he was so besotted with you that he did not see the power you wielded over him. I am not your father. To assist you to understand me, I will be more specific, my lady. If ever again you attempt to flee from me, I will tie you to my bed. I will spread your legs wide, and I will use you until I am tired of your skinny body. Now do you understand?"

"I understand," she whispered again.

"Good." He released her and calmly began removing his clothing. He paused a moment, then strode naked to the door and opened it.

"Evian."

The small boy scampered up from his pallet. "Aye, my lord?"

"Fetch me a goblet of wine, boy."

Graelam turned and stood by the open door, as if daring her to look at him. "You do not wish to look upon your husband?"

Kassia felt a frisson of alarm. She moistened her lips. "I am looking," she said.

"Do you feel no quickening between your thighs? No desire to share your husband's bed?"

The sneer in his voice made her forget her fear, just as he guessed it would. "Shall I get Nan for you, my lord?" she asked. "Perhaps the wine will help you, for I do not believe you are ready for her."

He drew in his breath, his eyes glittered. "Wine my lady wife, has not that effect. A drunken husband is an impotent one. But that is what you would prefer, is it not?"

"Allow me, my lord, to have a cask sent from Belleterre for you."

He threw back his head and laughed. "You don't break, do you? Particularly if you are more than ten feet away from me. My distance gives you courage. Ah, my wine. Thank you, boy. Go back to your bed now."

He shut the door with the heel of his foot, downed the wine, and walked to his bed, knowing that she was looking at him. He stretched upon his back and turned dark eyes toward her. "Let us test the power of the wine. Remove your clothes, and then we shall see."

She shook her head, mute.

"You fear me again?"

She nodded, hating herself, hating him.

"Very well. Blow out the candles to preserve your modesty. I will not tell you again, Kassia."

She doused the candles. She looked toward the unshuttered windows. Moonlight flowed full and free into the room. She picked up her bedrobe and ran to the far corner of the chamber. She worked clumsily at the fastenings of her gown. She did not understand him. There had been no ladies in her life to guide her in dealing with a man such as he. But how to deal with a man who mocked and laughed, a man who seemed at one moment to despise her and the next to threaten her when she had tried to escape him?

She drew her bedrobe tightly around her.

"Kassia, I'm waiting."

She shivered. He knew she feared him, knew that she was helpless against him. She slipped between the covers and lay perfectly still.

"Come here."

His voice was soft, even beguiling. It was the same voice he'd used when she had first come to Wolffeton. That time seemed so long ago now. He had been gentle, drawing her trust. She remembered teasing him, smiling at him.

"Please," she whispered, even as she forced herself to turn toward him.

His arms closed around her, drawing her against him. He felt the tension in her, could hear her short, gasping breaths as she tried to still her fear of him.

One of her hands was drawn into a fist and lay against his chest.

Graelam frowned at himself as his hand gently began to knead the nape of her neck. If he wanted to take her, he should simply rip aside her clothing and do it. A promise to a woman meant nothing. A promise, he reminded himself, gave a woman power. He felt the delicate bones of her shoulders as his hand continued kneading. As the minutes passed, he felt her tension ease. Her tight muscles relaxed under his fingers. His promise to her. He smiled into the darkness. No, he would not force her again. He would make her beg for him. Was it possible?

He continued to stroke her until her heart slowed and her breathing evened into sleep.

He turned on his side, facing her. He gathered her against him, and grew hard at the feel of her belly. He smiled, harshly, and willed himself to sleep.

When he awoke early the next morning, Kassia was wrapped in his arms, one of her legs between his, her cheek burrowed into the hollow of his neck. Slowly he eased his hand inside her bedrobe and began to caress her. She felt like soft satin. His body hardened. Her legs were slightly parted, easing his way, and he rested his fingers against her, savoring the feel of her.

As his fingers stroked and caressed her, she sighed in her sleep and drew closer to him, her arm tightening over his chest.

Kassia moaned, and the sound from her own throat brought her awake. She was first aware of the warmth, then a bolt of pleasure in her belly. She lay very still, not understanding, her mind still heavy with sleep and the dream that had made her want to burrow within it. She felt his breath against her temple. Graelam. She stiffened, aware of his body, his fingers.

"Hush," she heard him say, his lips feathering against her ear.

She felt the pleasure burn deep within her, and her body, without her permission, moved against his fingers. She felt the hair on his chest against her breasts, and wanted more.

"That pleases you, doesn't it, Kassia?"

She moaned, her hands clutching.

Suddenly his fingers were gone, and he had left her. She watched him as he rose from the bed and looked down at her. She stared up at him, her body bereft, not understanding. Suddenly she knew what he had done to her.

"Aye," he said, his dark eyes on her face. "Will you beg me to take you now? You must beg me, you know."

She hated herself, hated her weakness. "And I hate you," she whispered.

He threw back his head and laughed, the bastard.

She felt so humiliated, so light-headed with rage at what he had done, she lost her control. She jumped from the bed, oblivious of her nakedness, and flung herself at him, pounding his chest, yelling.

He clasped her hands easily. "Remind me, Kassia, to tell you how to hurt a man." Carelessly he picked her up in his arms and tossed her back onto the bed.

"I hate you!" she shrieked at him. "You're cruel, an animal. I want to kick your head in."

"Oh no, wife," he said, his eyes narrowing on her

pale face. "A possession does not harm its master, particularly his head or his cock."

She closed her eyes against the utter hopelessness his words brought her.

"I wish to break my fast," he said, his voice matter-of-fact. "Dress yourself and see to it."

Kassia talked with desperate gaiety as she rode beside Blanche. Then she saw the pity on the other woman's face, and grew silent. Whatever had happened to change Blanche was a blessing. She had been naught but sympathetic and kind during the past several days. Kassia was grateful to her when she suggested that they ride this morning. She wanted nothing more than to escape Wolffeton, for even a brief period of time. Escape her husband and escape his knowing.

"Evian is a kind boy," she said, breaking the silence. "The men have taken him under their wings."

"He worships Graelam," Blanche said. She saw the pain in Kassia's eyes and quickly said, "Forgive me. It is a lovely morning, is it not? And the sea is so calm, like polished glass."

"Aye," Kassia said. "Let us ride to the east, Blanche."

"I do not know if we should." Blanche appeared to hesitate, a frown between her brows.

"You were the one who didn't want an escort, Blanche. We are well on Wolffeton land. There are none to harm us."

"I suppose you are right," Blanche said. "I worry because your husband did not give us permission to ride out. I do not wish to anger him."

He is angered no matter what I do, Kassia thought.

* * *

Dienwald de Fortenberry sat easily on his destrier, calmly eyeing the two riders coming toward him. He recognized Blanche readily enough, but it was the other one who held his attention. She wore a cloak and a hood covered her hair. Blanche was undoubtedly correct. No man who cared for his wife would allow her to ride unprotected, even on his own lands. She was a shrew, Blanche had told him, spoiled and sullen, and Lord Graelam would be glad to see the last of her. He had been tricked into taking her to wive, forced to recognize her.

The two men who had accompanied him were bored. He looked back and frowned them to silence. He would play the game according to Blanche's rules. Some minutes later, he waved his men forward. They rode out from the cover of the trees toward the two women.

Kassia saw the men coming and felt alarm. The man at their head was richly dressed. When he raised his hand and waved at them, she drew up Bluebell.

When the man drew close enough for her to make out his face, she knew she had been wrong. He was looking intently at her, and his eyes were narrowed and cruel. For a moment she could not draw a breath. "Blanche. Flee."

She wheeled Bluebell about and dug her heels into her mare's sides. The wind tore the hood back from her hair. She felt her heart pound frantically against her breast. How could she have been so stupid as to ride out without men to accompany them?

She saw the shadow of the man as he closed beside her. She tried to jerk Bluebell away, but Blanche was riding close on her other side, hemming her in. She screamed as the man leaned over and grabbed her around her waist and lifted her easily. She fought him, kicking wildly, her fists flailing at his face. He drew to a halt. "Hold, my lady," he said, and shook her.

Kassia was beyond reason, and she continued to kick at him.

"If you do not stop your struggling, I will throw you facedown over the saddle."

Kassia went limp. He gathered her against him, sheltering her in the crook of his arm. She saw the two other men surround Blanche.

The man wheeled his horse about, shouting at the other two men to bring Blanche.

She was such a fool. Such a fool. She heard herself ask in a small, thready voice, "Who are you? What do you want?"

Dienwald said nothing, merely spurred his destrier to a faster pace. They rode east for some twenty more minutes. When he waved his men to a halt, Kassia was dumb with fear.

He kicked free of the saddle and eased her to her feet. "You will stay here, my lady," he said. "If you try to leave, I will beat you senseless."

Dienwald watched her carefully, to judge if she would obey him. Her face drained of color. She would obey him, he had no doubt about it. "What is that woman's name?"

"Blanche de Cormont. Please do not harm her."

His brows lowered a moment. "Lady Blanche," he called out. He motioned the two men to stay with Kassia, then strode toward Blanche.

"Please," Kassia called after him, "do not harm her."

"Come," Dienwald said to Blanche.

He took her arm roughly and led her into a copse of thick oaks.

"You have done well, my lord," Blanche said and shook off his hand.

"Of course," he said. "The jewels."

"Ah, certainly." Blanche pulled a leather pouch from the pocket in her cloak. She opened it slowly and spread out a heavy barbaric necklace of thick pounded gold. Diamonds and rubies glittered from their settings, huge stones that made his eyes glitter as bright as the jewels.

"It is beautiful, is it not? Certainly valuable enough to take her to Brittany."

"Lord Graelam brought it from the Holy Land?" Dienwald asked, fingering a large ruby.

"Aye. But neither you nor I, my lord, have anything to fear. Lord Graelam will think his wife stole it to escape him."

Dienwald raised his eyes from the beautiful necklace. "If it is so valuable," he said slowly, "will he not try to find her, just for its return? I would, were I he."

Blanche smiled easily. "I doubt that he will realize it is missing for at least a few days. And when he does, it will be too late. He will likely believe her dead at the hands of her cohorts." She shrugged. "That, or he will believe her returned to her father in Brittany, in which case he would assume that she had long rid herself of the necklace." She cocked a brow at him. "There is nothing for you to fear, my lord."

"You have planned this well, my lady." He gently wrapped the necklace back into its leather pouch and slid it into his tunic.

"Aye. I have had naught but time to do so."

"It is odd," he said, looking back at Kassia. "The little chick was afraid for you."

Blanche laughed, but it had no joy in it. She had to still her ridiculous guilt. Kassia would certainly be better off back with her father. Graelam had made her life a misery. Blanche was but doing her a favor. Her eyes did not quite meet Dienwald's as she said, "Kassia believes me her friend. You will find her something of a fool. But you will not harm her."

"Oh, but that is the rub, is it not? Whatever am I to do with her?"

"Return her to her doting father," Blanche said sharply. "The necklace is worth your trouble to send her to Brittany. There is no reason to kill her or harm her in any way."

Dienwald smiled. "Do you not fear that Graelam will go to Brittany to fetch her? Perhaps he will believe her story that she was kidnapped."

"Nay. I know him. His pride will not allow him to go after her. In the unlikely case her father demands that she return to Wolffeton, he will never believe her foolish story. Never, I promise you. And you, of course, my lord, would not be so careless as to tell her who you are."

"Nay, I would not be so careless, Blanche. But what if her father forces her to return? Will that not spoil your plans, my lady?"

Blanche smoothed the sleeve of her tunic. "I am not certain her father will force her back. But in any case, it will be a long time before Graelam learns that she is in Brittany. He cannot stand the sight of her. He treats her like a servant. She is nothing to him. He will have the marriage set aside quickly enough when he learns that she lives. The Duke of Cornwall will help him."

"And you will wed him?"

"Of course."

"When you return to Wolffeton, my lady, what will you tell Lord Graelam?"

"Why so much interest in my plans, my lord?"

Dienwald shrugged. "I have no desire to have the powerful Graelam de Moreton breathing down my neck, all through the carelessness of a woman."

"I will tell him that his wife hired two men to help her escape from him. She feared killing me, and thus I was bound and left."

"And, of course, you managed to free yourself before you came to harm. It would seem that there is nothing more to discuss. I suggest, my lady, that you scream a bit, for the benefit of the little chick."

Blanche frowned at him, then shrugged. "Perhaps you are right, though I do not see that it matters much."

Dienwald was quiet a moment, as if in deep thought. "Scream, my lady. One never knows."

Kassia heard Blanche's frantic screams. "No." She would have run toward the copse, but one of the men grabbed her arms and held her still.

Some minutes later, she saw the man come striding toward her, straightening his clothes. She paled, realizing what had happened, and moaned softly in her throat.

He stopped in front of her.

"You filthy animal. How could you harm a helpless woman?" She tried hard to struggle free.

"Perhaps," Dienwald said, "you should think of yourself for a moment."

Kassia looked up at him. She had remembered thinking he looked cruel. But he didn't look cruel now. His hair, brows, even his eyes, were the color of fine brownish-gray sand on the beach. There was even a line of freckles over his high-bridged nose. He was not overpoweringly large like Graelam, but he was built solidly, and she knew she would be no match against him.

"What did you do to Blanche?"

"I raped her," he said, "and let her go."

He watched her stiffen her shoulders. "What will you do with me?"

"We shall see, little chick," he said. Dienwald felt an unwonted surge of guilt at the miserable show of defiance from this pitiful little scrap. "Come, we ride now. No, you will not ride your mare, you will sit before me."

He would rape her. But what did it matter? Nothing mattered.

She allowed him to lift her in front of him. His destrier pranced to the side, disliking the extra weight, but Dienwald spoke softly to him, and he quieted.

They rode in silence for an hour or more.

"Who are you?" Kassia asked at last.

"You may call me Edmund," he said. "And I will call you Kassia. That is your name, is it not?"

She nodded, and he felt her hair graze his chin.

He frowned over her head, his eyes between his destrier's ears. She had not once mentioned her powerful husband. It was as Blanche said. Graelam despised his wife, and she knew it well.

"Your husband, why was he not with you?" he asked. "It is not wise for two women to ride unescorted."

She laughed. The man who had raped Blanche and stolen her was lecturing her. "My husband," she said, not hearing the helpless bitterness in her voice, "did not know we would be riding. It was my fault. We are still on my husband's land. I thought no one would dare—"

"You were wrong, and you are something of a child in your reasoning, are you not?"

"It would appear so," Kassia said.

"And also a shrew?"

He looked into her face as he spoke, and saw the incomprehension in her eyes. "A shrew," she said. She sighed deeply. "Mayhap I am. My lord makes me so angry sometimes. I fear that I am sometimes unable to moderate my feelings or my words."

Why was she speaking to him as she would a person she had known all her life, and trusted? It was idiocy. She was an idiot.

She did not realize that two tears had welled up in her eyes and were sliding down her cheeks.

"Stop it. I have given you no reason to cry."

She blinked, and knuckled her eyes with her fists. "I'm sorry," she said. "I'm afraid."

He cursed, some of his words more coarse and descriptive than Graelam's.

"Will you not tell me where you are taking me?"

"Nay. Keep your tongue behind your teeth. We have some distance to go before we rest for the night." His actions did not match his harsh words. His arm curved more protectively around her. "You're tired. Sleep now."

To her surprise, she did, nestled against Dienwald's chest. He heard her soft, even breathing, and realized that she was stirring feelings in him that he had thought well dormant for years now. He was a fool to be drawn to this pitiful little female.

She awoke with a cry, and struggled until he said, almost unwillingly, "I won't hurt you, little chick. We will stop for the night."

"Why do you call me 'little chick'?"

He gave her a twisted smile, lifted his hand, and touched her curls. "Because your hair is soft and downy and you are small and warm."

For an evil man, Kassia thought, growing more bewildered, he was not behaving as he should.

Dienwald called a halt some minutes later. He dispatched his men to hunt their dinner, and motioned Kassia to sit quietly beneath a tree. He watched her fidget a moment, then said, "The ride was long. Go relieve yourself." His eyes narrowed. "Do not attempt to flee me, or it will be the worse for you."

She believed him, just as she believed Graelam.

It was not long before she was helping Ned, a short, wiry man who looked as fearsome as her childhood images of the devil, pluck and prepare the rabbits. She stared at him when he said in a kind voice, "Nay, lass, ye cannot skewer the beast like that. Watch."

She sat back on her heels, blinking at his seeming kindness. The smell of the roasting rabbits filled her nostrils, and her stomach growled. She knew that she should likely be fainting or at least wailing in fear, but oddly enough, it did not occur to her to do so. Whatever they wished to do with her would be done. It was not in her power to stop them.

"Eat, little chick," Dienwald said, handing her a well-cooked piece. He ate silently beside her, saying nothing. Afterward, he left her a moment, his eyes a

silent threat, and spoke to his men. They moved
away, to protective positions, Kassia supposed, about
their small camp. The evening was warm and the
sky clear. The skimpy meal sat well in her stomach.
She waited.

Dienwald stood over her, his hands on his lean
hips. "Well, little chick, do you think it time I
raped you?"

18

She stared up at him, her eyes helpless upon his face. "I wish you would not," she said.

"Then what should I do with you?"

She moistened her lips with her tongue. "I don't know."

He eased down beside her, and sat cross-legged, staring into the dying fire. "Nor do I," he said more to himself than to her.

He turned to face her. "How came you to wed Graelam de Moreton?"

She looked at him uncertainly a moment, then shrugged. There was no reason not to tell him. "He did not wish to wed me," she said. "It was my father who convinced him to do so."

Dienwald stiffened. At least about that Blanche had told him the truth. "A man like Graelam is not easily convinced," he said.

"You sound as if you know my husband."

"Let us say," Dienwald said, "that I have a healthy respect for de Moreton. But continue."

"You're right, now that I know him better, I wonder how my father accomplished it. You see, I was dying, and have no memory at all of wedding him."

"I think," Dienwald said, his eyes never leaving her face, "that you will tell me the whole of it."

She repeated to him all that her father had told her. She paused a moment, then said calmly, unaware of the thread of bitterness in her voice, "Then I thought perhaps he cared for me, just a little, you understand. But it was not true. I don't understand him. It is likely that I'm too stupid to understand his motives."

"You are not stupid," Dienwald said, even as he mulled over what she had told him.

"Then unfit to be a wife."

He ignored that. "You tell me he refused to annul the marriage in the face of the Duke of Cornwall's wishes?"

"Aye. I have come to believe that he bears with me only because he cares for my father, and, of course, for Belleterre. He is now my father's heir, and Belleterre is a very rich holding."

"If he put you aside, Belleterre would still be his. At least he could battle your father and your greedy cousin for ownership."

"You are likely right," Kassia said, and turned to face him. "Edmund," she said, unaware that she had used his name, "are you holding me for ransom?"

"And if I were?"

She shrugged, a helpless smile kicking up her mouth. "I only wondered. I don't know what Graelam would do."

Saint Peter's teeth, she was as innocent and trusting as a child. He had thought to rape her—what man would not? He had thought even to keep her until he tired of her, mayhap even kill her to save the expense of sending her to Brittany. The surge of protectiveness he felt for her alarmed him. He jumped to his feet.

"You weary me with your chatter."

She flinched at the harshness of his voice, and he felt like a man who has just kicked a tethered animal.

"Kassia, sleep now. We will speak further in the morning."

He tossed her a blanket and walked to the other side of the fire.

She wrapped herself in the blanket and curled up in a tight ball. Why had he not raped her as he had Blanche? She shivered. Perhaps he still would rape her. Perhaps his seeming kindness was all a sham. She shook her head, wondering if she would ever understand any man. Her last thought before she slept was of a bloody battle between her father and Graelam for possession of Belleterre.

Dienwald handed her a hunk of bread. "Eat," he said, and turned to speak to his men.

She chewed the dry bread slowly, wishing she had a goblet of milk. Her fear, in abeyance the night before, had returned full measure when he had awakened her at dawn. She swallowed the bread and waited for him to return.

"What will you do with me?" she asked, looking up at him.

"I will tell you whilst we ride," he said.

Ned tossed her up into Dienwald's arms. She settled herself, and waited for him to speak.

"Why don't you let me ride my mare?" she asked at last.

"I don't know," he said.

"I cannot escape you."

"I know."

"Edmund, please tell me what you intend. I am very afraid."

She felt his arm tighten around her and winced.

"Kassia, if I gave you the choice, would you prefer to return to your father in Brittany or to Wolffeton, to your husband?"

"If you are asking me who is more likely to pay you a ransom, I don't know."

"I'm not asking you that. Answer me."

She sighed. "I cannot allow my husband to claim Belleterre and fight my father. If you gave me the choice, I would return to Wolffeton. It is where I belong."

"Do you care for your husband?"

Dienwald expected a vehement denial. For many moments she said nothing.

He slowed his destrier to a walk, and Kassia found herself staring unseeing at the sharp-fanged boulders in a near hillside. She swallowed, remembering yet again Graelam's kindness to her when she had first come to Wolffeton. His gentleness when he had taken her to his bed. His concern at her pain. What had she done to make him despise her? The stupid material she had taken to sew him a new tunic? She wasn't aware that tears were slipping down her cheeks.

"I'm stupid," she said.

"Ah," he said.

Suddenly Kassia stiffened. "Edmund, you are going in the wrong direction. We are on Wolffeton land."

"I know."

She tried to twist around to look at him, but he held her still. "We are still several hours from Lord Graelam's keep. Sleep. I believe you will need your strength."

"I will never understand men," she said.

He smiled over her head. "Mayhap not," he said gently, "but you will not change. You must not change."

"I would not know where to begin," she said, and leaned back against him, trusting him, and fell into a light sleep.

"Little chick. Wake up."

Kassia straightened, looking around her as she shook herself awake.

"Wolffeton lies just beyond the next rise. I can take you no farther." He laughed. "I have no wish to face your husband. I fear he would peel off my hide."

He pulled his destrier to a halt and jumped to the ground, Kassia held firmly in his arms. He set her down gently.

There were so many questions in her eyes that he began to shake his head in answer. "Listen to me, Kassia," he said, stroking his hands over her arms. "You will take care when you return to Wolffeton. Do you understand me?"

He knew that she did not. He ground his teeth, but self-interest kept him quiet.

"I will try to do as you say, Edmund," she said, her head cocked to one side, her eyes on his face.

"Go now." He leaned down and lightly kissed her mouth, then quickly released her. "Ned, bring her mare."

He tossed her onto Bluebell's back. "Remember

what I told you," he said, then thwacked the mare's rump.

He stood quietly, watching her ride toward Wolffeton.

"My lord," Ned said, coming up to stand beside him.

"Aye?"

"The lass rides into hell, methinks. Ye did not tell her of the woman's plot."

"No, I did not." Dienwald turned and grinned rakishly at his man. "As I told the wench, Ned, I have no wish to have Lord Graelam after my hide. If she knew who I was, the chances are that sooner or later her husband would find out, and not be content until he had me roasting in hell's fires."

"But that other lady. She knows ye, my lord."

"Aye, but to harm me, my friend, she would be doing herself in. And I have the feeling that Lady Blanche cares as much about her pretty hide as I do about mine."

Ned spat onto the rocky ground.

Guy ran a weary hand through his hair. His was beyond tired, yet he knew he would ride again within the hour to continue the search, this time northward. He walked down the steps from the keep into the inner bailey, pausing when he heard men shouting. Had Graelam found her? He galloped down the steps, and came to an abrupt halt at the sight of Kassia, alone, riding her mare into the inner bailey.

"Guy." She waved to him wildly even as she slipped off her mare's back. "Guy."

She ran toward him, her hands outstretched. Guy

wanted nothing more than to crush her against him, so great was his relief that she was safe, but he saw the men closing about them, and grasped her hands, holding her away from him.

"You came back," he said roughly.

"He brought me back. I thought he would rape me or kill me, but he did not. He was kind, Guy. He brought me home."

"What," Guy said, startled, "are you talking about?"

"Where is Graelam? He is all right, is he not?"

"He is searching for you. I expect him to return shortly."

"Blount. Rolfe." She pulled away from Guy. "How good it is to see you again." She had no time to realize that the men were gaping at her, for she saw Blanche standing on the steps leading up to the Great Hall, her son, Evian, at her side.

"Blanche? Are you all right? I was so worried for you."

Kassia started toward her, but Guy grabbed her arm. "Wait," he said.

She responded to his voice, and turned slowly to face him. "What is the matter, Guy? Did everyone believe me dead? I was afraid, but he wasn't evil as I thought at first. Indeed—"

She broke off, hearing the thundering sound of approaching horses. She felt Guy take her arm and hold her still beside him. Why had Blanche not come to welcome her? Why were the men regarding her like she was a ghost?

Graelam rode at the fore of his dozen men into the inner bailey. He was so bloody tired he could scarce see straight. His face was gray with worry, and fear, and anger. He raised his head, his hand upraised to halt his men, and saw her standing beside Guy. He felt a spurt of sheer relief, before rage flowed through him.

He leapt off Demon's back, his hands now fists. He held himself still for an instant, drawing control.

Kassia pulled free of Guy and ran toward her husband. "Graelam. I am home. I'm safe."

He caught her arms and stared down at her.

"You are unharmed?"

She nodded happily. He closed his eyes a moment, nearly choking on his rage. "Aye," he said, "I see that you are quite unharmed. Why did you come back?"

She cocked her head to one side in question. "He brought me back, my lord. He did not harm me, I promise you."

Graelam was aware that every servant and all of his men were watching. He should take her inside, away from all his gaping people, but he couldn't seem to move. He saw Blanche from the corner of his eye, her face white, her hand clutched over her breast. "He, my lady?" he asked, turning back to her. "The man you hired to help you return to Brittany brought you back?"

"Hired—" Kassia said. "I don't understand, my lord. I was kidnapped, but the man, Edmund is his name, felt sorry for me, I think. He brought me back."

Graelam took her arm, saying as he drew her forward, "Come, we shall go into the hall." He heard Guy call to him, but he ignored him.

Kassia took double steps to keep up with him. What had he meant about her hiring men? She darted a glance upward to his set profile. She could see the lines of weariness on his face, and felt a spurt of hope. He had been searching for her. He must care something for her.

He released her suddenly, and pushed her down into a chair. He stood over her, frowning. He said, "So you think, wife, to return to me, and have me smile at you and forget what you did?"

She shook her head, even as she said, "You searched for me."

"Aye," he said, "I have spared nothing trying to find you. That appears to please you."

His voice was calm, but his eyes, dark as a cloudless night, were cold, so cold that she shivered.

"It surprises me," she said.

Graelam's eyes narrowed to slits. He turned away from her and called out sharply, "Blanche."

Kassia felt a wave of relief to see Blanche walk slowly toward them.

"Blanche," Kassia said, "you are all right? That man, Edmund, he didn't harm you?"

Blanche smiled at her—a pitying smile. "The man did not harm me, Kassia." She is like a cat, Blanche thought, always landing on her feet. By God, what was she to say, how was she to act? What would Graelam do if he discovered the truth? That made her still any guilt she felt. Why, she wondered, does everything I do end up in disaster? She had no choice now but to brazen her way through this.

"Tell her, Blanche," Graelam said, "what you told me."

She looked down at Kassia again, and said slowly, "Perhaps I was wrong, Graelam. Perhaps she did not hire those men. It simply appeared so to me."

"What are you saying, Blanche? You know I did not hire those men. How could you ever believe that? You saw them come after us. Surely you knew that they meant us harm. Their leader, Edmund, he raped you. Surely you realized they—"

"Yet you are returned safe and unharmed," Graelam interrupted her smoothly.

"Kassia," Blanche said, "you are here again, safe. It is obvious that they meant you no harm." She shrugged. "I was not certain if you were fleeing from them when they rode toward us. I thought that you were—" She paused, leaving a delicate, damning silence.

"That I what, Blanche?" Kassia said, disbelieving this idiocy.

"That you had hired them to help you escape Wolffeton and your husband. Forgive me if I misjudged you."

Kassia stared at the circle of disbelieving faces around her. Edmund had warned her, but she had not understood. "But the man raped you, Blanche. How could you believe that they would do less to me?"

"He didn't rape me, Kassia. No man save my husband has ever touched me. He merely—fondled me for a moment, and that made me scream. I believed he was in a hurry to return to you." That, she thought, must surely have been the truth.

"Kassia," Graelam said very quietly, "you will cease your act."

Act? What am I acting?

She struggled to her feet and looked at the faces around her. She saw Guy reach out to take her hand, saw her husband shove him away.

"Listen to what she has to say," Guy said to Graelam.

"I will listen," Graelam said. "Sit down, my lady. And talk."

Kassia sat down again in the chair, staring ahead. It was a nightmare, in a moment, she would awake, and she would be safe and warm.

"Speak," she heard Graelam say.

She raised her eyes to her husband's cold face and said, "Blanche and I went riding yesterday morning. We were without escort, but on Wolffeton land. Three men came toward us. We tried to escape them, but they caught us. The leader, Edmund, told me he had raped Blanche and let her go. He took me up on his destrier. I thought he would rape me or kill me, or hold me for ransom, but he did nothing. He was kind to me. He brought me home."

Graelam just looked at her. "Such a pitiful little tale. Surely you had ample time to invent something more believable." He turned to Guy. "Well, have I given her enough of a hearing?"

Guy had been watching Blanche's face. He saw fear and something else in her eyes. Kassia's story had been so unbelievable as to be the truth. He said quietly to Graelam, "If Kassia hired these men to return her to her father, what did she pay them?"

Blanche smiled, her relief so obvious that she quickly lowered her head so no one would see it.

"And why did she have them return her to you, my lord? If indeed she did hire them to escape you, the fact that she changed her mind must mean something."

"Perhaps," Blanche said, knowing that she must say something, hating herself for the damning words even as she spoke them, "she paid the men with her body."

"No."

Blanche scented victory. She must not succumb to pity or regret now. She said calmly, her eyes thoughtful on Kassia's face, "And perhaps they didn't like the prize and let you go."

She'd been such a fool. Such a fool. Slowly, she said, "My lord, I did not try to escape you."

"I have heard enough for the moment," Graelam said. "Go to our bedchamber. I will come to you soon."

Guy, who knew his lord much better than did Kassia, was alarmed at Graelam's passionless voice. He touched to Graelam's sleeve. "I believe her," he said.

"Do you indeed, Sir Guy? Do you not question why a man would kidnap a woman only to return her unharmed? It is foolishness."

"I believe her," Guy said again.

"You," Blanche said, wanting to hit him, "are a besotted fool."

Kassia grabbed up her skirts and ran up the stairs to the bedchamber. She should have begged Edmund to send her to Brittany. She shook away the thought. No, she would convince Graelam of the truth. After all, she was his wife. Surely that must mean something.

19

Graelam listened to the dozen voices raging around him, but said nothing. Had he been capable of it, he would have smiled to hear Blount, that hard-nosed old goat, who never gave an inch, vociferously defend his lady. And Guy. Aye, had she come back because she could not bear to be separated from him?

He rose from his chair and said in a voice that chilled Rolfe to his bones, "You will go about your duties now." He saw worry etched in many of the faces. "I have heard all of you. Go now."

He did not wait to see if they obeyed him. It was only Kassia who had ever dared to disobey him. He walked up the stairs to his bedchamber. He paused a moment, hearing Kassia's old nurse, Etta, sobbing.

"Why, my baby?" the old woman was saying, her voice hoarse from her crying. "Why did you do it?"

"Etta," Kassia said, sighing, "I did nothing. You, of all people, should believe me."

Graelam pushed open the door. He said nothing, merely motioned to the old nurse to leave. She slithered past him, her eyes puffy from her weeping.

He stood for a moment, looking at his wife. She was pale, but that little chin of hers was lifted. He wanted to wrap his fingers around her white throat, but instead he asked, "Did the men rape you?"

Kassia shook her head. "Nay, I told you that they did not harm me."

"I would think that such ruffians as Blanche described to me would not leave such a tempting morsel as yourself with her legs together and her belly empty."

She winced, but said firmly, "Their leader, Edmund, was no ruffian. Indeed, his men called him 'my lord.' "

"I know of no Edmund who is a lord in these parts."

"I don't believe it was his real name."

"Tell me, Kassia, what did this Edmund look like?"

She took heart at the quiet, interested tone of his voice. "He was not of your size, my lord. His hair and eyes and brows were all of that strange hue, of silver and brown. He knew of you. Indeed, I believe he feared you."

Despite himself, Graelam searched his memory for a man of that description. There was none that he knew of. "And that is why he returned you to me? He feared retribution?"

"Nay," she said. "I told you, I believe he felt sorry for me." She paused a moment, then said, "He asked me if I would prefer going to Brittany or returning here."

"And what was your reason for returning?"

"He told me that even if I returned to Belleterre, you would still hold claim. That if you wished it, you could wage war upon my father for your rights. I could not allow that to happen."

"Ah, so you are the sacrificial little lamb."

The sneer in his voice made her close her eyes. "Please," she said, desperate now, "you must believe me, Graelam."

He regarded her, watching her pitiful show of bravery begin to crumble.

He said, "Do you recall, my lady, what I told you I would do to you if you ever again tried to escape me?"

She remembered suddenly, and without thought, realizing what a fool she was, she dashed frantically toward the door.

She felt his powerful arm lock around her waist and heave her up as if she were naught of anything at all. If she struggled against him she would only hurt herself. She knew it well, but could not stop herself. She tried to twist away, but he tightened his hold, and for an instant she couldn't breathe.

Graelam eased her down upon her back on the bed. He sat back and regarded her intently, his fingers touching her throat.

"You do not wish me to have you," he said, his voice almost meditative. "Did you enjoy this Edmund's caresses? Did he give you a woman's pleasure?"

He saw the look of utter incomprehension in her eyes, and knew at least that she had told the truth about not being raped.

Kassia gulped. "Why will you not believe me? I have never lied." Her expression flickered, and she quickly said, "At least I haven't lied since I was a child."

"Kassia, what did you use for payment?"

"There was no payment. Why will you not believe me?"

He frowned suddenly. "Don't move." He strode purposefully to his large chest. He jerked open the lid and riffled through the contents. Beautiful cloth rippled through his fingers. He dug to the bottom and pulled up a large leather case. His fingers weren't quite steady as he opened it. The necklace, worth a king's ransom, was gone. All hope dissolved in that moment. The depths of his disappointment startled him. He had wanted to believe her. But she had lied.

He slowly replaced the leather case in the bottom of the trunk, slowly straightened all the glittering cloth, and shut the lid.

Without a word, he strode back to the bed. "You were a fool to come back."

"I don't understand."

"The necklace is gone."

"What necklace?"

He leaned over her and ripped away the skirt of her gown.

Kassia tried to jerk away from him, but she was no match for him, and he easily subdued her. She watched him as he tore the wool into strips. He clasped her hands and drew them over her head.

"Graelam," she said, "what are you going to do?"

"I told you, told you quite specifically before you left me again."

"No." But she couldn't move; he'd tied her wrists above her head.

He rose and stared down at her for a long moment. He saw the terror in her eyes, the pleading. Her small breasts were heaving against her tunic.

He quickly spread her legs wide, binding each ankle. He drew his dagger, and sat down beside her.

"Please," she said, nearly beyond reason, "don't hurt me."

Slowly he sliced the dagger blade through the material. He cut each layer from her body, until she lay naked on her back.

He straightened over her and looked at every inch of her. "You have filled out a bit," he said. He touched a fingertip to her breast, and felt her quiver. In fear.

"I wonder if that tiny little belly of yours will ever fill with my child?"

Kassia closed her eyes against his words, against what she knew he was going to do to her. She was a fool. Such a fool.

She heard him undressing, felt the bed sink down as he eased beside her. He splayed his hand over her belly.

Graelam looked at her, at the straight legs drawn so widely apart, followed their woman's shape to the soft curls between her thighs. He touched her and she whimpered, but not with pleasure. Never pleasure with him.

Damn her. The devil take her and all women. He came up between her legs and picked up her hips. She was bound so securely that she couldn't struggle against him. He did not mean to take her, merely to frighten her, merely prove to her that he would not allow her to make a fool of him.

He drew away his hands and sat back on his haunches, looking at her face. She was as pale as death. Tears streamed from her closed eyes. He jerked away from her, her distress burning deep into him. He picked up a blanket and smoothed it over her.

He turned away from her, wishing he could close out the sound of her choking on her own tears. He cursed loudly and fluently, grabbed a towel, and wiped her face with it.

"Stop it. Stop those damned tears."

She sniffed, and unwittingly brushed her cheek against his hand. He felt her hot tears wet his palm.

He could not bear it. He untied her wrists and ankles, cursing himself for a weak bastard, even as he rubbed feeling back.

She lay passively, her sobs now noisy hiccups.

He rose. "At least you did come back," he said, "for whatever reason."

"I never left," she said.

He turned and quickly dressed, cursing his trembling hands. He walked to the chamber door, paused, and said over his shoulder, "You are mistress of Wolffeton. I expect a decent meal. Rouse yourself and see to it."

He added harshly, "And bathe yourself. You smell of horse sweat."

And fear, he added silently. She smelled of fear.

"Did you hurt her?" Guy said.

"If I killed her, it would be no more than she deserved," he said, eyeing his knight.

"My lord, she told the truth. There is naught but honesty in her. If I can see it, you, as her husband, cannot be blind to it."

"Guy, you are a fool," Graelam said, so weary he wanted to lie in the corner and sleep. "The necklace is gone."

"The necklace from Al-Afdal's camp?"

"Aye. Damn her, I would have given it to her."

Guy studied his master's face. He is suffering, Guy realized, shocked with his insight. For the first time in his life, he is suffering for a woman. He said no more, wanting to think. If Kassia had not taken the valuable necklace, then who had? The answer was not long in coming to him.

The evening meal, if not excellent, was at least more palatable than it would have been had Kassia not been at Wolffeton. But her movements, her instructions, were mechanical. She saw vaguely that there was pity and concern in some of the eyes that looked at her. In others, there was puzzlement. Nan regarded her with contempt and triumph.

And there was Blanche. It had taken her benumbed brain several hours before she had realized what Blanche had done. She didn't know what to do. If she confronted Blanche, she would sneer at her and call her a liar. If she told Graelam what she believed—No. In his eyes, Blanche was everything Kassia was not. Never would he believe her. She didn't know what to do.

Her silence that evening in the great hall was seen by most as the proper response of a chastised wife. She avoided Graelam's eyes, not wanting to see the distrust, even the hatred he must feel for her. She ate little, unable to stomach much.

"So, you will dwindle away with your sulking?"

Her head snapped up at her husband's voice.

"I'm not sulking, at least I haven't for some five years now."

"Just as you do not lie. Then eat." He eyed her

closely. "When I told you you had filled out a bit, I did not mean that you had grown presentable. You still scarce have a woman's body."

So that was why he hadn't forced her. He found her so repulsive that he could not bring himself to take her, even in his rage.

She knew she should be ecstatic, but tears hung on the tips of her lashes.

"If you cry in front of everyone, I shall truly give you cause to do so."

"You already have," she said, gulping.

"You amaze me, Kassia," he said, leaning back in his chair, his arms crossed over his chest. "Do you never tread warily?"

She said nothing, merely stared into her goblet of wine.

"Perhaps I should return you to your father. At least your absence would bring me some peace."

The response he knew he would gain was swift in coming. "Nay, please do not."

"Ah, anything to save your father. Anything to save Belleterre. This man who felt so sorry for you, Kassia, you say it was he who told you that to return to Belleterre would lose all?"

"Aye, that is what I said to you." She raised weary eyes to his face. "Why do you torment me? I have told you everything." But she was lying, not telling him about Blanche, and he saw the lie in her eyes.

A surge of rage swept through him, and he gripped the arms of his chair until his knuckles showed white.

"Leave me," he said finally, "and know, my lady wife, that I can make your life a hell if you do not admit to your lies."

*   *   *

Blanche ate daintily, savoring every bite of the tender pork. I am safe, she thought. She was so relieved that she could not long sustain her fury at Dienwald de Fortenberry. Graelam would never believe his wife. And of course Kassia, little fool that she was, was too proud, too unbending to convince her husband otherwise. Blanche had looked closely at Kassia, searching for bruises. It had surprised her to see none, for she would have sworn that Graelam was furious enough to kill her. Again she stilled her guilt. Kassia had returned safely, and Blanche had but to bide her time.

"I hadn't realized that you knew of Lord Graelam's treasure trove."

Blanche's heart skipped a beat at Guy's words, but none of it showed on her lovely face. She arched an eyebrow. "You spoke, Sir Guy?"

"Aye, Blanche. You took the Saracen necklace and you hired those men to remove Kassia from Wolffeton. Did you expect them to kill her?" He shook his head. "No, you are not without some pity. But you wanted them to take her back to Brittany, did you not? Were you dismayed to see Kassia returned with nary a scratch?"

"Your imagination rivals the minstrels', Guy. Pray, have you other, equally interesting tales?"

Never, he knew, would he succeed in getting her to tell the truth. He would have to do something else. He stroked his jaw with his fingers, realizing that Blanche was single-minded, if nothing else. She had failed this time to rid herself of Kassia. He had no doubt that she would try again, and that frightened him. How could Graelam be so damnably blind? He said, "Blanche, even if Kassia were dead, Graelam would not wed you."

She laughed. "Ah, Guy, is that jealousy I hear in your voice?"

He looked at her for a long moment. "Jealousy, Blanche? Mayhap, you are onto something."

"It is a message from the Duke of Cornwall. He comes within the week."

Kassia quickly set aside the ledger of accounts, uncertain of Graelam's reaction to what she was doing, and forced a smile. Blount certainly delighted in her skills. "I shall see to his comfort, my lord."

"You may recall that his retinue is vast."

"Aye, I remember."

Graelam eyed her with growing irritation. "Must you leap out of your white skin whenever I am about?"

She looked at his darkly handsome face and felt a wrench of pain. "I believed you wished proper submissiveness in your wife."

"You are about as submissive as my destrier. You cannot even play the role well."

She said nothing, her eyes on her hands that lay clasped in her lap.

"What are you doing?"

He leaned to the table and picked up the ledger, rifling through it. "Ah yes," he said, "I had forgot that your father taught you to read and write. Does Blount know that you poach on his preserves?"

"Aye."

He tossed the ledger back onto the table. "Does it please you to make fools of us all? Nay, do not say it again, Kassia. Your lies have filled my craw to overflowing."

He strode from the small workroom, not looking at her again. She returned to her figures, wishing she could tell him that Wolffeton was becoming a rich holding. But hearing her say it would only anger him, for he would doubtless believe that she was angling for new gowns, jewels, or the like. She finished her task and called all the indoor servants together in the Great Hall.

She looked at their faces, some of them dear to her now, others, like Nan's, implacably hostile. Seeing Blanche sitting near the great fireplace, her expression chillingly serene, Kassia told them of the duke's impending visit. "Marta," she said to an older widow who was now in charge of the spinning and weaving, "we will speak of new clothing for the women. We have enough surplus cloth now to see to our own needs."

All but Nan smiled at that.

"Aye, my lady," Marta said, nearly singing she was so proud.

"Blount will give up his chamber to the duke. Nan, Alice, you will see to its thorough cleaning. I hope to have finished new cushions for the duke's chair."

She heard Nan muttering, but ignored her. She gave other orders, then dismissed the servants, all save the cooks. She spent another hour planning meals with them.

Kassia rose and rubbed her neck. She wanted to ride, but doubted Graelam would allow it. Indeed, he would likely humiliate her in front of his men if she even tried.

"Kassia."

She jumped, startled, for she had not noticed Guy entering the hall.

"I have news, my lady. You shall be the first to congratulate me."

She smiled. "What is your good fortune?"

"My father has died. His lands and keep near Dover are now mine." He raised his hand, seeing the shock in her eyes. "Nay, do not give me your condolences on his demise. He was a rotten old lecher, mean-spirited and cruel. It is a relief to all his men and servants, and to my poor sister who lived with him."

"Then I do congratulate you, Guy. You are now a knight of substance. You will leave us?"

"Aye. The keep is nothing to compare to Wolf-feton, of course, but it is a beginning." He paused a moment, a smile lighting his blue eyes. "I begin to believe in fate."

Kassia cocked her head to one side in question, waiting for him to explain, but he only shook his head and smiled at her.

"Aye," he said, "it is indeed fate."

To Kassia's relief, Graelam showed no hesitation in his well wishes to Sir Guy. The ale and wine flowed to the early hours of the morning. Graelam, good-humored in his drunkenness, tried to press Nan on Guy, but he refused, shouting to the company that he doubted his ability to raise either his interest or his member.

Kassia quietly left the hall, hopeful that her husband would fall asleep below. She turned on the stairs at the sound of rustling skirts.

"How sad for you that the handsome, so malleable Guy leaves us."

"It is sad for all of us," Kassia said. "I suggest you find your bed, Blanche. You are slurring your words as badly as the men."

Kassia could tell that Blanche would have liked to sneer at her, but the wine and ale had dulled her wits. She left her, shaking her head at her own stupidity. Blanche, her friend.

Blanche was indeed dull-witted. She frowned at Kassia's back, then made her way carefully to her own small bedchamber. It was close and warm, but she was too befuddled to slide the shutters away from the one window. She undressed and slipped into her bed. Her head was swimming and her thoughts were warm. It was almost as if she had willed him to come. She watched the door open slowly. In the darkness, she could only make out that it was a man, a tall man.

"Graelam," she said.

He quietly closed the door and stood a moment, tall and straight. Then he was coming toward her, shucking off his clothing.

"I knew you would come," she said, and held out her arms toward him.

"Aye," he said, "I came."

20

Blanche shuddered when he took her into his arms and pulled her onto his lap. He kissed her deeply, thoroughly, until she was trembling with her need for him, and her triumph.

His flesh beneath her questing fingers was smooth as silk, hard muscle beneath.

"It has been so long," she said, her fingers trailing down his chest to his belly.

"No man since your husband died?" he asked, his words punctuated with nipping kisses down the side of her neck.

"Nay. And he was a beast."

"I'm not," he said. He pressed her onto her back and came down beside her. "What a woman you are," he said, his fingers cupping her.

"So long." Blanche arched up against his hand, wanting him so much she could scarce restrain herself. She found him, hard and ready, and inhaled sharply at the feel of him.

"You will have me in your bed every night," he said. "Never will you want for a man again."

Her mind reeled with his promise, and she pulled him down over her, opening herself to him.

His fingers drove her to the edge before he eased into her. He sucked in his breath at the heat of her, and thrust deep.

"Now," Blanche said, and she met his every thrust, drawing him deeper and deeper until he lost control. But he held himself back until she yelled into the stillness of the chamber.

He took his own release and fell over her, his head beside hers on the pillow.

It took a long time before Blanche brought herself back into focus. He is inside me, his seed is filling me, she thought, and felt a moment of panic. She wanted to shove him away, to cleanse herself, but he would not move. She felt him kissing her on her ear, and smiled into the darkness.

"You are mine at last," she said. Oddly enough, even though she had found great pleasure with him, she was thinking of another, a knight with golden hair and blue eyes. She was stupid. "When will you send her back to Brittany?" She stroked her hands over his chest.

He said into her mouth, still kissing her, "You will never worry about her again, Blanche. You will be mistress of my keep, and my wife. Very soon now. Very soon." She felt him growing hard within her once again, and she was surprised when her body wanted to sing with pleasure.

He took her more slowly this time, until she was pleading with him.

He laughed, and gave her what she wanted. She fell asleep in the crook of his arm, so sated that she was beyond words, beyond caring that his seed still filled her, beyond the niggling feeling that she wished it had been another to share her bed. I have won, she thought. At last I have won. I am safe, my son is safe.

Blanche awoke the next morning with no splitting headache from all the wine she'd drunk the previous night. Graelam was gone, but that did not surprise her. She bathed herself, so pleased that worry of him seeding a child within her was only a minor thought. She dressed herself in her most becoming gown, a russet wool with a golden-threaded belt that emphasized her breasts and waist.

She hummed softly as she made her way to the hall. She saw Kassia seated alone, nibbling on a slice of bread. She frowned, wondering how she should act. Had Graelam told Kassia that he was setting her aside? She remembered his words. *Very soon*, he had told her. *Very soon*. She decided to hold her peace. Kassia would discover the truth soon enough.

Kassia raised tired eyes to Blanche, mentally preparing herself, but Blanche, to her utter surprise, only smiled at her.

She noticed Blanche's lovely gown and frowned, wondering why Blanche was wearing one of her best gowns. She herself was wearing an old gown of faded gray, for she planned to oversee the cleaning of the stables herself. And the jakes. They were foul and needed a river of lime to mask the smell.

"You look like a serving wench," Blanche said, unable to keep the triumph from her voice.

"Aye," Kassia said. "But then, I am mistress of Wolffeton, Blanche. It is my responsibility to see that all is ready for the duke."

Blanche laughed; she couldn't help herself. Blind little fool. So Graelam had said nothing to her as yet. It was on the tip of her tongue to tell Kassia that her brief stay was soon to be over, when she heard Graelam's deep voice. He was speaking to Guy about the final repairs on the eastern outer wall.

"Will you break your fast, my lord?" Kassia asked, rising from the bench.

"Aye," Graelam said. "And a goblet of ale to clear my aching head."

Kassia immediately left the hall to do his bidding.

Graelam stretched. His eyes fell upon Blanche. There was a very soft smile on her face, and he nodded at her.

"You have the look of a cat who has been well fed," Guy said.

"Aye," Blanche said, never looking away from Graelam.

"One should never allow a cat to go hungry for too long a time," Guy said as he sat himself beside Graelam.

Blanche looked at him uncertainly, wondering if he knew of his master's visit to her chamber. Somehow the thought made her feel ashamed. "Is there anything I can do to see to your comfort, my lord?" she asked Graelam.

"Nay," Graelam said, turning again to Guy.

Why didn't he say something? She eyed him with mounting frustration. Why didn't he ask to speak to her alone?

She looked up to see Kassia, a serving wench following in her wake, carrying a large tray.

Kassia motioned for the girl to set it in front of Graelam. "I have brought enough for you also, Guy," she said.

"Thank you, my lady," Guy said. "I need to keep up my strength."

"When must you leave us, Guy?"

Graelam thought he heard distress in his wife's voice, and slewed around to look at her. He saw only weariness in her eyes, and dark smudges beneath them. She'd not rested well the previous night. What the devil did she want? He attacked the cold beef with a vengeance. After all, he hadn't bothered her.

"I will leave when the duke does, my lady," Guy said. "I cannot in good conscience remove myself until Graelam has found another warrior to protect Wolffeton. I fear what would happen if I did go."

"Conceited fool," Graelam said without heat. "You know I have written to the duke. It is likely he will have a knight in his train who is a landless lout, just as you were."

"How sorry we will be to see you go," Blanche said.

"It warms me to hear you say so," Guy said.

Kassia heard something odd in Blanche's voice, something that she couldn't define. She herself would miss Guy terribly, but of course, she could say nothing, especially in front of Graelam. Her one protector. She shuddered at the thought of how alone she would be when he left.

"What ails you?" Graelam asked, his voice sharp.

She shook her head.

"Have you eaten?"

"Aye, my lord. If you will excuse me, there is much that needs my attention."

He nodded, and watched her walk slowly from the hall, her head bent. She is thinking of Guy, he thought, and frowned. She continues to elude me, to treat me as if I were naught but a heavy burden to be borne. He turned and smiled at Blanche.

The night was dark and mysterious as the depths of a woman. But still he waited until he knew she would be asleep. Quietly he eased open the door to her small chamber and peered inside. He could hear her breathing and knew she was deep in sleep. A lone candle was close to gutting on the small table beside her bed. So she had waited for him. He undressed quickly and leaned over to blow it out.

Blanche lay on her side, one leg drawn up to her chest, her face pillowed by her open hand. He was able at last to make out her outline in the darkness. She was beautiful.

He eased beside her, lifted her heavy hair, and began kissing her neck, his hands caressing her back. Blanche stirred, froze, then smiled.

"I did not think you would come to me," she said and parted her lips for his kiss.

"I told you that you would never sleep without me again."

Blanche frowned a moment. Her mind was clear of sleep now and there was no wine to tangle her thoughts. His voice sounded odd. A searing bolt of pleasure spread through her belly, and she sighed and gave herself over to him.

"Allow me to rise," she said when they were done.

"Nay, love. You will go nowhere."

"I must."

He nibbled on her breast, and smiled when he realized the reason for her urgency. "Nay, Blanche, my seed will spring to life in your beautiful belly. You will give me sons, many sons."

She froze. "But there is Evian," she said, only to feel him push deep inside her, again, holding her still.

She lay exhausted, and still he moved within her. Something wasn't right, and it nagged at her. He seemed more lean than she remembered. She fell asleep even as her hand roved over his thigh, searching for the long, jagged scar.

Blanche eyed Kassia closely the next day, noting her pallor, the pinched look about her mouth. Graelam had told her, finally. "You do not look well, Kassia," she said.

"I did not sleep well." Kassia didn't look at her.

"What you require is some exercise. Since it no longer matters, why don't you go riding?"

What no longer mattered? She shook off Blanche's question, and nodded. "Indeed, I would like to. All is ready for the duke."

Still she hesitated, and Blanche said, "Graelam will not mind, I promise you. Mayhap this time you will not return."

Kassia looked at her wearily. "You will never tell him the truth, will you?"

"The truth?" Blanche arched a beautifully plucked brow.

"What was his name, Blanche? Not Edmund, I think."

"You surprise me," Blanche said. "He is not a gentle man, at least by repute, yet he released you. Certainly it was not because of your womanly endowments."

"Nay," Kassia said. "And he was gentle, and quite kind to me. What is his name, Blanche?"

"I am tempted to tell you, now that it makes no difference. Graelam no longer cares. Mayhap he would even ask him to take you away again."

"I'm going riding, Blanche." Kassia turned and walked quickly from the hall. She nodded to the men she met in the inner bailey, noted a scattered pile of refuse in a mud puddle from the brief shower the night before, and called to one of the servants to clean it up.

She raised her face to the bright morning sun. Even now, she thought, unhappiness searing through her, my father is gazing upward, just as am I. The sun is warming his face. She thought of Blanche's words about Graelam, and knew them to be true. If she rode out and never returned, he would not care.

To her utter surprise, the stable groom, Osbert, a feisty old man with grizzled hair and a hook nose, shook his head at her request. "Forgive me, my lady, but my lord said ye were not to ride out, not without him."

"When did he give you this order, Osbert?"

"Yesterday, my lady. Again. He told me he'd stretch my neck if I bowed to your pretty face."

Pretty face? She wanted to laugh. "Where is Lord Graelam?"

"Here, my lady."

She spun about, paling as she saw him leaning against the open doorway, his arms crossed over his chest. She ran her tongue over her lips, and her eyes fell to the strewn hay at her feet.

"You wish to ride out?"

She wanted suddenly to demand where he had spent the past two nights. But when she raised her face, she saw that he was frowning at her, his dark eyes narrowed.

"Aye," she said. "If it pleases you, my lord."

He straightened and nodded toward Osbert. "Ready her mare. You may come with me, Kassia." She forced herself to stand quietly as he approached her. "Guy will ride with us," he said. "That is certain to please you."

Guy. She blinked, thinking absurdly that she was a bone, and two dogs were fighting over her. "Aye," she said, tilting her chin upward. "That would please me."

He wheeled away from her. "I will await you outside," he said, and left her.

There were six men in their party. Rolfe told her they were to visit the merchant Drieux in the newly chartered village of Wolffeton. To Kassia's surprise, Graelam said nothing when Guy reined his destrier beside her.

Guy smiled at her. "I was telling my master," he said, leaning toward her in the saddle, "that the jakes are no longer offensive to the nose."

"Lime," she said.

"The duke will be pleasantly surprised," Graelam said, looking back toward Wolffeton. "Have you finished cushions for him?"

She nodded.

"His old butt will be well content," Guy said, laughing.

"You have done well, my lady," Graelam said.

She felt herself flushing with pleasure at his unexpected praise.

"Gallop with me, Kassia," he said, and slapped the flat of his gloved hand to Bluebell's rump.

She laughed aloud with pleasure, feeling the soft summer breeze tangle through her hair. She breathed in the salty sea air deeply.

When they slowed to a walk, Graelam turned to her. "I had intended that you come with me this morning. Now that your cheeks are red and your eyes bright, you do not look so ill."

"I'm not ill," she said.

"Tell me his name, Kassia."

She felt a deadening pain in her chest. "I asked Blanche," she said, "but she would not tell me."

"Blanche." His hands tightened on the reins, and Demon snorted, dancing sideways.

She saw his face darken with anger, and drew in her breath. But he said nothing, merely dug his heels into his destrier's sides and galloped away from her.

The village of Wolffeton lay nestled in a valley not a league from the castle. A dozen men were building the defensive wall that would rise some eighteen feet into the air, shielding them from sea attacks. The ground was deeply rutted and muddy, and piles of refuse were stacked around at least a dozen tents. The only completed structure was the merchant's house. Drieux stood in the doorway waiting for them. He was an ascetic-looking man, his face thin, his pale eyes deeply set, and nearly the age of her father. He had been exquisitely polite to Kassia when he had met her some weeks before at the castle.

"My lord, my lady," he said, bowing deeply from the waist.

Graelam nodded, and dismounted. "All goes well, I see," he said, looking about the growing village. "You do need more men," he said, pointing toward the wall.

"A dozen more families will be arrriving within the week," Drieux said. "By the end of the year, we will be self-sufficient."

Graelam turned to Guy, and Kassia watched him and the men ride toward the wall.

"I have brought my wife to see the goods we settled upon," Graelam said.

Goods? What goods? Kassia felt Graelam's hands close about her waist as he lifted her off her mare's back and set her on the ground. "Come, Kassia."

Graelam had to bow his head as they entered Drieux's house. Actually, Kassia saw, the main chamber housed his goods. The beamed ceilings were high, the floor still earth-covered. All smelled of freshly cut lumber. There were several long trestle tables, and on each were piles of material, boxes of spices and herbs and shining new tools. "It's a beginning," Drieux said. "Here is the carpet, my lord."

Kassia watched as a young boy helped Drieux unroll a magnificent red wool rug.

"Oh, Graelam, it's beautiful."

He smiled down at her, his eyes lightening. "Does it match your cushions?"

She turned glowing eyes to his face. "I will make new ones if it does not."

He watched her finger the thick wool, exclaiming to the merchant as she traced each swirling pattern. "From Flanders?" she asked.

"Aye," said Drieux.

"And the other, for our bedchamber," Graelam said.

The other carpet was a vibrant blue, so soft that Kassia could imagine her bare feet sinking into it. "It is so very fine." Suddenly she frowned, thinking of the cost, thinking of the valuable necklace stolen from Graelam's chest.

"It does not please you?"

She swallowed. "We really do not need it, my lord. It is so very valuable."

"It matters not. I want it."

She smiled up at him shyly, and he returned her smile, until he realized that he was playing the fool, seeking to please her.

"Shall we put it in the duke's bedchamber until he leaves?"

"An excellent idea," he said. "The duke will doubtless believe that you are just the mistress Wolffeton needed."

He left her then, to see to the village's fortifications.

Kassia followed him outside and stood quietly, watching the men work on the wall. Drieux came up to stand beside her. "The carpets are indeed from Flanders, my lady," he said.

"However did you get them so quickly?"

"From a rich merchant in Portsmouth. Lord Graelam wanted them."

Kassia smiled up at him. "Doubtless you will become a wealthy man, monsieur."

"With Lord Graelam's strength and protection, I believe it will be so."

Graelam returned and helped Kassia into the saddle. After giving Drieux instructions to have the carpets brought to Wolffeton that afternoon, he wheeled Demon about.

As they neared Wolffeton, Graelam sent Guy and his men to the castle and motioned for Kassia to follow him.

He saw her hesitate briefly, and raised a brow. "You do want to ride, do you not?"

He led her to the protected cove, the place where he had taken her virginity many weeks before.

"I wish to speak to you," he said.

He lifted her from her saddle, tethered the horses, then left her to walk along the rocky beach. He gazed out over the billowing waves, watching them crash, sending spumes of white over the jutting rocks.

He turned back to her and said, "When I asked you the man's name, you said that Blanche would not tell you. Why do you bring her into this, Kassia?"

Her chin rose. "Because it had to be she who hired those men. I did not guess it until you told me of the missing necklace. I knew then that it had to be someone within the keep. Since it was Blanche who accompanied me that day, there was no one else. I asked her to tell me the man's name, but she merely laughed at me and refused."

"That is ridiculous," he said. "There is no reason for Blanche to do such a thing."

"Aye, there is. She wishes to wed you, and she loves her son mightily and seeks to ensure his future."

Graelam was silent a moment. He remembered the night Blanche had come to his bedchamber, into his bed.

Kassia knew that he didn't believe her, but she said, "I do not know if Blanche hired them to kill me. I trust it is not so."

"You weave fantasies, Kassia," he said. "It is not me Blanche desires, it is Guy. Indeed, Guy will announce their betrothal this evening. He has spent the last two nights in her bed."

Kassia swayed where she stood. Guy and Blanche? "No."

"Aye, that distresses you, does it not, my lady? Your gallant Guy desires another woman. And Blanche is a woman, with a woman's needs, and a woman's soft body."

"But she is older than Guy."

"Two years. It's nothing. She will breed him many sons, which, of course, is the only reason for a man to wed, that and to add to his coffers or land to his holdings. He could not ask her before, since he owned no land. As I said, Blanche is a woman, and she is honest in her need for a man."

Kassia was beginning to doubt her sanity. If Blanche loved Guy, then why would she hire those men to take her away from Wolffeton? There was no answer.

Graelam saw the changing thoughts on her expressive face. He remembered Guy telling him the previous evening, "It is best for your wife if Blanche is gone from Wolffeton," but he said nothing to Kassia. He saw the unhappiness in her eyes, unhappiness she would not hide at losing Guy, and wanted to hurt her. Even as he spoke, he knew he was being unfair and unnecessarily cruel. "Guy is lucky, is he not? He is wedding a woman who is soft and giving. A woman who welcomes him gladly to her bed." He saw her become still as a stone. That damned chin of hers went into the air.

"I believe it time for you to breed me sons. Even though you are frigid, you will do your duty by me." He clasped her shoulders and drew her against him. He cupped her face in his large hands, and kissed her roughly. Her lips were cold and tightly pursed.

"Please," she whispered against his mouth, "don't hurt me again. I have done nothing to deserve it."

He cursed and pushed her away from him.

"Have you not? Perhaps I should send you back to Belleterre and get myself a wife who is also a woman."

He made her blind with fury. "Perhaps you should," she said quite coldly.

"Enough. Mount your mare, wife. At least there is something you are good at. You may return to Wolffeton and order preparations for a feast tonight. You would not want Guy to feel unappreciated, would you?"

She shook her head, mute, and climbed on Bluebell's back.

21

Kassia stood quietly while Etta tightened the soft silk belt around her waist, drawing in the bright blue silk tunic. She would have preferred dull gray wool, but knew Graelam would be furious with her if she did not appear well-garbed this evening. She had seen nothing of Blanche during the day. It was probably just as well. She winced as Etta drew her tortoise shell comb through her hair, tugging at a tangle. There was no reason at all for Blanche to tell her the truth. What was the truth?

"It's lovely you look, my baby," Etta said, stepping back to admire her mistress. "The duke does not arrive until tomorrow. Why do you wear your best gown tonight?"

Kassia gave her a pained smile. "You will see, Etta. Be in the hall."

Blanche, as had been her habit the past two days, also appeared in one of her best gowns, and looked utterly beautiful, even to Kassia's jaundiced eye. No wonder Guy loved her.

Blanche eyed Kassia closely, dark brow arched upward. "You have nearly the look of a gentlewoman this evening, Kassia. May I ask why?"

"To honor your betrothal, of course."

Blanche blinked at that. "You know? Graelam has spoken to you?"

"Aye, he did this morning. I suppose that I must congratulate you."

Blanche felt that the world had taken a faulty turn. "Are you not upset? You did understand what Graelam said?"

"Aye, I understood, and I am only upset because it seems an unlikely match, at least to me. I had no idea you cared for each other."

Blanche was momentarily speechless, wondering if the little snit was blind. She was not loath to gloat, just a bit. "And I had thought that you cared for him. It was all an act? Come, I do not believe you."

"I do care for him." Kassia shrugged. "However, since I have no say in the matter, it is foolish to rant and rave. It is his decision, after all." She raised her chin. "I hope, Blanche, that you will be a good wife to him."

"You may be certain that I shall. He has been quite pleased to share my bed the past two nights."

"Aye, I know. Graelam also told me of that."

Blanche could only shake her head. She wanted to gloat a bit more, but in the face of Kassia's calm acceptance, she was left without a word to say. "You are mad," she said, and left her.

Mad, am I? Kassia frowned at Blanche's back, then turned to direct the servants. The hall filled quickly, the men seating themselves along the long trestle tables. Blanche stayed back until Guy smiled at her and motioned her to her place beside him.

"I don't know," she said and tried to catch Graelam's attention. But he was speaking to Kassia and did not heed her.

"Sit down, Blanche. You will see, it is better so."

She could scarce eat a bite, her eyes continually going to the high table, questions tumbling through her mind. When will he tell everyone? Why is he waiting? What is he saying to Kassia?

"Patience, Blanche," Guy said, slanting her an amused look.

At least, she thought, turning to Guy, she could show him her triumph. If Graelam had told Kassia, it was likely Guy also knew. "Everything has worked out just as I said it would," she said, her voice sounding shrill and defensive to her own ears.

"I think so," Guy said.

"There is nothing you can do about it. In a few minutes Graelam will make the announcement." Why did he seem so indifferent to what had happened, so uncaring?

"He told me he would," he said.

She cursed him under her breath, her unspoken disappointment making her say angrily, "It is your hope to take Kassia yourself? Will you volunteer to see her back to her father in Brittany?"

"No," he said.

Blanche turned at the sound of Graelam's bellow for silence. At last, she thought, straightening. At last.

Graelam rose from his chair. "Attend me," he called out. He paused a moment until the hall was quiet. "I have happy news to give you. Blanche, will you please come here? And Guy, of course."

Why Guy? She walked gracefully to the raised dais, Guy beside her.

"Everyone wish the couple well," Graelam said, grinning at Guy. "Blanche and Guy will be wed the day after tomorrow, in the presence of the Duke of Cornwall."

"No." The small word scarcely spoke itself when Guy grabbed her and kissed her hard, smothering her cry.

There was a chorus of shouts and congratulations and calls for more ale. "It is done, Blanche," Guy said into her mouth.

"You whoreson." She tried to pull away from him, but he was too strong.

"You didn't think that when I was in your bed," he said into her mouth. "Indeed, you enjoyed yourself much, Blanche. And I did promise you that you would never sleep alone again. You are well caught, my love. Graelam is pleased. You will not gainsay me now."

"No." She still couldn't believe what had happened.

Guy heard shouts and kissed her again, allowing his hand to slip down her back. "Mayhap my son already grows in your belly, my love. Chitterly is not so grand as Wolffeton, but you will grow content, you will see. Now, Blanche, smile, else when I come to your bed tonight, I will take you without thought to your pleasure."

"You planned this." She felt his hand on her hips. "May you rot in hell, Guy. I will never wed you, never. It's Graelam I want, and I shall have him."

Guy was profoundly grateful for the lecherous calls and lewd jests from the men, and Graelam's oblivious presence. "I think, my love, that you and I will leave the hall for a moment. There is much that you must come to understand." Without another word, Guy hoisted her onto his shoulder and strode through the laughing men out of the hall.

She struggled, but it was no use. She was panting in fury when he set her down and took her arm, pulling her along with him into the inner bailey. He took her into the warm, dark stable. Only Osbert was there, and Guy dismissed him.

He gave her a light shove and she fell onto a pile of hay. He stood over her, hands on his lean hips. "Listen well, Blanche. It is my intention to turn you into a sweet, loving wife. If you fight me, I shall beat you, doubt it not." He saw the fury in her eyes, and added, his voice hard, "Graelam does not want you. He never has. How you could be so blind astonishes me. You know as well as I that there are problems between Graelam and Kassia, but you will not be here to add to Kassia's unhappiness, or, I might add, my love, to hire more men to rid Wolffeton of her presence. No, do not bother to deny it. Now, I believe it time to consummate our betrothal."

He began shedding his clothing, and for a moment Blanche simply stared at him. Pain filled her, and she said, "You told Graelam that I willingly bedded you?"

"Aye." He paused a moment and regarded her closely. "It is odd. Graelam still believes you modest and submissive. That you managed to keep him blind for so long is amazing to me." He laughed. "I assured him that you were quite a woman in my bed."

"You do not want me," she said, her eyes against her will going over his body as he bared himself. "It is that little slut you want. You know Graelam does not want her. Damn you, you know it."

He stood before her, naked. "Graelam wants her, all right," he said. "He merely does not know it yet. And with you gone from Wolffeton, he will come to understand her quickly enough, and himself. Do you like my body, Blanche? Last night you searched for the scar on my groin before you fell into a sated sleep. And Graelam is a much larger man. I was surprised that you did not recognize me last night, for you were drunk only on lust, and not on wine."

"I was a fool," she said.

Guy didn't like the defeat in her eyes. "It is likely," he said, dropping down beside her on the hay. "But you have won me, Blanche. You do account me a good lover, do you not?"

"I believe you a nasty, cocky whoreson." He smiled and pressed her upon her back. "You're a witch, do you know that? Come now, Blanche, I know you are not indifferent to me, no more than I am to you." He kissed her deeply, his hand going downward over her belly. He felt the ripple of pleasure in her as she arched her hips up. "No," he said into her mouth, "not indifferent at all. You are a delightful bargain, my love. I will easily make you forget Graelam and Wolffeton."

"You could pretend that you are pleased," Graelam said to his wife.

"I will miss Guy," she said. "He has been kind to me."

"Aye, so many men are *kind* to you. Even Drieux sings your praises." He leaned closer to her. "Have you entertained the good merchant in your bed?"

"Since my bed is also yours, my lord," she said,

"you know you speak only to fan your dislike of me." She shrugged. "Of course, since you have not been in your bed for several nights, you cannot really know, can you?"

She felt gooseflesh rise on her arms at his deep laugh, and wished she had kept her mouth shut. Why did she allow him to bait her? "You sound lonely. But I wonder how that can be so, when you are still a child, and have no use for men." He sat back in his chair, his arms folded over his chest. "I imagine that at this very moment Guy is between Blanche's thighs. That bothers you, does it not?"

She shook her head, not looking at him.

"Kassia, you believe I dislike you. Damn you, look at me when I speak."

She obeyed him. "Aye, I believe it," she said. "Not at first, but you changed."

"I, wife? It is only that I discovered my sweet, innocent wife was a deceitful bitch."

Was there never to be an end to it? "I did not hurt you, my lord. Nor have I ever been deceitful."

He cursed, aware that Blount was looking at him.

"May I be excused, my lord?"

He waved her away. He watched her walk gracefully through the hall, stopping to speak to various of his men, and felt his irritation grow. He thought again of the conversation he had had with Drake, his armorer, that afternoon. He admitted to himself that he had been wavering in his beliefs until Drake had matter-of-factly stated in his even, emotionless way that women, even the best of them, couldn't help themselves. "They spin tales, my lord," he said as if he were discussing the weather. "Lady Kassia lied to you, but again, she is but a woman. How could she tell you the truth?" Drake shrugged, and spat into the corner of the armory.

"Mayhap," Graelam heard himself say as if from a great distance, "she did not lie."

"She is young, my lord. Wolffeton is vastly different from her home in Brittany. Why did she try to escape you? Why did she come back? Why, my lord, does any woman behave in ways that make our heads spin?" He picked up a hauberk and began to pound methodically at the iron fastenings. "You might as well forget it, my lord. Accept your lady for what she is."

Graelam knew that he should have cut off Drake's impudence, but he had wanted to hear what he had to say. He was a man who had lived many years and known many women. He treated Kassia's duplicity as if it were naught. Damn her, he thought and drained his wine.

"Well, well, my lord," the Duke of Cornwall said to Graelam as he looked about the great hall of Wolffeton. "It is quite an improvement. Even a carpet." He turned a smile upon Kassia.

"You have done more than I thought possible, my lady. It appears you have tamed this big brute. Ah, even cushions on the chairs. Aye, Graelam, you chose your wife wisely."

Graelam grunted and Kassia kept her head lowered.

She felt the duke's bony fingers cupping her chin and slowly raised her head. "And you, my lady, have much benefited from your husband, I see. More meat on your delicate bones. No babe as yet?"

Kassia, her eyes held by the old duke's piercing gaze, could only shake her head.

"You'll see to it, my lord," the duke said, and patted her cheek. He turned slowly, his joints creaking in his own ears, and called out, "Sir Walter. Come and meet your new lord."

Kassia watched the tall, thin knight stride forward. He was well-garbed, and as she listened, she realized that he said all the right words, showed due respect to Graelam. But there was something about him, something that she distrusted and disliked. When he at last turned to her, she realized that it was his eyes. They were dark blue, but cold and flat, without feeling.

"My lady," Sir Walter de Grasse said.

She felt naked, even her thoughts stripped bare before him. "Sir Walter," she said. "Welcome to Wolffeton."

"Sir Walter comes from Cornwall," the duke said, "Now, unfortunately, he must make his own way."

Sir Walter said, "Aye, it is true. My family's home was destroyed by the father of that viper Dienwald de Fortenberry."

Graelam gazed at the man thoughtfully. He heard venom in his voice, and saw the gleam of hatred in his eyes. He said very calmly, "Whatever de Fortenberry has done, Sir Walter, he has not come near to Wolffeton. I do not count him an enemy. I pray you will not forget that."

Sir Walter bowed slightly. Kassia shivered. She became aware of her husband's eyes upon her, and immediately broke into speech. "My lord duke, we have prepared a chamber for you that has its own carpet. Allow me to show you."

When told later at dinner of Sir Guy's betrothal, the duke said, "A good lad, and worthy. Lady Blanche, I understand, is Graelam's sister-in-law?"

"His first wife's half-sister," Kassia said.

"The boy, Evian," the duke continued to Graelam, "is he not Blanche's son?"

"Aye. Sir Guy has decided that the lad will remain here at Wolffeton. He is performing his duties quite well. I have hopes that one day he will squire me."

Kassia wondered how Blanche felt about leaving Evian at Wolffeton. They had not seemed particularly close, but still, shouldn't Blanche be the one to decide the future of her son?

"Likely the boy will have many brothers and sisters," the duke said, casting his rheumy eyes toward Blanche and Sir Guy. "The lady looks to be a fine breeder."

"At least she is a proven breeder," Graelam said.

"Do you consider wives to be as cattle and horses, then, my lord duke?" Kassia asked, and immediately wished she'd kept quiet. Graelam's opinion of women she knew well. Likely now she had insulted the duke.

"Nay, my dear wife," Graelam said, leaning toward her. "Cattle and horses know but one way to mate. Wives, if they but show a little interest, can find breeding very pleasurable."

The duke overheard Graelam's words and laughed. "Well said, my lord. But forget not that your lady has many other talents as well." He patted the cushion and sighed in contentment. "My old bones feel like they've melted and gone to heaven."

When at last the sweetmeats and fresh fruit were set in front of the duke, he turned to Graelam, and said, "I've a surprise for you, Graelam. Quiet the men, and I will announce my news."

Kassia cocked her head to one side, wondering wearily if the duke had another heiress for Graelam.

The Duke of Cornwall rose and stood quietly for

a moment, then burst out heartily, "Edward the First, King of England, returns shortly. His coronation and his queen's will take place in Westminster Abbey in October. My lord Graelam, your presence is requested at the ceremony."

There was wild cheering, and Kassia discreetly motioned for the servants to bring in more ale and wine. Her head whirled with excitement for Graelam. She turned to her husband. "Graelam, you will go, will not you? I must sew you new tunics. You have but one fine one. And a new robe, of purple velvet, I think. For the king, you must look very grand."

Graelam smiled at her enthusiasm.

"And what of you, Kassia? Do you not have need of new gowns and the like?"

She raised wide eyes to his face. "Do you mean that you wish me to accompany you?"

He felt a brief wrenching pain at the pitiful stirring of hope he saw in her eyes. "Of course you will come with me," he said. "Who else would see to my comfort?"

Any of the female servants, she wanted to yell at him, but her excitement at traveling to London quickly overcame her ire at his words. "I will really meet King Edward and Queen Eleanor?"

"Aye, you will meet them. And you do have need of some new gowns, Kassia. Unfortunately, the duke, as usual, gives us little time to prepare."

"I will do it," Kassia said. "Whatever needs to be done will be done."

Graelam fiddled with his wine goblet for a moment, frowning at himself even as he spoke. "There is a bolt of gold-threaded silk in my trunk. You will sew yourself a gown from it."

She blinked at him.

"It's a pity you gave the necklace away, for you could have worn it with the silk."

He saw the light go out of her eyes as if he had struck her. St. Peter's bones, why should he feel guilty? She was the one who had played him false. She was the one who persisted in her lies.

"Nan," he called. "More wine."

Kassia sat very quietly. In her excitement, she had forgotten momentarily how much he disliked and distrusted her. But of course he would not forget. He would never forget.

She lay curved into a small ball some hours later, the raucous laughter from the hall below not breaking into her dream. A man's voice spoke, "It's time to see if my little wench can breed." She sighed and turned onto her back. Suddenly she could hear the man's breathing. She blinked and came awake.

"Hold still," Graelam said, his hands on the belt of her bedrobe.

He was drunk. "Please, Graelam," she said, pressing her hands against his bare chest.

"Hold still," he said. He jerked up her bedrobe, giving up on the knot at her waist, and fell on top of her. He grasped her head between his hands and kissed her, his tongue in her mouth. Kassia felt him against her thigh. She knew she couldn't fight him, and lay perfectly still.

He raised his head until he could focus on her face in the dim light. Her eyes were tightly closed. "Damn you," he said. He felt her quiver beneath him. "I will make you respond." He got control of himself and pulled himself off her.

Her eyes flew open, and she saw his harsh face above her, his mouth grim.

"You want me to force you," he said. "Then you can hate me all the more."

"I don't hate you."

He lightly stroked his hand over her throat. "Take off the bedrobe, Kassia."

He controlled her. He would do just as he pleased with her, despite her wishes. A flicker of rebellion rose. "You tell me I am a child, that I do not have a woman's feelings. Why do you bother? Why do you not return to your mistress? Does it please you to hurt me? If so, then just get it over with."

Graelam was drunk. He was also sober enough to make sense of her words. He realized that he was likely too drunk to make her respond to him, and now her mind was locked against him. He rolled off her and rose. "Very well," he said, reaching for his bedrobe. Oddly enough, he felt no anger at her for spurning him. "If I return during the night, you need have no fear of me." He turned on his heel and strode from the bedchamber.

22

Kassia turned away from the cooking shed, mulling over again the words she had overheard Sir Walter say to Guy just before Guy and Blanche had left Wolffeton. "It is a pity that I do not have a father to die and pass me his estates." Guy, who was distracted, had said only, "Aye, it is unfortunate."

"But there are other ways," Sir Walter had said after a moment. "Soon, I believe, I will no longer be landless. I will gain what should have always belonged to me."

Kassia remembered how cold and emotionless his voice had been, though, objectively, they could simply reflect Sir Walter's ambition. She wished she could tell Graelam of her feelings, but she guessed he would simply look at her like she was a stupid woman and dismiss her out of hand. She paused a moment, looking at Drake, the armorer, at his work. She missed Guy. She remembered his words at his leave-taking. "Now, my lady," he had said, lightly touching his fingertips to her cheek, "the way is clear for you to live at Wolffeton happily and safely." Her eyes flew to his face, but he had shaken his head at her, smiling. "Blanche is a handful, never doubt it, Kassia, but she will please me. You may be certain of that."

Kassia was not so certain that would be the case. Although there seemed to be a new softness about Blanche, she nonetheless stared through Kassia, ignoring her completely when they took their leave of Wolffeton.

Kassia paused a moment, hearing her husband's voice from the practice field. He had not returned to their bed that night nearly a week before, and since then he had slept with her every night without touching her. She imagined that after taking his man's pleasure with Nan, he wanted the comfort of his own bed. She wanted not to care, but couldn't manage it.

She made her way to Blount's accounting room and began another coward's letter to her father. Not wanting to worry him, she had never mentioned her unhappiness or her husband's obvious distrust of her. She paused a moment over the piece of parchment, thinking about his last letter to her. "Geoffrey is quiet," he had written. "Too quiet. Like a snake that is slithering about until he can find a protected place from which to strike." The rest of his letter had merely recounted the day-to-day events at Belleterre. Kassia told him of the upcoming coronation, and left it at that.

"Ye believe ye're so above us all, don't ye, my fine lady?"

She turned to Nan and frowned. The girl stood in the doorway, hands on her hips, her hair tossed back, long and thick down her back. Normally she did not allow Nan's insolence to bother her, for after all, the wench did bed with Graelam. But this attack was both unexpected and beyond the line.

"What do you want, Nan?" She rose.

"That old crone Etta told me ye wanted me to scrub down the trestle tables."

"Yes, that is what I wish you to do."

"We'll see about that." Nan flounced away.

Kassia frowned. She frowned again several hours later when she finished sewing on her silk gown and went into the Great Hall. The trestle tables hadn't been cleaned. Furthermore, Nan was sitting in Kassia's chair, waving her hands, giving outlandish orders in a loud, shrewish voice in an effort to mimic her. Kassia felt rage, and strode into the hall.

The other servants saw her before Nan, and quickly lowered their heads, bending to their tasks.

"Get out of my chair," Kassia said. "Now."

Nan jumped, and slithered out of the chair, responding to the voice of authority. But she quickly straightened and faced Kassia.

"You will do your assigned tasks, Nan, else you will go into the laundry shed or the fields."

"Nay, my lady," Nan said, eyeing her with open contempt. "Ye haven't the power to do that. My lord would never allow it." She ran a hand through her gleaming long hair. "Aye, ye haven't the power. It's hard work, cleaning the trestle tables. My lord wouldn't want me to use my energy and become too tired for him."

Kassia heard a snicker behind her. She closed her eyes for a brief instant. She was the mistress of Wolffeton. Nan could not be allowed to speak to her thus, else she would lose all control. She drew up to her full height.

"You will still your insolent mouth, Nan, and do the work I ordered you to do. Now."

"Nay, my lady. It is too hard a task. My lord won't want me to harm his child." She clasped her arms about her belly, and smiled.

Child? Graelam's child. Kassia felt dizziness wash over her. Even she could now see the slight bulge at her waist. If she had had a knife, she would have stabbed it into Nan and then into Graelam.

Graelam stood in the shadows of the great oak door. Nan's words surprised him, but it was not she who held his attention. Kassia looked both ill and furious. He knew that he could not allow Nan to gainsay her mistress, knew it as well as he suspected Kassia did. He strode forward, drawing all eyes.

Kassia saw him and wondered dully how much he had overheard. She stood, waiting for him to complete her humiliation.

"My lord." Nan said, and started toward him.

Graelam raised a hand. "What is happening here, my lady?" he asked Kassia.

He knew exactly what had happened, and he was baiting her. He would make her say what she believed in front of the servants, then say exactly the opposite. She forced herself to meet his eyes. She said in a cool, clear voice, "I have given Nan a task, my lord. She does not wish to do it because she carries a child." *Your child.*

"I see," he said. He turned to Nan. "What is this task that would be so wearing on you?"

"Scrubbing the trestle tables, my lord. The duke's men were pigs, and left them filthy."

Graelam looked back toward his wife. He saw her hands fisted against her sides. He smiled. "Begin the task, Nan, as your mistress instructed. My lady, you will please accompany me now."

Begin the task. Kassia looked at him warily. Nan cocked her head to one side, but realized enough to keep her mouth shut. Perhaps he simply didn't wish to embarrass his skinny wife in front of all the servants. Nan probably should have told him of the child before she attacked Kassia.

"Very well, my lord," she said. "I shall begin the work."

"Come, Kassia," Graelam said, and walked from the hall.

Kassia knew she had no choice. She trailed after him, shoulders square, chin raised.

He waited until she was inside their bedchamber, then closed the door. He said nothing for a long moment, merely watched her. That little chin of hers was raised again for battle.

"It is your child, of course," Kassia said, hearing the anger in her voice.

"I suspect so."

"I suppose you expect me to thank you for not humiliating me in front of the servants."

"You could, but I doubt that you will."

His utter disinterest sent her over the edge. "I am the mistress of Wolffeton."

"Are you?" he asked. "In some ways I suppose that you are. In others, my lady, you are sorely lacking."

"Just as are you, my lord."

To her surprise, he nodded. "It is true. Now, you will heed me well. I put a stop to Nan's insolence for the moment. I will handle the wench to your satisfaction if you will agree to become the mistress of Wolffeton in all ways."

"What do you mean?"

"I see I have your full attention. Here is the bargain I propose. You will come to me willingly in my bed. You will no longer act the outraged maiden or the passive victim. If you refuse, I imagine your life could be particularly unpleasant."

He expected her to draw back in disgust, but she didn't move. Her eyes remained wide and questioning on his face. "What do you mean that you will handle Nan to my satisfaction?"

"Ah, the terms of the agreement. You are wise to have everything clear before agreeing or disagreeing. I will marry the wench off and remove her from Wolffeton. You will never have to deal with her insolence again. That is, if you agree."

Kassia could easily imagine what would happen if Nan gained the upper hand. She raised her chin even higher. "I do not think that it is your right to interfere at all in how I manage the servants. And that includes your precious mistress."

"Then I take it that you do not agree to my bargain?"

He thought he heard her curse, and it made him want to smile.

"You have not the right. Will you take everything from me?"

"On the contrary, I wish to give you more. A woman's pleasure, for example. Such pleasure truly does exist, I promise you."

"Give it to your slut, damn you."

He said, "How I envy Guy. I heard Blanche's cries of pleasure on their wedding night. Would you grant to Guy what you refuse to grant to me?"

"I would grant none of you anything."

"Enough, Kassia. What is your answer?"

"If I refuse, will you release Nan from all her duties and make her the mistress of Wolffeton?"

Of course he would not, but he saw that Kassia did not realize that. He merely shrugged, looking bored and impatient.

She looked away from him, her hands clenching and unclenching in front of her. "I don't know what to do."

"All I desire is your cooperation. I will teach you the rest. Come, my men await me. What is your answer?"

"I—I agree," she said in a whisper.

He made no move toward her. "Very well. Now you will come with me back into the hall and give Nan her orders. I will endeavor to find her a husband."

Kassie followed him. Why did he even bother? Why was it so important to him that she enjoy coupling? She did not understand him.

Nan gasped in disbelief, her eyes pleading on Graelam's face. She pleased him, the whoreson, and now he was choosing his skinny wife over her. It occurred to her that she had pushed Kassia too hard, challenged her too openly. She saw it in the eyes of the other servants. They were enjoying her downfall, rot them. She had to speak to Graelam alone.

Graelam took Kassia's hand and drew her with him to the inner bailey. "You will begin to fulfill your bargain this night." He squeezed her hand, and left her to stare after him, gooseflesh rising on her arms.

Later Graelam watched Sir Walter wash down his head and torso at the well. "All goes well, Walter?"

"Aye, my lord."

"I wish you to ride with three men tomorrow morning to the demesne farm that lies due west three miles. The farmer's name is Robert, I believe, and he has recently lost his wife. I want you to bring him to Wolffeton."

Walter readily agreed, not caring why Graelam wanted the farmer brought to Wolffeton. He only wished he could travel farther than the three miles, toward Dienwald de Fortenberry's stronghold.

Graelam decided wisely not to speak to Nan until the following day. He had no real faith that Kassia would hold to the bargain. He felt nothing in particular about Nan or the fact that she carried his child. He would provide support, of course, and pay the farmer well to marry her. It was his second bastard. The first, a girl, had died in her first year of life. His father had bragged about the wenches he had gotten with child, and claimed more than a dozen children. However, Graelam had never seen any resemblance to himself in any of the peasants around Wolffeton. He thought of Kassia's small belly filled with his child and felt a jolt of pleasure. He was becoming a half-wit, and he roared at one of his men-at-arms who had bungled his lance.

"Your hair is growing quickly, my baby," Etta said as she wielded the brush. "I believe it is thicker than before your illness. Still, you should not wear a wimple or even a snood."

Kassia looked into the polished silver mirror. Her chestnut hair fell in curls nearly to her shoulders. "Aye," she said. "I begin to look like a female again." Oddly enough, she remembered how she had liked her husband touching her and kissing her, until he had hurt her. Until he had shown how much he despised her. How could anything be different now?

"Your lord dealt well with Nan," Etta said as she straightened the chamber from Kassia's bath. "You will no longer have to put up with her tantrums."

"No, I will not," Kassia said.

"I have also heard that the new knight, Sir Walter, is not as popular with the men as was Sir Guy."

"Where did you hear that?"

Etta shrugged. "From one of the men, likely. I do not remember. I find Sir Walter a cold lout, and a secretive one."

"I wonder what Graelam thinks of him," Kassia said.

"Your lord is an astute man. If Sir Walter is not what he appears, he will soon be ousted."

"I trust you are right, Etta."

"Right about what?" Graelam asked as he came into the chamber.

Etta said, "Right about Sir Walter."

"Perhaps," Kassia said, "he is not what he appears to be."

Graelam's brows drew together. "Has he bothered you?"

"Nay, my lord, it is just that I do not completely trust him. He reminds me somewhat of Geoffrey."

"I see," Graelam said. He dismissed Etta and stood quietly watching his wife fidget about the room, her hands going again and again to the sash at her waist.

"Are you still of the same mind, my lady?"

She nodded, not meeting his eyes.

"I promised you once that I would not force you

again. You still believe that you will have to bear pain and pretend to enjoy me, do you not?"

"I have known nothing else," she said, her eyes focused on her bare feet, sinking down into the soft carpet.

"You will tonight."

"I—I will try, Graelam."

There was a soft rap on the door and Graelam opened it. Evian handed him a tray that held wine and two goblets.

"You do not have to make me drunk, my lord."

He smiled at her. "Nay, but I do think you need to relax a bit. Here." He handed her a goblet of wine, then poured himself one.

She sipped slowly, wondering how it slipped down her clogged throat. She felt her face grow warm as she downed a second goblet. Everything seemed softer, her tongue loosened, and she spoke her thoughts aloud. "Why is it important to you that I—that I like coupling with you?"

"I don't want my child conceived in fear," he said, knowing he wasn't being honest with her.

"Does it matter?"

"To me it does." He did not want to probe his own reasons, and said abruptly, "Enough wine, Kassia. Get into bed now."

She obeyed him, forcing herself not to burrow under the covers.

He watched her from the corner of his eye as he quickly undressed. Indeed, he thought, why did it matter what she felt? She was but a woman, and his wife. But it did matter, and for whatever reason, he was pleased that he had thought of a way to ensure her compliance. He saw her pale when he eased into the bed beside her. She thought he would savage her now. He stretched on his back, and pillowed his head with his arms. After a moment he asked, "Did Nan do your bidding?"

"Aye, but unwillingly."

"Good."

It was time to see if she would hold to the bargain. "Kassia, come here."

He felt the bed sink down as she moved toward him. "Now," he said, turning his head to look at her, "I want you to kiss me."

Kassia frowned a moment, wondering at him. He hadn't moved. His hands were still pillowed beneath his head. Slowly she rose on her elbow, leaned down, and quickly pecked him on his mouth.

"Excellent." Still he did not move. "Now I want you to kiss me again, only this time, part your lips just a bit."

He felt her warm breath, sweet from the wine, as her lips brushed his mouth again. He looked up into her eyes and smiled. "That wasn't so terrible, was it?"

She shook her head.

"I want to feel your tongue on my mouth. It will not hurt, I promise you."

As Kassia, filled with embarrassment, did as he bid her, she became aware, very slowly, of her body pressed against him. He was so large, and she felt his tongue touch hers. She drew back, but as he made no move, touched her tongue to his. It was the wine that was making her feel warm. She was unaware that her hand now rested on his chest, and her fingers were caressing his chest.

When she raised her head, she was panting, and

there was a look of profound worry in her eyes. He wanted to laugh and at the same time to crush her against him, but he did neither. "Again, Kassia," he said.

He allowed her to do just as she wished, and was delighted when she deepened the kiss, her hand now on his shoulder, her fingers digging into his flesh. He felt her breasts pressing against his chest, and wondered if he could control himself. Very slowly he brought one hand from beneath his head to rest lightly on her back. He felt her start to draw back, wary again. He began to stroke her hair.

He thought he would explode when her hand went downward to his belly.

"Do you like the way I feel?" he asked her, the words warm in her mouth.

Her answer was a small gasp as she whipped her hand away. She didn't know why she had wanted to touch him. It was as if her body was no longer taking orders from her mind.

"I—I don't mind kissing you."

"I'm pleased," he said. St. Peter's bones, this was a torture he could never have imagined.

She was kissing his chin now, her fingers sliding beneath his head to bring him closer to her.

When she made another foray into his mouth, he felt her quiver when his tongue touched hers. Her bare thigh was rubbing lightly against his. If he allowed her to continue, he knew that he would lose control.

He brought his other hand down and clasped her shoulder, pushing her away from him. "You have done well," he said, looked closely into her eyes. "Go to sleep now, Kassia."

She stared at him, aware of the heat in her belly, aware that her breasts felt swollen, aware that she didn't want to stop what she was doing. "I—I don't understand."

"Go to sleep," he said. He rolled over onto his stomach, his head turned away from her. He knew that she hadn't moved. He smiled painfully, and said, "I want you to take off your bedrobe. When you become cold during the night, I want you to come to me for warmth. Good night, Kassia."

She pulled at the belt, throwing it away from her. She slipped out of the bedrobe, and utterly confused, curled up on her side. "I will never understand you," she said into the darkness.

Perhaps, he thought, still striving to calm his breathing, he would never understand himself.

23

The farmer Robert was delighted with the offer of a new wife. That she carried the lord's child bothered him not a bit. She was a comely wench and quite young. With the sons she would doubtless bear him, his farm would prosper, and him along with it. As for the lord's child, that one would be well taken care of. He realized quickly that she was not at all pleased with the prospect of becoming his wife, but he thought tolerantly, that would quickly change.

Nan was disbelieving, then furious. But it was all no use. As for the farmer, she hated him on sight, though, objectively, he was neither old nor ill-looking.

Wolffeton's priest, Father Tobias, married the couple with dispatch, and Graelam presented the farmer with a cask of his finest wine, as well as a dowry for Nan.

If Kassia believed Graelam to be rather cold-blooded about casting off his mistress, she had to admit to relief that the girl would be gone. Even during the brief ceremony, she found her thoughts going over and over what had happened the previous night. She'd felt something whilst she had kissed him, something that made her feel very warm and urgent. Yet Graelam had pushed her away. Rejected her. This morning when she had awakened, he was gone, and he had greeted her in the hall as if nothing out of the ordinary had occurred between them. For a moment she'd felt an overwhelming urge to kick him.

She stood quietly beside him, watching Nan and her new husband ride in an open cart from Wolffeton, the cask of wine set up beside Nan like a plump child. She toyed briefly with the notion that she would tell him the bargain was off. He could no longer threaten her with Nan's insolence. She bit her tongue. She was no longer certain that she didn't want the bargain to continue, if continue it would. Why hadn't she asked her father to explain men to her?

Graelam wanted a fight. His energy was inexhaustible, his mood violent. He would have even welcomed Dienwald de Fortenberry pillaging his lands if only he could meet the man in battle. Since his wish wasn't to be granted, at least that day, he rode off with a dozen men to the village of Wolffeton, and worked to finish the defensive wall. He was exhausted when he returned late that afternoon, pleased that he had exorcised his wife from his thoughts during most of the day.

But he didn't feel as exhausted as he had believed when Kassia entered their bedchamber while he was bathing.

"I have come to assist you, my lord," she said, not meeting his eyes. He was relieved that the water level hid his sex. He was hard as a stone.

"You may wash my back," he said and leaned forward.

Kassia stared at the broad expanse of back. She could feel the movement of muscle beneath the bathing cloth. To her surprise, she felt warmth, coming directly from her belly.

"What did you do today?" Graelam said, trying to distract himself.

"I finished your new tunic. I trust you will approve."

"What about your gown?"

"I will begin it shortly."

Her hand dipped down below the water toward his hips, and he whipped his head around. "That is enough, Kassia. Go see to our meal."

He thought he saw a flicker of hurt in her eyes, but it was quickly masked.

"I will be down shortly."

She nodded, unable to speak, for there was a knot of misery forming in her throat. She left the bedchamber, and berated a serving wench when she carelessly dropped a silver platter.

Sir Walter de Grasse looked toward the raised dais, to Lady Kassia. He sensed her dislike of him, and it angered him. So proud she was, the lord's wife, who had willingly taken up with Dienwald de Fortenberry. He had heard the description of the man Edmund she had given her husband in her attempts to appease him. Features the strange color of silver and brown. Aye, it could be none other than de Fortenberry. Just how she had managed to meet him was beyond Walter, but he supposed that women were devious and more capable of deceit and cunning than most men believed. He leaned for-

ward, resting his elbows on either side of his trencher. Soon, as soon as he had the opportunity, he
would bring de Fortenberry here to Wolffeton. He
wondered how the proud Kassia would react when
she saw her lover. He frowned a moment, thinking
of the men who had professed to believe her unlikely tale. No, he was certain she had lied. He only
wondered why Lord Graelam seemed so gentle with
her. Had she been his wife, he would have beaten
her to death.

He wondered if he should simply tell Graelam the
identity of the man. Graelam's rage would likely lead
him against de Fortenberry. Sir Walter downed his
goblet of ale and continued his thinking.

"Do you wish to play a game of chess with me?"
Graelam asked Kassia.

"I think so," she said, fiddling with a piece of
bread.

"You aren't certain? As I recall, you have beaten
me more times than not."

She remembered wanting to kick him, and said
now, "Aye, I should enjoy it, my lord."

When they sat across from each other in their bedchamber, the chess table between them, Graelam
leaned back in his chair, watching Kassia concentrate
on the position of her pieces. Very slowly he
stretched out his legs, allowing his thigh to brush
against her. She jumped, her eyes flying to his face.

"See to your bishop, Kassia," he said, ignoring
her reaction.

"My bishop," she said.

"Aye, your queen's bishop." He smiled at her,
stroked his chin, and his eyes gleamed. "Why do we
not make the game more interesting?"

"How?"

"We have yet to trade even a pawn. Let us say that every piece you lose to me, you will kiss me."

Kassia became very still. "And what would happen, my lord, were you to lose a piece to me?"

"Ah, in that case, I suppose I shall just have to kiss you."

• "Do you really wish to?"

"Wish to what? Kiss you?"

She nodded, still not looking at him.

"Let us just say that you will suffer my kisses as I will yours. Agreed?"

"I—Very well."

On Graelam's next move, he took her king's knight. He sat back and waited. "Well, wife?"

"That was not a wise move, my lord," she said. "You will lose both a bishop and a pawn."

"I will suffer the consequences," he said, and patted his thigh. "Come and pay your forfeit, Kassia."

What disturbed Kassia as she slowly rose from her chair was that she wanted to kiss him. She stood beside him a moment, then allowed him to draw her onto his lap. She closed her eyes and pursed her lips. She felt his large hands holding her loosely about her waist. Slowly she leaned forward and pecked him on his mouth.

"That, Kassia, is hardly a kiss. Try again."

She ran her tongue over her lower lip. "I believe this game could last a very long time."

"Aye."

She looked into his eyes, very aware of him, and wanted to ask him why he was being so kind to her. Was it possible that he finally believed that she hadn't stolen the necklace, that she hadn't tried to escape him? She leaned against him. He allowed her the kiss, leaving his hands about her waist, not forcing her at all. He felt her small breasts pressing against his chest, and wondered as her tongue touched his lips if she could feel his sex hard beneath her hips.

She was breathing fast when she broke off her kiss. He made no move to continue it, merely smiled at her. "I believe you're learning," he said.

She leaned toward him again, her eyes on his mouth. He quickly lifted her off his lap. "Onward, Kassia. I believe it is your move."

Kassia shook her head as she sat again in her chair, and tried to force her attention back to the chessboard.

Her brain cleared, and she smiled, the dimples in her cheeks deepening. "It's now your move, my lord."

"Perhaps not such a long game," Graelam said. She had not taken his bishop, merely moved her king pawn forward another square.

Without a thought, he took her pawn, laying himself open to at least a check. He said nothing, merely patted his thighs again.

When Kassia leaned away from him this time, she wondered if he could hear her heart pounding. She squirmed a bit on his thighs, and felt his muscles tighten beneath her. She hung her head. "I—I don't know what's wrong with me."

"We will see," Graelam said, and again lifted her of his lap.

She was forced at last to take one of his pieces. She raised her head. "I don't believe I can hold you in my lap, my lord."

She looked so very worried that he was hard pressed not to laugh. "Then you must come here, I suppose."

When she was settled again on his thighs, he said, "Remember, wife, this is my kiss. You are not to caress me or move against me."

"But I didn't." She sucked in her breath when his mouth closed over hers. She felt his hand on the back of her head, tangling in her hair, bringing her closer. "Just relax," he said in her mouth. "You have nothing to do but close your eyes and let me kiss you."

He didn't press her, merely deepened the pressure slowly, as he felt her begin to respond to him. To his delight, when he gently cupped her breasts in his hands, she moaned and arched her back. He released her immediately.

Never, he thought, somewhat dazed himself, had he seen such a look of disappointment on a woman's face. Woman. Aye, he thought, tonight he would make her a woman. As he watched her move back to her chair, he wondered if she wouldn't attack him before the game was through.

He continued to study her as she regained her wits and gazed at the board. He remembered, with some pain, how she had been so open and trusting of him before he had forced her. Would she admit the truth to him once he regained her trust? He wanted her to beg him to take her. His jaw tightened, and the next kiss he gave her was quick and passionless.

After some fifteen more minutes, Kassia had lost all but her king and two pawns.

"An exciting game," Graelam said. "I'm tired." He rose and stretched. "I wish to go to bed." He saw her look warily at him, but ignored it. "Unless you wish for another game?"

"Nay," she said, plucking nervously at the folds of her gown.

"One final kiss for the winner. Come here, Kassia."

She walked slowly toward him, her eyes never leaving his face. He gathered her to him, leaned down, and lightly touched her mouth. She parted her lips without any instruction from him, and despite his intentions, his hands cupped her buttocks. He drew her up until her belly was pressed against him. She wrapped her arms about his neck, unthinking now, only feeling. And wanting to feel more, much more. "Please," she said.

"Please what?" He molded her more tightly against him, his fingers caressing her.

"I don't know," she said, her voice nearly a wail.

"And if I give you what you want, will you finally admit the truth to me?"

She stared up at him blankly; then her face flooded with color, and her arms fell away from him.

If he could have kicked himself, he would have. She was stiff and cold and withdrawn.

"Come to bed," he said, and turned away from her.

He lay on his back, staring up into the darkness. He heard her sobbing in harsh little gasps, and imagined that she had stuffed her fist into her mouth. He listened until he could bear it no longer.

"Kassia," he said. "Come here. I promise I won't hurt you."

He waited until she rolled toward him, drew her into his arms, and felt the wet of her tears against his chest.

Her sobs eased as he stroked her back.

"I will say nothing more about it," he said finally.

But you will never believe me.

"I want to come inside you, Kassia. I don't think I can hold back another night."

He felt her quiver at his words, but he didn't know whether it was in fear or in anticipated pleasure. He had spoken the truth. He hurt. He quickly pulled off her bedrobe, brought her naked body against him.

"You are so small, so delicate," he said against her temple as his hands stroked over her breasts and belly. "Part your legs, Kassia."

She felt his finger ease inside her and her muscles clenched. "You're ready for me," he said.

He wanted to caress her, kiss her until she was wild, but he was wound tight as a bowstring. When she moved against him, he thought he would lose control. "I can't wait," he said, and moved between her legs. Slowly he eased inside her, felt her stretch for him, felt himself slide into her. He moaned at the unbelievable sensation, and thrust his full length into her. He leaned over her, cupping her face in his hands. He wished he could see her eyes. "Am I hurting you?" he asked into her mouth.

She shook her head. "It feels odd." Actually, she thought, as he moved slowly over her, if coupling were always this way, it was quite bearable. The thought was surprising, but more surprising was the slow ache that was building low in her belly, separate from him, yet also a part of him.

"Graelam, I—" He thrust his tongue into her mouth, just as his sex was pushing deep into her belly. The heat built deep inside her, and she moved, arching her back upward, her arms tight around his waist.

"Kassia, don't!" But it was too late. He could no longer hold back. For an instant, as she felt him convulse, she felt a pounding need to respond. But as he quieted over her, the need slowly faded, leaving her vaguely disappointed, not knowing what it was that she sought.

She stroked her hands over his back, kneading the hard muscles, enjoying the feel of his man's body. His breathing slowed, his body relaxed over her. His weight was great, but she didn't mind. No, she thought, coupling was not too bad. It didn't hurt.

Graelam raised himself on his elbows and looked down at her shadowed face. He knew he had moved too quickly, that she had not gained a woman's release. He cursed at his loss of control.

"I'm sorry," she said. "I don't know what to do."

"Hush," he said, "it was I who raced ahead like a randy boy."

She shook her head against his shoulder.

"You're soft and pleasing, Kassia, and I wanted you very much. Soon, I promise you, you will want me equally."

He could picture the bewildered question in her eyes at his words. He kissed her, and rolled onto his side, bringing her with him.

She fell asleep with the very strange feeling of his sex resting inside her.

Kassia awoke at dawn, her eyes drawn to the bright slivers of pinkish light coming through the shutters. She stirred slightly, and quieted quickly, aware that she was half-lying on Graelam, his thigh between her legs, her cheek pillowed against the mat of hair on his chest. She blinked away the remnants of sleep, allowing a procession of images from the night before to flow slowly through her mind. With the intimate images came a flood of feelings. She still did not move. She felt the thick muscles in his thigh pressing up against her and the feelings were no longer memories. She felt a stirring deep within her, awakening her body as surely as she had awakened with the dawn, making her move slowly and quietly against him. She slid the palm of her hand over his chest, and felt the slow, regular pounding of his heart. She breathed deeply, relieved that he slept. She should move away from him, but her body had no intention of obeying her. Her hand slipped down to his flat, hard belly. She stroked the ridges of smooth muscle, and moved still lower. Feeling the edge of the scar at his groin, she followed its roughness over his thigh. When her arm brushed against his sex, lying soft against him, a warmth spurted through her, making her move once more against his thigh. She squeezed her eyes shut at the unbelievable sensations it brought. Her breathing quickened, and her body continued its moving, knowing instinctively what to do.

She realized that she wanted to touch him, to feel the texture of his flesh, to try to understand why his body, with no effort from him, was making her feel the way she was. Slowly, tentatively, her heart pounding too loud in the silence of the chamber, her fingers closed around him.

She didn't realize she was moving rhythmically against his thigh, deepening the pressure, but Graelam did. He didn't move. When her fingers closed over him he thought he would lose control, but he held himself still. He lifted his thigh very slowly, and the pressing, upward motion made her cry out. Never had she taken the initiative, and he smiled with pleasure, then grimaced in the next moment, not certain how long he could remain quiet under her touch.

In a moment her hand could no longer close over him. Her head flew up to his face, and she saw him looking at her.

"You're awake," she said.

"Aye," he said, and forced himself to be still.

"I—Your leg, it makes me feel so—"

He moved his thigh against her, feeling the growing moistness, and reveling in it. "You feel so what?"

She ducked her head against his chest. "I don't think I can stop moving against you."

Her fingers fell away from his sex, and he wanted to weep. He thought vaguely that men were utterly physical, with no modesty, born, it seemed, with the need to have a woman stroke them and caress them. Whilst women— The thought left him when Kassia kneaded his belly.

He lifted her onto her back. Her eyes flew to his face, but he only kissed her mouth, teasing her with his tongue, but not forcing himself upon her. His hand cupped her breast, his thumb stroking over her nipple, and still she stared up at him, unmoving. He smiled down at her, knowing well what she needed. His fingers found her, and he sucked in his breath at the warmth and wetness of her. His stroking was rhythmic, his fingers pressing deeply, then lightly teasing her, making her wail in frustration.

"Graelam," she said, clutching his shoulders.

"Aye?" he said, watching her face.

"I can't bear it." Her hips lurched up against his fingers, and he gave her what she wanted.

He had pleasured women many times in this fashion, but never had he felt so involved, as if all he felt depended upon her feelings.

"Kassia," he said, and the sound of her name on his lips sent her over the edge. She felt things she never imagined existed. She bucked and twisted against him.

He watched every expression on her face, from the utter surprise to the dazed sheen when her woman's pleasure took her, making her unaware of him, unaware of everything except the incredible pleasure coming from his fingers. At the height of her release, she screamed his name, and he felt the pleasure of it to his bones.

For a moment, she seemed senseless. He kissed her, feeding on her soft mouth, enjoying her small gasps of breath. To his immense delight, he felt her quiver again when he cupped his hand over her. She seemed hardly aware that she was arching her back upward, moving against him. He brought her to pleasure again, and this time she clutched him to her, sobbing into his shoulder.

She was filled with passion, utterly responsive to him. He wondered if he could bring her to pleasure yet again, but decided against it this time. She was unused to this. Soon, he thought, gathering her against him and stroking her back, soon he would see.

He realized that he had not thought of his own need even once. He was becoming a half-wit, yet he was smiling when he kissed her ear and pressed her against the length of his body. He did not fall asleep again, but Kassia did, a deep, sated sleep.

—Whilst women, his thinking of many moments before continued, women were more complex. At least Kassia was. He realized that she had to trust him completely before she could open to him. But what man cared about a woman's trust? What man cared if a woman enjoyed coupling? He did, unfortunately, and he knew well that he could not retreat from her now.

24

Graelam smiled at the sound of Kassia's bright laugh. No longer was she the pale, silent little ghost of the week before. She was full of energy, full of laughter, and full of desire for him. He had never before wanted to be with a woman, other than to couple with her, but everything seemed different now. He enjoyed her teasing, enjoyed watching her care for Wolffeton and all its people, enjoyed the excited look in her eyes whenever she looked at him. Invariably when that happened, she blushed, and he would smile wickedly and whisper intimate words to her, causing her to blush even more.

He learned that she could not respond to him in bed if something was on her mind, a problem with a servant perhaps, or a new project taking shape in her thoughts. Thus it was that he was beginning to learn how she thought, how she felt about her thoughts, and how she came to decisions about problems within the keep. He recalled the first time he had wanted nothing more than to fling her onto the bed and love her until she was mad for him. She hadn't refused him, but he saw a frown on her forehead as he was kissing her. At first he was insulted and infuriated with her, and had said, "What is wrong with you, Kassia? Where is your mind?"

She cocked her head at him. "It is Bernard," she said. "I don't know what to do about him, and I must do something."

"Bernard," he said, finally picturing the quiet, shaggy-looking boy who had come to the castle to tend the dogs after ten years with his father's sheep.

She nibbled thoughtfully on her lower lip, then burst into a wide smile. "Why did I not ask you immediately? You will know what to do."

Thus it was that they discussed the problem of Bernard and his odd and painful reaction to dog lice until they found a solution that pleased them both. Her response to him afterward was something he could not have imagined.

He gave her free access to all the material in his trunk, telling her to do with it as she wished. But of course she did not. She always asked him, and he knew it would take a long time for her to forget his initial reaction when she had taken material to make him a tunic.

He realized also that he liked his wife. It was a strange thing and he didn't like to think about it. A wife saw to her husband's comfort, both in his keep and his body, most men of his acquaintance believed and parroted religiously. He turned again, hearing her laughter, and realized that it was coming from the practice field. Whatever would Kassia be doing among his men? He strode to the wide field and drew to an abrupt halt. There she sat, wearing a white wool cloth over her hair and a faded green wool gown, his men gathered around her. If he had not recognized her laugh, he would have thought her a serving wench.

"Nay, Bran," he heard her say, the laughter still in her voice, "the remaining pie is for my lord. You have already had your share."

He saw that she was holding a tray and his men were either eating or wiping their mouths.

Her lord. Any thought of chastising her for interrupting his men disappeared from his mind. When she saw him she skipped toward him, startled and pleased to see him.

"I had thought you buried with Blount," she said. "Here, my lord. It is an apple tart, freshly baked."

He accepted the pastry from her, realizing belatedly that his expression was probably just as besotted as the rest of his men's.

He wiped his mouth and smiled down at her. "It was delicious, Kassia. But I don't believe that these shiftless louts deserve your consideration."

He heard loud guffaws from behind him. Kassia was laughing with the rest of them. Without really wishing to, he lightly touched his fingers to her smooth cheek. "Go now, little one," he said, "else I might be tempted to toss you over my shoulder and show you how delicious you are."

She flushed, disclaimed, smiled wickedly at him, and sped from the practice field. Sometime later, Rolfe said to him, "You are a lucky man, my lord. Aye, very lucky."

"Aye," Graelam said, wiping the sweat from his brow and gazing toward the fortified eastern wall. "Wolffeton is a castle to be proud of. The jakes no longer stink, and Bernard does much better in the stables with the horses." He stretched, eyeing his master-at-arms from the corner of his eye. Rolfe could not recognize a jest if it kicked him in his lean butt.

Rolfe cleared his throat. "Aye," he said, "that is true, my lord, but I was speaking of your lady wife." He drew himself up, frowning at the slight smile on his master's lips. "She brings joy to us, my lord. It pleases me—all the men—to see her smile again."

She didn't betray you. He immediately quashed the thought. He had decided many days before that he had been as much to blame as she for her leaving him. And, he had thought over and over, she had returned to him. *But why wouldn't she tell him the truth?*

He shook his head, realizing vaguely that it brought him a measure of pain to think about it. He said aloud, "There is enough pain in life without adding to it."

Rolfe pulled on his ear. "She is a dear child," he said at last.

"Nay, my old friend. She is not a child," Grae-lam said.

Late that night as he caressed her belly, feeling her response to him, he said quietly, "You are no longer a child, Kassia."

Her answer was a cry that made him harder than the bricks in the ramparts. He wanted to bury himself within her. He pushed her to the edge of her climax, then came into her. Her release was immediate and rending. She cried out into his mouth, her back arched up against him, so beyond herself in that long moment that she could think of nothing, only feel. He was held spellbound in her pleasure before his own need consumed him. He moved slightly, afraid that his weight was too much for her.

He felt her arms clutching around his back. "Nay," she said, "do not leave me."

He slipped his arms around her and rolled onto his back, bringing her on top of him. She laughed, surprised, for he was still deep inside her. "You are now to be ridden, my lord?"

"Aye," he said, cupping her face in his hands and bringing her down to him, "in a moment, Kassia. In a moment."

"I feel so—" She paused, her eyes caressing his face, as her lips curved into a smile. "Not so full as I did."

"Mouthy wench." He stroked his hands over her back. Gently he eased her off him and laid her on her back. He leaned over her, balanced on his elbow.

Kassia brought her hand up to cover herself.

"What is this?" he asked, surprised. He pushed her hand away. "You are filling out nicely, Kassia."

His callused fingers moved lightly over her breast. "Very nicely," he said, and leaned down to caress her with his mouth.

"Do you really think so?"

He raised his head.

She flushed. "I mean—I was so skinny."

He looked down the length of her, his eyes pausing a moment on the soft triangle of curls between her thighs, still damp. "You are," he said, his voice rough and deep, "as I want you to be."

"As are you, my lord," she said. "As you are."

Dammit, he did not want to leave her. He eyed the messenger from Crandall, knowing he had no choice but to return and stem the rebellion there. I'll take her with me, he thought, only to reject his decision almost immediately. He wanted her kept safe, above all. Damn Raymond de Cercy, nephew of the former castellan. He had not been overly impressed with the man, yet more fool he, he had made him governor of the small keep on the southern edge of Wolffeton. What had the fool done to bring the peasants to revolt so quickly?

He dismissed the tired messenger and strode to their bedchamber. He found her there, seated by the window, sewing. He remembered suddenly the last time he had left her, and flinched at the memory. He had been back less than two days before he had hurt her.

"I must leave," he said without preamble.

She jabbed her finger with the needle, and cried out.

"I'm clumsy," she said, watching a drop of blood well up.

He dropped to his knees beside her chair and took the finger in his hand. Gently he lifted the finger to his mouth and licked away the blood.

"Where do you go, my lord?" she asked, breathless, instantly wanting him.

He lightly kissed the finger and rose. "To Crandall. De Cercy's messenger tells of a revolt amongst the peasants."

"Will there be danger?"

"Perhaps, but not likely," he said, shrugging his shoulders indifferently.

Kassia was not fooled. She saw the gleam of anticipation in his dark eyes. "How long will you be away?"

"A week, perhaps longer. If de Cercy is the fool I begin to believe him to be, I will have to find another man to be castellan of Crandall."

"May I come with you, Graelam?" She saw that he would tell her no, and immediately said, "I can care for you, you will see. I don't tire easily, and I will not bother you. I can cook your—"

He leaned down and lifted her out of her chair. "Hush, Kassia," he said, and drew her against his chest. "I will take no chance with your safety." She clutched at him, as if she wanted to become part of him, and he felt a wave of protectiveness so strong he shook with it. He grasped her arms and pushed her away.

He saw the bright glimmer of tears in her eyes. "Do not," he said, trying to sound stern, but failing.

"I will miss you," she said.

He cupped her chin with his hand. "Will you really?"

Kassia rubbed her cheek against his palm, and he felt the wet of her tears on his flesh.

"I will not leave until the morrow," he said, and pulled her against him.

"You look like a lost lamb," Etta said. "This is no way to behave, my baby. What would your lord say if he saw you wandering about pale and silent?"

"It has been four days," Kassia wailed. "And I have heard nothing. Nothing. He promised to send me word."

"So," Etta said, her rheumy eyes narrowing on her mistress's face, "it has finally happened."

Kassia abruptly stopped her pacing and whirled around to face her old nurse. "What has happened?"

"You love your husband," Etta said.

"Nay. That is, perhaps it is just that—"

"You love your husband to distraction," Etta said again.

To Etta's surprise, Kassia looked at her blankly, turned on her heel, and walked quickly from the chamber. She went to the stable and asked Bernard to saddle Bluebell for her. Sir Walter stood in the inner bailey when she emerged from the stable leading her mare.

"Sir Walter," she said, hating even to say his name.

"You wish to ride, my lady?"

"As you see."

"Lord Graelam bade me never to leave your side if you rode out of the keep."

She wondered why Graelam had left Sir Walter at Wolffeton whilst he took Rolfe with him to Crandall. Was it because he did not wish the man to fight beside him? She wanted very much to be alone, but it appeared she had no choice but to suffer Sir Walter's company. She nodded. "Very well," she said.

She pushed Bluebell into a gallop, leaving Sir Walter and his three men behind her. At the protected cove, she dismounted and stared out over the churning water. A summer storm was building to the north. It would strike tonight, when she would be alone in the great bed. She shivered.

"If you are cold, my lady, perhaps we should return to Wolffeton."

She jumped, for she hadn't heard Sir Walter approach. She shook her head. "Nay, I wish to walk about for a while."

"If you wish," he said, and offered her his arm.

She ignored him and walked to the edge of the cliff.

"Is it your lord you miss, my lady?"

At his snide tone, she stiffened. Her hand itched

to strike him, but she said only, "My feelings are none of your business, Sir Walter."

"Perhaps not, my lady, but I heard about your misadventure. Perhaps you did not plan your escape well enough."

"I wish to return to Wolffeton," Kassia said, and walked quickly away from him.

Sir Walter wanted to shake her and wring her proud neck. Little bitch, treating him as if he were vermin, of no worth at all. He watched one of the men help her into her saddle. Soon, my lady, he thought, very soon now.

Kassia felt a brief surge of excitement as she stood at her post in the crenellated embrasure in the eastern outer wall, watching the riders come nearer. Then she recognized Sir Walter riding at their head. He had left the day before, claiming that there had been an attack on a demesne farm. She had not believed him, and seeing him now, she wondered where he had gone and what he had done.

One man was huddled over his saddle as if he were hurt, and three men were obviously dead, slung over their horses' backs like bags of wheat. As they drew nearer, she could see that the hurt man was bound with heavy rope. Speeding down the narrow stairs, she made her way into the inner bailey. As Sir Walter shouted to the porter, she prepared to step forward, but something she could not explain stopped her. She waited in the shadows of the cooking shed and watched the men enter the inner bailey. The smile on Sir Walter's face chilled her.

He pulled the bound man off his horse. The man

staggered, then stood straight. "Behold," Sir Walter called out to the gathering men. "We have caught a prize." He pulled the hood back from the man's head. "Dienwald de Fortenberry, knave, murderer, and thief."

Kassia went cold. It was Edmund. She remembered Sir Walter's venomous words about de Fortenberry, remembered clearly Graelam telling him that de Fortenberry had made no forays onto Wolffeton land, and was thus of no interest to him. Somehow Sir Walter had discovered that Dienwald de Fortenberry was the man who had taken her. She saw Sir Walter draw back his fist and smash it into Dienwald's ribs. That decided her. She ran forward.

"Hold, Sir Walter."

Sir Walter spun around, as did the other men.

"My lady," he said, bowing to her deeply, the sarcasm in his voice clear for all to hear.

"Is it a knight's code to strike a bound man, Sir Walter?"

"It is a knight's code to crush vermin, my lady."

She drew herself up to her full height. "I believe you called this man Dienwald de Fortenberry. I remember my lord telling you that he was no threat to Wolffeton. Why have you brought him here, Sir Walter?"

He could denounce her in front of everyone. But no, the proud little bitch was too popular among the men and the servants, and he couldn't be certain of their backing. Oh no, he would wait for Graelam to return. Graelam would be enraged; he would kill the miserable de Fortenberry for him, and, Sir Walter thought, he would be thankful to him for bringing the whoreson to him. Land, he thought, his chest expanding in anticipation; Graelam would doubtless award him land and his own keep.

"I have brought him here, my lady," he said, quite calmly now, "to be held for Lord Graelam's return."

Kassia felt a surge of relief. Dienwald de Fortenberry would tell Graelam that it was Blanche who had hired him. At last he would know the truth. At last he would believe her.

She turned to Dienwald de Fortenberry, who was struggling to regain his breath. She wanted to go to him, to help him, but she knew she would be a fool to do so.

Dienwald knew that several of his ribs were broken. He met Kassia's eyes for a moment before a pain ripped through him and he fell to the cobblestones.

Kassia listened as Sir Walter ordered the men to carry de Fortenberry to the dungeon.

"Sir Walter," she said in a loud, calm voice, "I trust that Dienwald de Fortenberry will be alive when my lord returns."

"Slut," Sir Walter said between his teeth. Did she believe she had that much power over Graelam? Tales of Graelam de Moreton's prowess were legendary. He could not imagine such a warrior allowing his wife to escape unscathed when he was confronted not only with her lover but also with the man she had hired to help her escape him.

Kassia went directly to her bedchamber, closed the door, and sat in her chair to think.

At the evening meal, she appeared serene and concerned only with the taste of the roast pork and the fresh cabbage. She chatted with Blount and Father Tobias, aware that many eyes were watching her closely. She could feel the dislike rolling off Sir Walter, but she could also sense his uncertainty at her calm behavior. You will pay for this, she wanted to yell. It was odd, she thought as she replied to a question from one of the serving wenches, but she should be thanking him. Were it not for his hatred and his bitterness, she would never have known that Edmund was Dienwald de Fortenberry.

She returned to her bedchamber to wait. It was near to midnight when Etta slipped into the chamber, nodding silently.

"There was but one guard?"

"Aye, my baby, and soon he will be fast asleep. There is no need for any guards down there," she continued, shivering. "The saints could not escape from that place."

"Sir Walter is taking no chances," Kassia said. "How very surprised that knave will be when Dienwald tells my lord the truth of the matter."

Etta gripped Kassia's arm. "Must you go to him, my baby? Can you not wait for Lord Graelam's return?"

"Dienwald de Fortenberry is many things, Etta, I know that, but he was kind to me. Had Blanche paid another man to take me, I would likely have been raped and killed. If he dies from his wounds, I will gain nothing. And I must speak to him. I must be certain that he will speak the truth to Graelam."

Etta knew she could not sway her mistress. "All the men are asleep. I heard no one."

"Excellent," Kassia said. "I don't want you to wait for me, Etta. Go to bed now."

She waited until her old nurse had left, then drew on her cloak. Saying a silent prayer, she slipped from her bedchamber and made her way out of the Great

Hall. The dungeon was in the base of the southern tower.

Soundlessly she moved beyond the thick oak door, freezing when she saw the guard. But he was fast asleep, his head cradled on his arms. Carefully she eased the huge iron keys from his tunic and dropped them into the pocket of her cloak. Then, clutching the lone candle, she walked down the deeply worn stone steps to the lower level. The air became more fetid and foul, and she could hear the rats scurrying from her path. It smelled of human misery, though she knew that no prisoner had been held here for many years. Her hand shook as she fitted one of the keys into the rusting lock. It grated so loudly that she expected to see all of Sir Walter's men bursting in upon her.

But only rats were about.

The door swung open and she stepped into the cell, holding the candle high. She felt nausea at the stench. The stone walls were green and slimy with dampness, the earth floor was strewn with ancient straw reeking of human excrement. She raised the candle higher, gasping when she saw Dienwald de Fortenberry. His arms were pulled away from his body, his wrists manacled to the walls.

"Dienwald," she said.

Slowly he raised his head. For a long moment he stared at her blankly. Then a slow smile twisted his mouth into a painful grimace.

"Little chick," he said. "Why did you send me a message begging that I help you?"

25

Kassia stared at him. "I do not know about any message," she said.

A spasm of pain wiped his mind of words and it was some moments before he said, "No, I do not suppose that you do. I was a fool, and now I will pay for it."

"No, you won't." She rushed to his side and quickly unlocked the heavy rusted manacles from his wrists. He managed to steady himself and sank down onto the straw.

"It was Sir Walter," she said, dropping to her knees beside him. "He hates you, but I had no idea that it was you he hated."

He raised his head and smiled at her. "Only I would know what you mean, little chick."

"When my lord returns to Wolffeton, all will be well, I promise you, Edmund—Dienwald." She touched her hand to his shoulder. "You will tell him it was Blanche who hired you, will you not?"

"You have had a difficult time making your husband believe you?"

"Very few people here believe that I am innocent, but now, Dienwald, they will know the truth."

"Ah, Kassia, you are so innocent and trusting."

"No," she said firmly, "no longer. I will see that my lord punishes Sir Walter for what he did to you. Where are you hurt?"

"Several ribs are broken. Sir Walter is a vicious man. I begin to see now why he did not simply kill me as he did my men."

"I don't understand."

He lifted his hand and touched his fingers to her soft hair. "No, likely you would not understand. I will explain it to you. Sir Walter wants land. What landless knight does not? And it is true that my father killed his and took his birthright, though from what I remember, his action was justified. But had Sir Walter killed me there would have been no reward for him, no gain at all if, that is, he kept his neck in place. Your husband, little chick, is a very powerful man with very powerful friends. Were he to kill me, there would be no retribution, and Sir Walter would most likely gain from his trickery."

Kassia shook her head. "Graelam would not kill you."

Dienwald gave her a tender look that held pity. Slowly he drew her forward, and before Kassia knew what he was about, he had fastened one of the heavy manacles about her wrist.

"Little chick," he said, "I beg you will forgive me, but I do not wish to die. If I stay, your husband will kill me without a second thought. Even if I were able to fight him with all my strength, he would still likely put an end to me."

"He has no reason to kill you. Please, Dienwald, you must not leave me."

"Kassia, listen to me, for I must escape, and very soon. Your husband believes that you paid me to help you escape him. If I were to tell him it was Blanche, he would still kill me, for I accepted his barbaric necklace as payment to rid Wolffeton and Blanche of your presence." He gave a pained laugh. "Were I your husband, I would kill me. I know that when you are found here, in my cell, you will be blamed for releasing me. I'm sorry for it, but your husband will not kill you. Were there another way, I would not leave you. But there is no choice for me. Forgive me, Kassia."

She looked at the harsh manacle about her wrist. "I forgive you," she said. "But you have sentenced me to hell."

He grasped her chin in his palm and lightly kissed her. "I can take you with me."

He saw the helpless pain in her eyes, and drew back. "Ah, so that is the way it is." He rose and stood over her a moment. "Graelam de Moreton is a harsh and ruthless warrior. He can have no understanding of something as delicate and honest as you. Please, Kassia, do not scream until I am gone."

"It would do no good," she said. "My old nurse drugged the only guard. Evidently Sir Walter believed no more guards were necessary."

"I will leave you the candle," he said. "Good-bye." She watched him slip through the cell door and pull it closed behind him. She leaned back against the damp wall as the rats moved closer to her, their small eyes orange in the wavering candlelight. When the candle sputtered out and the cell was plunged into blackness, she closed her eyes and drew her legs up to her chest.

She heard heavy boots approaching, and then the cell door was shoved violently open. A rushlight torch filled the darkness with blinding light. Kassia had prayed that Etta would come for her, but her prayer was not answered. For a moment she could only make out the outline of a man. Sir Walter, she thought. What would he do to her?

"Kassia."

She froze and pressed herself closer to the slimy wall. "What are you doing here?" she asked.

Graelam gave a harsh laugh. "No, I do not suppose you expected me until tomorrow night. I missed you and pushed my men to return." He laughed again, hard and cruel. He handed the torch to a man behind him and strode toward her. She cowered away from him. He dropped to his knees and unlocked the manacle.

"Did your lover really need to chain you? Could not even he trust you?"

Kassia rubbed her bruised wrist, concentrating on the pain to block the terrible words from her mind.

"Look at me, damn you." Graelam grasped her shoulders and shook her.

"I'm looking now," she said, staring directly into his furious eyes.

"Dienwald de Fortenberry. Did he appreciate your calling him Edmund, my lady? How very surprised you must have been to see him. Sir Walter is something of a fool, unfortunately. He never dreamed that my soft fragile lady would be so daring as to release her lover. He is now distraught."

"Dienwald de Fortenberry is not my lover," she said quietly, hopelessly. "He was never my lover."

His fingers tightened about her shoulders and he felt her small bones twisting beneath his strength. Damn him for a fool. He had ridden back to Wolf-feton like a maniac, his only thought of Kassia and holding her, seeing her, listening to her laugh, feeling her soft body beneath him, opening to him. He released her abruptly and stood.

"Come," he said. "I don't wish you to die from a fever."

She staggered to her feet and pulled her cloak more closely about her. She saw Sir Walter standing in the narrow doorway, a look of hatred contorting his features. She said in a loud, clear voice, "Did Sir Walter tell you how he managed to capture Dien-wald de Fortenberry? Did he tell you how he beat him viciously whilst he was bound and could not defend himself?"

Graelam turned slowly to face his knight.

"Did he tell you that he trusted you to kill de Fortenberry and then reward him for bringing him to you?"

Graelam said in a cold voice, "I will speak to Sir Walter, wife. Now, my lady, you will come with me."

He drew away from her a moment and spoke in a quiet voice to Sir Walter. The man nodded and withdrew. He hated her because she was a woman and thus not to be believed or trusted. She said aloud, "I did not betray you, Graelam. I have never betrayed you."

She saw the fury building in his dark eyes. She threw back her head, raising her chin. "Will you kill me now? Just as you would have killed Dienwald?"

He looked at that proud chin of hers and turned quickly away, his hands clenched at his sides. He did not want to strike her, for if he did, it would likely kill her.

"That is why he escaped, Graelam. It is true that I released his chains, but my thought was only to spare him more pain. I trusted him to tell you the truth, that it was Blanche who had paid him the necklace to be rid of me, but he said you would kill him regardless of what he told you. He did not wish to die."

"So he left you here, chained, to face me. An honorable man."

"Was he right? Would you have killed him?"

"Come, Kassia," he said, striding to the cell door. She followed him silently, feeling blessedly numb. She did not wonder about the future; it could be naught but the cold misery of the present.

There was utter silence as she walked beside her husband through the great hall. She felt the servants' eyes upon her. She imagined that she could even feel their fear for her. But she felt no fear. She felt nothing. Everything was over now.

Graelam paused a moment and gave orders for hot water to be brought to their bedchamber. She saw the lines of fatigue in his face for the first time, and the filth of his chain mail and tunic. She wanted to ask him if he was all right, then almost laughed aloud at the wifely spurt of concern she felt for him.

When they reached their bedchamber, Graelam ignored her. Evian helped him strip off his armor. After he dismissed the boy, he peeled off the rest of his clothes and sank down naked into his high-backed chair. Still he said nothing.

Two serving wenches came into the room and poured hot water into the wooden tub. Graelam rose and walked to the tub even as they filled it, oblivious of his nakedness. He dismissed them with a curt nod and climbed into the tub.

He felt the hot water seep into his muscles, easing his soreness and bone-weariness. He wondered vaguely whether Sir Walter would have left her locked in de Fortenberry's cell if Graelam had not returned until the following night. No, the knight would not have dared. Graelam eased his body deeper into the water. Thoughts of his joy at seeing Kassia mingled with knowledge of her deception, and he felt suddenly old and very tired. His father was right. Drake, his armorer, was right. He had been a fool to have begun to doubt his sire's wisdom. Women were good for breeding, and only if a husband kept his wife away from other men to ensure whose seed filled her belly. Had de Fortenberry taken her before he had escaped? He sat up in the tub and turned his head to see her sitting quietly, as still as a statue, in a chair. "Kassia," he said, "take off your clothes. I wish to see if de Fortenberry's seed is in your body."

She could only stare at him, paling, as his words gained meaning in her mind.

"Damn you, do as I say."

"Graelam," she said, clutching the arms of the chair until her knuckles showed white, "please, you must believe me. Dienwald de Fortenberry was not my lover."

"If you do not obey me, I will rip off your clothes."

"Why won't you believe me?"

His jaw clenched. He quickly washed his hair and

his body and just as quickly rose from the tub and
dried himself. From the corner of his eye he saw her
rise from the chair and run toward the chamber door.
He caught her as her hand touched the brass handle.

"Please," she panted, "for once, please believe
me."

"Do you want me to rip your clothes off?"

She stared up at him, knew he was implacable. She
would not let him cow her again. Slowly she shook
her head. "You will not humiliate me," she said. "My
only crime was feeling concern for a man who was
kind to me." Her chin went up. "I am glad he was
wise enough to escape. I am glad he did not stay so
you could kill him."

He drew back his hand, but then got a grip on
himself and slowly lowered it to his side. Very slowly
he turned away from her. He said over his shoulder,
"If you leave this room, you will wish you had not."

He tossed on his bedrobe, belted it, and returned
to her. "Take off your clothes."

"No."

He shrugged, and very deliberately tore away her
olive-green wool gown. She tried to struggle against
him, but it was useless and she knew it. She would
only hurt herself. When she was naked and
trembling, he stepped back, a cruel light in his dark
eyes, and thoughtfully began stroking his chin. "Aye,
you have become quite the woman, have you not,
Kassia? Such lovely breasts you have now. And that
soft little belly of yours."

She did not try to cover herself. Instead, she clapped
her hands over her ears to block out his words.

He laughed, picked her up in his arms, and carried
her to the bed. He tossed her down upon her back.

"Hold still," he said. There could be no greater humiliation, she thought, as he pulled her legs apart and looked down at her. She flinched when he ran his hand over her.

"So," he said, straightening. "If a child does grow in your belly, it will be mine. At least this time."

Kassia rolled over onto her side and drew her legs up. Great sobs tore from her throat.

Graelam stared down at her, hating himself for the pain he was feeling at her suffering, hating himself for wanting to gather her into his arms and stroke her and soothe her and caress her.

"Get under the covers," he said. When she didn't move, he lifted her and placed her beneath them himself.

"There is no choice, my baby. You cannot remain here longer."

Kassia nodded, knowing Etta was right.

Still, she clutched Etta's arm before she stiffened her back and walked down into the Great Hall. She heard the clatter of horses' hooves from the inner bailey and wondered with a mixture of relief and pain if Graelam were leaving again. She stood quietly at the top of the steps and watched Sir Walter and three men preparing to ride out. Had Graelam dismissed the man from his service? She started forward, only to stop when Graelam, as if sensing her presence, turned to look at her. The bright morning sun gleamed down on his thick dark hair. For a brief moment she saw him as she had when he had held her so tightly against him, whispering love words whilst he gave her pleasure. Her hands clenched, remembering the feel of his flesh, his muscled body.

He strode toward her and she remained where she was, watching him in silence.

He said nothing, merely looked at her, his face expressionless. Finally he said, "Do you not wish to know where Sir Walter goes?"

"Aye," she said.

He remained silent.

"Have you dismissed him?"

"Nay, wife, I have made him the new castellan of Crandall. He goes to relieve Rolfe, who now holds the keep."

"You have rewarded him? After all that he did?"

"Tell me, Kassia," he said, striding up the steps toward her, "tell me once again why you had Dienwald de Fortenberry return you to Wolffeton. Tell me why you did not stay with him or have him take you back to your father. Tell me why you did not leave with him last night."

She closed her eyes against the anger in his eyes. "I never left you, Graelam. When he asked me if I wished him to take me to Brittany, I told him that I wanted to go home." Her voice was singsong, as if she was reciting a litany.

"And did he refuse to take you with him last night?

She shook her head.

"Ah, so he did want to take you with him when he escaped?"

She stared at him like a wounded animal who knows that the hunter waits to deliver the killing blow. She nodded. The blow came quickly.

"Why did you not go with him?"

"I told him that he was sentencing me to hell if he escaped."

"Why did you not go with him?" The repeated words, though softly spoken, made her shiver.

It did not occur to her to lie. She said quietly, "I couldn't go with him because you are my husband, and I love you."

Graelam sucked in his breath as if he had been struck in the belly. For an instant, something deep inside him seemed to expand, filling him with inexplicable joy. The feeling quickly shriveled and died. "That was quite good, my lady," he said. "So, your handsome lover did ask you to go with him. Did he suggest to you that you might tell me that lie to calm my anger?"

"No."

"Lies, quite good ones actually, flow so easily from your pretty mouth. Such a pity that you did not wed a man who is a gullible fool."

Up went her chin. "I did not marry any man. If you will recall, my lord, I had no choice in the matter. And it appears that my husband is a fool."

"Get out of my sight," he said in a deadly voice. "Go, before I thrash you."

She clutched her gown in her hands and fled back up the stairs.

Kassia did not see him until the early-evening meal. The tension among the men was palpable, as thick and tangible as the slabs of beef on the trays. Graelam said nothing to her, and she listened while he and his men discussed the situation at Crandall. There had been some fighting by the few soldiers loyal to the castellan, de Cercy, who held the keep.

She heard Ian, a young man-at-arms who worshiped Graelam, say reverently, "You dispatched that whoreson so quickly, my lord. He was no match for you."

Who, Kassia wondered. De Cercy?

"He had become lazy from greed," Graelam said.

She wanted to ask him what he expected Sir Walter to do, but she held her tongue. As the men recounted in great detail each bout with the enemy, Kassia lost what little appetite she had. She left the table very quietly while Graelam was held in close conversation with Blount.

The gown she was sewing awaited her, but she didn't touch it. Why should she? There would be no place she could wear such a beautiful garment. And it was beautiful, special. Blue satin, its sleeves long and closely fitted, its skirt flowing, fitted to her waist with a leather girdle threaded with gold and silver. She paced across the thick carpet, her thoughts black, numb.

"I thought I had made it clear to you, Kassia, that you were not to leave unless I gave you permission."

How could he walk so silently, and he was so large?

"Forgive me," she said. "You appeared very interested in your talk. I did not wish to disturb you."

Graelam said nothing. His eyes lit upon the luxurious blue satin material, and he walked to it and lifted it, stroking it in his hands. "You will look quite lovely in this. I told you, did I not, that the cloth came from Acre?" He continued to caress the material, looking thoughtful. Suddenly he tossed the material aside. "You will need some ornament to wear with it. I believe this will look quite dramatic." He pulled something from the inside of his tunic and tossed it to her.

She caught it, and stared down at the heavy golden necklace studded with gems of incredible beauty. "It is lovely," she began. She raised bewildered eyes to his set face. "Why do you give it to me, my lord?"

"Will you forever playact with me? I fancy you recognize the necklace. You should. It has caused you a great deal of difficulty."

She dropped the necklace as if it were a snake to bite her. "It is the necklace Blanche gave to de Fortenberry," she said dully, staring at the tangled heap of gold on the carpet at her feet. "Where did you get it?"

"A groom found it in de Fortenberry's cell, hidden in some straw. I imagine that it must have dropped from his clothing. I also imagine that he was bringing it back to you."

Kassia raised pain-filled eyes to his face. "Aye," she said. "He must have forgotten about it."

Graelam regarded her silently. He was a fool, he realized, to feel cold and sad at the sight of her pain. He said finally, "Have you bathed away the stench of the dungeons?"

She nodded.

"Get into bed. I have gone many days without a woman."

She did not argue with him, or attempt to plead with him. It would gain her naught. Slowly she removed her clothes, folding each item carefully. She slipped into bed, naked, and closed her eyes.

She felt his hands stroke over her. She thought he would simply force her quickly and be done with it. But he did not. He was undemanding, finding her mouth and kissing her slowly, gently, while his hand cupped her breast, his thumb caressing her nipple. To her shock, her body leaped in reponse. He had taught her well, too well, and her body was not in her mind's control.

Her arms went around his back, and he smiled grimly as he kissed her throat. He knew how to arouse her, and he watched her face as his fingers found her. She moaned, arching against him. He moved down her body, touching and stroking every inch of her. When he gathered her hips in his hands and lifted her to his mouth, he looked at her face. He could see the building passion in her eyes, and something else, a flicker of pain. He lowered his head and brought her closer to her release. She cried out, beyond herself.

But he did not allow her release. He left her abruptly, raised himself above her, and came into her. He cupped her face between his hands, holding her still, willing her to look at him.

"Tell me the truth, Kassia. Tell me, and I will forgive you."

Her body froze, and all pleasure disappeared as if it had never awakened.

"Tell me."

"I have told you the truth."

He had filled her, made himself a part of her, and she hated it and him and herself. She lay cold beneath him, suffering him in silence, unmoving. She was separate, apart from the helpless woman who lay beneath the man.

Graelam cursed her, his words catching in his throat as he took his release. He rolled away from her immediately and lay panting on his back.

"Your love is short-lived, I see," he said, not turning toward her.

"Yes," she said. "I suppose it must be. How can love survive cruelty and distrust?"

He cursed again softly.

Kassia rose from the bed, walked to the basin, and quickly bathed herself. She knew he was watching her, but she said nothing, did not acknowledge him. She hugged the side of the bed, pulling the covers to her chin, but she could not get warm. She realized vaguely that the coldness was coming from deep within her. She would probably be cold for the rest of her life.

26

"Edward's coronation is in a week and a half."

"When will you leave, my lord?" Kassia asked, finishing the roasted woodcock from her trencher.

"I, my lady? Do you not recall that the both of us are invited? Do you find my company so distasteful that you would even forgo such an exciting event?"

She raised pitifully hopeful eyes to his face. He watched her pink tongue flicker over her lower lip, and cursed himself silently for wanting her, wanting her simply because she sat beside him, and in a hall full of people.

"I am to come with you, my lord?"

"I do not dare risk leaving you here," he said. He saw a flash of anger in her eyes. "And do eat more, wife, else I will have naught but sympathy from Edward when he sees I am wed to such a skinny child."

He watched with great interest when her hand closed about the stem of her goblet. "Go ahead," he said, "toss your wine in my face. I, at least, would enjoy my retaliation."

Her hand fell away from the goblet as if burned. He laughed, harsh and cold. "It matters not, Kas-

sia. Coupling with you gives me little enough pleasure. If you continue as you are, you will soon
enough look like a boy. Then perhaps I will think of
myself as a pederast."

She gritted her teeth so tight her jaw ached.

"What? You will not even raise that little chin of
yours?"

Kassia picked up a ribbed piece of pork, raised it
to her mouth and slowly began to nibble off the
meat. She heard him suck in his breath, and let her
tongue lick the gravy from the bone. She eased it
deeper into her mouth, sucking at the tender meat.

Once, so long ago, it seemed, he had taught her to
give him pleasure. He had laughed at her, teased her,
until he had moaned, and laughed again at her obvious delight. She saw his eyes fasten on her mouth,
and felt the momentary power of revenge. She withdrew the bone and tossed it carelessly to her trencher. She raised her chin.

"Bitch," he said.

He rose from the table and strode from the hall.

It had begun to rain, and she nearly called to him.
She was such a stupid fool, worrying that he will
take a chill.

Graelam strode at a furious pace up the winding
wooden stairs to the ramparts. He leaned forward
against the harsh cold stone and looked toward the
sea, but the sliver of moon showed him no more
than an occasional white-topped wave. The rain was
warm on his face. At least it cooled his passions.

He realized that he was tired, tired to the depths
of his being of baiting Kassia, tired of watching her
show her fear then her hatred of him. None of it was
his fault, damn her. But he knew that it was. She

would never have left him if he had not driven her to it. The events of the past months careened through his mind. The weeks of warmth and caring they had shared when he had decided to forget what she had done, forget her lies, excusing her by blaming himself. Dienwald de Fortenberry. The knight's name rang like a death knell in his mind. *I did not leave with him because I love you.* His eyes darkened, anger at himself flowing through him for believing her even for a moment.

Graelam pounded his fist hard against the stone. He hated himself for his feelings of deep uncertainty. He had never experienced the emotions she had evoked in him. If Edward called for another crusade, he would have agreed immediately. On the heels of that thought he saw her face, her dimples deepening as she smiled at him, saw her eyes widen with bewildered astonishment when he had first brought her pleasure.

"Saint Peter's bones, but I am weary of all this." He strode back into the keep, shaking off the rain like a huge mongrel dog.

It would take them six days to travel to London, but Kassia didn't mind. She was filled with excitement, and even her husband's indifference did not overly upset her. He had simply ignored her, leaving all preparations to her. The string of details and decisions to be made allowed her to bury her feelings for him, and her hurt, until she lay in bed at night, listening to his even breathing. The day before they were to leave, Graelam had walked into their bedchamber unexpectedly. He paused a moment, watching Kassia twirl around in her new blue satin gown. She looked more beautiful than any woman he'd seen in his life. Her hair lay in thick soft curls about her small head, now falling to her shoulders. Her laughter died in her throat when she saw him.

"My lord?"

"The gown becomes you, my lady," he said.

Her face went carefully blank. "Thank you, my lord."

"You will wear the necklace with that gown." He could see the distaste in her eyes before she lowered her head.

He walked to his trunk and dug it out. He held it up, watching the precious gems gleam in the sunlight that poured through the small windows. "Come here," he said.

She walked slowly to him and turned around, lifting her hair off her neck. She felt the weight of the necklace as it rested upon her chest, felt the chill of the thick gold against her bare neck. He fastened the clasp and stepped back.

She looked like a barbaric princess, a precious, beautiful barbaric princess. He watched her lift her hand and touch the necklace. It did not particularly surprise him when her fingers fell away from it as if it burned her.

"You will be thus gowned for the coronation," he said, and left the bedchamber.

He took her that night, quickly but not roughly, and she thought she heard him curse her when he stiffened over her. She lay very still even after he had rolled off her. When she made to rise to bathe herself, he closed his hand around her waist, pulling her back.

"Nay," he said, "you will not wash my seed from your body."

She was shocked when she quivered at his words, and had to remind herself that he saw her now as naught but a brood mare. She tugged and he released her wrist.

"Go to sleep, wife, we leave early on the morrow."

They arrived in London a full week later, filthy and weary, their horses and wagons splattered with mud. Kassia had ridden most of the way, even when it had rained, once she had convinced Graelam that riding in a wagon made her ill.

She didn't know what to expect, but the sight of so many people packed into such a small area made her stare. And the filth. There was a constant stench of human excrement and rotting food. And there were the vendors, screeching at the top of their voices at passersby.

"All towns of any size are like this," Graelam said when he saw her cover her nose. "It is not so bad where we will stay. The compound is on the Thames, but north of the city."

"This is the house the Duke of Cornwall gave to you?" she asked.

"Aye, he deeded it to me upon my betrothal to Lady Joanna."

Her eyes flew to his face.

"He insisted I keep it once he had deemed you worthy."

A fine, misting rain was falling steadily and the ground was slushy mud. Bluebell slipped and Graelam's hand shot out to grasp the reins and steady the mare.

Kassia started to thank him, but he said merely,

"You are filthy enough. I do not wish you to have a broken leg as well."

"Then you would have to wear that wretched necklace yourself," she said under her breath.

"There," Graelam said to her, pointing to his left, "is Westminster Abbey, where Edward will have his coronation."

"It's beautiful."

"Aye, King Henry spent much money to reconstruct it. He is buried there."

They passed the White Tower, where Edward and Eleanor were now staying. "I don't know when Edward returned to London," Graelam said. "But I imagine that immediately the Duke of Cornwall heard he was coming, he set the coronation into motion."

Kassia was weaving in the saddle, so weary she couldn't keep her eyes open. At last they reached a high-walled fortress. A thick-barred iron gate swung slowly open and their caravan passed into a muddy, utterly dismal yard. The two-story wooden building in front of them was square and looked gray and uninviting in the growing darkness.

"You will see to the inside, Kassia," Graelam said as he lifted her off Bluebell's back.

She nodded, imagining with growing depression what awaited her within. To her utter astonishment, inside the house there were scores of lighted candles and a huge fire burning in a fireplace at the far end of the long, narrow lower chamber.

"Lady Kassia?"

A plump gray-haired woman gave her a deep curtsy.

"I am Margaret, my lady. The duke told us to expect you."

"I am so pleased you are here," Kassia told the woman with a tired smile.

Margaret clucked around her, much in Etta's manner, and Kassia allowed herself for some minutes to be cosseted. She was led upstairs to a comfortable chamber, where another fire burned.

"For you and your lord," Margaret said.

There were fresh reeds on the stone floor and a tapestry of vivid colors covering one wall. A large bed was set upon a dais, and there were several high-backed chairs surrounding a small circular table.

"I believe I have died and gone to heaven," Kassia said.

"I will kiss the duke's feet," Etta said.

"I will kiss the duke's feet myself. I will have the wenches bring you hot water for a bath," Margaret said. "My husband, Sarn, will assist your lord to see to the horses and wagons. You need do naught, my lady, but see to yourself."

Etta hurrumphed when Margaret started to assist Kassia out of her wet cloak, and the woman merely smiled, curtsied again, and left the chamber, saying over her shoulder, "The duke sent an entire wild boar for your first meal. After you have rested, my lady, we will have the evening meal."

After Margaret left the chamber, Kassia said, "Etta, you are wet through! You see to yourself. I am not helpless, you know."

Kassia was immersed to her chin in a wooden tub filled with blessedly hot water when Graelam entered the chamber.

She forgot the bridgeless expanse that lay between them, forgot she was naked, and said happily, "The duke must be the most thoughtful man in all of England. I do not even have to see to the preparation of dinner. And this room is so pleasant and so very warm. Was all as you wished, my lord?"

He smiled at her wearily. "Aye, everything is fine. I will give you five more minutes in that tub, Kassia."

She flushed, and quickly ducked her head underwater to wet her hair. When she climbed out of the tub, Graelam was wearing his bedrobe, seated in front of the roaring fire. She quickly toweled herself dry and wrapped a small linen towel about her wet hair.

"I was very dirty, Graelam," she said, eyeing the bathwater.

"I called for clean water," he said, not turning.

Kassia heard the heavy footsteps outside their chamber and quickly pulled on her bedrobe, drawing the belt tight.

She was combing out her hair in front of the fire when Graelam said from the tub, "We will have our meal here this evening. Tomorrow we will go to the tower."

Kassia paused a moment in her combing and said tentatively, "I should like to see everything, my lord. I fear I was too tired today to appreciate England's capital."

"Aye," he said, closing his eyes, "it has been a long time since I was here. I remarked changes. We will see everything you wish to see."

"Thank you," she said. "Do you wish me to assist you, my lord?"

"Bring me a towel," he said, rising.

She tried to avoid looking at his body, but failed dismally. Her fingers itched to tangle themselves in the hair on his chest, to stroke over his smooth back. It had been so long. Her mind warred with her body, and in that moment she hated him for teaching her pleasure, for teaching her body to respond to him. Her eyes fell to his groin and she wanted to jump on him. But he hated her, she reminded herself, forcing her eyes upward. She met his eyes and gulped.

"The towel, Kassia," he said, holding out his hand.

She thrust the towel at him and quickly turned back and sat before the fire.

She knew he had seen the lust in her eyes, and she wanted to kick herself. She heard him say very calmly from behind her, "I will part your sweet thighs, my lady, and caress you until you scream with pleasure, if you will but admit, finally, the truth to me."

She wanted to yell, to plead her innocence yet again. But it would do no good. Why not simply tell him what he wanted to hear? She froze at the thought, for she knew what the result would be. He would possibly forgive her, but he would never trust her. He could never really care for her if he distrusted her. At least there would be peace of a sort between them. From the corner of her eye she saw him pull off the towel and stand quietly, stretching in front of the fire, oblivious of his nakedness. His sex was hard, and she gulped, quickly turning away from him. He would slake his desire in another woman's body. The thought made her jump to her feet, the pain of her spirit shimmering in her eyes.

"Graelam, I—"

There was a knock on the chamber door. She

closed her eyes, and trembled with the knowledge of what she had been about to say to him.

"Enter," she called, her voice high and shrill.

Two serving wenches came into the chamber, carrying trays. Their eyes went immediately to Graelam, who was languidly reaching for his bedrobe. Both the women eyed him openly. Would he take one of them?

"Set the trays here," Kassia said, pointing to the small table.

She gritted her teeth as one of the women, quite pretty, with thick black hair and full breasts, gave Graelam a look that promised anything he wanted.

"You may leave now." She stepped in front of her husband.

He watched her, a gleam of satisfaction in his eyes. But he said nothing until she was seated across from him, her mouth full of roast pork.

"That was quite a display of wifely jealousy."

She choked, and downed half the wine in his goblet. She could not speak for several moments as she gasped for breath. But she shook her head.

"Odd," he said. "I had the impression that you were about to tell me something of great interest when the wenches interrupted us."

She stared down at the wooden plate. Her face was very expressive, and Graelam saw all the myriad emotions. Was it pride that kept her silent?

"You are very young, Kassia," he said after a moment, remembering Drake's words. "When one is young, one makes mistakes. And one is reluctant to admit to mistakes."

"Do not older people also make mistakes, Graelam?"

"Aye." He sat back in his chair and crossed his arms over his chest. "But heed me, Kassia, I do not intend to hear more mewling protests from you. They now weary and bore me."

"Very well, my lord," she said, "I will say nothing."

The decision was made. Was it pride that kept her silent? Honor? Stupidity?

In the next instant he was towering above her, jerking her out of her chair.

"No." She leaned back as far as she was able.

He laughed and lifted her over his shoulder. "Would you prefer that I bed that pretty wench who brought our meal?"

"Aye. I care not what you do."

He dropped her onto her back and stripped off her bedrobe. When he released her to rid himself of his own bedrobe, she rolled onto her knees and tried to escape him. He caught her by her ankle and flipped her again onto her back.

"No," he said. "I am not yet sated with your sweet body. But there will be no pleasure for you, my lady." He pulled her legs apart and came into her. His eyes widened and flew to her face, for she was moist and ready for him.

Kassia stared at him. She felt him deep and throbbing inside her, felt him grinding against her belly, and she cried out, beyond herself.

It would not stop, and cry after cry burst from her mouth.

Graelam felt her clutching at his shoulders, felt the furious arching of her hips to match his rhythm. He kissed her deeply, and moaned his own release into her mouth.

He crushed her against him, utterly confused by her response to him. The punishment he had given had failed abysmally. It both angered him and, oddly enough, pleased him.

Damn her. He said, as his hands stroked and caressed her hips, "So yielding and passionate—did you think of him when I came into you?"

He felt her go still, but he didn't release her. "Go to sleep, Kassia. I will not allow you to bathe yourself. My seed will stay in your belly."

Graelam finally fell into an exhausted sleep, the wet of her tears on his shoulder.

27

I must remember everything, Kassia thought as she looked upward at the high vaulted cathedral, for someday I shall tell my grandchildren that I attended the coronation of King Edward the First of England. She took in the gorgeously arrayed lords and ladies and the splendid stained-glass windows. All was overladen with religious solemnity. The prelates, their flowing robes as beautifully sewn as those of the king and queen, recited the ceremony in Latin, their voices hushed and reverent. Kassia leaned forward when Edward accepted his scepter and crown. All too soon, the ceremony was over. The new king and queen of England were whisked away, and the lords and ladies moved quietly out of the abbey. Kassia heard Graelam sigh in relief. She looked up at him, but he merely nodded at her, saying only, "At least our king is home. Now, Kassia, we will shuck all the religious trappings and you will meet Edward and Eleanor."

She looks beautiful, Graelam thought, unconsciously comparing Kassia to the other noble ladies assembled in the huge lower chamber of the White Tower. "Do not look so awestruck," he said to her, "else everyone will believe you a country maid."

"I am trying to memorize everything," she said quite seriously.

"We will doubtless come to London again."

She nodded, and spoke before she could censor her thought, "Aye, but this is the coronation. We will be able to tell our grandchildren about it." Her hand flew to her mouth. She waited for him to blight her.

"I had not thought of that," he said. "Come, Kassia, there are many people for you to meet."

It was indeed odd, Kassia thought after meeting so many lords and ladies, that her mouth seemed frozen into a permanent smile, but she had not felt at all intimidated as she had expected to. Graelam was playing the husband's role well, pretending he was pleased to have all his friends meet his wife. And it was also the necklace, she thought. Although she hated its weight on her neck and all the pain it had brought her, it nonetheless gave her a very rich, slightly exotic appearance that, strangely, gave her confidence.

"By all that's precious. Look what Cornwall has spit up, Chandra. My lord Graelam."

Kassia raised her eyes to meet the blue ones of one of the most handsome men she had ever seen. He was nearly as tall as Graelam, wide of shoulder and lean of waist and hip. His hair was burnished gold and his face lightly tanned and exquisitely formed. Standing next to him was a very beautiful lady, the perfect mate for such a man. Kassia felt suddenly skinny, ugly, and tongue-tied, her confidence utterly destroyed when faced with this unbelievable creature with her long golden hair and her utterly perfect woman's body.

"So you and Chandra have traveled from the northern wilds for the great occasion," Graelam said, slapping the other man on his muscled arm. "Chandra," he continued, his voice dropping slightly as he took her hand, "how is it you manage to appear more beautiful each time I see you?"

Chandra laughed. "This beast, Jerval, has kept me off the practice field for the past month so I would not embarrass him at court with my bruises and scratches."

Practice field. What, Kassia wondered, was she talking about?

"Don't believe that tale, Graelam," Sir Jerval said, his long fingers resting on his wife's shoulder. "The only thing that has slowed her down at all was the birth of our son but four months ago."

"I do not suppose," Graelam said, "that you named the lad after me?"

"Not likely, Graelam," Chandra said. "He is Edward. Jerval believed that there should be an Edward in London and one in Cumbria. I had no choice in the matter."

"And for once she was flat on her back, too tired to argue with me," Sir Jerval said. "Of course, I learned that technique of gaining her compliance long ago."

Kassia wished Graelam would introduce her to these people, yet afraid of making a fool of herself if he did so. She felt so insignificant.

"The necklace. My God, Graelam, I had forgot all about it."

It was as if, Kassia thought, her husband had just remembered her presence. "Aye," he said, "it is the same one, from Al-Afdal's camp. And the little one wearing it is Kassia, my wife."

Lady Chandra's expressive blue eyes widened in surprise. "Good heavens, Jerval, you and I now have a son, but Graelam has got himself a wife. My dear, I trust you buffet this great beast at least twice a day. He doubtless tries to play the tyrant over you."

Kassia felt bereft of speech at this unexpected advice, but Lady Chandra continued smiling at her, and she said, "I suspect he is as much a tyrant as he ever was."

"Kassia," Graelam said, "this is Sir Jerval de Vernon and his wife, Lady Chandra."

"My wife," Sir Jerval said to Kassia, "is always offering advice that she herself ignores. She adores me so mightily that I am always having to lift her from her knees—"

Lady Chandra poked him in the ribs. "Pay him no heed, Kassia. He is like most men, crowing and bragging and praying others will believe him."

"Ha," Sir Jerval said.

Chandra said to Kassia, "Has Graelam told you of our adventures in the Holy Land? How long ago it seems. The history of the necklace you are wearing is particularly— Ah, let me just say it was an adventure I don't want to repeat."

"You tried to kill me, Chandra, then saved me," Graelam said. "Neither tale bears repeating, particularly to a wife who—" He broke off, not really knowing what he would have said, and fearing that it would show his bitterness.

"Well," Chandra said, "I shall tell her all about it."

"You tried to kill my husband?" Kassia asked.

She saw Chandra's eyes fly to Graelam's face.

"It was a long time ago," Lady Chandra said and patted his hand. "And of no importance at all now."

"Jerval, Chandra, how long do you remain in London?" Graelam asked.

"Another week or so," Jerval said. "Chandra has accepted a challenge from Edward on the archery range. I fear I am relegated to the role of holding her quiver."

"It will be a close contest," Graelam said. "I will bear you company and the two of us will cheer her on." He turned to his wife. "Come, Kassia, it's time you met your king."

"Lady Chandra will go against the king?" Kassia asked, disbelief so clear in her voice that Graelam laughed.

"Indeed," he said. "Chandra is a warrior."

"But she is so beautiful."

"I learned with her that the one only enhances the other. She is a woman who holds honor dear. And at last it appears that she holds her womanhood dear as well."

The tone of his voice altered slightly, and Kassia frowned down at her blue leather slippers. She remembered him telling her that a lady had given him the scar on his shoulder. Chandra? Had he loved her? Did he still love her? At the very least, he admired her. She was everything Kassia wasn't. She wouldn't know the end of an arrow from its beginning.

They entered a line of nobles that would pass in front of the newly crowned King Edward and Queen Eleanor. Kassia smiled, curtsying to a Sir John de

Vescy, another noble who had been with Graelam in the Holy Land.

She thanked the Lord for the coolness of the October day, for with the press of people, heat would have made it unbearable.

She moved closer to her husband, comparing him to the other noblemen. He looked as magnificent as a king, as he threw back his black head and laughed aloud at a comment from a gaunt-looking man with bushy black eyebrows. Graelam's robe was of rich gold velvet, full-cut, its flowing sleeves lined with ermine. About his waist was a thick black belt from which hung a slender gem-studded sword. The robe fit across his massive shoulders perfectly. She had sewed many hours to make it thus.

"Ah, my lord Graelam."

Graelam bowed deeply. "Sire, welcome home. Your throne has grown dusty in your absence, and your barons morose without a king to complain about."

"Aye," the king said, "but I venture you have told them enough stories to blacken my reputation. My love, here is the Wolf of Cornwall to greet you."

Queen Eleanor laughed with pleasure. "Graelam. So many friends come to see us. You look more handsome than my poor lord, Graelam. I fear foreign lands have added gray to his hair."

"But who is this, my lord?" Edward said, his brilliant blue eyes going to the small woman at Graelam's side.

"Allow me to present my wife, sire, Kassia de Moreton."

"My lady," Edward said smoothly, and took her small hand into his large one.

"Sire," Kassia said, curtsying. She said, "You are so tall. I had believed my lord the largest of men, yet you can see over his head."

Eleanor laughed. "He has oft told me that he grew to such a height to better intimidate all his nobles. My lord's uncle, the Duke of Cornwall, has told us of you, Kassia. So romantic and dramatic a story. We will speak, for I wish to hear all about you and your taming of the Wolf of Cornwall."

Taming? Ha, Kassia thought as she walked beside her husband to greet other acquaintances.

The afternoon faded into evening and by the time the great banquet was served, Kassia was very tired. She toyed with the vast variety of foods, sampling only the delicious stuffed pheasants, garden cress, beets and turnips. The wine, she was certain, came from Aquitaine.

"The queen is very gracious," she said to Graelam when he turned away from conversation with Lord John de Valance.

"Aye," Graelam said. "It is the only love match amongst royalty I have heard of. Eleanor saved Edward's life in the Holy Land when he was attacked by an assassin with a poisoned dagger."

"She killed the assassin?" Kassia asked.

"Nay, Edward killed the man and collapsed. She sucked the poison from his arm. I wasn't there, but Jerval and Chandra were. Edward's physicians were supposedly furious at the queen's interference."

She toyed for a moment with her goblet. "You knew Lady Chandra before she wed Sir Jerval?"

"Aye," he said. "I knew her."

"She stabbed you in the shoulder?"

"She did not stab me. Actually, she flung the dagger from a goodly distance. Had she been less furious and closer to me, I would likely be dead."

"How—" Kassia said, but Graelam's attention was drawn back to Lord John. Questions flew about in her mind, but she had no opportunity to speak privately to Graelam until they arrived at their compound. To Kassia's delight, Margaret had hot spiced wine awaiting them in their chamber.

"I feel like royalty with all this attention," she said as she carefully removed the necklace.

Graelam stretched, rubbed his neck. "The ceremony went well. I am pleased that Edward is home again. We return tomorrow to the tower. I will be meeting with Edward along with many other nobles. You, Kassia, will become better acquainted with the ladies."

He paused a moment. He had seen Lady Joanna, but had managed to avoid her. He supposed he was a fool for worrying that she wouldn't be kind to Kassia.

"Graelam, would you tell me about Lady Chandra?"

He sat down in one of the high-backed chairs. "There is little to tell, but if you wish it—I had wanted to marry her, but her father, a Marcher baron—" he broke off a moment, seeing her confusion. "A Marcher baron is a noble whose holdings and fortresses defend the border of England from the Welsh. In any case, Lord Richard refused me. Through trickery, I managed to capture both Chandra and their castle of Croyland. She would have wed me, for I held her younger brother, save for the timely arrival of Jerval. I was routed and managed to leave with but a wound in my shoulder. Chandra's father then forced her into marriage with Jerval, the son of a close friend of his."

She was staring at him. "But you are all friends."

"Now we are. Much happened in the Holy Land to reconcile our differences. And from what I can tell, that is where Chandra decided to become a real wife to her husband."

Kassia fiddled with the fastenings on her gown. "Did you love her?"

Graelam stared into the glowing coals in the fireplace. "It was a long time ago. No, I did not love her, but I wanted her. She is unlike any woman I have ever known. She knows a man's honor and a man's loyalty." He raised brooding eyes to her face. "She is capable only of truth. Aye, rare in a woman."

Kassia couldn't believe the pain his words brought her. She walked slowly to the far corner of the chamber and began to remove her clothes. He watched her from beneath slitted eyelids, feeling a pang of guilt. He had spoken the truth about Chandra, but not all of it. Before Jerval, she had been more unbending than the most ruthless of men, spurning the meaning of compromise. Even now, Graelam imagined that Jerval waged a constant battle with his beautiful wife to keep control.

He sipped the warm wine, waiting for Kassia to get into bed. It was odd, he thought, but when he had seen Chandra, he had felt no rush of lust for her. Indeed, he had felt nothing save friendship for both her and Jerval. He saw a flash of soft white flesh before Kassia pulled the covers over herself. He shifted in his chair, angry at himself for the lust he felt for his wife. He thought about the passion he'd felt for her the evening before, passion he had forced himself to ignore.

After a while Graelam rose to his feet and stripped off his clothes. He strode to the bed, lifted the lone candle high, and stared down at his wife. Her hair was spread about her head on the pillow, her mouth slightly open as she breathed evenly in sleep. Could he blame Dienwald de Fortenberry for being taken with such an apparently guileless, fragile girl? He slipped into bed, forcing himself to stay a goodly distance away from her.

Queen Eleanor sat among her ladies in the solarium. The interested, attentive smile never left her face as she looked toward Kassia de Moreton. She continued to weave the intricate tapestry, watching the girl from the corner of her eye as Chandra de Vernon approached her.

Events might well prove interesting. Her ears perked up when she heard a snide comment from Lady Joanna, daughter of the Earl of Leichester.

"You should have seen her," Joanna was saying to Lady Louise de Sanson, "when she first arrived at Wolffeton. I could tell that Lord Graelam was appalled, but of course there was nothing he could do about her."

"He really married her on her deathbed?" Louise asked, her sloe eyes lighting avidly.

"Aye," Joanna said. "The look on his face when the skinny little thing arrived, looking for the world like a dirty little boy. And her hair so short."

"Scandalous," Louise said.

"You can see that she has not much improved," Joanna said.

Eleanor, seeing that other ladies were beginning to listen and then look toward Kassia de Moreton, decided it was time to intervene. "I think her quite lovely," she said in a clear voice. "Lord Graelam is very lucky."

Joanna paused a moment, judging the waters. She said in a hushed whisper that carried a goodly distance, "But that is not what Lord Graelam thinks, your highness. I was told by Lady Blanche de Blasis, the half-sister of Graelam's first wife, that Lady Kassia even tried to escape him. It would not appear that he made such a good bargain."

The whispering had reached Kassia's ears. She flushed with anger even as she tried to heed Lady Chandra's words. Suddenly Chandra's strong fingers closed over her arm. "Leave the bitch to me," Chandra said, and strode toward the little group.

"Ah, Lady Joanna. I understand that you were to be married. How very unfortunate for you that the groom escaped."

Queen Eleanor hid a smile behind her hand.

There was a loud rustling of silk skirts as the ladies moved closer.

Joanna knew of Chandra only by reputation. She had believed that she must be an Amazon, but faced with the beautiful creature staring at her with contempt, she was forced to revise her opinion. "My father is relieved that I did not marry Lord Graelam." She gave a small shudder. "He did not wish me to be immured in Cornwall."

"But how terribly embarrassing for you, dear Joanna," Chandra said, "to lose your first choice."

"Graelam had no choice," Joanna said in a shrill voice. "He was forced to keep her."

Kassia moved quietly to stand beside Chandra. She could not allow Chandra to defend her.

"He did have a choice, Joanna," Kassia said. "You see, our marriage had not been consummated."

"Then why did you try to escape him?" Louise said.

"I believe," Kassia said slowly, "that Lady Blanche claims this as a fact. It is not true. I owe my loyalty to my husband and always will."

"How you have changed your stance." *Why am I still baiting her? Do I so fear that Graelam will learn that I was the one responsible?* It was true, Blanche knew as she watched Kassia whirl about at the sound of her voice. She feared Graelam would take revenge upon Guy.

"Blanche—" Kassia said.

Very soon, Eleanor thought, she would have chaos. She set aside her thread and rose from her chair. "Ladies, I believe it is time for me to tell you of the court in Sicily. And I will show you some of the treasures I brought back with me."

"Come," Chandra said to Kassia. "If I stay longer, I will break Joanna's neck. And perhaps Blanche's arm."

"Why did you defend me?" Kassia asked. "You don't know me."

"A penchant for fairness," Chandra said. "Joanna from what I hear, is a vicious, mean-spirited bitch. Graelam would likely have killed her had he married her."

Kassia said, "You sound as though you have forgiven Graelam for what he tried to do to you."

"So he told you about that, did he?"

"Aye, I asked him last night. He admires you."

"Well," Chandra said after a moment, "had we wed, I don't know who would have survived. Graelam is used to ruling all within his power. He won't tolerate his wishes gainsaid. And unfortunately, he cannot seem to accept a woman's going against him in anything. Am I right?"

"Aye," Kassia said, "you are right. There was a time when I believed that he—" She broke off. "It matters not. Nothing will change his opinion of me now."

"Walk with me," Chandra said. "I would hear about this adventure of yours."

"—and so I cannot blame Dienwald for escaping," Kassia concluded after some time. "Graelam would have killed him. And now Blanche is here, and still persists in despising me, and lying. There is nothing I can do or say to convince him otherwise."

"Hmmm," Chandra said.

"If I were more like you," Kassia said, "he would likely love me. At least he might believe me, for he spoke about your honor and your honesty."

Chandra smiled down at Kassia. "I have an idea," she said. "Why do you not come with me to the archery range? I have a contest with the king tomorrow and must practice. And while I am at it, I can show you how to shoot."

28

"You are meddling, and I don't like it."

Lady Chandra de Vernon snuggled closer to her husband. "But she is innocent, Jerval." She drew in her breath as her husband's hand moved down over her belly. "I only wish to help."

"She does bring out one's protective instincts."

"Aye, but don't think she's a fragile helpless little flower. There is a core of strength in her. She will bend, but will not break. If only Graelam were not such a—"

"Proud, cynical, arrogant, distrustful—"

"All of those things, I suppose," Chandra said on a sigh. "You should have seen her on the archery range this afternoon. She looked at my bow as if it were a snake that would bite her. But she quickly got over that. She hasn't much physical strength, but she does have a good eye and a steady hand."

"So you would turn her into a warrior?"

"No, but just perhaps I can make her feel that she has more worth."

Jerval said as he drew her into his arms, "I will

speak to Graelam tomorrow, and also Sir Guy de Blasis. He seems a decent man."

"I cannot say that much for his wife."

"Hush now. I wish to have my way with you."

"I wonder," Chandra said before kissing her husband, "what Blanche is saying to her husband? Do you believe he knows the truth?"

Sir Guy knew all there was to know about his bride. He had realized even before he had tricked her into marrying him that her relentless pursuit of Graelam had been primarily because of her fear for her son's future. But Evian's future was now assured. Guy felt a good deal of affection for her, even enjoyed her tirades, for he knew that once in bed, she would forget everything but him. She was a passionate woman, one who was not always logical, and, unfortunately, quite single-minded. But that would change. He smiled at her now, lazily, listening to her rant. She never bored him.

"I don't want to be pregnant."

"But you are, my dear," he said, "and you will remain that way. After you have given me two or three sons, I will allow you to take that vile potion again."

"You are a beast."

"A virile beast, it appears. I should keep you in bed all the time—it would save your temper and my ears and patience."

"I don't want to be ugly, fat, and swollen. I don't want the pain of birthing another child."

"Blanche," he said, leaning over the small table between them, "I am truly sorry about the birthing pain. If I could prevent it, I would, but I cannot. As to your appearing ugly, you are being foolish. You will see that my desire for you will not diminish. You are my wife and my lover. It will remain thus, I promise you."

"I'm not a fool, Guy," she said.

"I trust not, at least not anymore."

She jumped to her feet, splaying her hands on the table. "I know why you married me. It's that skinny little girl you love, not me." She paled at her words, and she whirled about, giving him her back.

Guy leaned back in his chair, clasping his hands behind his head. "At last," he said with deep satisfaction. "You have finally admitted it."

"I have admitted nothing. Admitted what?"

"That you love me, of course. It warms my heart, Blanche. Don't you realize there's no need for you to insult Kassia further?"

At her silence, he said, "Please turn around, my love."

Blanche slowly swung about, but she kept her eyes on her soft leather slippers.

"You are doubtless the most stubborn woman in England. Come, at least yell at me."

"I'm not stubborn, and she was with that bitch Chandra de Vernon."

"Are all the ladies at court bitches, Blanche? My poor love, how very trying for you."

"I must admit that I did not like being in Joanna's company," she said.

"Forced to take sides, my dear? And, it appears, you have chosen the wrong one, again."

She wanted to tell him that she had baited Kassia because she was afraid for him. Afraid of what Graelam would do if he discovered her perfidy. *I have been fine and fairly won,* she thought. *I love him, yet I am afraid to tell him so. Afraid that he really thinks me a spiteful witch.*

Guy rose and walked to her, clasping her shoulders in his hands and shaking her a little. "Listen to me. It's time for you to forget Graelam, Kassia, and Wolffeton, to forget your disappointment. It is time, you know, for you to accept me as your husband." He paused a moment, examining his thoughts to make them into words. "I don't love Kassia. I felt protective of her, for a more innocent maid I have yet to see. But I wanted you, Blanche, despite what you did." He shrugged. "I gained you, and saved Kassia from further of your machinations."

Her eyes flew to his face. "I . . . I did nothing."

He caressed his fingertips over her lips. "I am not blind, love. There is no reason for you to pretend to me. I will admit that it would please me mightily if you would willingly go to Graelam and tell him the truth." His eyes darkened, narrowing in thought. "Of course, Graelam, being as blind as he appears to be when it comes to women, would likely assume that I put you up to it. And seeing you soft and lovely after I've taken you, I could not blame him. Perhaps it's best to leave matters as they are, at least for the time being. I have a feeling that they will work out things between them without any more of your interference, or mine. But attend me, Blanche. I will not allow you to direct any more mischief toward Kassia. Do you understand me?"

"I cannot help but understand you."

He didn't let her go. "Perhaps in five or ten years you will come to believe me. Together, Blanche, you and I will build Chitterly into a great holding." He chuckled, and leaned down to kiss her. "Our children will never believe their mother a spineless wench."

"You mock me, Guy," she said, "and you are slippery as the wettest fish. I don't like you."

"Nay, but you love me. I will accept that for a while. I trust that you will not go against my wishes."

"You would likely beat me if I did."

He touched his hand to her slightly rounded belly. "No, but I would find other ways to punish you."

She buried her face against his shoulder. "I don't mean to say bad things, Guy," she said. "I was just so afraid."

He kissed her temple. "But not now. Not ever again. And, love, I enjoy your fishwife's tongue. Now I will take you to bed and make you forget everything but me."

The afternoon was clear and sunny, the air crisp. Lords and ladies were gathered in the huge tower courtyard to see the competition between King Edward and Lady Chandra de Vernon. Graelam left Kassia with the queen and joined Jerval de Vernon and his friend Sir Mark. There was much good-natured jesting and prodding until Jerval tore off part of his tunic sleeve. "An adequate favor for my lady?" he asked, and the men dissolved into more laughter.

"My lord is quite cocky," Queen Eleanor said with a smile, "but I think he will soon become quite serious about it all. You watched Chandra practicing yesterday, Kassia?"

"She is unbelievable," Kassia said. "I never

dreamed that a woman could be so—" She sought for a word.

"Complete?" Eleanor said.

"Perhaps. And she is so beautiful."

"Actually, Kassia, her completeness came only when she went to her husband. She was not always as happy as she is now."

But her husband always loved her, Kassia wanted to say. Instead, she spoke of the match. "She is concerned that the third round will do her in. The distance requires a great deal of strength, and she says that only the king can shoot so far with accuracy."

"Aye, I know," Eleanor said. "I believe my lord insisted upon it. He does not like to lose."

Kassia laughed. "At least he is honest about it." She looked toward Chandra, who was grinning as her husband wrapped a piece of material about her arm as his favor. I would be like her, Kassia thought. If I could but learn a little of what she does so effortlessly, perhaps Graelam would admire me. She tried to see herself wielding a lance, riding a mighty warhorse, and failed. Nonetheless, the thought stayed with her.

Eleanor turned to speak to the Countess of Pembroke. Kassia looked about her and smiled at a slight, light-haired girl whose belly was rounded with child. "You must be tired," she said. "Come and sit beside me."

"Thank you. I do not have the energy that I used to have."

Kassia felt a brief twinge of envy, then looked toward Chandra. "Does she not look utterly beautiful?"

"Aye. You should see her in her armor, though.

It's a sight that boggles the mind. I grew up with Chandra, you see."

"Were you at Croyland when Graelam de Moreton came to take her?"

The girl stiffened, but said, "Aye, I was there."

"Did Lady Chandra truly hurl a dagger at Graelam?"

The girl nodded. She turned at the sound of a bright child's laughter. "Ah, my daughter, Glenda." She took the child from a nurse and lifted her in her arms. "Glenda, I would like you to meet a lovely lady." She looked inquiringly at Kassia.

"Kassia is my name. She is a lovely child. You're very lucky." Kassia gazed at the little girl's thick dark hair, then into her large gray eyes. Suddenly Glenda leaned toward Kassia, her small hand clutching at the ermine of her cloak. The child laughed as she stroked the fur, and Kassia froze. The expression was Graelam's.

"Are you all right, Kassia? You look very pale."

Kassia said, "I do not believe I know your name."

"Mary. My husband, Sir Mark, is yon, standing with Sir Jerval and Graelam de Moreton."

Was Mary a former lover of Graelam's? It seemed impossible. Mary appeared so sweet, her face so gentle and innocent.

Mary said, "I hear that Lord Graelam has wed. She is, I am told, an heiress from Brittany."

"Aye, she is from Brittany."

"I can't but feel sorry for her," Mary said in a low voice. "I can't imagine that Lord Graelam is an easy man."

"No, he is not," Kassia said. "Your daughter, does she resemble her father?"

"I don't think so," Mary said after a brief pause. "Why do you ask?"

Kassia closed her eyes a moment as she said, "My name is Kassia de Moreton."

"I see," Mary said in a voice so low Kassia barely heard her. "Do you see such a resemblance, then? I didn't want to bring her to London, but my husband said no one would notice. He assured me that Glenda looks not one whit like Graelam."

"It is not her features, but the expression when she laughed. Forgive me for making you uncomfortable. I will say nothing, I promise you."

Mary forced a smile. "Thank you. Look, Chandra is preparing to shoot."

To Kassia's amazement, Chandra won the first round. The straw-filled circular targets stood at a distance of thirty feet. For the second round, the distance was doubled. The king won, by dint of a very lucky shot that split one of Chandra's arrows. Kassia heard Chandra's bright laughter as the targets were moved to an even greater distance.

"Sire," she said, "you have much improved. You are at last providing me with decent competition."

"Ho, my lady," the king said, drawing himself up to his full giant's height. "We will see now who is the better."

"I need my husband to provide some brawn," Chandra said, shading her eyes as she looked at the distant targets.

Edward's smile lasted only until he stepped forward. His eyes narrowed in concentration and his arm was steady. His arrow arched through the air and landed near the edge of the black center of the target.

"It's a pity the target is so distant," Sir Jerval said

to Graelam as he watched his wife prepare to shoot. "She has the eye of an eagle but not the strength for this distance."

Chandra released her arrow and it soared gracefully toward the target, landing close to Edward's.

"Well done," Jerval shouted.

More haggling bets were laid, and Edward had to shout for silence before he took his next turn. There was a loud thud as his arrow embedded itself once again just inside the black center.

Chandra's next arrow was carried by a sudden shift of the slight breeze to the outside edge of the target.

"I can hear her cursing from here," Jerval said.

The same shifting breeze caught Edward's arrow, and it missed the target altogether.

"By all the saints," Graelam said. "I didn't believe it possible!"

There was complete silence as Chandra released her final arrow. It landed with a light thud near her first arrow, at the edge of the black center. Loud applause and shouting followed.

Edward grinned at her and blew her a kiss. "Forgive me, my lady," he said, and released his final arrow. It smacked in the middle of the bull's-eye, its feathered tip vibrating for some moments at the power of the shot.

"I do not suppose, sire," Chandra said, "that you will believe I allowed you to beat me?"

Edward tossed his bow to one of his men, clasped her about her waist, and twirled her high above his head. "My lady," he said, lowering her gently to the ground, "I would believe anything you chose to tell me."

"You are too much the sporting winner, sire. Nay, the victory is yours."

"Jerval, you lucky hound, come and rescue your wife before I abduct her."

Kassia saw the admiration in Graelam's eyes as he watched Lady Chandra. A knot of resolve formed in her. He would look at her like that, she would make it happen. She turned about, but Mary was gone, her small daughter with her.

"I see that your bitch protectress is well-occupied," Lady Joanna said from behind Kassia.

Kassia's hand itched to slap her face, but she said quite mildly, "Must you show your jealousy, Joanna? It makes your face appear quite plain, you know."

She felt a moment of satisfaction when Joanna quickly raised her hand to her face.

"Kassia."

Graelam's dark eyes glittered with anger at Joanna, but his smile was gentle as he looked down at his wife. "Come, Edward wishes to celebrate his victory."

She walked quietly beside him, her thoughts on the little girl, Glenda.

"Don't let her distress you," Graelam said.

"She is like a bothersome insect," Kassia said. "I do not heed her."

"Then why is your face flushed?"

Kassia stopped, turned slowly, and studied her husband's face. "I met your daughter."

If she expected to see guilt, she was doomed to disappointment. Graelam merely looked at her blankly, a black brow raised in silent question.

"Did you meet Sir Mark, a friend of Sir Jerval's?"

"Aye, but what has that to do with this daughter of mine?"

"His wife, Lady Mary, grew up with Lady Chandra. She was at Croyland when you took the castle."

Slowly memory righted itself. "It was long ago," Graelam said slowly. "A very long time ago."

"Was she your mistress?"

"Nay. I took her by force to gain Chandra's compliance."

"You forced a lady?"

He flushed, and it angered him. A man could do whatever he wished, without the condemnation of his damned wife. A muscle jumped in his jaw. "That is enough," he said. "It was a long time ago, as I told you, and I do not wish to hear you rant at me anymore." He added, seeing the horror still in her eyes, "I am sorry for it. I was very angry at the time, and frustrated."

"As angry and frustrated as you were with me?" Kassia asked.

Again his face darkened, but he didn't answer her. After a long moment he said, "I seem to do little that pleases you. Will this news send you plotting again to escape me?"

She shook her head.

"At least you no longer protest your innocence. Do not tell me that Chandra is teaching you the value of keeping your tongue behind your teeth? Ah, there are Sir Guy and his lovely bride."

"You are looking well, Kassia," Guy said, briefly touching her hands.

"And you, Guy. Does all go well with you?"

"Aye, and soon I will be a father."

Kassia was surprised at the jealousy she felt at his words. She turned to Blanche and said quietly, "Congratulations, Blanche. You are very lucky."

Guy saw the dilemma in his wife's eyes, and quickly pulled her close. He kissed her cheek, whispering as he did so, "Easy, my love. Let Graelam and Kassia see your winsome side."

"Thank you," Blanche said. Then, to her own surprise, she smiled, her eyes going inadvertently to her husband's face.

"Guy," Graelam called, "bring your conceited butt here. I wish you to meet Sir Jerval."

Blanche looked after her husband, shaking her head as if to clear her thoughts. "You don't look well, Kassia," she said. "Joanna remarked it to me yesterday."

"Joanna remarked many things. Indeed, she dominated, did she not, with her vicious tongue?"

"Aye," Blanche said, "she did."

"Are you happy now, Blanche?"

Blanche narrowed her eyes on Kassia's face, but could see no hidden meaning there. "A husband is a husband," she said, shrugging, her words sounding false even to her own ears.

"Nay, I find Guy very kind."

"He is *my* husband," Blanche said.

"I know. Please, Blanche, I have never taken anything of yours." Kassia did not realize that Blanche's words were spurred by jealousy, and added, a touch of sarcasm in her voice, "Incidentally, Dienwald de Fortenberry sends you his greetings."

Kassia heard Blanche's hiss of breath, and turned away.

Graelam remained occupied with his friends, and

it was Rolfe who accompanied Kassia and Etta on a tour of London. So many beautiful things, she thought, fingering bolts of exquisite material. But she had no coin, and was too ashamed to admit it to Rolfe.

Late that evening Kassia lay huddled in the soft bed, wondering where Graelam was. When she at last heard the door to their bedchamber open and close, she closed her eyes tightly. She felt the bed sink under Graelam's weight, and tried to pretend sleep.

"I know you're awake, Kassia," he said, his words slurred from too much ale.

"Aye," she said. "I am awake."

"Tell me, Kassia, when I left you alone with Blanche, were you again unkind to her? I saw her standing alone, her head bowed, after you left her. What did you say to her, Kassia?"

"I said nothing untoward to her."

"Why don't I believe you?"

Kassia could no more prevent her actions than stop the sun from rising. Lurching up, she drew back her arm and slapped him as hard as she could. He looked at her with blank surprise, then his eyes darkened. She cried out and rolled off the bed. Naked, she ran toward the bedchamber door.

He caught her about the waist and jerked her around to face him. His fingers bit into her flesh but she made no sound. She stared numbly at his chest and waited.

"If I thrust myself between your lovely legs, will I again find you warm and ready for me?"

She shook her head, afraid to speak, afraid of what would come from her mouth.

He entwined his fingers in her hair, pulling her head back.

"Will you yell your pleasure before I have scarce begun to couple with you?"

She saw the vague imprint of her palm on his cheek. "Will you strike me?" she asked.

"You deserve it," he said, his eyes falling to her small white breasts. "But no. There is a more effective punishment for you, is there not? I must simply ensure that your fear of me douses your lust."

"You will force me again, rape me like you did poor Mary?"

"Why not?" he asked, hating himself for the lust he felt for her. "I can do anything I wish with you. You are my wife."

"Please, Graelam," she said, trying to pull away from him, "don't hurt me."

He carried her to the bed. "No, I won't hurt you, but neither will I allow you pleasure." He pressed her onto her stomach and spread her legs. She closed her eyes against the humiliation. She knew he was staring down at her, and when his fingers touched her, she cried out. Suddenly he released her.

"Go to sleep," he said. "I don't want you."

She curled into a ball, drawing the covers to her chin. She felt tears, and quickly and angrily dashed them away.

One moment she was sleeping soundly, and the next, she was moaning into the darkness. Her legs were quivering, and there was a pleasure deep inside her. She felt his mouth, hot and wet, kissing her, caressing her, and both sleep and the humiliation she had felt fled her mind.

He took her, and she climaxed once, then again.

She was sated, but so confused she wanted to scream with it. How could she respond to him so easily after what he had said and done? She was nothing but a simple fool.

29

The heavy cloak made her clumsy, but she ignored it and took another arrow from Evian. She set it in its notch and slowly drew it back until her bunched fingers touched her cheek. She released it, her eyes never leaving the target. To her immense pleasure, she heard a satisfying thud and saw the arrow embedded firmly in the straw target.

"Well done, my lady." Evian clapped his hands.

She wanted to shout her own pleasure. She would never be Chandra, but she had hit the target, and from twenty feet.

"I have improved, have I not?" she asked, her eyes sparkling. The boy nodded enthusiastically. Kassia saw that he was shivering with cold. "Oh, Evian," she said, "you are freezing. It is enough."

But Evian saw her looking toward the remaining arrows in the leather quiver. "Nay, my lady," he said, "you have six more arrows to shoot."

"I can see your breath even as you speak."

"We will not have sunlight for much longer." He handed her another arrow.

Rolfe rubbed his arms as he rounded the naked-branched apple trees in the orchard. Saint Peter's bones, he thought, it is getting cold. He started to speak, then stopped and watched Kassia shoot three arrows. All three hit the target firmly, one of them close to the dark blue center. He smiled, remembering his shock when Kassia had approached him during their return trip from London. She had pulled her mare in beside him.

"My lady?" He turned in his saddle to face her.

"Rolfe," she said, "will you teach me how to use a bow and arrow?" He would have laughed had he not seen the intense, pleading look in her eyes. He was not stupid. His young mistress had met the exquisite Lady Chandra, had watched her with all the other nobles in her match with the king. He had been in Lord Graelam's service when he had decided he wanted to wed Chandra de Avenell, the warrior princess, as he called her. He had accompanied him to Croyland and witnessed the first success and final failure of his plan to wed the girl.

He asked very gently, "Why do you wish to learn a man's skill, my lady?"

Her eyes fell for a moment; then that chin of hers rose. "I wish to be complete," she said. She knew it odd of her to speak thus to her husband's master-at-arms, but she did not have a choice. She doubted he would help her if she was not honest with him.

"A lady such as you is complete. You manage a great keep, help Blount with the accounts—aye, he told me that—direct the preparation of meals that keep our bellies happy, and play an amazing game of chess."

"It is not enough," she said. He saw the flash of pain in her fine eyes, and wished for a moment that he could kick his master off his destrier and pound some sense into his thick head.

Rolfe said finally, hoping his young mistress wouldn't take offense, "She was nothing more than a dream, spun in my lord's imagination and fed by the minstrel's foolish songs. I doubt that she has acquired your skills, my lady."

Kassia did not pretend to misunderstand him. "She is all that Graelam wants and admires, Rolfe. Nay, please don't look away from me. I must speak what is in my mind. He told me about her, of course, when I asked him. He spoke of her honor, of her honesty, and of her amazing skills as a warrior. In his eyes, Rolfe, I have none of those things. Perhaps if I acquire some skill, the other qualities will follow." She lowered her head a moment and Rolfe saw her clench the reins tightly in her small hands. "I must do something."

But not mold yourself into Lady Chandra's elusive image, he thought. "In most of the men's eyes, my lady, you are all that is good and honest and honorable. Very few believe that you betrayed Graelam."

"He does," she said.

Rolfe said before he could stop himself, "He is a fool, particularly when it concerns a woman."

"He is also my husband. If I cannot change his thinking, it is likely that I will betray him and return to my father. I cannot bear the pain of it, you see."

Rolfe wanted to demand if Graelam had beaten her, but he could not. Even speaking to her so honestly was improper.

"He knows only anger at me." She gave him a sad smile. "I don't blame him for what he believes. Sometimes I wonder if I did not imagine it all."

Rolfe looked between his horse's ears, wishing yet again that he could beat some sense into his ruthless master's head. To his surprise, he saw Graelam turn in his saddle, a look of suspicion narrowing his eyes. My God, Rolfe thought, startled, he is jealous. Of me, an old man. He thoughtfully chewed his lower lip. "My lady," he said finally, "I will teach you."

"Graelam must not know of it."

"Nay, he will not know, not until you have the skill to impress him."

"Thank you, Rolfe." She gave him a radiant smile, and he was stunned at the pure sweet beauty of her face.

Rolfe waited now until she had shot her final arrow, then strode forward. He could see his breath in the still, cold air. Fallen leaves crunched under his booted feet. He worried that she would catch a fever, standing for so long in the silent winter afternoon. But he also knew that to say so would wipe the pleasure off her face. He said, "You must hold your right arm more stiffly. Here, let me show you."

He helped her until he felt the cold seep through his thick clothes. She must be freezing, he thought, and stepped back from her. "That is enough, my lady. My old bones need the warmth of a fire."

"And some hot ale," Kassia said. "For you too, Evian."

Evian tucked her bow and the leather quiver beneath his arm, as if it were he who was practicing so faithfully. Rolfe had told him only that his lady's practice was to be a surprise for Lord Graelam.

Kassia entered the Great Hall, still smiling. She drew up at the sight of Graelam, his arms crossed over his chest, watching her. He had returned the evening before from a visit to Crandall. He had not asked her to accompany him, and she had said nothing. It had given her nearly a week to practice without worrying he would come upon her. She felt bone-deep pleasure as she stared at him. He looked vigorous, and splendidly male, his thick black hair tousled around his head. And then her face became a careful blank when he said, "Where have you been?"

Her eyes fell. He had been so busy with Blount. It had not occurred to her that he would miss her, and she had practiced but an hour.

"Would you care for some mulled wine, my lord?"

"What I would care for, my lady, is an answer from you."

"I was walking in the orchard."

She saw the distrust in his eyes. "Evian was with me. I am thinking about planting some pear trees in the spring."

Why was she lying to him? Pear trees, for God's sake. "Come and warm yourself," he said, his voice roughening. "Your nose is red with cold."

She obeyed him after she had given orders for some mulled wine.

"Sir Walter," she said, relieved that Graelam did not question her further, "how fares he at Crandall?" She could not keep the dislike from her voice.

"He is a bit overbearing with the peasants, but I doubt not that he will settle in."

Kassia had hoped that Sir Walter would show his true colors to Graelam, but it appeared that he hadn't yet. She said, "Did Blount show you the message from the Duke of Cornwall?"

"Aye, and it worries me. All his talk about growing old. One would think that with Edward safely on the throne, the duke would relax a bit and enjoy life."

"He has no more responsibilities to keep him young. It would seem, as you have said, that once the heavy burdens are lifted, a man could enjoy his peace. But it is not so. Sometimes I think that Geoffrey and his threats of treachery keep my father healthy."

"Let us hope that your father has enough to keep him busy during the winter. If Geoffrey plans something, he will not execute it until spring."

"How I wish Geoffrey would forget his disappointment. I can't bear the thought of Belleterre being threatened." She moved closer to the huge fireplace and stared into the flames. Her father and Belleterre had been the two constants in her life. Geoffrey had always seemed but a mild nuisance. Belleterre and her father were her refuge, even now, if Graelam no longer wanted her. Two tears spilled onto her cheeks and trailed downward. She didn't have the energy to brush them away.

"Stop crying," Graelam said. "You are not a child, Kassia, and there is no reason to worry about Geoffrey."

Oddly enough, he understood vaguely what she was feeling. He cursed when she raised her face and looked at him with such hopelessness.

He gathered her into his arms, pressing her face against his warm tunic. "Hush," he said more gently, his strong fingers kneading the taut muscles in her shoulders.

He felt a surge of need for her. He well understood lust, but what he felt for Kassia was tempered with other emotions, deep, swirling emotions that he was loath to examine. Damn her, he thought, holding her more tightly. He had bedded several serving wenches during his stay at Crandall, hoping that the next one would give him release and wipe Kassia's image from his mind. But after his stark passion had peaked and receded he had lain awake staring into the darkness even as the woman who had pleasured him lay sleeping beside him.

He felt the delicate bones in her shoulders, so fragile beneath his fingers. He closed his eyes, breathing in the sweet scent of her. No other woman smelled like her. He lowered his head and rubbed his cheek against her hair. Lavender, he thought. She smelled of lavender. His hands dropped lower, cupping her hips. He felt her stiffen. He laughed and pushed her away from him. "I will not take you here. Dry your tears and see to our evening meal."

Kassia brushed away her tears, cursed herself for desiring his strength and his comfort even for a moment. "Aye, my lord," she said and left him. She smiled and spoke throughout the long evening, seeing to Graelam's needs, while wishing that she could creep away someplace and brood. She listened to him speak to his men, listened to him laugh as they traded jests. He hadn't touched her the night before, and she knew that he would take her this night. She wanted him to take her, make her forget, if only for a moment. But not in anger. Not as a punishment.

She excused herself and went to their bedchamber. It took her some time to rid herself of Etta. She bathed in hot scented water, forcing herself to accept the conclusion she had fought against for so long. Pride and truth yielded nothing but empty misery.

She thought of all her practice with the bow and arrow, and laughed at her foolishness. Perhaps Graelam would admire her, but likely it would not bring him to trust her, to believe in her. Only a lie would change how he treated her.

When Graelam entered much later, she was lying in their bed propped up against the pillows.

"I had expected you to be asleep," he said as he stripped off his clothes.

"Nay," she said. "I have missed you."

His heat shot up. She saw the gleam of pleasure in his dark eyes before he quickly made his expression impassive. "Why?"

He stood by the bed, naked, his eyes intent upon her face.

"I don't want strife between us, Graelam," she said, trying not to look so hungrily at him.

But she failed, and he knew it. "You know what I demand from you," he said as he slipped into bed beside her.

"Aye, I know." She wouldn't cry, she wouldn't. "You said you would forgive me."

"I will forgive you."

"Then it was as you believe."

He felt a blow of contempt at himself, and a surge of disappointment as well. He had wanted her to admit her guilt, admit that she had hired Dienwald de Fortenberry and given him the necklace, but facing the fact of her doing it made him almost physically ill. He rose on his elbow beside her and looked down into her pale face. He saw tears shimmering in her eyes.

"I told you I would forgive you if you but spoke the truth. Why do you cry?"

I am so lonely. I cannot bear my loneliness. I will gladly take whatever part of you you wish to give me.

She could think of nothing to say to him. With a small, helpless cry, she flung herself against him, wrapping her arms about his back and burrowing her face against his shoulder.

"So," he said, his bitterness sounding in his voice, "it is my body you wish." He felt her soft mouth pressing light kisses against his chest.

"Please," she said, "no more anger. I can bear no more anger from you."

"It isn't anger I feel for you now, Kassia. I will give you your woman's pleasure, and we will speak no more about the past." He gently pressed her onto her back and drew the covers down to her waist. Her heart was pounding so loudly she thought he must hear it. She felt him looking at her, and it both alarmed and excited her.

"Your breasts seem fuller," he said. He stroked a fingertip around a pink nipple. She wanted to yell it felt so wonderful.

"You do not find me too skinny?"

Oh no, he found her all that he wanted. "You are fine," he said. He lowered his head and kissed her. His hand slipped under the covers and began kneading her belly. "I like the feel of you."

"Please, Graelam." She lurched up as his fingers caressed lower.

He touched her moist flesh. "You are so delicate," he said into her mouth. "And you're ready for me." She felt his fingers deepen their primitive rhythm.

Kassia was wild with lust. "Please, love me. I cannot bear it."

To her surprise, Graelam rolled onto his back and

brought her with him. "I would have you ride me," he said.

She felt him deep inside her, felt his hands about her waist, lifting her and lowering her. "Draw up your legs. You may move over me as you wish."

Kassia had never imagined that she could feel such things. When his fingers found her, she lost all hold and yelled, her head thrown back, her back arched.

She vaguely heard him say her name, felt his fingers tense over her even as her body convulsed in release. He was deep inside her when she felt his seed. She fell forward, her mind emptied of all regret and pain.

Graelam held her close. He straightened her legs. She fell asleep, covering him, her hand nestled in the hollow of his throat. He stroked her tousled hair and tried to close his mind to its tortured thoughts.

It is not enough, Kassia thought, aware yet again that Graelam was watching her, his expression brooding. He wants to hate me, but his honor keeps him to his promise. She wanted to shriek and cry at the same time, but she could not. She had done it to herself, and must now live with it.

He continued to be kind to her. At night she could imagine that he loved her as he took her. She was so aware of him that if his eyes darkened, her body leapt in response. And he knew it. She wondered if he hated her for that too.

It was time to concentrate. Kassia urged Bluebell into a gentle gallop, drew back the bow, and released the arrow at the target. It hit the center, and she turned in the saddle at Evian's shout, his fist raised in triumph.

They were on the beach, a good mile from Wolffeton. She did not want to take the chance that Graelam would come by chance upon her. In this, she would surprise him. He would be pleased with her prowess. He must be pleased. It was the only thing that kept her practicing so diligently.

But he had missed her. She immediately saw the distrust and anger in his eyes.

"You plan more trees for the orchard?" he watched her dismount from Bluebell's back.

Her chin rose. "Nay, my lord. I plan a surprise for you!"

His eyes narrowed. "Explain yourself."

She shook her head, and tried to tease him. "Nay, my lord. You must wait."

"I promised to forgive you the past, not the present," he said.

She could only stare at him. "But I have done nothing to displease you."

"Have you not?" he asked, then turned on his heel and left her.

If she had had a rock in her hand, she would have hurled it at his back. "I will show you," she said, and waved her own fist at his back, not in triumph.

Three days later, on a bright, cold afternoon, Kassia planned to surprise him. She felt excited, hopeful, and proud of herself.

30

"Rolfe. You promised."

Rolfe scratched his head and wished he was any-where but here at Wolffeton. "I don't think it is a good idea," he said.

"But Graelam will be surprised and pleased. You know he must be, Rolfe. I will be just like Lady Chandra and he will admire me." If naught else, that must be true. "You said yourself that I have improved beyond all your expectations. You have already arranged the competition."

"Aye, I have," he said. "I will probably be hanged for a fool."

"Mayhap," she said, "the minstrels will hear about me and write their *chansons* to praise my skill."

"I don't know what will come of this," Rolfe said.

"I must change my clothes." She lowered her voice. "Do not forget what you will say to my lord."

Rolfe watched her run up the stairs into the great hall. He scuffed the toe of his leather boot against a cobblestone and cursed.

"So, Rolfe," Graelam said with some amusement

to his master-at-arms as they walked side by side toward the practice field, "do you also expect me to give a prize to the winner?"

"The men have practiced hard," Rolfe said, not blinking. "Some sort of recognition from you would not be amiss."

"Then I shall think of something." Graelam shaded his eyes and looked over the course. "You are lucky it hasn't rained in a week," he said. "The targets are arranged wide apart. I think most of the men will complete it with a perfect score. Why is it so easy?"

So your lady won't break her neck. "The men competing have little practice in shooting their arrows from horseback," he said. "I wanted to be as fair as possible to them."

Graelam cocked a black brow at him. "I believe you grow soft in your old age." He saw his men lined up on the far side of the course, drawing lots to determine the order. He moved into position beside Rolfe, waiting for the competition to begin.

Rolfe saw him glance back toward the keep and wondered if his master was looking for his wife.

"Kassia takes great pleasure in surprising the men," Graelam said, as if in answer. "I wonder if she will bring the winner a tray of pastries."

Rolfe's eyes were on Kassia, dressed in boy's clothes, sitting proudly astride a bay stallion. She was wearing a short mantle that fastened with a brooch over her right shoulder, its hood drawn up and clipped securely over her hair. It had not occurred to either of them until the day before that Graelam would immediately recognize Bluebell if she rode her mare in the competition. Thus the bay stallion, Ganfred. Rolfe watched the stallion prance sideways, and closed his eyes in a silent prayer. The horse was not as placid and obedient as Bluebell, and Kassia had ridden him but once. She had not seemed at all concerned, but Rolfe was not deceived.

"Only eight men to compete?" Graelam asked, turning to Rolfe. "Have I counted aright?"

The other men had moved away to take positions along the course. The truth was out. "Aye, it's primarily the men who have not done much of this." Indeed, he had handpicked the men who would not make Kassia look bad. Most of them were big men, clumsy with a bow, men who were trained to the lance and mace.

"I imagine," Graelam said, "that I am about to be vastly entertained," for he had begun to recognize the men, even from this distance. "I didn't know that Joseph even knew how to notch an arrow."

"He has been practicing," Rolfe said. "Come, my lord, I believe they are ready to begin."

They'd erected a small dais, wide enough for only two men. Graelam jumped into it and gave Rolfe a hand.

He turned at a shout and watched the first man, Arnold, ride into the course, his bow aimed at the first target. The arrow struck the target with more strength than accuracy, and Graelam shook his head. By the time Arnold had completed the course he had managed to hit the bull's-eye on six of the twelve targets.

There was much good-natured laughing and cheering from the men.

"Arnold the ox!"

"He'll eat the targets he missed for his dinner!"

"Fascinating," Graelam said to Rolfe. "By all means, let's see more."

The next two men did no better than Arnold, and Graelam was beginning to believe that Rolfe had arranged this ridiculous competition as a jest. He started to say as much to his master-at-arms, but Rolfe was staring toward the next rider.

Graelam didn't recognize the man—boy, rather. But the stallion, Ganfred, was from his stable.

"At least the lad shows more ability than the rest," he said, watching the boy draw his bow smoothly back and gently release the arrow. It hit the center. He frowned. "Who is he, Rolfe? A new fledgling you wish to take under your wing?"

"He does well," Rolfe said, trying to postpone the moment of reckoning as long as possible. "Look, my lord, another bull's-eye."

Rolfe swelled with pride. She was doing well, despite the problems she was having with the stallion. By the end of the course, she had struck nine bull's-eyes out of twelve.

"The boy is undersized." Graelam watched him ride back to the far side of the field. "I begin to believe that you arranged this competition just to make him look good. You gave him Ganfred to ride? Who is he, Rolfe?"

"My lord, look. Here is Bran."

Graelam shot a sideways glance at Rolfe. Something was brewing. He decided to wait and see and simply enjoy himself in the meanwhile. The wiry, graceless Bran made Arnold look like a master archer. Graelam joined the laughter as Bran finished the course, smiling widely, showing the huge space between his front teeth.

"I will challenge any jongleurs to beat this act," Graelam said.

Perhaps, Rolfe thought, he shouldn't have picked such utter dolts to compete. Even if Lady Kassia won, it wouldn't be much of a victory. He realized that the men competing had, of course, recognized her, for their performance became even worse. All the men were very fond of her, and were shielding her. He saw the men whispering to each other, passing the word along, and he realized that he had made a grave mistake in allowing this.

Graelam would skin him alive.

He cleared his throat. "The lad appears to have won the first round, my lord." The men slapped Kassia on the back, congratulating her. "The men will pair up in the second round and compete for the targets."

Rolfe saw that Kassia was paired with Bran, the worst of the lot. He waited until the two of them rode toward the first target, jockeying for position as they drew close.

"The lad, my lord," he said, touching Graelam's sleeve to gain his attention, "he did win the first round."

"Aye, and he does not do so badly in this one. But he had better watch Bran's horse. The brute hates Ganfred."

Rolfe drew in his breath. The plan had been to have Kassia ride smartly up to her husband, pull back her hood, and demand the prize from him. He watched helplessly as Bran's horse reared up, kicking his hind legs at Ganfred just as Kassia, as vulnerable as possible, raised her bow to shoot at a target.

"We must stop this!" Rolfe shouted.

"Why? You are growing soft as an old man, Rolfe. Let's see how much talent the lad does have."

"The lad, my lord, is your wife. She did not ride Ganfred until yesterday."

"You're mad," Graelam said. "The jest goes too far, Rolfe."

But Rolfe had jumped from the dais and was running toward the course, waving his hands. The men had quieted, watching Bran try unsuccessfully to rein in his mount. The stallion, his eyes rolling with challenge, bit Ganfred on the neck, reared again, and smashed his hooves into Ganfred's sides.

Graelam was running, all thought frozen, fear coursing through him, raw and cold. He watched helplessly as Kassia's bow and arrow went flying from her hands to the ground. He saw her desperately try to pull away from the maddened stallion, but she did not have the strength to control him. Ganfred turned on the other horse and attacked.

"Kassia, jump off." He heard his own shout, knowing it was lost in the shouts of his men.

Kassia was not afraid, she was furious. She must have been born under an unlucky star. "Bran, pull the beast away." When Ganfred reared up and attacked, she realized that all had gone awry. She struggled to bring the huge stallion under control, but it was no use. She felt Ganfred jerk the reins from her hands at the same time she heard Graelam shout at her.

But she knew if she jumped she might be crushed under the horses' hooves. She hung on, clutching frantically at Ganfred's mane.

"Bran," she yelled, "pull him away!"

Ganfred gave a mighty heave, rearing up again to attack, but the other stallion was running away. He snorted in fury and dashed after him. Kassia lost her hold. She realized that she should roll once she hit the ground, but when the hard earth crashed against her side she was stunned, unable to move, the breath knocked from her.

She lay perfectly still, trying to clear her wits and regain her breath.

"Kassia."

She looked up to see Graelam above her. "It's not fair," she said. "I would have won. It's not fair."

He dropped to his knees beside her, his hands going methodically over her body. "Can you move your legs?"

"Aye." She felt suddenly dizzy and nauseous. "Graelam, I would have won."

His hands were bending her arms, then prodding at her belly.

She sucked in her breath, not wanting to retch. That would be the ultimate humiliation. She saw the shadows of the men above her, heard them talking.

Graelam clasped his hands about her shoulders. "Kassia," he said, gently pulling her up. "Look at me. Can you see me?"

"Of course," she said. "I'm all right."

Graelam lifted her in his arms. "The competition is over," he said.

She closed her eyes against the waves of dizziness, her head falling back against his arm. "I wasn't afraid. If it had not been for that wretched horse—"

"Hush," Graelam said. He carried her to their bedchamber, shouting for Etta. After laying her on the bed, he gently straightened her legs. She closed her eyes tightly.

He felt utterly helpless.

"My baby." Etta scurried to the bed, ignoring Graelam as she sat beside her mistress.

"I am going to be sick, Etta," Kassia said.

When the spasms passed, she lay pale and weak. Her head ached, but the waves of dizziness were lessening.

"I will prepare her a potion, my lord," Etta said, and slowly rose.

"Will she be all right?"

"I trust so," Etta said. "It is just that—"

"Just what?"

"Naught of importance," Etta said, and hastened from the bedchamber.

Graelam sat beside his wife, took her small hand in his, and noticed the calluses on the pads of her fingers for the first time. But he said nothing, merely watched her pale face for signs of pain.

Kassia opened her eyes and looked into her husband's face. "I would have won," she said, sounding a litany.

"Why did you do it?" His grip tightened on her hand.

"I wanted to make you admire me as you do Lady Chandra. I thought if I won you would be pleased."

"I do not want my wife aping men."

She stared up at him, hopelessness in her eyes. "I wanted only to gain your approval, to make you proud of me. I could think of nothing else to make you care for me, to make you forget that you so dislike me."

Graelam said nothing. Guilt flooded him. "I don't

dislike you. But what you did was foolish beyond permission."

"Please do not blame Rolfe," she said. "Or any of the men. They could not have known that Bran's stallion would attack Ganfred."

He wanted to bash all their heads in, but he said, "Very well." He unfastened the brooch and pulled off her mantle. "You will likely be sore for a while from your fall." He fell silent, then smiled at her. "Compared to your competitors, you did very well indeed. This was my surprise?"

She nodded. "They were not really competitors," she said. "Rolfe didn't believe I could gain your attention if I went against the better men. He did not want me to look bad."

"You didn't look bad. Did Lady Chandra give you this idea?"

"Nay, though she showed me how to handle a bow. She is so beautiful."

"Kassia," he said, "I wanted her, I told you that. But I did not love her. There was no reason for you to be jealous of her skills." He lightly touched his palm to her forehead, and relaxed. She felt cool to the touch. "Kassia, does it matter so much to you what I think?"

She looked up at him, remembering that she had once told him she loved him. Had he simply ignored her words? Believed that she was telling but another lie? And now, of course, since she had admitted that she had lied to him, he would likely believe nothing she said. She said only, "Aye, it matters to me."

"There has been much between us." He broke off as Etta came into the bedchamber. He moved aside and watched her give Kassia the vile smelling potion.

Etta straightened. "She will sleep now, my lord. I did not know what she planned, else I would never have allowed her to do it. I pray that she will be all right."

"I will stay with her until she sleeps," he said. "I will call you if she worsens, Etta."

He stroked her hand. Her lashes fluttered, closed. He listened to her breathing as it evened into a drugged sleep.

He undressed her, smiling at the boy's clothes. He eased her beneath the covers, pulled them to her chin. He found himself studying her, comparing her to Chandra. There was, he decided, no comparison at all, and he was pleased.

Kassia slept the afternoon away, awakening briefly in the evening. She felt oddly heavy, and dull.

"It is the potion Etta gave you," Graelam said. "I fear that you must rest a few days before you again take up your bow and arrow."

"You do not mind?"

"Nay," he said, smiling at her. "In fact, I will give you better competition than poor Bran. The fellow is frantic with worry. You must get well and reassure him."

"Aye, I will." She fell asleep again, hope filling her at his words.

She awoke to darkness, her throat dry and scratchy. She slipped from the bed and made her way slowly to the carafe of water on the table. She reached for the water, only to whip her hand to her belly at a sudden fierce pain. She felt wet stickiness gushing from her body. She looked at herself, not understanding, then doubled over as another cramping pain ripped through her. She cried out.

Graelam bounded out of the bed. He quickly lit a candle and strode toward her.

"Kassia, what is it?"

"Graelam, help me. I'm bleeding." She doubled over as another pain clutched at her.

He saw crimson on her white chemise, rivulets of blood flowing down her legs. Her monthly flow? No, it was not that. He felt his guts turn cold.

He grabbed her to him. Her hands clutched at his shoulders, and she stiffenend with another cramp. "Help me. What is happening?"

He knew then that she was miscarrying a babe. He heard himself saying to her quite calmly, "You will be all right, Kassia. Let me help you into bed. I will get Etta."

He lifted her gently into his arms and laid her on the bed. She stared up at him, eyes wild with fear.

"You will be all right," he said again, more for himself than for her. "Don't move."

She watched him jerk open the door, and bellow for Etta.

Etta paid no heed to Lord Graelam's nakedness. She was panting hard, still pulling on her bedrobe.

"Blood," Graelam said. "I fear she is losing a babe. Is she with child?"

Etta felt the blood drain from her face. "Aye," she said. She looked down at Kassia, saw her mistress lying in a pool of blood. "Oh, my baby." She clutched at Kassia's hand.

"What can I do?" Graelam asked from behind her.

Etta pulled herself together. "Clean cloths, my lord, and hot water. We must make certain she does not bleed her life away."

Graelam turned immediately, pausing only when he heard Etta call after him, "My lord, your bedrobe."

31

"You knew she was with child?"

Etta's kind face contorted with pain. "Aye, I knew, my lord, and I was going to tell her if she did not come to the knowledge soon."

"It is a pity that you did not tell before she played the man today."

"You had no knowledge of it, my lord?"

Graelam made a slashing motion with his hand. It was on the tip of his tongue to shout at her that he was a man and paid no heed to women's concerns. But he held himself quiet. It should have occurred to him that she'd had no monthly flow. And had he not noticed that her breasts seemed fuller?

"How far along was she?" he asked instead.

"Early days," Etta said. "Two months, I should say."

He looked down at his wife, asleep now from another potion Etta had given her. She was so pale her face looked as if it had been drained of blood. Her chemise, stained with streaks of crimson, lay wrapped in cloths on the floor. "She will be all right?"

"Aye, the bleeding is stopped." Etta rubbed her gnarled hands together helplessly. "I should have told her. I thought that since she was now a married lady, and you a man of experience, she would realize that—"

Graelam cut her off. He felt impotent and angry. "I married a child," he said. "How could anyone expect her to know a woman's function?"

"She has had other concerns of late, my lord," Etta said, looking directly at him.

"Aye, riding astride and learning men's sports."

"It was not her fault," Etta said.

"I don't suppose that she finally admitted to you that she lied? About everything?"

"My lady does not lie, my lord."

Graelam laughed. "Little you know her. It matters not now. Go to bed. I will call you if she awakens."

Etta gave him a long look, tempted to tell him he was a fool, but she saw the pain in his dark eyes and held her tongue. He did care for Kassia, but how much? She shuffled from the chamber, her bones creaking with tiredness.

Kassia awoke, blinking into the bright sunlight that streaked into the bedchamber. Memory flooded back and she tensed, waiting for the terrible pain, but there was none. She felt tired and sore, as if her body had been bludgeoned. She smiled, remembering well that it had. But the blood. What had happened to her?

"Here, drink this."

She turned her head slowly on the pillow at the sound of her husband's voice. She felt his hand slip behind her head to lift her, and sipped the sweet-tasting brew.

"How do you feel?" Graelam asked as he carefully eased her down again.

She managed a smile. "I feel as though you must have beaten me, my lord. But I don't understand. All the blood, the pain in my belly."

"You lost our—a babe."

She stared up at him. "I was with child?" At his nod, she felt herself grow cold. "I didn't know. Oh no!"

Tears filled her eyes, fell onto her cheeks, but she didn't have the strength to dash them away.

Graelam wiped them away with the corner of the bedcover. He wanted to comfort her, but bitterness flowed through him and he said, "I daresay even your mentor, Chandra, knew enough to curb her men's sports when she was with child."

The unfairness of his words numbed her. Did he believe that she lied about not knowing? Did he believe that she had willfully endangered their babe? It was too much. She slowly turned her face away from him and closed her eyes tightly against the damnable tears. She would weep no more. "Perhaps," she said so low that he had to lean closer to hear her, "it would have been best had I died."

Graelam reeled back. "Do not speak nonsense," he said. "There will be other babes."

Would there?

"You will not blame Rolfe? He did not know, I swear it."

"I'm not a monster," he said, forgetting for a moment the tongue-lashing he had given his master-at-arms. "You must rest now and regain your strength. Your nurse is hovering outside to attend you. I will see you later."

She watched him stride toward the door, so powerful, so unyielding. He did not look back at her.

The evening meal Etta served her was prepared for an invalid's flagging appetite.

"Come now, my baby. The cook made the stewed beef especially for you, using cummin and hysop just as you taught him. And here is hot, freshly baked bread with honey."

Kassia ate. When she was too exhausted to lift the spoon, she leaned back against the fluffed pillows. "Where is Lord Graelam?"

"In the hall." Etta eyed her mistress. "Everyone is very worried about you. Poor Rolfe was ready to kill Bran."

"It wasn't Bran's fault." Kassia closed her eyes. "He blames me," she said flatly after a long, silent moment.

Etta did not pretend to misunderstand her. "Your lord is very concerned for your welfare."

"Do not spin tales, Etta. He believes a wife's only worth is in breeding children. I was stupid, and forgot that."

"You will carry another child, my baby. I could see no harm done."

"Aye, it is my duty to do something my lord approves of," she said. "I will not be so stupid as to want something more—ever again."

"You will cease this silly talk," Etta said. "It's a man's kingdom." She searched for the right words. "It's men who rule, men who make the rules."

"Aye, and it is a woman's duty to give birth to

more of them so they may subjugate the lot who have the misfortune to be born girls."

Etta tried to think of something soothing to say. Her thinking halted abruptly at the sound of Lord Graelam's voice. Oh God, how much had he heard?

"You speak the truth, my lady, but your words are overly harsh and bitter. Men rule because they are the only ones fit to do so. A woman does have worth, you are right, for men cannot continue unless women birth them."

"Now I have no worth," Kassia said matter-of-factly. She felt oddly devoid of feeling, and blessedly numb.

"I did not say that," Graelam said evenly. "I trust only that you now will see to your woman's duties."

She looked at him straight, all hope in her quashed, and said, "If I but knew how to get a message to Dienwald de Fortenberry, I should be tempted to offer him that wretched necklace to take me away. That would please you. It's a pity that Blanche is no longer here to wed you."

He clenched his teeth, feeling a muscle in his jaw jump. "But you do know how to reach Dienwald de Fortenberry, do you not?"

"My lord," Etta said, rising to face him, "she is overly tired. She must have rest."

Graelam remembered how he had come to comfort her, to spend time with her while she mended. But her words had made him angry. "I will leave her to your care," he said, and left the chamber.

"You must not say things like that," Etta said.

"Why? It matters not, Etta. Nothing matters, not anymore."

*   *   *

The inked quill hovered over the parchment, but she knew she could not write to her father of the despair in her heart. She inquired after his health and the winter weather in Brittany, then detailed all the household improvements she had made. She did not ask him about Geoffrey, knowing that if he were to plan anything, her father would send a message to Graelam, not her. She wrote nothing of the lost babe or the indifferent war that existed between her and Graelam. She had just finished sprinkling sand on the parchment when Blount entered the small chamber.

"You write your father, my lady?"

"Aye, it is done, Blount."

He looked at her and then down at the parchment. "My lord will read what you have written, my lady."

She took his meaning well, but merely smiled wearily at him. "I know. There is naught within to anger him." She rose and shook out the skirt of her wool gown. "Indeed, it is so boring, perhaps my lord will think it useless to send." She walked slowly to the small window and drew back the wooden shutters. "It does not feel like the end of February. There is the sweet smell of spring in the air."

"Aye, it is uncommonly warm today." Blount eyed his mistress, worry drawing a deep furrow in his brow. "Why do you not ride out, my lady?"

"Perhaps I shall," Kassia said. "Aye, it's a good idea."

Though the weather was mild, Kassia dressed warmly, choosing a velvet mantle lined with miniver. A month, she thought, walking slowly to the stables, a month waging a war without fighting. She smiled grimly. She should be used to it by now. During her short marriage she had endured more bitter than sweet, and now the bitter seemed unending. She greeted servants and Graelam's man-at-arms, all of whom, had she but noticed, held sympathy in their eyes.

Bran was in the stables. At the sight of her he paled. "My lady, you must forgive me. Those damned horses, and it was all my fault."

Kassia raised a hand. "You will not blame yourself, Bran. It was my decision to compete and my decision not to ride my mare. No, say no more. It's over and best forgotten. I am well again. Indeed, I am riding out now to enjoy the lovely weather."

No one tried to stop her. She waved to the porter, but did not slow Bluebell's pace. The sky was a vivid blue with fat clouds drifting slowly overhead. The breeze grew stiffer the closer she drew to the sea. She threw back her head and breathed in the crisp, salty scent of the water. She guided Bluebell down the rocky path to the small cove, the place where Graelam had taken her so slowly, and held her so gently. No, she would not think of that. She slid from Bluebell's back and tethered her to a bare-branched yew bush that thrust out of a rocky crevice.

Kassia walked along the beach, watching the water slowly rise closer as the tide came in. It was so peaceful here. If only, she thought, raking her hand through her hair, she could know this peace all of the time. She sat down on an outjutting boulder, tucking her feet beneath her to protect them from the encroaching waves that pounded against the lower rocks, spewing white mist upward. Her mind flitted to many things, always returning to Graelam and the bitterness of her life with him. She accepted that she loved him, knowing she was a fool to do so, but

unable to change the feelings that seemed so deeply
embedded within her. He would always blame her
for losing the babe. After all, what else was she good
for? She should not allow herself to forget what excellent meals he and his men now enjoyed.

And he would always believe her guilty of trying
to escape him and of freeing Dienwald. After all, had
she not stupidly admitted guilt to him? All to spare
further anger, further recriminations. What a fool she
had been. Dienwald. His face formed in her mind
and she did not allow it to fade. Peace, she thought;
she could hope for nothing more now. Brittany and
her father. The irony of this thought nearly made her
cry. She rose to her feet and shook out her velvet
mantle. Her idea burgeoned and she nourished it,
not thinking for the moment how she would accomplish it. She thought of the barbaric necklace and
laughed. If Blanche could manage it, then so could
she.

Graelam read the message from the Duke of Cornwall, bidding him to come to him. He frowned, for
the duke gave no indication of any urgency. Damn,
he was a warrior, trained to fight. Affairs in England
had been more interesting when he was a lad. Aye,
he would even be pleased were one of his neighbors
to try some pilaging. He sighed, wondering what the
duke wanted. He decided to leave immediately, for
there was nothing to hold him here. Having made
his decision, he called Rolfe, gave instructions, then
went in search of Kassia. She was not in their bedchamber, nor could he find her in any of the outbuildings. He saw Bran approach him and paused.

"My lord," the man said, "I hear you search for Lady Kassia. She went riding, I know not where."

Graelam felt his jaw tighten, for he had given orders to Osbert that she was never to ride out without his permission. The man had obviously disobeyed him. He was on the point of going to the stable when he saw Kassia's still face in his mind. She was not foolish enough to ride from his lands. Let her mend, he thought, let her regain her health and her spirit. When he returned from the Duke of Cornwall's, he would go more gently with her. She had not, after all, known she was with child; though she had been foolish—Here his thinking stopped. She had tried to impress him, believing he would admire her if she could be like Chandra. He felt pain, and hated it. It made him feel uncertain about himself and what he wanted. A man who was soft with women was weak and despicable. He forced his mind to picture her body—her flesh, the warmth of her when he was deep within her. He would once again enjoy her in his bed and see her smile.

Kassia still had not returned when he left Wolffeton, twenty of his men with him. He instructed Blount merely to tell her that he was visiting the Duke of Cornwall and would return to Wolffeton soon.

He looked back at Wolffeton once before a steep hillock obstructed his view. He would miss her, he realized, but it was for the best that he be apart from her for a while. Being with her constantly made him want her. And it was still too soon. He wanted her well first.

* * *

Kassia was crushed when Blount, unable to meet her eyes, told her what Graelam had instructed him to. For a moment she couldn't draw enough breath into her lungs. Graelam had left. He had not cared enough even to see her, to tell her of his business or when he would return. Any niggling doubts she felt were gone. She cursed him, and it made her feel better.

She rode with Bran and an escort of six men the same afternoon to the village of Wolffeton. The merchant Drieux would help her. The small wrapped package would indeed be delivered as soon as possible to Dienwald de Fortenberry, Drieux assured her. That the package contained the necklace and letter to Dienwald would remain her secret.

To Bran's pleased surprise, his mistress laughed on their ride back to Wolffeton.

32

"Little chick, may I say that you have surprised me more than I ever believed possible?"

Kassia smiled at Dienwald de Fortenberry, quite unaware that it was a sad smile, one that tugged at his heart. "But you did come," she said.

"Aye, though I was tempted to believe it another ruse on the part of that whoreson Sir Walter."

"My husband rewarded Sir Walter by making him castellan of Crandall," she said. "At least he is no longer at Wolffeton. He disliked me as much as he did you."

Dienwald looked at her closely for a long moment, then moved his destrier closer to her mare. "Your message said only that you needed me. I see you have some baggage with you. And you sent me the necklace. What is it you wish?"

"I want to return home to Brittany, to my father. The necklace is payment."

Dienwald stared hard at her, saw that she was quite serious, then threw back his head and roared with laughter. He quieted quickly enough. "So," he said, "that fool husband of yours has finally driven you away. The irony of it can't have escaped you, Kassia."

"Aye, it has made me laugh as well. I would have been much wiser to let you return me to Belleterre the first time."

He saw the bruised shadows beneath her expressive eyes, and said in a savage voice, "Did that bastard beat you?"

Kassia shook her head wearily. "I lost a babe through my own foolishness. I cannot really blame him for being angered, though I did not know I was with child."

He saw her hands tug convulsively at her mare's reins. "I'm sorry, Kassia. If you are certain this is what you wish, I will take you to your father."

"It is what I must want."

"He will come after you."

"Perhaps, but I beg leave to doubt it. He is blessed with many powerful friends. It is more likely that he will have our marriage dissolved and marry a proper English lady. One who will most willingly accept her place."

Dienwald cursed, making the men behind him stare at him in surprise. She was so damned helpless and vulnerable and trusting. St. Peter's teeth, how he wished he could knock some sense into Graelam's thick head. He knew well enough that she loved her husband, else he would have begged her to let him care for her, to wipe the sadness from her eyes. He grew silent.

"Will you help me, Dienwald?"

"You are not content with what he gives you," he said. "What is the place you cannot accept?"

"Being treated as though I had no more importance than a brood mare—No, that is not precisely true." She slashed her hand through the still air. "He does not love me and never will. I thought perhaps I could gain his trust, his esteem, but it was for naught. I can bear no more. I ask you again, Dienwald. Will you help me?"

"Aye, it seems to be my fate to have my life intertwined with yours. I do not want the necklace, Kassia. I think the damned thing is cursed."

"Nay, it is yours. I fancy that it will cost you to get me to Brittany."

He glanced at her oddly for a long moment. "You trust me not to take advantage of you?"

She looked surprised and cocked her head to one side. "Should I not trust you?"

"I did leave you in my cell at Wolffeton to face your husband."

"Aye, but I understood. I would likely have done the same in your place. It is over now, and there is no need to speak of it again."

"Very well. We will return to my keep for supplies. I will have you safe in your father's hands within two weeks, I promise you."

"Thank you, Dienwald. Please, keep the necklace. Any merchant will pay you greatly for it." She saw him still hesitate, and said, "I wish never to see it again."

He nodded, then asked, "How did you manage to leave Wolffeton without your husband's knowledge?"

She gave a short, bitter laugh. "He left to visit the Duke of Cornwall, for what reason I know not. He was growing restless at Wolffeton. Perhaps there is some dispute the duke wishes him to settle. I did not even see him."

"Good. Now I do not have to look over my shoulder. Come, little chick. We have some distance to go."

"So, Graelam, you came more quickly than I had expected," the Duke of Cornwall said as he eyed the younger man over his wine goblet.

"As your loyal and dutiful vassal, is it not what you would expect?"

The duke chuckled. "Aye, you are in the right of it, of course. Actually, I wished to have your opinion on Edward's grandiose plans."

"Ah, he chafes already under the weight of his kingly robes? I take it he is ready to journey to Wales?"

"Aye, I imagined he had spoken to you of it. He is ready to begin building. Unlike his father, his plans do not include cathedrals."

"It is well," Graelam said, sipping at the sweet red wine in his golden goblet. "The Marcher barons have not the strength to keep the Welsh raiders in check." He grinned at the duke. "Now that you have my opinion, my lord duke, you wish me to leave?"

"Nay, you impudent rascal. Actually, I have planned a tourney and wish you to take part. Does that interest you?"

Graelam rubbed his hands together, his dark eyes lighting up. "It interests me. I have grown bored with naught to do but see to the reparations of Wolffeton. When will the tourney take place?"

"I had thought of April. It gives me no pleasure

to think of knights floundering about in foot-deep snow and slush."

"Will Edward come?"

"Can you doubt it, Graelam? This castle building of his will cost dearly, and his nobles, of course, must dig into their coffers."

"I imagined as much. Still, it is wiser to have his nobles bashing each other's heads in a tourney sponsored by the king's uncle than attacking each other without his permission."

"What do you think your lady would say to your fighting, my lord? She would accompany you, would she not?"

Graelam's dark eyes narrowed. He forced himself to sip at his wine again before answering. "She has been ill. We will have to see when the time grows near."

"Ill? Does the child do better now?"

"She lost our babe," Graelam said. "She is well now, at least in body."

"A pity, but she is young and appears quite healthy. She will bless you with many sons."

Graelam held himself silent, and the duke said after a moment, "I have heard from Sir Guy. It appears that his new bride, Blanche, is with child. He is pleased."

"I will visit him soon. He is a good man and a valiant warrior. I miss him sorely."

"But it pleases you that he is now landed, does it not?"

"Aye, it pleases me."

"How did your lady lose her babe?"

Taken off guard, Graelam said, "She was playing at being the man. My master-at-arms, Rolfe, had taught her how to shoot the bow. He arranged a competition with the most clumsy of my men, to make her look good, of course. One of the horses attacked her mount and she was thrown."

The duke leaned forward in his chair, eyes alight with interest. "I don't understand. What made her do such a thing?"

"She met Lady Chandra at Edward's coronation. She was impressed with Chandra's prowess. She thought to impress me."

"And did she?"

Graelam sighed, the truth coming easily now, for he was beset with guilt. Still, his voice was hesitant. "Aye, but it wasn't necessary. I was coming to admire her without such ruses."

The duke felt as though the world had taken a faulty turn. He knew he was staring, but he could not help it. He had always believed Graelam a warrior without equal, a proud man, a man who took what he wanted, be it possessions or women. But there was always a part of Graelam he knew to be lacking. He said quietly, "My lord, to love a woman does not weaken a man or make him a fool. The stronger the man, the more gentle he is with his lady. Your father was quite wrong, you know."

Graelam snorted. "You sound like the troubadours, my lord duke. Can you see me kneeling before a lady and vowing her eyes are brighter than the stars and her complexion a rival to the fairest rose?"

"Does your wife demand such nonsense?"

Graelam ran his hand over his brow. "Nay, but she demands more of me than I am able to give." Even as he spoke the words, he knew they weren't true. What had she demanded of him? Naught save gentleness and kindness and affection. *She left you. She lied. She is not to be trusted. She lost your babe.* He rose abruptly and paced about the duke's solarium. He stilled momentarily at the sound of the duke's voice. "And just what, Graelam, does your gentle wife demand of you?"

He should have known the old man would pry. "I believe," he heard himself say, "that she wants me to love her." He slammed his fist against his open palm. "Damn her! I told her I forgave her lies."

The duke raised a bushy gray brow. "Lies? What is this?"

Graelam saw no hope for it. He eased himself into the high-backed chair opposite the duke and quickly related the happenings at Wolffeton, omitting nothing. When he had finished, the duke was silent for many moments. "Odd," he said, "I would have thought that Dienwald de Fortenberry would be merciless, even with a gently bred lady. But no matter. Why, my lord Graelam, don't you believe your wife?"

"Do you know," he said, astounded at the words that were taking form, "I have come to think that it matters naught, not anymore." But for the first time, he allowed himself to consider that Kassia had been telling him the truth.

"Excellent. I might add that it is possible you saw Blanche as she wished you to see her. I myself received the impression that she was not at all what she seemed, at least in her dealings with you." The duke actually had no idea if this were true or not. But he had overheard Queen Eleanor say something to her husband of Blanche's unkindness to Kassia.

Graelam shrugged. "I did not come here to speak

of my marital problems, my lord duke. She is my wife and will remain so, no matter what her feelings."

"And what of your feelings, my lord?"

"Dammit, I wish to speak no more of it. Mayhap I will fall in your damned tourney. If you believe my wife to be such a paragon, you may take her."

The duke merely smiled, pleased with what he saw. They proceeded to discuss in detail Edward's plans, then enjoyed an excellent meal. The duke offered Graelam a girl for his bed, and to his amusement, Graelam refused.

Graelam didn't leave the duke's fortress for a week. During the days, he forced his thoughts to planning the duke's tourney, but at night, alone in his bed, he couldn't prevent Kassia's face from coming into his mind. He could practically feel the softness of her body, hear her cries as he gave her pleasure, smell her woman's scent. He jerked upright in his bed. He thought to rut the girl the duke offered him. He shook his head in the darkness. Nay, there was but one woman who would satisfy him. The admission surprised him, and at the same time brought him a great measure of peace. *I love her.* He began to laugh, seeing himself for the first time as Kassia must have seen him. Gentle and loving one day, harsh and unforgiving the next. How could she have come to love him when he had treated her thus? He remembered his rape of her so long ago. Yet she had forgiven him that.

He jumped from the bed and strode naked to the shuttered windows. He opened them, and breathed in the crisp cold night air. The moon was a sliver in

the black sky, as clear from Wolffeton as it was from
here. Are you thinking of me now, Kassia? Is there
anger at me in your mind? I will win you back when
I return to Wolfeton.

It was a woman's place to yield, to surrender; a
man's place to demand and dominate. He had spent
twenty-eight years without a thought to a woman's
needs. Oh, her physical needs, to be sure, for that
but added to his sense of dominance. It chilled him
to admit that he had acted the ass, utterly selfishly.
Telling himself it was not too late, he felt a surge of
confidence. Soon he would yield to her. The unexpected thought gave him great pleasure.

Dienwald rode beside Kassia up the winding path
to Belleterre. He had journeyed in easy stages, trying
not to weary her too much. He felt the tension mount
in her as they neared the mighty keep.

"Be easy, little chick," he said. "All will be well,
you will see."

Nay, Kassia thought, nothing would ever be well
again. She thought of Etta's anguish at finding her
gone from Wolffeton, even though she had tried to
explain her actions in a message to her old nurse.
Would Graelam care? She shook her head. It did not
matter. She must put him behind her. She must look
to the future.

The muted gray stone of Belleterre gleamed in the
afternoon sunlight. Kassia tried to take pleasure in
her homecoming. She gazed at the naked-branched
trees she had climbed in her childhood, at the deep-
cut embrasures in the wall along the north tower
where she had played so many years before. What

would her father say? Would he forgive her? Would he insist she return to Graelam? She refused to consider those possibilities.

They pulled to a halt in front of the mighty gates.

"I will leave you now," Dienwald said. "I do not intend to wait and see if your father wishes to thank me or slice my head from my body. I am not, after all, your esteemed husband."

Kassia turned in her saddle, and clasped her hand over his. "I am lucky to have a friend such as you," she said. She reached out her hand and he grasped it in his. "Thank you. God go with you, Dienwald."

"Good-bye, little chick. If ever you have need of me, I will come to you."

With those words he whirled about his destrier and galloped down the winding path to where his men waited.

Kassia looked up and saw the surprised faces of the men who had known her since she was a child. Shouts of greeting rose even as the great iron-studded gates swung open to admit her. She rode into the inner bailey. These were her people. They loved her, trusted her, and respected her. Children cavorted around Bluebell and she leaned down to speak to each of them. She was dismounting from her mare when she heard a welcoming shout from her father.

"Kassia!" He gathered her into his arms, squeezing her so tightly that she yelped. She felt her father's love flow into her, and began to know again a measure of peace and comfort.

"Where is Graelam, poppin?" He held her back as he asked his question, studying her weary face.

Kassia's eyes dropped. "Can we speak alone, Father? It's a long story, and one that should be talked of in private."

"As you wish." His arm tightened about her shoulders as they entered the great hall. "My love—" he said, then paused, clearing his throat. "There is something I must tell you."

"Aye, Papa?"

"I was on the point of sending you a message."

"What message?" Kassia stared at her father.

"I have someone I wish you to meet," he said. "She is my wife."

"*Wife?*"

Maurice nodded, not quite meeting her eyes. "Her name is Marie, and she hails from Normandy. I met her in Lyon, actually. She is a widow—My dear," he called.

Kassia's mind reeled with her father's unexpected news. She had a stepmother. She watched a graceful woman of some thirty-five or so years walk toward them. Her hair was as black as a raven's wing, her eyes a soft brown, her complexion fair. There was a smile on her face.

"My love," Maurice said, releasing his daughter. "This is Kassia, come for a visit."

"How very lovely you are." Marie said, holding out a beautiful white hand. "Maurice speaks so much of you—and your husband, of course." She looked around expectantly.

"My husband did not accompany me," Kassia said, fighting tears. She wouldn't make a fool of herself in front of her father's new wife.

"No matter," Marie said complacently, as if a wife traveling without her husband were the most common occurrence. "I hope we may be friends, Kassia.

Come, my dear, I will take you to your chamber. You must be weary from your journey." She smiled at her husband. "We will join you a bit later, Maurice."

"You are quite a surprise," Kassia said as she accompanied her new stepmother up the winding stairs to the upper chambers.

"Your father and I just returned to Belleterre three weeks ago. I believe he intended to send a message to you and your lord in the next day or so. Oh dear, I had hoped we would have a few moments of quiet."

Three children, two young boys and a girl, were racing toward them.

"My children," Marie said, lifting her dark brows. "I fear now we shall have little peace."

"They are beautiful," Kassia said as she stared down at a little girl of about seven years. The two boys hung back. "How very lucky you are."

"Now I am," Marie said. "Gerard, Paul, come and greet your sister. And you, Jeanne, make your curtsy."

"Oh dear," Kassia said, bursting into merry laughter. "I am overcome."

"My lord, there is an encampment ahead."

Dienwald drew in his destrier. "Are they French? Did you see a standard?"

"Aye, my lord. Three black wolves, upright and snarling against a background of white."

Dienwald shook his head, bemused. "The Wolf of Cornwall," he said. Graelam. Well, he had told Kassia her husband would come after her. It would be easy enough, he thought, to ride unseen around

Graelam's camp. It was on the tip of his tongue to give that order, but he did not.

Graelam stretched out on his narrow cot, pulled a single blanket over himself, and commanded his weary body to sleep. Tomorrow, he thought, watching the lone candle spiral its thin light to the roof of the tent, he would see Kassia. His fury at her disappearance had faded, leaving only a numbing emptiness. He thought again of her message, and it chilled him. "You must not worry about my safety, my lord," she had written, "for I will be well-protected." By whom? But he knew. She had hired Dienwald de Fortenberry once; she had done it again. "It is likely that my father will not blame you for my failure. Belleterre will doubtless be yours in any case. I trust, my lord, that you will find a lady who will please you."

And that was all. Nothing more. Did she really expect him to let her go? Did she really think so little of herself that she believed Belleterre the only reason he had kept her as his wife?

He gave not two farthings for Belleterre at the moment. He wanted his wife. He wanted to beat her, kiss her and crush her against him. He wanted to hear her tell him that she loved him, that she forgave him. He laughed. How he had changed, and all of it wrought by a skinny little girl whose smile would melt the heart of the most hardened warrior. Except his. Until now.

Graelam heard a soft rustle as the tent flap raised. He sat up, instantly on guard, and reached for his sword.

"Hold, my lord Graelam," he heard a man's deep voice say. He saw a flash of silver steel.

"What is this?" Graelam's hand tightened on his sword.

"I mean you no harm, my lord. I am not your enemy. I have too healthy a wish to keep my body intact."

"Who the devil are you?"

"Dienwald de Fortenberry. Your wife spared me the only other opportunity I had of meeting you."

Graelam's eyes glittered in the dim light. So he had been right. The bastard had taken Kassia back to her father. "Just how did you get past my men?"

"A moment, my lord. I beg you not to call for you men. I have no wish to run you through."

Graelam released his sword, and Dienwald watched it fall to the ground. "Thank you," he said. He looked at Graelam de Moreton closely. He was naked, save for the blanket that came only to his loins. He was a powerful man, chest muscled and covered with black hair. Dienwald could see the ribbed muscles over his flat belly. Aye, he thought, a man women would admire, and desire. His eyes roved over Graelam's face. It was not a handsome courtier's face, but it was strong, proud, and at the moment harsh, the dark eyes narrowed on Dienwald's face. His mouth was hard, the lower lip full, his teeth gleaming white and straight. Dienwald was probably a fool to take this chance, slipping into this man's camp, but he had decided it was a debt he owed to Kassia. He was aware that Graelam was studying him just as closely.

Graelam eyed the man. His features were silver and brown, just as Kassia had told him. "What do you want?" he asked. Oblivious of his nakedness, he rose and poured two goblets of wine. He quirked a black brow toward Dienwald.

Dienwald accepted the goblet of wine. "Please sit down, my lord. You must excuse my distrust, but I am not the fool I must seem. When my men told me of your encampment, I was pleased that you came so quickly for your wife. Of course, she did not believe me. She fancied you would be pleased to see no more of her."

Graelam's eyes narrowed. He wanted to leap at the man and tear his heart from his chest with his bare hands. But Dienwald held the upper hand, for the moment at least, and Graelam had no idea how his men were situated outside his tent.

"You have interfered mightily in my life," he said. "So she paid you yet again to take her from me."

Dienwald gently caressed the razor-sharp edge of his sword. "You are a fool, my lord. Your wife's gentle heart is pure and honest. If she would have me, I would willingly take her from you. I crept into your camp for one reason only. I owe a debt to your wife."

"What did she use for payment this time?" Graelam hissed. "The necklace again?"

"Aye," Dienwald said, his lips a twisted smile. "I did not want the damned thing, but she insisted. I have laughed at the irony of it, my lord. Now, you will heed me, for I imagine that I have not much more time. Your wife has never lied to you, at least to my knowledge. It was Blanche who first paid me the necklace to rid herself of your wife. But I could not do it. When I asked her what she wished, she told me to return her to Wolffeton, to you, her husband. Then that whoreson Sir Walter captured me by

a ruse, using Kassia's name. She released the manacles, my lord, because she hated to see me in pain.
She was, of course, too trusting. I had to leave her
there, for I had no wish to die by your hand." He
paused a moment, then said, "I asked her to come
away with me, but she would not. She loves you,
though I don't think you deserve it."

"You could be lying for her even now," Graelam
said. "Perhaps you are even her lover, as I have always suspected."

Dienwald smiled, encouraged at the show of fury.
"I could certainly have ravished her. Perhaps it is
what Blanche expected, even wished me to do. But I
found that even I, a rough and conscienceless rogue,
could not harm so gentle and trusting a lady. It is
you she loves, my lord, though by all the saints in
heaven you do not deserve such tender feelings from
her." He fingered his sword edge for a long moment.
"I first believed her the most gentle, biddable of crea-
tures. But it isn't so. There is a thread of steel in her,
and a pride that rivals any man's. She left you because she could see no more hope for herself living
as your wife. Her sadness would smite the most
closed of hearts. As I said before, you are a great
fool."

To Dienwald's surprise, Graelam looked straight at
him and said, "Aye, you are right. I realized it myself
but days ago. It is more ironic than you believe, de
Fortenberry. I found I no longer cared if she had lied
to me or not. I want her, and if I can convince her
of the truth of my feelings, I will take her back to
Wolffeton with me."

Very slowly Dienwald sheathed his sword. "I trust

you have a smooth tongue, my lord, for she is adamant.''

"She will obey me."

"I foresee a battle royal. Forget not, my lord, that she is in her father's keep, not yours. I imagine he would protect her if she wished it."

Graelam began to pace furiously about the small space, his powerful naked body gleaming in the candlelight. Suddenly he turned to Dienwald and smiled. "Aye, you've the right of it. But she will obey me. I am her husband." Graelam paused a moment, chewing at his lower lip. "How did her father greet her?"

"I did not enter the fortress with her, fearing some retribution from her father. I have learned never to count on a peaceful welcome from a stranger."

"It goes against the grain to thank a man I have recently considered my enemy. Now that you are no longer a stranger to me, Dienwald de Fortenberry, I will welcome you at Wolffeton. Keep your sword sheathed."

Dienwald smiled, shaking his head. "Can I really be assured that you will not wish to see my body severed in bloody pieces for your sport?"

Graelam stretched out his hand to Dienwald. "I call you friend. And I thank you for protecting my wife. You are welcome at Wolffeton, I swear it."

"Thank you, my lord."

"May I now know how you managed to get into my camp and into my tent without any of my men noticing?"

Dienwald chuckled. "It's not so difficult for a lone man to enter where he wishes, my lord. But leaving intact is a different matter. I am mightily relieved you don't wish to see the color of my blood."

"Nay," Graelam said, smiling easily now, "your blood can remain in your body, at least until the tourney. It would please me to face you on the field."

"A tourney, my lord?"

"Aye, the Duke of Cornwall plans one for April."

"Then I shall see you there. I bid you good-bye and good luck."

Graelam stood motionless as Dienwald slipped quietly from his tent. He shook his head, bemused, and returned to his cot. If only, he thought, snuffing out the gutting candle, he had known the truth months ago. Now it didn't matter. He pondered on the vagaries of fate before he fell into the first sound sleep he had enjoyed in more than a week.

33

The evening meal was boisterous, Maurice having allowed his stepchildren to join them. The men-at-arms pelted Kassia with questions she did not precisely answer, and all the servants stayed close, wishing to tell her all that had occurred to them during her absence. No one mentioned her husband. Kassia felt her father's eyes on her, but she resolutely kept a happy smile. Indeed, she was inordinately pleased to see him so happy with himself and his new family. Marie was good-natured, and she loved Maurice. Kassia was pleased.

"The stewed beef does not please you, Kassia?" Marie asked her after some time of watching her new stepdaughter push the food about on her trencher.

"Oh, of course, Marie. It's just that I am too excited to eat. I shall be ravenous on the morrow."

Marie was silent for a moment, then leaned close to Kassia. "I trust, my dear, that you are not displeased with your father's marriage."

Kassia said honestly, "I'm happy that my father has found someone to care for. My mother died so long ago, and I fear he has been particularly lonely after I left for England. And the children bring new life to Belleterre."

"I would not have you or your husband concerned that Belleterre will pass from you to my children," Marie said quietly. "Indeed, both my boys will have lands of their own, bequeathed to them by my late husband. As for Jeanne, she will have sufficient dowry."

"My husband will be pleased that he will not lose Belleterre," Kassia said.

"Maurice has told me much of Lord Graelam, particularly about your lord saving his life in Aquitaine. He holds him in great esteem."

"As do I," Kassia said, her eyes on her trencher. She waited for Marie to ask her the obvious question, but her new stepmother said nothing further, merely spoke of the servants and their efficiency and kindness to her, their new mistress.

It was very late when the Great Hall quieted. Kassia saw Marie nod to her husband; then she approached Kassia and hugged her. "I will bid you good night, Kassia. If you are not too tired, I think your father would like some private words with you." With those words, she left, shooing her very tired children in front of her.

"You are to be congratulated, Father," Kassia said. "Marie is enchanting, as are the children. You are most lucky."

"Aye, I know it well. I am pleased, and relieved, that you approve, poppin." Maurice slicked his hand through his gray hair then eyed his daughter. "Kassia, do you wish to tell me why you have come to Belleterre alone?"

"I did not come alone, Father," she said. "A dear friend brought me. My safety was never in question."

"My men told me about this 'dear friend' of yours, poppin. Why did he not come to greet me?"

"He is not my husband. He feared you would not be overly pleased to see him."

"Aye, likely," Maurice said. "Come and sit down, Kassia. My old bones are weary, and you are looking none too spry yourself."

Kassia did as he bid her, and eased into the chair opposite her father's. "Does Marie play chess?"

"A bit. She has not your quickness with the pieces or your strategy of the game."

Maurice studied her for a long moment, noting the dark shadows beneath her expressive eyes and the tenseness of her hands, now clutched together in her lap. "You have left your husband?"

Kassia could only nod. Were she to speak, she knew she would cry and shame herself.

Maurice turned to look at the dying embers in the fireplace. "I hope you will forgive me, poppin. It is my fault, wedding you to a man I knew scarce a week. But I truly believed him honorable, my love."

"Papa, you believed I was dying," Kassia said, hating his guilt. "And Lord Graelam is honorable. It is just that—"

"That what, poppin?"

"He does not love me."

Maurice had always believed his daughter one of the most beautiful girls he had ever seen. He tried now to see her objectively, to see her as a stranger might. Her glorious hair was in loose curls to her shoulders, thick, lovely. She had filled out again, but she was still very slender. But the impish, whimsical quality about her was lost. "Then I must believe," Maurice said, "that Graelam is something of a fool."

"Nay, Papa," she said, wondering why she was defending her husband, "he simply has no place in his heart for a female. And I miscarried our babe."

"Are you well?"

"I am well. Indeed, I did not even know I was with child." She rose. "Please, Papa, I don't wish to speak more about it now. He will not come after me. He is likely well-pleased that I left him."

He heard the pain in her voice, and felt utterly helpless.

"May I stay here, Papa? I swear to you that I will not interfere with anything Marie does."

"Of course. This is your home, Kassia."

"Thank you, Papa."

"You are weary, my love. We will speak more about this when you are rested." He drew her to him and hugged her. He felt her womanly curves, her woman's softness. It amazed him that he had not noticed earlier that his little girl had matured. Had Graelam abused her? He pictured the huge man naked with his daughter, taking her as a man took a woman, and wanted to snarl. He leaned his head down and kissed her cheek, wet with her tears.

"Kassia, don't cry, poppin. All will be well now, you will see."

"I don't deserve you," she said, sniffing back the hated tears.

"Well, we are even, for your husband does not deserve you." He patted her back and released her.

"In the morning, poppin. Everything always looks brighter in the sunlight."

Kassia smiled. It had always been one of her father's favorite sayings. She turned to go, when his voice stopped her in her tracks.

"Do you love Graelam?"

She turned slowly back to face him, and Maurice hated the sadness in her expressive eyes. She said very quietly, "I am sick with love for him, Papa. I'm a fool." She turned quickly, lifted her skirts, and fled up the stairs to the upper chambers.

Maurice stood still for many long moments, listening to her light footfalls on the stairs. He had met Marie and lost his heart to her. How could any man not do the same for his daughter? Was Graelam so hardened a warrior that there was no giving, no softness in him? Maurice shook his head and walked slowly to his chamber, knowing that Marie would be there in his bed, ready to comfort him with all the kindness in her heart.

There were no more conversations with her father. Kassia knew she was purposefully avoiding him. She saw the questions in his eyes when she chanced to look at him, but it was too soon. The pain was too sharp. She spent the next day to herself, walking about Belleterre, searching out all her old childhood haunts. She spoke to all her old friends, savoring their words, for they evoked happier times, when her life was simple and filled with love. How odd, she thought, walking up the steep wooden steps to the eastern tower, that she had always taken everyone's love and approval for granted. Several times the ser-

vants had come to her with questions, out of long
habit, and she had sent them to Marie. She had no
intention, just as she had assured her father, of
wresting the management from her new stepmother.

She gained the watchtower and threw back her
head to feel the breeze from the sea and the bright
afternoon sunlight on her face. She heard the men-
at-arms joking with each other on the practice field.
In other days, she would have gone down to watch
them, never questioning that she was welcome.

She saw a group of men riding toward Belleterre.
Her heart began to pound. No, it could not be Graelam. Still, her feet moved along the walkway
toward the great gates of Belleterre. She stood motionless, watching the clouds of dust kicked up by
the horses' hooves. She recognized Graelam's standard, recognized his mighty destrier. He looked utterly resplendent in his silver mail and black velvet
surcoat. He had come. But why? To assure himself
that Belleterre would still be his upon her father's
death?

She stood directly above the gates, looking down
at her husband as he halted his men. She heard
Pierre, the porter, shout down, "Who are you, my
lord? What do you wish at Belleterre?"

She watched Graelam jerk off his helmet and pull
back the mesh hood from his head. "I am Graelam
de Moreton. I have come for my wife."

It could not be true, she thought, doubting it even
as it passed through her mind. Her husband was a
possessive man. Had her leaving him hurt his pride?

"I am here, my lord," she shouted down at him,
leaning forward so he could see her.

Graelam looked upward, and to her consternation,

he smiled. "Madam wife," he called up to her. "I trust you are well after your harrowing journey."

"It was not at all harrowing," she said. "Dienwald was careful of my well-being."

There, she thought, let him realize the truth. She waited to see the fury turn his face to stone. His smile, to her utter surprise, grew wider.

"Have your men open the gates. My men and I are weary."

She stood a moment, irresolute. He had but a dozen or so men with him. He could not force her to return with him. Her father would protect her. She called to the porter. "Allow my lord to enter, Pierre."

She found herself smoothing her hair, wishing that she was garbed in a more becoming gown. Fool. It mattered not if she looked like a dairy maid. She marched down the stairs to the inner bailey.

He rode in like a conquering master, she thought, her eyes narrowing as she watched him. Her chin rose.

Graelam drew Demon to a halt some feet from his wife and dismounted. He handed the reins to one of his men, then looked back at her. It was not going to be easy. He was so pleased to see her that he had to hold himself back from grabbing her and riding away with her. He was aware of men and servants closing about them, all of them ready to club him to death if he threatened her in any way. Their show of loyalty pleased him.

"My lady," he said, stopping in front of her.

"Why are you here, Graelam?"

"It is as I said, Kassia. I have come to take you home to Wolffeton."

"There was no reason for such an action, my lord. I assured you that you would not lose Belleterre."

"I don't give a flying damn about your father's possessions, my lady."

Her chin rose higher. "Dienwald de Fortenberry brought me here. I paid him with the necklace."

"Aye, I know it well." He reached out his hand so quickly she had not time to jerk away from him. He cupped her chin in his palm. "Your pride pleases me, Kassia. Now, I would like something to drink, my men also. We have ridden hard this day."

He released her chin, and she backed away. "You will follow me, my lord."

Graelam watched her walk up the steep oak stairs into the Great Hall.

What were his plans? Would he continue toying with her?

Graelam's eyes narrowed upon the black-haired woman who approached them.

"My stepmother, Marie, my lord," Kassia said. "Marie, this is my husband, Lord Graelam de Moreton."

Marie eyed the man who looked utterly fierce and unyielding. "My lord," she said. "Kassia, your father is in the solarium with his steward. Would you please fetch him?"

Kassia nodded, thankful to Marie for the chance to escape.

"So," Graelam said after Kassia had left, "Maurice has found himself a new wife."

"And three stepchildren, my lord."

Graelam remembered Maurice telling him that his seed was lifeless. He had done well for himself. "Excellent," he said.

"Will you not be seated, my lord?"

Graelam sat himself in Maurice's chair, and

watched Marie give orders to the serving wenches. He wondered idly what Kassia thought of her father's new wife.

"My lord." Graelam rose from his chair to greet his father-in-law. Maurice was looking at him warily, uncertain, Graelam imagined, just how he should greet his son-in-law.

"Maurice, it is a pleasure to see you again." He clasped the older man's shoulders and hugged him briefly.

"You have come to see your wife?"

"Aye, more than that. I am come to take her home to Cornwall."

"Why?" It was Kassia.

He drank in the sight of his wife. She was looking at him as warily as her father.

"Because," he said quietly, "you are mine and will always be so. Your father gave you to me." He saw her eyes narrow, and smiled at her. "However, I understand your wish to visit with your father and your new stepmother for a while. If it pleases your father, we will remain here at Belleterre for several days before we return to Wolffeton."

Kassia looked helplessly toward her father. Maurice, for the first time in his life, had not a clue as to what he should do. He had to admit to great admiration for Graelam, for the man had ridden up to Belleterre, seemingly without a worry in the world. He would have known, of course, that Maurice's men could have cut down him and his men had he wished it. But there was his daughter to consider. It was Marie who spoke.

"We are pleased to welcome you, my lord. You may, if Kassia wishes it, speak to her."

Maurice said, "Aye, Graelam, but you'll not force my daughter to do anything she does not wish to."

"It is not my intention ever again to force Kassia to do what she does not want to do."

Marie said, "Would you care to bathe, my lord? The evening meal will be ready soon."

Graelam nodded. "Thank you, my lady." He said to his wife, "Would you please show me to the proper chamber?"

Maurice saw Kassia hesitate, but he knew that Graelam had no power in Belleterre. "Aye, daughter," he said. "Accompany Graelam."

Kassia knew she had no choice. She marched toward the stairs. She heard Marie giving orders for a bath. She led him to her chamber, pausing a moment inside the room.

"Come in, Kassia," Graelam said. "I need assistance with my armor."

"I am not your squire."

"True, you are my wife. Surely the sight of my body will not surprise you or offend you."

She felt a wave of heat. It had been so long. She dropped to her knees and untied his cross-garters. He pulled off his chaussures and stood naked in front of her. He did not move to cover himself when two serving girls entered, bearing buckets of hot water.

She wouldn't look at him. She watched the tub filled with steaming water. When he stepped into the tub, she tossed him a bar of lavender-scented soap.

Graelam didn't notice the scent. He leaned back in the tub and closed his eyes. "Ah." He began to rub the soap over his chest, his eyes still closed. "You have led me a merry chase, Kassia."

She said over her shoulder, still not looking at him, "Nay, my lord. I did nothing but leave a most unhappy situation."

"With Dienwald de Fortenberry."

"Why not? After all, he has helped me on previous occasions. Surely you cannot doubt our devotion to each other."

"I certainly don't doubt his devotion to you."

"Then why are you here? I have proved to you that I am not trustworthy, that I have no honor, indeed, that I have lied to you from the very beginning."

"I suppose I could regard it in such a light."

He was toying with her. She gritted her teeth. "I won't return with you, Graelam. I want no more of your anger or your indifference to me. I won't play brood mare to your stallion."

Graelam opened one eye and regarded her. "But you have not yet proved to me that you can even fulfill that role."

"I have no intention of playing any role for you, my lord. And you cannot force me. My father will protect me."

"I imagine that Maurice would," Graelam said, and began to lather his hair, as if he had no other concern in the world.

"I repeat, my lord, why are you here?"

He merely continued washing his hair, then rinsing it, cupping his hands in the hot water, and splashing it liberally. He shook his head, sending droplets of water flying toward her, then asked, "Will you scrub my back, Kassia?"

"No. Your dirt is your own, my lord. I will have nothing to do with it."

He sighed. "You left Wolffeton in something of an uproar, my lady. Your nurse was so noisy in her tears that she could only hand me your message to her. As for yours to me—" He shrugged. "Well, it made me want to thrash you."

"You won't touch me, my lord."

"I would not be too certain of that, Kassia."

He rose in the tub, and his sex was hard. She couldn't help staring.

"You are quite beautiful," she heard him say behind her. "I have found that more generously endowed women no longer appeal to me." She felt his fingers touch her hair. "So soft. You will give me a daughter, Kassia, endowed with your beauty."

"Please, Graelam, I don't want—"

His arms closed around her, and he drew her back against his chest. She stood stiffly, willing herself to stand firm. He didn't love her. She was a woman, a wife to breed.

"Release me, my lord."

He did, much to her disappointment. "Have you a bedrobe for me, Kassia?"

She shook her head, mute.

"No matter. I'm weary, wife, and would like to rest for a while." He drew her toward the bed.

"I won't let you take me, Graelam. It will have to be by force. But then again, you are quite uncaring of how you take a woman."

He drew in his breath. "I have not been a very loving husband to you," he said, turning her to face him. "But that will change. You see, Kassia, I have never before wanted a woman as I want you. I never believed a man could truly love a woman, yield to her without losing the essence of his strength." He gently stroked his hands over her arms, and his voice deepened. "I have not known much gentleness in my life, Kassia, yet I know now that I would never willingly hurt you again. I love you, and because I love you, I want you to come home with me."

She gazed up at him, her breath caught in her throat. "But you cannot love me," she whispered. "You do not trust me!"

"I would trust you with my life."

"Has Blanche finally admitted the truth to you?"

"No, I have heard nothing from Blanche."

"Then why? Why are you acting this way? Why are you saying these things to me? I told you that you would not lose Belleterre. Do you wish my father also to assure you of that fact?"

"I see that if there is trust to be gained, it is you to learn that I can be believed. No, don't raise that little chin of yours at me, though it is a delightful part of you. Will you consent to believe me, Kassia?"

She stared at him numbly.

"Will you consider forgiving me for all I have done to you? Can you still love me?"

She lowered her head. "I have no choice but to love you. But—but I am not Chandra. I have not the talent to be as she."

He drew her close, pressed her cheek against his chest. She could feel his laughter as he stroked his hands down her back. "I once told Guy that Chandra is a prince among women. I wish to be with a princess, my lady. I wish to love you, watch you smile and laugh, watch your small belly grow with our children.

"I want to hear you yell your passion for me when I love you. Kiss me."

She felt her heart expand with such happiness she could scarce think straight. She raised her head. His hands cupped her and raised her against him, fitting her belly against him. He kissed her, lightly nipping at her lower lip. She loved what he did, and parted her lips.

She felt his powerful body tremble with need for her. Her breasts felt swollen, as if he had caressed them. "Graelam," she whispered into his mouth.

He laid her on her back onto the bed. "Will you let me love you now, Kassia?"

He made no move to touch her, but waited patiently for her to answer him. "Aye," she said. "I want you to love me. It has been so long. You taught me too well."

She saw his dark eyes leap at her words. Slowly, as if she were a precious treasure, he undressed her, pausing as he removed each article of clothing to caress and kiss her. When her breasts were bare to his gaze, he smiled down at her. "You are more beautiful than I remembered. So delicate." Slowly he began to kiss her breasts. When he heard her moan, he eased off the rest of her clothes. "By all the saints," he said, his voice deep, his hands following his eyes to stroke her ribs and belly, "you are the most lovely of God's creations."

"Not so beautiful and perfect as you are," she said, looking down his body.

"And just how many men have you seen naked?"

"If ever I see another man naked, I should likely laugh, for no man could look as you do."

His fingers found her, and her hips arching up.

"You are so warm, so ready for me," he said, and fit himself beside her. He continued to caress her rhythmically as he looked directly into her eyes. He watched them grow smoky with her urgency, and felt his entire being expand with pleasure when she cried out for him. But he held himself back. Slowly, with infinite care, he eased himself between her legs. He lifted her hips in his hands and lowered his mouth to her. She jerked upward, crying out. He reveled in her pleasure. She was shuddering in the rippling aftermath when he slowly rose over her and eased into her. She raised her hips to receive him, and wanted to yell with the pleasure of it when he filled her. Her hands clutched his back as he went deeper. She whispered his name again and again, and when he tensed over her, she felt herself opening even more to him, welcoming him deep inside her, making him a part of her.

She welcomed his weight, holding him tightly against her.

"Nay, love," he said, "I'm too heavy for you." He eased out of her and turned her on her side to face him.

"Thank you," Kassia said, turning her face into his shoulder.

"For what?"

"For loving me."

"You will never doubt it again. Now I will let you sleep before I hear you go mad with pleasure again. The shadows under your eyes are interesting, but I would prefer you lost them."

"I too." She fell asleep in a cocoon of warmth. She woke slowly, disoriented, until she felt a surge of pure pleasure. Graelam was deep inside her, still facing her, his fingers stroking her.

"I love you," she whispered, and pressed herself tightly against him.

He gently drew her hand down between them and let her feel his fingers caressing her. Her embarrassment was a brief illusion. "Feel how you want me," he said against her lips.

She moaned in his mouth and he smiled. She moved her fingers down his belly and touched him. At his sharp indrawn breath, she smiled. "I feel how you want me, my lord."

34

They walked together in the sunlight, Graelam's arm about his wife's waist, his head lowered to hear her speak.

"Graelam, my father knew. He looked at me so oddly this morning."

Graelam chuckled. "At least he didn't believe that I was holding you in your bedchamber, beating you. The glowing smile on your face testified to my innocence."

"Speaking of smiles, did you see how Rolfe looked at us? And the rest of the men?"

"Aye, they are very pleased, and relieved that I am no longer a braying ass."

Her eyes twinkled, her dimples deepened. "Aye, my lord, as am I."

Graelam was silent for a moment, looking thoughtfully on the bare-branched trees in Belleterre's orchard. "I wish to tell you something, Kassia."

She tensed at his tone, and he felt it. "Nay, love, it's not a bad thing, but a confession of sorts. I wish there only to be truth between us." He paused a moment, then lifted her in his arms and kissed her soundly on the mouth. "That is to assure you that my feelings have not changed and never will."

She wrapped her arms about his neck and pressed hard against him. "I need no confession, my lord."

He set her down. "Nay, Kassia. Listen to me. When I left Wolffeton to visit the Duke of Cornwall, many things became clear to me. I will admit to you that the duke—the interfering old goat—did call me a fool whilst we spoke of you. But he did speak the truth. To love a woman well, to yield to her, does not weaken a man. It has been a difficult truth for me to accept, but accept it I did. When I returned to Wolffeton, I intended to tell you of what I felt for you. But you were gone.

"Two nights ago I was lying in my tent, as miserable as a man can be, when Dienwald de Fortenberry entered. When he told me who he was, I was ready to break his neck. He told me, Kassia, that he owed you a debt, and to pay it meant he must speak the truth to me. We parted friends, my love. No, do not draw away from me. Had he told me that you had hired him a dozen times to remove you from my hold, it would have changed naught. You see, it no longer mattered. It was up to you to forgive me my distrust, not the other way around. So you see, Dienwald or no Dienwald, it made no difference in my feelings for you."

Graelam looked thoughtful. "I think he would have liked to return that damned necklace to me."

"He has been kind to me, Graelam," Kassia said, "and I hoped that when Sir Walter brought him to Wolffeton, he would tell you the truth then. I released him only to spare him pain. But he had to escape. He felt very guilty about it."

"He did indeed. Do you believe me, Kassia? Believe that I did not change my feelings for you because of what he said?"

"I believe you, my lord. Now, if I could see Blanche. How I should love to clout her."

"Why not ask her and Guy to visit Wolffeton? You can challenge her to an archery match."

Because she was so happy, she threw her arms about his waist, squeezing him with all her strength.

"Attacked by a fly," Graelam said, leaning down to nibble at her ear. "Ah, my love, I see your father eyeing us. Shall we assure him that I'm not coercing you in any way?"

Geoffrey could scarce credit his man's words. Graelam de Moreton, his enemy, the only man who stood between him and Belleterre, was in Brittany. Over the past months he had ground his teeth in frustration, especially when it had become clear to him that to assassinate Graelam in Cornwall was a plan doomed to failure. The man was always too well-protected, his men too loyal. But now he was here, and with but a dozen men guarding him.

Geoffrey knew every hillock in Brittany, every likely spot for an ambush. He wondered idly if Kassia would care if he butchered her husband. If she did, it would take him a bit more time to bring her around. If she threatened to denounce him, he would simply lock her away and beat her, for he would force her to wed him immediately. He smiled at the thought. His proud little cousin would not long go against him. He was, after all, a man who knew women well. They were simple and easily led.

He rode from his keep, wanting to avoid his

mother. He hadn't seen her for many weeks now, having just returned from the court in Paris, for her black-worded tongue was enough to drive any man mad. She would change her stance once Kassia was his wife, and Belleterre would be his after his uncle had died.

Graelam and Kassia left Belleterre three days later. Early-spring weather blessed their journey, a sign, Graelam assured Kassia, straight from the Duke of Cornwall. That wily old man believed he had the direct ear of the Lord Almighty.

"Mayhap Papa also talks into that same ear," Kassia said. "I have never seen him so pleased."

"Don't forget your stepmother. It was her influence that kept your father from beating down your bedchamber door that first evening I arrived. Aye, she's a wise woman. She doubtless recognized me as your proper master, and knew you would yield quickly enough to me."

"Conceited brute," Kassia said, laughing.

"I was forced to tell her that you would not allow me out of your bed. Likely she was concerned that you would exhaust me."

Kassia flushed to her eyebrows. She decided it was her turn. "You know, my lord, I must admit that suffering your great body is a mighty chore."

"And a nightly one, Kassia. I also have wondered how your skinny little parts accommodate me so nicely. I think you forget my mighty size once you're yelling to the rafters."

She struck his shoulder, laughing as she did so.

Rolfe smiled as he watched his master and mistress play. Never had he believed Lord Graelam could be so much at his ease with a woman. Life was much improved, he thought, aye, much improved indeed. In the next moment, all thoughts of improved life fled his mind at the sound of one of the men screaming in pain.

"Brigands!" Rolfe shouted at the top of his lungs, twisting around in his saddle, his hand already upon his sword hilt. "An ambush!" He looked wildly about at the narrow passage, at the boulders rising high into the air, surrounding them.

Long years of training kept panic at bay. Graelam coolly analyzed their situation, a fraction of a second passing before he shouted orders.

"All of you, dismount and press under the over-hangs in the cliffs. The whoresons will have to come in to get at us."

Graelam grabbed Kassia off Bluebell's back, protecting her with his body. An arrow tore through the chain mail at his side, but did him no harm. He pulled her to an indentation between two boulders and shoved her inside. "Crouch down and cover yourself with your cloak."

Kassia obeyed him. Brigands? She heard the scream of a horse, of a man. Graelam moved away from her, his back pressed against the stones, until he was crouched next to Rolfe and three of his men.

"We must discover the leader," he said. "James there is a small cleavage between those boulders yon. Think you that you can ease through it? See the number of men who are there?"

"Aye, my lord," James said, fear and excitement nearly overflowing his craw. He was fairly new to Lord Graelam's service, and now he would prove himself. He inched away, licking his suddenly dry lips, and squeezed upward through the narrow passage.

Kassia was terrified at the sudden silence. The horses had calmed, for there were no more arrows raining down. She began to pray, calling upon every litany she had learned since childhood.

The wait seemed an eternity. Graelam held himself perfectly still, listening to any sound that would give him information. He heard a slithering noise and twisted about to see James slip down beside him.

"It's some sort of lord," James said. "I saw him seated on his destrier, dressed in gleaming armor, a man beside him holding his standard. An eagle, my lord, its beak blood-red."

Graelam frowned. Something Kassia had said many months ago stirred in his memory. "Don't move, any of you."

He slipped in and out of the protective crevices until he reached Kassia.

"It is all right," he said, seeing her white face. "A standard, Kassia, one with an eagle on it."

"Geoffrey," she whispered, scarcely believing her own words. "I don't understand, Graelam. It's madness."

"I know," he said. "Stay here, Kassia. All will be well, I promise you." He kissed her hard, and was gone.

He moved in the shadow of the boulders until he was nearly at the end of the narrow passage. He shouted out, "Geoffrey. Geoffrey de Lacy. Show yourself, you puking little coward."

Geoffrey jumped at the sound of his name on his enemy's lips. One of his men had suggested he not fly his standard, even that he not garb himself in armor. He had scoffed, and done as he pleased. Now he was frowning. If he did nothing, and waited, perhaps Graelam and his men could slip out under cover of darkness. He bit his lower lip. Damn the overhanging cliffs and the protection they provided from his men's arrows. Why hadn't one of his damned men told him they offered enough protection from arrows?

"Your father whelped a voiceless coward as well," Graelam shouted. "Fight me, you pathetic little bastard. Do you have guts only to clear the food in your belly?"

Geoffrey roared with fury. "You come to me, Englishman. I will show you how a real warrior fights."

"What, coward? And have your men cut me down? Your treachery is wide known, you lying scum."

"Damn you, pig of an Englishman. You shall not keep what is mine."

Graelam was silent a moment. The man evidently did not know of Maurice's marriage, that it was no longer just he who stood between Geoffrey and Belleterre.

"You're an ass, Geoffrey. Go home to your own keep, for it is all you will ever own. Maurice has remarried and has blessed himself with two healthy stepsons."

"A likely tale! I heard nothing of such a marriage. You're a coward and a liar, Englishman."

Kassia could keep quiet no longer. "It is true, Geoffrey. I swear it to you. Leave us go in peace."

Geoffrey gnawed at his lower lip. The unfairness of it all made him want to yell.

"My lord," one of his men said beside him. "Mayhap it is the truth."

Geoffrey growled obscenities. Thoughts swirled through his mind, until finally he smiled. "Kassia," he called, "come to me, in safety, and tell me to my face."

Graelam froze. "Kassia," he said, but he was too late. His wife moved away from her protection and rose to her full height, in full view of all of Geoffrey's attacking men.

"Here I am, Geoffrey," she called out in her sweet, clear voice. "Let this foolishness cease. If you can't believe me, I will ride back with you to Belleterre and you may meet my father's new wife and children."

Graelam determined at that moment to beat his wife. Without a thought to his own safety, he rushed out and grabbed her. He felt a searing pain go through his arm, and looked vaguely at the arrow sticking out of the chain mail. He tossed her to her knees and dragged her back into the shadowed overhang.

"You little fool."

But Kassia wasn't heeding him. She stared conscience-stricken at the arrow in his upper arm. "Hold still, my lord." She closed her eyes a brief moment, then drew a deep breath and laid her hands about the arrow's thick shaft. Quickly she jerked it out. Graelam made not a sound. He watched her lift the skirt of her gown and rip off material from her chemise. She bound it securely about his arm.

"Do not think that this wound weakens me, wife. You disobeyed me and imperiled your own life."

"But I only wished to spare you his treachery. I knew he would not dare to harm me." She saw quickly enough this was a bad reason. "Very well, Graelam. What shall we do now, my lord?"

"Wait until it grows dark. Then I will take great pleasure in killing that fool."

"Perhaps if I did return with him—" Kassia said, only to shut her mouth at the look on her husband's face.

As the time dragged on, Kassia began to think about how thirsty she was. Graelam had slipped away from her to speak with his men. The sun was setting in the distance, casting shades of gold over the rough-hewn boulders. Suddenly Kassia sat upright. She couldn't believe her ears. It was indeed her Aunt Felice.

"You fool," she heard Felice yell. "Lucky for you, imbecile, that one of the men told me of your lunatic plan. Since when do you act without consulting me?"

Kassia couldn't make out Geoffrey's reply, but she did feel a brief instant of pity for him. It wasn't right for a mother to belittle her son in front of his men.

"They spoke the truth," Felice yelled again. "Damn, Geoffrey, I have wept enough tears for the both of us. It's over."

Kassia turned to see Graelam slip down beside her. He was grinning. "Another prince among women," he said, laughing.

"Kill the Englishman and you gain naught. Do you wish to wed with your cousin so badly? She would come to you without any dowry, young fool. Think of your own neck, Geoffrey. The Englishman is powerful. There would be retribution."

Geoffrey stared impotently at his mother. "But he deserves to die."

"Fool," his mother said. "You will listen to me now, Geoffrey. When I discovered that Maurice had wed Marie de Chamfreys of Normandy, I began to change my thinking. I have found you a lovely girl, my boy, one who will bring us—you—valuable lands. Leave the Englishman with his skinny twit of a wife."

"What is her name?"

"Whose name? Oh, the girl. It is Lady Joanna. She is English and the daughter of the Earl of Leichester. She is ripe for the plucking, and I have had my good friend Orland de Marston speak to her father. He will dower you with rich lands in Normandy. You are to travel to London to meet your betrothed. Soon, Geoffrey."

"Very well, Mother, perhaps Lady Joanna will give me the respect I deserve."

Felice nodded not expecting any other reply. "Now, it would give me great pleasure to tell Lord Graelam what we—you—have gained."

She rode to the end of the narrow passage, pulling in roughly on her mare's reins. "My lord Graelam," she yelled.

"Lady Felice," Graelam said in greeting. "Have you come to take your bowel-less puppy home?"

"Don't be too amused, my lord," she said. "I wish my son to take no chances with his . . . health. He has far greater advantages offered to him. My lord, he will shortly wed Lady Joanna, the Earl of Leichester's daughter. She will bring him great wealth, and her beauty is renowned. Take your silly chit of a wife and leave Brittany."

Felice jerked her mare about and rode back to her son.

Graelam turned to look at his wife. Kassia was trying not to laugh, but it was no use. Graelam roared with laughter just at the look on her face. His laughter grew even louder as he heard his men laughing.

"Oh, it is too much," Kassia said.

"Joanna and Geoffrey."

"Nay, my lord. Joanna and Geoffrey and Felice."

"It is a fitting fate for your cousin, and precious Joanna."

"We must, my lord," Kassia said, "send my cousin and his betrothed a wedding gift."

"Aye," Graelam said and pulled her against him. "Mayhap a whip and manacles. I wager on Joanna's success."

Kassia raised her head at the sound of the departing horses. "Now, my lord, I wish to see properly to your arm."

"And I, my lady, once properly seen to, wish to beat you." Graelam drew her up against him and caressed his hand downward over her bottom. "Mayhap I could bring myself to do it in fifty years or so," he said, and kissed her.

Epilogue

Graelam quietly opened the shutters and breathed in the crisp early-summer air. A year and a half it had been, a year and a half since he and Kassia had returned to Wolffeton. And now he had a son. He turned slightly, a smile touching his mouth as he stared at Kassia, suckling their son, Harry, at her milk-swollen breast. Her hair was much longer now, curling softly about her shoulders. The color of gold and brown and copper, he thought, the colors of autumn.

He shook his head, suddenly remembering how such a short time before he was terrified she would die in childbirth. He said, "Just two hours, my lady, and you present me with a wailing son. I believe there must be peasant stock in you."

Kassia looked up, and thought she'd die of loving him. "You wanted a good breeder, my lord, and now you complain that I wasn't sufficiently delicate. I can hardly believe that the pain ended so quickly. Even now it's becoming a memory, now that I'm holding our boy in my arms." She was well and getting stronger, and so very happy that she wanted to shou her joy to all of Wolffeton. "He is beautiful, is he not, Graelam?"

"Aye, he will rival the vigorous looks of his father when he is a man, though I fear his eyes will be black as that rogue, Roland." Graelam looked thoughtful for a moment. "I wonder how Roland managed in Wales. He was going there, you know, to perform some sort of rescue."

"Roland is a man who lands on his feet because his tongue is so agile. Now, my lord, I wish to speak more of my beautiful son," Kassia said, putting Harry to suckle at her other breast. "I cannot see that he carries even the smallest bone of his sweet mother in him. Even his hair will be black as all the sins of Satan."

But Graelam didn't smile. He was back into his agonizing memories. "You scared the very devil out of me," he said, drawing close to the bed, his voice hoarse. "I was about to swear I would never touch you again if you but survived. And in the next moment, just before I was to take an eternal vow of celibacy, you smiled at me and bade me look at the miracle you accomplished."

"I wonder," she mused aloud, "if you would have kept that vow. 'Tis a mystery never to be solved." She hugged Harry to her and he looked up with blurry eyes, making her laugh. "He is a miracle, is he not, Graelam? He will be a great powerful man, just like his father."

"Let us trust so—if he is to protect the sisters he's certain to have in the next couple of years."

Kassia merely smiled at that, all the pain of Harry's birthing not yet relegated to the past. She lifted her now-sleeping son from her breast. Graelam took him, placing him gingerly in the crook of his arm. "I cannot believe I was once this small and fragile. It's alarming."

"And so dependent upon a woman's care."

"Ah, that I can believe. 'Tis a lesson I learned late in life from a mouthy little wench." He raised his eyes from his son's wrinkled face to study his wife. "You are feeling all right now, Kassia?"

"Aye," she said, and stretched. "But it is a pity he must look so much like you. It doesn't seem fair when I did all the work."

"Mayhap his eyes will become an impudent hazel."

"Ha. You're right—they'll be as black as Roland's. Mayhap he'll have dimples. I like the thought of that."

He laid his son into his cradle. He touched his fingers to his child's smooth cheek, feeling pride so strong he couldn't speak. In that moment he vowed that his son would never know the coarseness and cruelty he had known. When he sat beside Kassia on their bed he looked uncommonly serious.

"What troubles you, Graelam?"

"I want him to have your dimples," Graelam said, his voice gruff. "He will be a strong man, Kassia, but he will also learn that women are to be esteemed and protected."

"He could have no better teacher, my lord."

Graelam shook himself. "I grow too serious, and I had meant to make you laugh. We have a message from your father."

"Since you want me to laugh, I assume he is quite healthy?"

"Aye, as are Marie and the children. It concerns Geoffrey."

When he only grinned at her, she hit his shoulder. "Graelam, tell me. What has happened?"

"It seems your Aunt Felice and Joanna have formed something of an alliance. Geoffrey, a bridegroom of only three months, has fled to Paris to escape their plans to improve him."

Her laughter filled the chamber. "I can almost feel pity for him. Poor Geoffrey."

"Well, he did not leave until he got Joanna with child. At least he did something that must please that mother of his."

"Speaking of children, when will we see Guy's son?"

"Soon, I expect. Unfortunately, Blanche will not accompany him for she is breeding again." Graelam sighed. "Such an accommodating, submissive woman. So gentle and understanding of her master's needs and wants."

Kassia only smiled, for it was a jest of long standing between them.

He cupped his hand under her breast, weighing its heaviness. "Did I tell you how beautiful you are, Kassia?"

"Not since yesterday, I think. But—"

She grew silent yet again as her husband pulled down her shift, lowered his head, and gently suckled at her breast. She felt a ripple of pleasure that brought a flush to her face.

She caressed her fingers through his thick hair and held him close. He raised his head and stared at her for a long moment. "I cannot believe," he said in a thick voice, "that my greedy son received as much pleasure from his mother as I just did. Your milk is warm and sweet, like the rest of you."

"I pray you will always feel thus, my lord," she said.

"I think it likely, very likely."

The Song Series *by*

CATHERINE COULTER

~~~~~

Fire Song

Earth Song

Secret Song

~~~~~